OUR LADY
of
MYSTERIOUS
AILMENTS

By T. L. Huchu

Edinburgh Nights series
The Library of the Dead
Our Lady of Mysterious Ailments

EDINBURGH NIGHTS
BOOK Two

OUR LADY
of
MYSTERIOUS
AILMENTS

T. L. HUCHU

TOR

First published 2022 by Tor
an imprint of Pan Macmillan
The Smithson, 6 Briset Street, London EC1M 5NR
EU representative: Macmillan Publishers Ireland Ltd, 1st Floor,
The Liffey Trust Centre, 117–126 Sheriff Street Upper,
Dublin 1, D01 YC43
Associated companies throughout the world
www.panmacmillan.com

ISBN 978-1-5290-3952-8

1 3 5 7 9 8 6 4 2

A CIP catalogue record for this book is available from the British Library.

Typeset by Palimpsest Book Production Ltd, Falkirk, Stirlingshire
Printed and bound by CPI Group (UK) Ltd, Croydon, CR0 4YY

Visit **www.panmacmillan.com** to read more about all our books
and to buy them. You will also find features, author interviews and
news of any author events, and you can sign up for e-newsletters
so that you're always first to hear about our new releases.

For
Haggai Huchu

Principal Magical Institutions

Allied Esoteric Professions Council: The AEPC is a learned society that regulates the activities of professions adjacent to magic. These are typically professions whose practitioners do not hold qualifications from Scotland's four schools of magic. It was incorporated on 17 November 1945.

Calton Hill Library, incorporating the Library of the Dead: These are Scotland's premier magical libraries, both located under Calton Hill in Edinburgh's city centre. Together, they house an impressive collection of magical texts and books. There is an entrance by the pillars of the National Monument of Scotland, on the summit of the Hill. Alternatively, there's a further entrance via David Hume's mausoleum in the Old Calton Burial Ground. Those who don't practise magic are strongly advised against visiting as punishments for trespass are reportedly disproportionately severe.

Elgin (The): A term mostly used by the alumni of the Edinburgh School (see Calton Hill Library, incorporating the Library of the Dead).

General Discoveries Directorate: An independent division within the Society of Sceptical Enquirers. It supports the Secretary of the Society (currently Sir Ian Callander) in his role as Scotland's Discoverer General.

Our Lady of Mysterious Ailments: An exclusive holistic healing and therapy clinic on Colinton Road. Clients include aristocrats, celebrities and the cream of Edinburgh society.

Society of Sceptical Enquirers: Scotland's premier magical professional body. It is headquartered in Dundas House on St Andrew Square in the New Town.

Principal Places

Advocates Library: Formally inaugurated in 1689, the Advocates Library in Parliament House in the Old Town is the library of the Faculty of Advocates.

Camelot: A notorious tent city atop Arthur's Seat. The population of this place is difficult to estimate because of the transient tenure of most residents. Due to concerns about crime from local residents in the nearby neighbourhoods of Duddingston and Meadowbank, the city council has made several attempts to clear Camelot – but with limited success.

Dundas House: Designed by the architect Sir William Chambers and completed in 1774, this neoclassical building located at 36 St Andrew Square in the New Town was once the headquarters of the Royal Bank of Scotland. It remains the bank's corporate address and simultaneously serves as the headquarters of the Society of Sceptical Enquirers.

everyThere (The): This realm is a nonplace beyond the ordinary world. It is where deceased souls go before they can move on. Only a few of the living can reach and navigate it safely.

His Majesty's Slum Hermiston: This slum is located on farmland in the south-west of Edinburgh. It runs from the city bypass along the M8. The dwellings are a higgledy-piggledy assortment of trailers, caravans, shipping containers, garden sheds, etc.

Other Place (The): Little is known about this realm in the astral plane, but wayward spirits can be expelled there. It is believed there is no return for them from it.

Royal Bank of Scotland: Established in 1727, the RBS is a major retail and commercial bank.

RBS Archives: Located in South Gyle, the archives are responsible for collecting and preserving the records of both the Royal Bank of Scotland and the Society of Sceptical Enquirers. While the premises belong to the RBS, the archivists who work there are employed by the Calton Hill Library.

underHume: The basement area of Calton Hill Library. It houses practice rooms, laboratories and storage space.

Principal Characters

Bumblebeam, Boniface: An unregistered magical practitioner specializing in the field of astral tourism. He is an alumnus of the Lord Kelvin Institute in Glasgow.

Callander, Ian (Sir): Scotland's leading magician. Secretary of the Society of Sceptical Enquirers. His role in the Society also makes him the Discoverer General in Scotland.

Clan (The): This notorious gang is responsible for most of the criminal activities in both Edinburgh's Old Town and New Town. Its territory extends through to Leith and Tollcross, and it is considered the most formidable gang in the city.

Cockburn, Frances: Director of Membership Services at the Society of Sceptical Enquirers.

Cruickshank: Ropa Moyo's magical scarf. A gift from her mentor, Sir Callander.

Duffie, Douglas: Student at the Edinburgh Ordinary School for Boys.

Evelyn (Mr): Librarian at the Calton Hill Library.

Featherstone, Calista: Head teacher at the Aberdeen School of Magic and Esoterica.

Kapoor, Priyanka: Healer at the Our Lady of Mysterious Ailments clinic on Colinton Road. She studied healing and herbology at the Lord Kelvin Institute in Glasgow.

Lethington, Cornelius: Consultant Healer at the Our Lady of Mysterious Ailments clinic on Colinton Road.

Logan, Eilidh: Archivist at the RBS Archives in South Gyle.

Lovell, Theodosia: Fortune teller and matriarch of the Travelling Folk.

MacCulloch (Lord): Rory's father. Owns an estate in Clackmannanshire.

MacCulloch, Rory: Student at the Edinburgh Ordinary School for Boys.

Maige, Jomo: Trainee librarian at Calton Hill Library and Ropa Moyo's best friend.

Maige, Pythagoras (Dr): Head Librarian at the Calton Hill Library and Master of the Books for the Library of the Dead. He holds a doctorate in mathematics from the University of Edinburgh and is Jomo's father.

Mhondoro, Melsie: Ropa Moyo's grandmother.

Moyo, Izwi: Ropa Moyo's precocious younger sister.

Moyo, Ropa: A teenage ghostalker from HMS Hermiston in the south-west of the city. Ropa dropped out of school to support her little sister and grandmother by delivering messages on behalf of Edinburgh's dearly departed. Her activities, including finding and saving missing children, have attracted the attention of the Society of Sceptical Enquirers, an unusual feat for an unqualified independent practitioner.

O'Donohue, Gary: Resident of HMS Hermiston.

Rooster Rob/Red Rob: Leader of the notorious street gang called the Clan. He governs Camelot atop Arthur's Seat in the centre of Edinburgh.

Sneddon (Mr): Librarian at the Calton Hill Library.

Wedderburn, Montgomery: Rector of the prestigious Edinburgh Ordinary School for Boys.

Wharncliffe, Lewis: Student of Sonicology at the Edinburgh Ordinary School for Boys.

Wu, Bing: Max Wu's father.

Wu, Connie: Max Wu's mother.

Wu, Max: Student at the Edinburgh Ordinary School for Boys.

The Somerville Equation

$$y = w(c+a-N)/t$$

y – yield
w – practitioner's potential
c – combustible material
a – agitative threshold

N – natural resistance

t – time

Discovered in 1797 by the polymath Mary Somerville, from Jedburgh, when she was only sixteen. This elegant equation was the first mathematical proof of the Promethean fire spell. Somerville's work is considered by most scholars to have been a key development in the shift towards magic becoming a true scientific discipline. Scotland's four schools of magic also use it to derive their pupils' potential by working out the 'w'.

The Four Magic Schools

These are the only accredited schools of magic in Scotland. They are highly selective and have very competitive admission standards. Qualification at one of these institutions is a requirement for professional registration with the Society of Sceptical Enquirers:

Aberdeen School of Magic and Esoterica, Aberdeen

Edinburgh Ordinary School for Boys, Edinburgh

Lord Kelvin Institute, Glasgow

St Andrews College, St Andrews

I

So, I'm skint again. 'Nothing new there, Ropa,' I hear you say. Well, up yours. This time though, a lass is in luck – Sir Callander, Scotland's premier magical bigwig, has hooked me up with an interview for an apprenticeship. Free food and a proper *wage* – all for a wee bit of filing. Yay.

I'm sauntering through George Street in Edinburgh's city centre, headed towards the East End, and pass a beggar with matted hair sat on cardboard on the pavement, arms stretched out for alms. His trousers are folded and pinned just below the knees, where his legs have been amputated. Must have been a vet during the catastrophe or maybe just some civilian caught up in the crossfire. The bad old days were wild like that.

'Spare some change,' he says in a downtrodden voice. Makes me super sad.

'Sorry, pal, ain't got nothing on me,' I say, and it's a hundred percent true. Been lean times lately, and if I could spare a shilling, I would. I know more than most what it's like to be broke.

'God save the king,' he replies.

'Long may he reign,' I say.

I get away as quick as I can, hoping someone with deeper pockets might take pity on the gadge. Used to be, I ran a small business as a ghostalker, delivering messages around the city for the dearly departed, but certain shenanigans which I daren't recall in full saw that business go kaput. I went off Sherlocking around Edinburgh to find a missing kid for one of my spectral clients. Have to admit, I was pretty good at it, but it took up a bit of my time, and so I couldn't do my core job. The spectral community got miffed and I lost a ton of customers. Sigh. It ain't been easy building the business back up again. But you know what they say, one door closes and all that kind of jazz. This thing Callander's lined up for me is some next-level shit. Formal employment – who'd have thought a fifteen-year-old lass from Hermiston Slum without no school certificates or nothing like that would get a job with them suit and tie folks? My future's so bright I might just swap these plastic shades I'm wearing for a welding visor.

I don't normally dress all formal, but for this, I've gone full-on bougie. Found myself a black pair of tailored straight-leg trousers and a beige fitted shirt with long sleeves. Hell, even borrowed myself a pair of Clarks to make sure my shoe game's proper white collar. My old gig mainly involved tramping around like a postie, so I didn't need to dress up or anything like that. But for this new one, I read on the net you've got to look the part . . . especially for the interview.

It's a nice summer's morn, blue skies, not too hot, which is brill 'cause I don't wanna go in sweating like an oinker. The scent of ground coffee as I pass a cafe before crossing Hanover Street. Big old statue of George IV on a plinth to commemorate the geezer visiting Scotland back when. That was 'cause it had been ages before the king found it fit to visit this part of his realm. Our current monarch ain't been up here since his reign began during the catastrophe, but seeing as how old George's hair has turned white with seagull poop, I can't blame any of his successors for staying well clear of this shithole.

A couple of buskers are jamming acoustic guitars near the church on the opposite side of the road. Their voices carry across loud and clear, covering Dolly Parton's '9 to 5', and I know that's got to be an omen. I stop, take out a tissue from the handbag I nicked off my gran and brush dirt off my shoes. This apprenticeship's really gonna turn my life around. I don't know how much they're paying yet, but it's bound to be more than what I was on before. Means I'll be able to do more for Gran and my little sis, Izwi. Been a bit rough the last couple of years. Same goes for most, to be fair, but once I get paid, I'm looking to get us out of the slum we live in on the outskirts of Edinburgh, into a real house. Then I'll get treatment for Gran, who's a bit poorly, and maybe even a better school for sis. She's the brightest kid this side of the asteroid belt.

With so much on the line, I'm a wee bit feart. Happy and nervous at the same time – nervicited, like that moment before lift-off when the countdown's going and your dicky ticker's racing with the second hand. Mad. I check the time on my mobile. Great, it's only 09:40. Callander said to meet him on St Andrew Square for 10:00, so I've got a bit of time to kill and chill my nerves. I'm returning the phone to Gran's handbag when the ringtone goes off, startling me. It's only my pal Priya, though, so I pick up.

'I've got great news, Ropa,' Priya says so loud I might burst an eardrum. 'Well, not for *them*, but for you.'

'I'm all ears.'

'We've got this patient at my work and his case isn't looking good. It's been a struggle to make a diagnosis, which is hampering our treatment.' Priya's a healer, so I'm not too sure where this is all going. I don't know nothing about no doctoring. 'What we need is a proper investigation into what happened around the time he got sick so we can see if there's anything we've missed. Can you come round to my clinic? His parents are willing to pay you cash for the job.'

'Sorry, Priya, it's a no-go for me—'

'Huh? This gig is right up your street.' She sounds proper baffled. 'I thought . . . Is everything alright with you?'

'Hunky-dory. In fact, I've got a new job now.' Well, almost. 'Sir Callander's hooked me up, and so I'm going in for my first day just as we speak.' I hate to disappoint Priya since she knows I've been hard up lately, but I'm sorted now. Or at least I will be after today.

'You kept that one hush. Damn it, you'd have been the best person for this. After you solved all that drama with those other sick kids. But, hey, congrats. Well done, you. We should catch up soon so you can fill me in on this new J-O-B, baby. I'll be doing the skatepark in Saughton on Wednesday if you're about,' she says. 'Listen, I've got to go – rounds to do, patients to see. Speak soon, mwah – sloppy kiss.'

Wow, look at that, little old me turning down odd jobs. *Who'd have thought?* I wait for a shilly-shilly ferrying passengers to Leith to pass so I can cross the road into the garden on St

Andrew Square. It's nice and peaceful here, with the scent of newly mowed grass, though the small crescent-shaped pool's dry at the mo. I sit on one of the concrete bench mcthingies that run along the footpath, and veg. That's a relief 'cause the shoes I borrowed off Marie are half a size too small so my pinky toes are sore.

The New Town where I'm at just now is the nicer part of town, relatively speaking. If you go across the loch to the Old Town, it's unadulterated mayhem. The only thing kinda marring this side is the pockmarks on the walls of the grand old buildings surrounding the square. Bullet holes. That's from way back, when the king's men were going street to street, driving out the separatists from the city into the Forth where a good few drowned. It's legend out here how in the bleak midwinter of the war hundreds of diehard separatists were lined up on the great Edinburgh seawall with machine guns pointed at them. They were told to swim across the Forth to Fife – a good few miles in freezing water – or take a bullet to the back of the head. Only a handful made it, and to this day they remain His Majesty's guests in Saughton gaol.

Must have been quite the horror show then. Grown-ups don't like to talk about them days, almost like they can silence it out of existence. When I was growing up, if someone talked about being in a 'bullet or breaststroke situation', you knew they'd been put in an impossible position. This is what makes me a keen reader of books about war. It's so I can be ready to save my family if shit hits the fan again.

I'm seagulling away, coasting in the moment and watching

folks go about their business on the pavements, horse-drawn carts and electrics mingling, plus a shitload of cyclists hogging up the roads like this is eighties Beijing. Nah, Edinburgh's nowhere near as posh. China – that's the dream right there. Was a time, once upon, when everyone and their grandma was emigrating out that way, via Hong Kong, but the Great Wall's been put up again and so we're stuck here. Still, with the magic gig, there are deffo worse places to be.

I startle and jerk to the left 'cause a man's suddenly beside me. I look up, and it's Sir Callander, calmly staring ahead as though he's been tracking my gaze for a while. A soft wind blows east, and I catch a hint of tobacco smoke snagged in his three-piece tweed suit.

'Sir Callander, I didn't see you coming,' I say, a little uneasy 'cause I'm sure I've been spotting everyone in these gardens from my vantage point.

'No one ever does, Miss Moyo,' he replies matter-of-factly. 'You look distinguished.'

I'm taken aback, 'cause Callander's not normally one to offer compliments. He's Scotland's top magician, and a chance encounter with him a wee while back led to this moment right here. But I ain't a believer in blind luck. No sir, I've stayed up nights reading posts on prepping for a new job, and so even my pinky toes will forgive me one day when we're aboard the gravy choo-choo. Callander's not the type to hand over anything so easily.

'A position within the Society of Sceptical Enquirers is a much sought-after, seldom proffered affair, which you should take very seriously. You have come prepared?'

'Yes,' I say. I ain't done much else but dream of this since spring ended.

'And you've already fully mastered all aspects of the Promethean spell?'

Piece of cake, that one. I nod. I don't want to seem too enthusiastic, but inside I really want to burst out, *Yes, yes, yes, just get me started on the apprenticeship already.*

'It's almost time. The others will be waiting. Come with me, Miss Moyo,' Sir Callander says, getting up.

I'm in his shadow as I follow him out the garden. He's tall and confident, and moves like a great ship making people part like waves to let him through. I'm bursting with pride, trailing him. This is it, my dream about to happen, and my binoculars are wide open.

We cross the tramlines; hardly ever any trams about, so barring a few cyclists it's a quick walk to the building opposite. The one with the statue of a geezer and horse in the garden at the front. Dundas House, number 36 St Andrew Square, the main branch of the Royal Bank of Scotland in this city. I've never been inside. Never had to. I'm not sure what we have come out here for, but maybe Callander needs a bit of dosh before our appointment.

The road that runs inside the yard to the building arcs a U for vehicles coming in and out from St Andrew Square. Callander proceeds down the road directly ahead of the main door to the solid neoclassical building. It's got large windows, straight lines and simple geometric architecture appropriately reeking of money, though the walls are sooted badly from pollution layered over the years.

'This has been the home of the Society of Sceptical Enquirers for over two hundred and fifty years, Ropa Moyo. Or in other words, the home of Scottish magic. Mark me well, you always slip in via the extreme left of the door so your shoulder brushes against the frame. With your right hand, hold your thumb and index finger together and point the others down to the ground, like this. Arm by your side, palm facing your thigh.' I mimic him, and he gives a satisfied nod. 'And remember to be discreet so members of the public don't see you come in.' With this, we walk into the bank.

The air takes on a glassy tone. Everything kinda looks slightly reversed as if I'm looking into a mirror. My left is now my right and my right becomes my left, 'cause now we are on the *inside*.

II

We're in this liminal space, a haze-like distortion of reality where everything is almost normal but slightly off. And you can't quite grasp it, like being inside of the memory of a dream. I sometimes go off into the everyThere, the astral plane, but this is uncanny – it throws you off balance and your body doesn't know what's happening to it. Weird. You just sense you're in a different dimension. At least that's what it feels like to me. Marble flooring, classical white pillars and elaborate cornices up above showing attention to detail. A golden chandelier adds a sense of opulence to the history already on display. We are within the bank, yet someplace else.

Definitely not the sort of place for the likes of me. But it's all gravy at the end of the day and I'm getting on that choo-choo whether they want me or not. Hell, I'll be in the engine room, shovelling coal, if that's what it takes.

'Empty space,' says Callander, sweeping his hand in a grand gesture. 'I want you to think of hydrogen, the simplest atom of all. If you were to make the nucleus the size of a football, then you would find the electron orbiting some two miles away. Thus, with great effort and skill, Scottish magicians of old manipulated the fabric of this space to fold us into the unseen gaps. This allows the bank and our magical Society to exist and function independently while occupying the same geographical coordinates. If the bank is on the left, we are right. If they sit atop the x-axis, we fall below it. If they are tails, we are heads, the other side of the coin. It's a powerful piece of scientific magic, Miss Moyo – one few contemporary practitioners can comprehend, let alone dream of replicating.'

There's slight delay in his voice compared to the movement of his lips, as though it takes maybe a fraction of a second longer to reach me. A sort of Doppler effect, I guess. He halts to let me take it in. A wisp of a customer passes through me like a ghost heading towards the banking hall. While I see them, they don't seem aware of our presence, so if this were a mirror, it'd be one-way.

'If you want to truly understand how modern Scotland came to be, you have to understand the history of the bank. And to understand the bank, you have to understand the role of Scottish magic. Once, the Society of Sceptical Enquirers and the bank were inseparable. They didn't just inhabit the same space. And I hope they shall be again so we can regain our former influence,' Callander says.

I don't quite get that. What does banking have to do with magic anyways?

Sir Callander holds up his left hand, fingers open, and a second later, a thick grey book appears. Then he hands it to me.

'Money is power. Learn this well, and take this book back to the Elgin when you're done with it,' he says, heading into the main banking hall. 'There are a lot more resources available to you at the Library, as I'm sure you know.'

I read the cover: *Banking in Scotland: 1695 to 1995*, by Niall Munro. Seems like dry stuff to me. I wanna master magic and Callander's drawing me into the world of finance? Zzz. But I'll give anything a try at least once, I think, slipping the book into Gran's handbag. I follow Callander, but it's so awkward moving in here. It's like I've been wired wrong. When I try to lead with my right leg, it's actually the left that goes first, though my head's telling me I'm moving the right leg and vice versa. You can forget about chewing gum while doing this.

There's a big ol' knot in my stomach as we enter the main banking hall. The imprint of the real bank is still there, shadows of customers and staff moving, the semblance of their furniture. This side of the mirror, though, is an empty room with a man and woman waiting for us in the middle. I stay right at Callander's shoulder, desperate not to make an arse of myself with this sloshed gait of mine. *Back straight, Ropa, don't slouch.*

'Thank you for agreeing to do this,' Sir Callander says to the couple.

'I've never been one to turn down a curious proposition,' replies the man, who's wearing a golden monocle. Sounds super posh.

'So this is the girl you've been telling us about,' the woman next to him adds, looking me up and down as though trying to come up with the resale value of a bad investment. She's pencil thin, all cheekbones and angles, wearing a sharp grey business suit with shoulder pads. I feel cheap in my get-up.

'Ropa Moyo, meet Montgomery Wedderburn, rector of the

11

Edinburgh School, and this is Frances Cockburn, director of membership services here at our Society.'

'Pleasure to meet you,' I say, surprised at the distortion in my own voice.

I hold out my hand to greet them. Firm handshake – that's what the net told me to do, and I try it.

Montgomery Wedderburn is a striking man, with chiselled features and a prominent Roman nose. He has golden hair gelled to perfection, parted on the right side. His demeanour reminds me of a spider's web, something so light you may not see it until you walk right into it like a fruit fly. Any delicacy is offset by the fact that the silk web is stronger than steel. His hand is warm and soft. Can't believe I'm meeting the head of the best magic school in Scotland.

On the other hand, Frances Cockburn is cool, and she meets my firm grip with a vice-like response that turns my metacarpals into mush. Get the vibe of a dung beetle: strong, dependable, forever shifting piles of crap to God knows where.

Wedderburn gives Sir Callander a brief, knowing smile as I step back beside my mentor. I must have done something right already. My nerves lessen a notch, though I'm still on the edge. This opportunity means a lot to me. I'm a secondary school dropout, never been to no magic school or nothing like that, so this is my best shot at making it. *Calm yourself, lassie, you got this.*

'Shall we begin?' Sir Callander says.

'I'd like to repeat what I told you when you requested this induction. It's highly *irregular* for a non-practitioner to be given a role in the Society,' Cockburn says through thin lips.

'We've already been through this,' Callander replies with an air of annoyance.

'You're right, of course, Frances, but even the librarians would agree that as secretary, Sir Callander has wide-ranging privileges established by historical precedent,' says Wedderburn. 'It was not unknown in the past for the Society to impress young men of talent, usually the sons of local fishermen with no formal magical training, as storm-calmers aboard ships. And I for one agree that's analogous to this present situation.'

'You're reaching,' Cockburn replies sharply.

'It is not up to us to choose the secretary's apprentice.'

'Intern. Who *historically* has always come from your school, or have you forgotten that?' says Cockburn. 'Yet here you stand, ready to throw away that so-called precedent for this *ghostalker?*'

The way she says my old job really grates on me. It's like I'm dirt or something. So what if I talk to ghosts for a living – these guys don't consider that real magic. They come up with all sorts of highfalutin malarkey to claim it's less than. My piss is warming up to a boil already, but I keep cool, 'cause I feel like anything I say will be used against me. So annoying.

'That's why I was asked to assess if her independent learning satisfies established criteria. By this I mean, at a minimum, Ropa must demonstrate knowledge and skill equivalent to that of a novice pupil attending any one of the four schools of magic in Scotland today. We've already been over this, and I see no reason to rehash it. Apologies, Sir Callander, but we really ought to begin.'

The dung beetle's thrashing about in the web holding it fast. Wedderburn closes the argument, and I could run up and hug him. I'm not used to strangers fighting my corner so fiercely. Now it's up to me to prove Ms Paper-Lips here wrong – director of membership services, my buttcrack.

My hands are shaking, and I hide them behind my back so it don't show. It's easy to feel overwhelmed in this kind of joint. Here I am standing on this plush floor reflecting the sunlight streaming in from the incredible galaxy of star-shaped glasses that adorn the cupola. The intricate finishes show all the things money can buy, the very things I can't. I don't blame me for wanting in on this racket.

Sir Callander gives me a wee supportive nod, which buoys me like the jet stream.

'Ropa, describe for us the theories of magic as you understand them,' Wedderburn says in a gentle teacher's tone. I notice how he uses my first name and like him more for it, 'cause it means he's not so uptight.

Here goes: I've been reading up on this stuff all through the spring, so I lay it out the best way I can. I start with the ontological explanation of magic – classic gods and mortals stuff. It posits that the universe we live in was created by a god or gods, or that a god or gods exist within this universe, and their ability to manipulate the material world via a power we call magic is one we happen to share. I waffle about it for a bit then immediately launch into the scientific theory, which allows for an experimentally verifiable and replicable practice. Basically, a magician's cookbook: put the same ingredients in, get the same results out – voila.

'The scientific theory is my preferred proposition since it presents the only evidence-based description of how magic works,' I say, wading into the deep end.

Cockburn wears a haughty sneer, waiting for me to slip up. I don't let it faze me; even if I was on a unicycle with a monkey on my shoulder, I ain't about to fall off this tightrope anytime soon. The shadows of bankers and their customers going about their business in the regular dimension don't frighten me neither.

I break it down, starting with Thomas Young's famous 1801 double-slit experiment, running through wave particle duality and the implications observations have in quantum mechanics. These effects at a subatomic level scale up to the normal world of classical physics which we live in.

'And so magic is the conscious excitement of the quantum world by trained practitioners, triggering wave function collapses with verifiable results within the macro world,' I say, paraphrasing something I read.

I'm ready to go into the other hypotheses – magic as a result of simulated reality and what have you. There's lots of them. But Wedderburn holds up his hand.

'That's a satisfactory explanation, wouldn't you agree, Frances?' he says.

Cockburn rolls her eyes but refuses to be baited. It's like she grows more scunnered by me with each passing minute. Sir Callander remains impassive. The great ship anchored by my side.

'Your dominie tells me you've acquainted yourself with a little practical magic,' Wedderburn says. His voice is authoritative yet gentle. I reckon he was definitely one of those cool teachers that no one messed with back in his day. The kind who never had to shout or get angry in class since you can't help but want not to disappoint him.

'That's correct.'

'Have you mastered the basics of Promethean craftwork?'

'Come now, that's hardly a test of competence. You've lowered the bar to slip her through,' Cockburn says.

Wedderburn puts his thumbs in his jacket pockets, resting his hands on his stomach.

'I'm required to check she can perform at first-grade level. Anything more would be superfluous,' Wedderburn replies curtly. 'Ropa Moyo, show us the spark of your flame.'

I take a deep breath. This is my moment to show them all. Callander had warned me that the demonstration is a critical aspect of the induction, and I'm ready to give it to them. I take my shades out of my breast pocket and put them on. Ball my fingers on both hands into a fist and try to relax my mind. I choose an upper-illumination variant of the fire spell. Here goes.

'Spark of Prometheus from the fire of Mount Olympus, light the way ahead and shine bright upon this path.' With that I flick my fingers open, feeling something surge through my being.

There's a crackle and pop, then a white light appears in the air between us like a lit fuse throwing off sparks. Callander squints and turns his head from the incredible brightness. Both Wedderburn and Cockburn hold up their hands to shield against its brilliance. That's why I wore the shades. I'm sure

16

they're pretty impressed 'cause it's an amazing display. The air has a sharp chemical smell, which is what I've come to expect with this spell.

Sir Callander waves his hand, extinguishing all the sparks save for one, which he draws to himself until it's hovering just above his palm.

'Well, well,' says Wedderburn, eyebrows raised. 'Things just got a little more interesting in Scottish magic.'

'We haven't seen an áspro's colour in a very, very long time,' Sir Callander replies.

I read somewhere that the shade of a magician's flame is an indication of their potential to create powerful spells. Like there's colour charts and gradations running from blue, green, yellow, red, black, white and the unseen flame. There's shades in between too. It's all very complicated stuff, and I'm only just getting the hang of it.

'Be that as it may, the girl has failed the test. As director of membership services, I cannot admit her on the basis of this performance,' Cockburn says.

Wait a minute. Like, what the actual hell? I've just aced it here!

'You asked for a spark. A single spark, and what she's given you is an uncontrolled firework. Potential is two a penny – throw a stone onto Princes Street and you're guaranteed to hit someone who, with a good education, might turn in a flame. Control, dedication and discipline is what ultimately determines how a magician will fare. So it is with regret I must—'

'Wait, I can do it again,' I say.

'You have already taken your test, young lady. And this

17

outburst demonstrates the sort of loutish comportment we do not tolerate in this institution.'

'I say we offer the girl a conditional internship with the view to retaking her demonstration at a later date, since she has, in the main, met the baseline criteria,' Wedderburn cuts in. Callander glowers behind his thick eyebrows but says nothing. I guess he can't be seen to be interfering with the process, especially since he brought me here.

My bowels sink right to the floor, and Cockburn takes her time mulling things over.

'If we can't come to an understanding between ourselves, that means we'll need to get the librarians involved. Do you really want their tribunal telling you how to conduct Society business according to their *Rulebook*?' Wedderburn presses.

'Very well. It'll be an unpaid internship, since the girl doesn't fully meet our standards. That's as far as I am willing to go on this.'

'Fair compromise. As always, it's a pleasure doing business with you, Frances,' says Wedderburn, smugly checking his pocket watch. 'Sir Callander, we would love for you to drop by the school and give a lecture in the not-so-distant future.'

'I'll do that, Monty. And thank you both for your help in this matter.'

'As for you, young lady, it's hard enough to become a good magician, even with the benefits of a formal education. I trust you'll use this opportunity to the fullest, and the next time I do your assessment you'll have better mastery over your spellcraft. Remember, emotions have nothing to do with it. Let reason alone be your guide.'

My heart's sunk into the pits as they wind up my interview. I wanna tell them this is a load of bollocks, but instead I swallow hard and keep my gob schtum. Callander's saying something about how I should return next week to start my new role, but the blood whooshing in my ears muddles up his words. I thought I was getting an apprenticeship and that it came with an actual wage. Now all I've got is some crummy, unpaid internship working in a place with Knobhead McPaper-Lips, who obviously doesn't even want me there. Absolutely scunnered. I swear, story of my life.

III

Feeling like a right mug as I get home to His Majesty's Slum Hermiston near the bypass on the south-western outskirts of Edinburgh. Thick black smoke rises off burning tyres in the communal dump close to the M8. I'm passing by the allotments – folks here grow their own grub if they can – when old man Gary O'Donohue rises up from the patch he's weeding. Gives his back a good stretch and waves at me.

'Alright, mah wee pally?' he says.

'Aye, been a long day.'

'Yous looking worse for wear despite that dapper outfit.'

My trotters are killing me, and I had to do most of the walk home barefoot 'cause these borrowed shoes are a medieval torturing device. I'm wired and riled, so here I am scowling at Gary, who's one of the sweetest old geezers in this slum. Stays by himself in an old garden shed down yonder, so he loves to yak on if he can get your ear.

'Give this to your nana Melsie, if she's aboot,' Gary says, handing me a plastic bag filled with fresh vegetables from his allotment. Brill. I can make us a nice broth tonight.

I take it, thank him and flee, 'cause Gary'll talk till the cows come home if you give him half a chance. Reckon he's got the hots for Gran, since he's always got a wee parcel for her every time I pass by. Gran reciprocates with cooked food or knitwear every so often, but the two of them don't chat as far as I know.

This whole slum used to be farmland until the first squatters moved in, but now the farmer's given up chasing us out and instead charges us rent. It's a bomb site filled with caravans, trailers, refashioned shipping containers, tents, sheds and sheet-metal dwellings. Can get mad out here sometimes, but everyone knows everyone and we look out for each other. More so than the council estate across the bypass.

I get to our caravan and kneel down to say hi to River, my vulpine companion, who lives in a burrow somewhere beneath.

'Hey there, girl,' I say when she pokes out her nose.

Used to be River didn't much fancy being patted or any of that, but nowadays her and me are cool as cucumbers. I give her some scraps I dumpster-dived from the back of a restaurant in the city. My blouse has a few stains from the effort, and it was lean pickings. Not much I could use myself, but I figured River would appreciate the bones and stuff.

Soon enough, I'm up and go inside the caravan. Home sweet home. Gran's busy knitting but her face lights up and she breaks into a smile when I come in. Her face is brighter than the midday sun and warms me up so much I could melt into a puddle.

'I met your boyfriend on my way down,' I say. 'He's pretty dashing for an old fogey – even has his own teeth, too. You should have seen him in them dungarees and straw hat he was wearing.'

'Don't be silly,' Gran replies, laughing.

'Gary gave us a whole plastic bag filled with veg. I'd prefer

21

flowers and a box of chocolates myself, but, hey, your generation did things differently, right?'

'We even proposed with Haribo rings,' Gran retorts.

I plonk myself right next to Gran and rest my head against her shoulder. Lord, it feels good taking the weight off my feet. Next I wanna get out of this ridiculous outfit, but that can wait a while. My little sister's not here. She must be out playing with the other kids nearby.

'What you knitting?'

'Oh, this little thing? It's just a shawl for Linda Lyttleton. She's not been okay since she lost her bairn in the winter, and I thought this might give her some comfort.' She holds it up so I can see how it's coming along.

It's just like Gran to do stuff like that. Most of what she makes she gives away, but the folks in the slum keep her supplied with enough wool to keep things ticking over. Must be taking turns at the spinning jenny at the rate it keeps coming in. And just like that, I start feeling better already. At least I can veg here with my gran and shoot the breeze without worrying about the nonsense I've gone through. I swear if Frances Cockburn's skinny coupon pops up in my head one more time I'm going to scream.

Gran's got an episode of *Diagnosis: Murder* going on our little telly. I don't know how far in the show's gone, but it don't matter none 'cause Dick Van Dyke gets 'em every time.

'How was your day? Did you get the job you told me about?'

Knapf, that's the last thing I wanna talk about right now.

'Yeah, I got the job, Gran. I absolutely smashed the interview.'

What can I say, the damned thing was a train wreck.

IV

Wednesday morning and I'm cycling up Calder Road, feeling all sluggish. Like, who knew humble pie caused this much bloating? I need a bout of blether to get the interview out of my system. Good thing I know just the girl to talk to. There's the clippity-clop of horsemen headed uptown and the whirr of electrics driving round them.

I've got my left earphone plugged in, listening to an audiobook of *The Peloponnesian War*. Them Greeks sure got up to no good back in their day. I dig listening to stuff like this when I'm about. It's the only thing that stops my brain atrophying into full-on zombie mode. If there's anything I can put my ear to the keyhole and eavesdrop on, I'm game. It's the only method I know of teleportation and time travel too. Do enough reading and you come to realize this world's been insane right from the beginning.

It don't take long before I'm in Saughton and make my way into the park. A bunch of neds in jobby catchers lounge on the benches smoking, and I ride right past them. This place is a stone's throw from Murrayfield, and you've got the big prison nearby too.

I brake to a halt at the skatepark, take out my phone and

pause *The Peloponnesian War*. Ain't dressed fancy no more. Today I'm in my trusty steel-toecap boots, stonewash jeans and a vintage Garbage T-shirt with Shirley Manson looking fierce. I've dyed my dreads full-on amethyst but my lipstick is pure Henry Ford: I can wear it in any colour I like so long as it's black. I've also brought my backpack with my mbira in it, though I don't know why. Habit, I guess. The instrument helps me communicate with any deados bearing messages. Clients are thin at the mo, but a lassie can hope.

The sound of wheels on concrete and the clack of a board hitting the ground. I watch a bunch of skaters doing tricks in the park. It's like a tempest of rising halfpipes, spine transfers, vert ramps and handrails decorated with wild graffiti that adds verve to the grey. The best of the art is by some kid who thinks he's Basquiat and tags his futuristic Pictish pieces with the Crown of Scotland. Compared to this, the rest is by tossers with more paint than talent.

'Weeeeehey,' a girl's voice screams with delight. I spot a wheelchair rising high into the air, flipping a full 360 with a twist, before plunging back into the bowl and hitting the concrete hard.

That's my girl, Priyanka Kapoor. I cycle over and join a bunch of lads watching her zip through the bowl to the next edge. Her chair rises and she somehow manages to flip, hand on the edge of the bowl with the wheelchair dangling above her. Priya holds that position for a second, frozen picture perfect, and then, suddenly, she's back in motion, arcing left before righting herself and barrelling down again.

'She's blazing today – any hotter and we'll smell rubber.

Did you get that shot?' one of the lads beside me says.

'Dinnae micromanage me,' the one holding a camera says.

Priya takes the next ramp and goes back the way, gaining even more speed till she's hurtling towards our end of the bowl. Up the incline, she launches into the air, does a double backflip and lands on her left wheel. Precarious like. But Priya maintains her balance and comes towards us with a cheesy grin on her face. Her purple fringe is glued to her face from sweat, but the rest of her silver hair is totally messy after all the tumbling around.

Priya's a bit of a thrill-seeker, hellraiser, you know, that kind of thing. Likes her adrenaline shot in the morning before she gets her coffee. I, on the other hand, had my heart in my gob throughout her routine.

Check out those arms, though. She's well buff.

'You should have a go with that BMX of yours,' Priya says. 'It's a great bike, and if you ask Danny nicely, he'll let you use his workshop to mod it, just like I did with my chair.'

'You still owe me for that titanium tubing,' says a goth with oxblood lipstick.

'I'm good for it,' Priya replies.

'That's what they all say.' Danny hops onto his skateboard and takes to the bowl, his friend snapping pics.

'So, Ropa, how's the new job coming along? Congratulations again,' Priya says with such excitement my heart sinks.

There's no way of spinning it, so I come out with it straight. I thought Sir Callander was hooking me up with some sort of paid apprenticeship at the Society so I could actually learn magic. But all I got was a lousy unpaid internship. It's all down to bloody Cockburn's sleight of hand, because, as far as

I can tell, I still get to do the same thing, but apprentices get dosh whereas interns get shafted. An apprentice pretty much expects to get a job at the end of it all – interns get fuck all. An apprentice comes out with a recognized qualification; all interns get is a kick up the backside. I give Priya the full deets, including telling her what a fanny Frances Cockburn is.

'Hey, at least you got the gig – that's the most important thing. There's people who'd bite your arm off for an opportunity with the Society. Before you, Callander hadn't taken on an intern since, like, forever, so you should take that as a big plus. Seriously, it's a coveted prize you've got in your hands.'

'Yeah, but you know I need juicy bacon strips. I can't live off prestige,' I say. 'So, I was wondering if that job you told me about is still on the table.'

Priya grins and says, 'You're the first person I thought of. Let me grab my gear and I'll take you to the clinic so you can see what's what.'

Me and Priya make it up to Colinton Road, where her clinic's at. I've been down these ends on various jobs over the years, but I ain't never been inside this place. We go through the gates. The massive stone pillars on either side have the clinic's name, Our Lady of Mysterious Ailments, with a logo of praying hands. The air here smells of mint and lavender and much besides. And the riot of colours in the flower beds is incredible. They've got shrubs and herbs all over with small walkways between the beds. Hell, even the wee roundabout in the middle has something growing beneath a lime tree. Bees and insects flit in the air.

'We grow quite a lot of our own herbs, medicinal and

culinary. It's the same thing for us, because our treatments are holistic in nature,' Priya says. She studied healing and herbology at the Kelvin Institute in Glasgow, so I guess that means she knows all about plants.

'Smells ace out here,' I say.

'I know, right?'

There's something about this place. Right from when we rode in, I'm feeling a bit calmer, a little less stressed already. It's incredible. If you closed your eyes, you could even forget you were still in the city.

'Chamomile, ginkgo, aloe vera – don't leave home without it – lady's mantle, feverfew – that's a great one for migraines – burdock, centaury, echinacea . . .' Priya's rattling off a list of plants as we head towards the main door of the clinic.

I know Gran's sick. She's got problems with her ticker and waterworks, as well as diabetes. Basically, she's falling apart. Last night she said to me, 'If I was a cow, you could take me to the knackers.' I told her I wanted to but I was worried they'd end up charging us for the service. Wish I could get her seen at a place like this. It doesn't smell of disinfectant and death like the public facilities we use, where you can spend all day waiting to see the doctor.

I park my BMX in the rack and make sure I lock it. Dope as this place might be, this is still Edinburgh last I checked. And the bike's been stolen before, so I ain't taking no chances. The clinic is this tasteful-looking Edwardian building made of quarried sandstone, and it's three storeys high, with massive architraved windows. Not a hint of soot upon the walls, like we're someplace in the countryside.

'The old clinic was in Newhaven, but it was moved to this site just before the First World War,' says Priya.

She tells me the clinic was founded in the eighteenth century by the famous Catholic healer Mungo Arnot to encourage traditional methods, which were coming back into fashion in bourgeois circles at the time. He was even summoned to London to attend to George III – quite natural since the king took an interest in botany – when his maj was losing it, but alas the quacks had brought Arnot in too late to make a difference.

Kinda looks like a swanky spa inside. Pristine white walls, spotless floors and mellow Celtic music piped in at a volume so low it almost passes for subliminal. The receptionist is dressed in an orchid-colour tunic with the praying hands and 'OLMA' stitched on the left breast pocket. Her skin is flawless, nearly translucent, and a smile lights up like a reflex action when she sees Priya.

'You're early for the late shift, Priya,' she says.

'It almost sounds like you don't want me to be here,' Priya replies.

'As if.' The receptionist laughs. 'Mr Lethington said to find him when you come in. Something about the Wu case.'

'That's why I've brought this expert with me,' replies Priya, touching my arm. The receptionist raises her eyebrows and smiles at me.

We go through the doors opposite and take a left, past what looks like a massage room with a plinth, along a long corridor, past a gymnasium where an instructor is taking a group of old ladies through tai chi. Midway down the corridor, we stop by some lifts and take one to the first floor. There's green signs with white lettering telling you how to go round to the various departments.

'Most of the treatment rooms catering for our various therapies are downstairs. We get a mix of inpatients and outpatients. Our sickest clients stay on the first and second floors for the duration.'

'Poshville central out here,' I say.

'I know. When I started my training, I thought I was gonna be saving the masses, working with the homeless and people in need, but then I grew up. As you know, I try to do some voluntary work to make it up, but it's not the same thing, is it?'

I shrug. Volunteering ain't nothing I can even contemplate when I've got mouths to feed at home. Priya takes me into a staffroom.

'Wait here a moment, I need to get changed,' she says, leaving.

I plonk my arse down and twiddle my thumbs for a bit, before I spot a jumbo pack of Jammie Dodgers on the counter-top. I really shouldn't . . . Nah, screw that. I get up, make a beeline for it and check. There's still quite a few in there, so I take two and stuff another two in my pockets. Cycling sure takes a lot of energy. I'm stuffing my face when a bald man wearing a white lab coat walks in.

'Excuse me, are you lost?' he says, frowning.

'Nope, are you?' I reply. That leaves him flustered.

'Well, erm, no. I *work* here, and I was merely wondering what you're doing in my clinic, eating my biscuits.'

'That's the investigator you asked for on the Wu case,' Priya says, coming back into the room. She's got her hair all neat and tidy now and she's wearing a white lab coat too. 'Cornelius Lethington, I'd like you to meet Ropa Moyo.'

'Of what school?' he asks, narrowing his eyes.

'She's Sir Callander's new apprentice.'

'Codswallop. The secretary hasn't taken anyone on in years. And I am to believe he's now suddenly picked someone so obviously not of the Edinburgh School? Nothing trumps those old-boy networks, nothing. Those of us who studied at St Andrews – the superior institution, if you ask me – can attest to this situation which has ossified Scottish magic for far too long.'

'You're going to have to ask Sir Callander about that yourself,' I say.

I take another shameless bite from my pilfered Jammie Dodger, trying to come across hardboiled, but crumbs fall down my T-shirt. Not a great look; however, the coat rack on the wall catches my eye. I'll come back for it later.

'On your head be it, Kapoor. Let's get this done, shall we?' says Lethington, leading us out of the room.

I'm taken through another winding series of vinyl-floored corridors. There's a lot of artwork on the walls, abstract stuff in soothing tones. Unlike the crappy NHS hospitals, you get the feeling that folks come in here expecting to come out alive again. The lighting is a soft blue, making it feel like you're floating through the ocean. We pass by open doors where patients relax on comfy-looking beds, their wide windows allowing sunlight, while aromatherapeutic candles burn in glass jars. I couldn't afford it, but I sure wish I could bring my gran here for treatment. Maybe Priya can sort something out for me – call it voluntary work.

Lethington enters a room at the end of the corridor. I follow in behind Priya and take my spot near the door. It's proper Baltic in here, like, and I'm half expecting Thomas Abernethy, the polar explorer, to leap out in a fur coat. Brrr. Condensation forms with each breath I take. Don't take too long before goosebumps form on my flesh. It's as though there's an invisible line regulating temperatures between in here and out there, even though the door is wide open.

In the middle of the room, lying on a cushy bed, is a teenager, probably doing his Highers. He doesn't wake when we come in, and the only sign of life is the barest of wisps escaping his lips. Even prone like this, the fringe on his low-fade haircut is neatly in place.

'This is Max Wu, seventeen, a student from the Edinburgh School. He's been comatose for a week, and our various diagnostic attempts have not given us a satisfactory reason for his current state. This obviously impacts on his treatment, so it's imperative that we know more about his activities prior to this illness in order to make an informed assessment on his condition,' says Lethington. He has a clipped tone, old school.

'We suspect the condition may have an extranatural aetiology, which is why we called you in,' says Priya.

Now I don't know nothing about no medicine, so I say, 'What do you want me to do – kiss him awake?'

Evidently my quip doesn't land, given the look Lethington gives Priya. But, hey, I thought it'd be just the kind of thing

Sam Spade might say. I guess I ain't no smooth-talking Yankee detective, so I dial that shit down. I need the money, but thing is, if you show you're desperate, your rate goes down. Signals you can't be any good if your diary ain't full. Note to self: I need to go to the Library, see if they've got any good books on business. I need all the help I can get at the mo.

'We need you to find out all you can about Max Wu's activities in the days and weeks prior to this illness. What he did, ate, where he went; find out anything anomalous that may have a bearing on his case.'

Now, I have some prior experience in dealing with kids who've experienced 'extranatural' health issues, and so that's why Priya roped me in on this. Plus, I know how to spot an opportunity. If I nail this case, I might find myself with more work in the long run – and maybe I can get Gran seen. I deffo gotta behave myself now.

'That I can do,' I say in my most professional voice. 'We need to discuss my rates before I commit to anything.'

'This is an additional service Max Wu's parents will have to pay for out of pocket as it's not covered by their insurance. Priya will fill you in on the details. Is that okay? I really should be moving on to my next patient.'

There's a well-chuffed smile on Priya's face after Lethington leaves.

'I think he likes you, Ropa.'

She gives me the thumbs up and wheels herself to the other side of the bed, where there's a small cabinet with cards and various effects including a massive bouquet of flowers.

'I know you're looking for a needle in a haystack, but if

anyone can help us, it's you, Ropa,' says Priya. Her confidence in me is inspiring.

'Snooping around's my thing, and if the kid's parents pay well, then that's me sorted,' I reply.

But before seeing the kid's parents, I must have a nosey in this swanky five-star-hotel-looking room. As Miyamoto Musashi says in *The Book of Five Rings*, 'Become aware of what is not obvious.' Seems simple, don't it, but we go through our days checking out the obvious and missing the mundane muck in the fringes. Musashi was this badass samurai in Japan back in the seventeenth century. They say he won his first duel at thirteen and from then on went around the Land of the Rising Sun taking names and kicking arse. Never lost a fight, not one. Pure gangster, that. But Lord knows I've lost a good few scraps in my day, which is why I try to read up on the masters, see what I can steal from them. Doesn't matter whether it's feudal Japan or modern Scotland – some shit about people don't change, so I take what advice I can get.

'Careful not to disturb the crystals. They are laid out *very* precisely,' says Priya as I stroll around the room.

There's all these red, blue, green, black and ice-like rock crystals deliberately set on different parts of the floor. A couple are glued to the walls too. The smallest one is about the size of my finger and the largest is bigger than my noggin.

'What do these do?'

'Energies. It's complicated. I'd have to sit you down for you to get it.'

I walk up to the bed and stand directly in front of Max. There's a drip feeding IV fluids through a cannula in his arm and a nasogastric tube up his nose. This close up I can see tiny beads of sweat on his face. They've got ice packs wrapped in pillowcases around his torso and at his feet. I touch his forehead and withdraw, shocked by the sheer amount of heat radiating off him. You could cook an egg on there.

'I need to know everything you've got on him,' I say. I figure, cast a wide net, dredge the whole thing and see what comes up.

Priya gives me the rundown, right from when Max Wu was sent to Our Lady after the Royal Infirmary gave him zero chance of survival. Something about him being 'beyond conventional medicine'. Priya's kinda proud of that when she says it, and her voice rises an octave. She gives me all sorts of other information, his parents, the case history. Max was pretty sporty and in good health before this. Puberty hadn't dealt him so much as a solitary zit when his baws dropped. Good grades. Cheerful disposition, stayed out of trouble. Maybe that's possible in Poshville, not the ends I'm from. But this ain't about me. Need to remind myself of that sometimes, else you become one of those pricks who think the universe revolves around them.

'Could this be something he ate or drank, or caught off one of the kids at school?' I ask.

'You're thinking like a healer already, but no. We've already explored that avenue.'

Gran always used to tell me that when something weird is going on, you've got to eliminate every normal possibility first before you start blaming extranatural causes. It's a fine line, but if you went about spotting magical shit in everything, you'd be scuba-diving down the rabbit hole and liable to wash up in the loony bin. Then again, Priya and Lethington are the experts in this whole thing, so they have this covered. But I'll leave that on the scales till I make my own mind up. You can't let anyone else's notions cloud your judgement 'cause you're meant to be the fresh pair of eyes.

'So you guys think Max was bewitched, right? Some voodoo doll or the like?'

'No, Ropa, that kind of thing only works on telly. The human body is the most resistant thing there is to magic. As you should know by now, magic happens because of will. But the body is the ultimate vessel of will, so no magician can turn you into a pig, or cause you to get sick, without first manipulating you psychologically and binding you to their will. Even in this clinic, we need consent and compliance for our treatments to be truly effective. Little children are a different matter altogether because their wills aren't yet set. But, generally, a malevolent magician is better off dropping a brick on your head than trying to make you sick via magic.'

'No one likes a brick to the head either,' I observe.

I open the door of the bedside cabinet and crouch down so I can take a look. I go through Max's clothes, checking his pockets, and come up with nothing. Duh. These must be fresh clothes his parents brought in for him, so what did I expect? It's pretty optimistic, that – having clothes waiting 'cause they think their son'll need them when he gets better. Hope, simultaneously the most powerful and the most dangerous thing in this world.

The top drawer contains a few more personal effects, including a brown leather wallet with a hooded figure in front. The Grim Reaper? The universe ain't without no sense of irony. The wallet's light; the only coin in the pouch is a shilling.

There's a bank card, kinda retro since you can just pay for shit off your phone, but who am I to judge the whims of the moneyed. One ticket to a Mystery Fungus concert. Flyer for Bo Bumblebeam's astral tours. Shopping list. Receipts from a couple of supermarkets. Plenty of lint. My fingers are freezing just from rifling through this wallet. I need to get out of here before my toes fall off.

'So what d'you think?' Priya asks.

'Not a lot to go on, to be honest. Doesn't one of you lot have super-duper psychic powers or something?'

'LOL,' she says without laughing. 'That's not quite how it works.'

'How much time do I have on this?'

'A week, maybe two at the most. We can't keep him in suspension forever; his organs will start failing soon. Look at it like a patient with snakebite – the wrong antivenin may do more harm than good. That's why we need you to give us better clues so we can make the right diagnosis and treat him properly. A lot's riding on you, Ropa.'

No pressure then.

We leave the room and I find the warm corridor refreshing, though the goosebumps on my skin stubbornly stay. I tell Priya to get me the Wus' details so I can pay them a wee visit, seal the deal for the dosh and then get started on my enquiries. She takes me back through the maze and leaves me waiting in the staffroom while she gets a printout of the info. I notice the coat rack once again, and go through the white lab coats until I find a small one. Try it on and it fits me perfectly.

Looks like I work here too now.

V

The Wus live in a neat semi-terraced property on Morningside Drive, and I make sure to surprise them for eight. Appointments give people time to prepare a narrative, but I want raw sauce.

I've brought my number-one vulpine compadre, River, with me. She trots along next to my bike, occasionally disappearing behind this hedge and that as the spirit moves her. An extra pair of gnashers never hurt none, and I've taken to making sure she's with me more at night. She joins me in the day for emergencies only, 'cause there's more dogs about. And the owners don't much like it when I give their pets a taste of my catapult if they try to mess with River. Usually she forages her own meals at this time, so I make up for her help by sorting out her grub. You could say we have a compact.

The road has houses one side and Morningside Cemetery on the other, though the division between the living and the dead ain't as neat as this patch of tarmac suggests. I spot a couple grey ghosts trudging through the cemetery walls. Nothing to worry about though. In a graveyard this old, the ghosts there no longer have business with the living. These are the losers who can't seem to move on for whatever reason. It's the recently deceased you gotta watch out for, 'cause they're often miffed about one thing or another. That's my gift, seeing stuff like this. As far as superpowers go, it's a pretty lame one, so I'm right up there with Squirrel Girl, Arm-Fall-Off Boy and Jubilee. But, hey, gotta make the most of the hand you've been dealt in this grand old casino called life.

I get off my bike when I get to the Wus', which has a well-trimmed hedge and stairs cutting the front garden in half, leading up to the blue door. Through the turret windows I can see a TV playing in the living room. There's nothing to latch my BMX to, but I lock the wheel anyways. If anyone's gonna nick it then they at least have to put in a shift . . .

Feeling rather dapper in my white lab coat. It's got two side pockets with my katty and ammo in the right and my folded scarf in the left. Dagger sheathed at my side. Between all that gear and River beside me, I feel mighty confident waltzing about this crappy city. Fair enough, I don't anticipate shooting someone on a house call, but unlike Gaddafi and Saddam, I don't take my tactical options off the table.

I'm about to knock when a woman opens the door. She's short, about my height really, elegant and has a bob cut with a fringe.

'Mrs Wu?' I say. 'My name's Ropa, I work with the clinic.' *With* not *at*, so technically true.

'Connie,' she says, offering her hand.

I do the shakeroo and follow her inside after wiping my shoes on the doormat. Wouldn't wanna mess up the carpet. River, on the other hand, doesn't give a toss one way or the other. Just goes straight in as foxes are wont to do. Connie raises her eyebrows and blinks a couple of times.

'Is that your fox?'

'We're more of partners.'

'I see,' she says, regaining her composure.

We're led into the living room, and I sit myself on the leather recliner in the corner. For such an old house, the interior is proper done up to a contemporary standard. The fixtures and fittings have a chrome finish, and you can tell someone's poured in a bucket of dosh DIYing.

'My husband will be down shortly. Would you like a cup of tea?'

'With biscuits and some cold cuts, thanks,' I say. Always squeeze 'em for more. That's the way of the modern entrepreneur.

While Connie nips out, I scan around the bougie pad to get a feel for what sort of people they are, see if anything pops up. The mantelpiece above the fireplace has a few trophies, and one of them is a bronze face mounted on a marble cube. High achievers? The artworks on the walls look original, so they don't do prints; instead, they must choose reasonably priced stuff by local artists – the one of the grazing deer is pretty damn good. And if you combine that with the incomprehensible black-and-white flick on the TV, the arty-farty vibe is loud and clear.

'Thank you for visiting. Priya Kapoor told us you come highly recommended,' says a man walking into the room. He's geekish-looking in vintage grandpa glasses, wearing a light mustard sweater and dress pants. 'I'm Bing. You've already met my wife?'

Right on cue, Connie walks in with the tea. She places the

silver tray on a side table near me, and I thank her before setting down the plate with ham slices and Spanish chorizo for River. I swallow, wanting some of that for myself. These guys can afford to give out imported cuts so casually? My price instantly goes up by twenty percent.

'This tea's really good,' I say after taking my first sip. Normally it's just a thing you say for the sake of being polite, but this tea's actually the business. It hits the spot. Must be some pricey leaves to do my palate like that.

'It's just some premium Keemun tea, nothing fancy,' Connie says.

All I know's Tetley, Typhoo, PG and Yorkshire tea, so whatever. I nod along. For some reason the lady on TV's having her eyeball slit with a razor like it ain't no thing.

'The clinic says that if you can find out what happened to our son before he got sick it may help with his treatment,' Bing says. Down to business already. He gives off the sense impression of foggy dry ice and lights like an eighties B-movie.

'This is a very complicated case, you know. Lotta ins, lotta outs, lotta what-have-yous.' It's one of those meaningless lines you throw in and let people interpret however. 'I haven't decided to take on your case yet, 'cause of all that. I need to know more about Max. Anything at all you can tell me about him, up to the time he got sick.'

'He came home delirious, slapping his own face and saying he had to stop the "One Above All",' Connie says. 'It was horrifying.'

'A psychotic episode of some kind,' Bing adds.

'Time, day – give me the specifics,' I say. Detail is everything.

'Tuesday before last, maybe seven-ish. He'd been out with his pals all day.'

'Is there a history of mental illness in the family? Does Max do drugs?' I fire away.

'No, not at all. Our family is quite sound, on both sides. And we'd know if he was taking anything. We don't keep secrets from one another in this house.'

Yeah, right.

'Have you checked in with his friends?'

I need to know who they are and get them to corroborate Connie and Bing's story. Brother Musashi counsels, 'Do nothing which is of no use,' but at the moment I don't quite know what's useful and what's not, so I'm trawling. We'll open the net and sift through the contents later. For now I file away the reference to the 'One Above All' – whoever they are.

Through the Wus' meanderings I learn Bing is an effectician – a magician who does special effects on movie sets – and Connie is a corporate lawyer. Max is a student at the Edinburgh School, which might explain Priya's insistence on an extranatural cause. Problem is, I don't know much about magic school and all that.

'I need a list of his friends: names, phone numbers, addresses.'

'I'll give you Lewis Wharncliffe's details. That's his best friend . . . They go to school together,' Connie says.

'Max can be a bit of an introvert. He's really smart. I've always said he has his mother's brains,' says Bing, smiling at his wife. There's also an ounce of sadness in the gesture, and

I'm touched. I can only imagine what they must be going through, worry lines stencilled all over their faces like that.

'Will you help save Max, Ropa?' Connie asks desperately.

'I'll only do this if I think my work will be of some benefit.' Even though I need the wonga, I ain't about to con no one if I feel I can't do the job right. That ain't my style.

'What could be more important than saving my son's life?'

'Hun, I think she means that she has to gather all the facts and evaluate whether or not she—'

'I'm hearing her loud and clear, Bing.'

'I know this is a difficult time for you both, but I have to do this right,' I say, shifting on the sofa and leaning in. Agitating Connie's not in the plan. 'Just a few more things and then I can tell you what I think.'

When I'm done asking questions, I request to see Max's room. Bing takes me upstairs, and I check out the framed film posters on the wall. There's even one of Gran's favourites, *Mrs Hemel At The Grand Vic*, about a retired science teacher who saves a community hall from closing down by making a killing at casinos through blackjack. It's a classic.

'You helped make all of these?' I ask.

'A few. Most of them are just films I love,' Bing replies. 'It's not like the old days when effecticians were on every set. Nowadays I'd make more moving to South Africa to work as a rainmaker than I get from the pictures.'

'That's a bummer.'

'CGI will be the death of us. If it weren't for some fine producers who still believe in real effects, I'd be done for.'

And yet there he is in a picture, grinning like a Cheshire

cat with his BAFTA Award for the work he did on the World War One trench warfare epic *The Brisburn Brothers*. I've watched it, and never has a movie made me feel so claustrophobic in my life. My lungs were constricted by slow-rolling waves of phosgene gas majestically sweeping across no-man's-land, into the trenches where young men died gasping like fish out of water. I think I heard it termed 'gorgeously glorious gore' or something like that. Never pictured I'd be in the home of one of the guys who made the flick. My life keeps taking these incredible turns.

These folks have plenty of space. In this four-bedroomed house, Bing explains they've converted one into an office, the other's reserved as a guest room, main bedroom for Bing and Connie obvs, and the last is Max's, looking out into the back gardens of adjoining properties. His room's pretty messy, stacks of books and whatnot. The kid's got his own TV and gaming console. Mild adolescent pong, but who am I to judge? Socks on the floor. Dirty Converse trainers. K-pop posters of good-looking boy bands on the wall. If I had it this good in life, I wouldn't dream of checking out anytime soon.

Bing hangs back by the door while I snoop around. I start in Max's wardrobe, frisk his designer gear and come out with a couple of rubbers, still boxed, for my trouble. I work from there to his drawers, where nothing in particular catches my attention. Then I kneel by his divan and check the small gap under it, only coming up with sweet wrappers, a Rizla paper and some dirt. I do notice a few green granules of weed, and Bing and Connie may have lied about that, but I doubt that's the case. Most likely they don't know about his habit yet or they are in denial. Nothing conclusive either way – it's just normal teenage stuff: experimenting, hiding certain things from your parents, forging your own path . . . At least that's how I think it goes, seeing as I ain't got no parents. Only got Gran and my sis, Izwi, and that's all I need in this world. I don't have the luxury of forming bad habits 'cause them lot's counting on me to get by, and if I don't make it, we're all screwed sideways till the second coming.

Nothing under the mattress either. I still have to remind myself that in this game a negative result's as good as a positive. Not finding nothing means something in and of itself, and I'd like to believe I've gleaned aspects of the kid's character just by being here. I'm working Max's desk when Connie enters the room and sits on his bed. He's got loads of books and a laptop on his desk. Chandrasekar and Montague's *Advanced Aspects of Scientific Magic* catches my eye. Pretty good read, that one. *A Brief History of Time* – Stephen Hawking – ditto; I listened to the audiobook version, and while chunks of it flew over my head, there was a lot I got about physics in his day. The boy's also got a couple of other science and magic books which are standard scholarly type affairs.

At the bottom of the stack is a copy of *Daemonologie*, published in 1599 by James VI of Scotland . . . or James I of England as he was AKAed once he held the crown of both kingdoms. After he moved down to England circa 1603, he only ever returned to Scotland once, and then had the nerve to boast that he ruled Scotland with a pen. Textbook bellend if you ask me. Never read his *Daemonologie* myself, but I've seen it touched upon in various books about magic, usually in a condescending manner since the sort of necromancy, divination, sorcery, witchcraft and demonology it deals with are areas consigned to the loony fringes of unscientific magic. King James wasn't no magician, but he dabbled in esoterica, mixing in religion, folklore and superstition. It's the sort of mystical stuff they wouldn't be teaching at a proper magic school. So why does Max have it?

I look inside the book, and it alone doesn't have the library stamp from the Edinburgh School, which the rest of the books have. So he must have bought it or sourced it elsewhere.

'You mind if I borrow this?' I ask as Connie joins us. Poor lassie – she still looks so anxious.

'Go right ahead.'

I pop it in my backpack, then I try his laptop. But it's locked, and neither of them has a password for it. Well, I came, I saw, and I need the money since it's not like I'm getting that elsewhere, so I turn to Connie and Bing and offer my services.

'I can't guarantee anything, but I'll investigate some leads which may help your healers find the right treatment for Max,' I say.

'Thank you so much,' Connie replies.

Don't thank me yet, I think. With daily expenses and such, I'm gonna charge a Highland war chest for this job. I'm back, baby!

VI

It's after ten and me and River are nearly home, making our way through Wester Hailes, when a new ghost pops up in front of me. It holds out its vaporous hands in supplication. I can tell it's recently deceased 'cause it hasn't yet been able to find its form and it looks kinda smokey. Now I ain't done no ghostalking after my business tanked; it's been hard getting clients because the spiritualists have edged me out. This might be a blessing – the Wus ain't paid my retainer yet and I could do with a bit of extra cash to keep the family going – so I stop my bike and whip out my mbira from my backpack.

River draws near me, a bit edgy. She don't dig deados much, and I can't say I blame her. Used to spook me out before I got used to dealing with it.

On closer inspection, even though this ghost doesn't have a true form yet, he's just about managed to summon up a sort of tie with a complicated knot on his chest, even getting the crinkling in the spectral fabric right. That happens sometimes, but rarely, through a deep desire that spontaneously expresses a need. Must've really liked ties back in the day.

The ghost comes up to my face and goes, 'Booga wooga wooga.'

Give me strength.

Now, I'm a bit rusty and I can't hear ghosts unless I have an accompaniment, hence the mbira. Old-school musical instrument the Shona people use to commune with the souls of their ancestors. See, if you twang it just right, the harmonics synchronize with the spectral zone, and then me and the ghost can understand one another. I decide to play Sekuru Gora's 'Kufa Kwangu' 'cause I feel it's got the apt vibe for this deado who's just passed. You get a knack for sussing which track syncs with which ghost over time.

'Help me,' the newbie cries out once the waves hit him proper.

I can't just get into it straight like that. There's terms and conditions that I have to lay out or else I'm liable to lose my licence. So I give him the kauderwelsch:

'Okay, I can deliver a message from you to anyone you want within the city limits. There's a three-tier charge for this service, banded in a low flat fee, a middle flat fee and a high flat fee, plus twenty percent VAT. The band you fall into depends on the length, complexity and content of the message. If you cannot pay the bill, the fee will be reverse-charged to the recipient with a small surcharge. Please note: this service does not transmit vulgar, obscene, criminal or otherwise objection- able messages, but a fee may still be incurred if we decide to pass on a redacted version of the message. Do you understand?'

'Please, you've got to help me. I couldn't find no other medium nearby, so I had to come to you.'

'I'll take that as a yes, even though it sucks to know I'm the last resort.'

Anyways, the deado tells me about his situation and the errand he needs done, and I'm like, don't sweat it, man. RIP. I got this. That goes on my to-do for tomorrow morning. Between this commission, the Wu job and my internship, I can at least say I've diversified my portfolio.

'Something smells real nice,' I say, stepping into the cara. It's a warm evening and the windows are open, but I sniff tatties and spicy beans.

'Help yourself to a plate,' Gran says.

'Did you bring me anything nice?' Izwi asks.

'My day was great and I hope yours was too, sis,' I reply, retrieving Jammie Dodgers from my pocket and tossing them to her. Great, now I've got crumbs and jam to wash out too. Wasn't the brightest idea to pinch 'em without wrapping them first. Lesson learnt.

I grab a bowl of food and a spoon and plonk myself next to Gran on the berth. Coming from a big house like the Wus', our caravan feels even tinier than it did when I left this morning. I toss my phone to Izwi 'cause she likes to play games on it. Sometimes I find myself wishing I could get her a console and TV just like the ones Max has. Maybe once my Highland war chest is settled in full I can get the kid her own phone so she stops bugging me.

'You done any learning today, sis?' I ask.

'Give her a break. It's the holidays, Ropa,' Gran answers.

'She's got to stay on top of her books. The only break we get is when we're six feet under,' I reply. 'Maybe not even then.'

'Is the new job bothering you?' she asks.

'Nah, everything's on the up, Gran. Your hair couldn't turn whiter if you worried any more about me,' I reply.

She laughs, and it's loud and warm, filling the caravan. It's so infectious, soon Izwi joins in, and now I'm nearly choking on this potato 'cause I'm cracking up too. What the hell, I'm with my favourite girls, my belly's full, and I got work and cheddar to come. It's a good night.

Later, after both Gran and Izwi have gone to sleep, I'm lounging on my bunk when I take out King James VI's *Daemonologie*. It comes to me this was the same geezer who, after convening the Hampton Court Conference, dealt with the issues the Puritans had with various aspects of the faith, before getting round to commissioning a vernacular translation of the Bible. The King James Version of the Bible went on to become a smash hit worldwide. Can't say the same about *Daemonologie*, but it seems Jimmy Boy was all about them books.

I settle down to read the damn thing, so I can find out what Max wanted from this discredited text. There are all these notes scribbled in the margins of every page. Question marks and mathematical workings. Passages underlined. Seems to me he was deep into this text. It's hard for me to follow what exactly he was deriving from it, seeing as he has years of magical instruction behind him and I'm just starting out. But this is the antithesis of scientific magic, so why would a student from the Edinburgh School bother with it?

Might put on a podcast tomorrow so I learn a bit more about James VI from some experts. Couldn't hurt. Maybe that'll take me somewhere, maybe it won't. But right now, I feel what Sherlock Holmes would have called 'the present moment you thrill with the glamour of the situation and the anticipation of the hunt', or something smartish like that.

Wahey, the hunt is on.

VII

The worst thing about death is how inconvenient it is for everyone involved. It seldom picks that beautiful made-for-TV moment: the patriarch lying in bed, after a long life well lived, giving his adoring family his last words of wisdom before drifting off with a gentle sigh. Mediums would be out of work if shit went down like that.

The tie knot guy is called – was called? – Arawn McNulty, and he was sat on the loo, doing his business, the evening before his daughter's wedding when his ticker went kaboom. He found the whole incident rather embarrassing. 'Not how I thought I'd go out at all,' he kept saying to me last night. Welcome to the club. No one's ever ready, and if they tell you they are, they're lying.

I get to the house in Westburn nice and early 'cause I gotta get this side hustle sorted before I begin bloodhounding away. The place is nestled behind dour-looking flats with its back to Wester Hailes Road, which creeps up onto the B701.

I press the doorbell.

Someone inside swears and opens the door.

'Fuck do you want?' says a woman with bags under her eyes.

'Arawn sent me,' I say.

'You taking the piss, hen?'

I show her my licence and she spends an incredible amount of time reading it. Even flicks it over to check the inscription on the back. I maintain a solemn face in keeping with the occasion.

'Who is it?' a man calls from inside.

'Some lassie – says she's a medium.'

'Ghostalker,' I correct her. Misrepresentation is an offence.

'Let her in,' the man calls out.

My boots are wet, but I don't bother taking them off as I enter. The carpet's so old and stained it's not worth the hassle. Every home has a unique scent, a signature of the occupants. Here it's old fags, farts and stale booze snagged in the fabrics. I follow the woman into the living room, where people are sat on the sofas, looking sombre.

'Is Cheryl in?' I ask.

'What do you want?'

'I know this is a bad time. My sincerest condolences.' I pause for a second. 'The message is for Cheryl.'

'Go on then. Out with it.'

'There's the small matter of payment. I understand your situation, but Arawn's well aware of the costs for the service.'

'You having a giraffe?' A young guy in one of the armchairs stands up; my hand rests on my lap next to my dagger. 'My dad's died and you're trying to scam us?'

The needle on the thermometer drops right in front of my eyes. The door's just behind me, if things go south, but I made the blunder of letting bag-eyes stand there, blocking my exit. I'm not feeling this vibe. These ends are full of neds you don't wanna mess with. They don't take too kindly to being taken for eejits. I should have done this thing at the door. I maintain my chill and pick my mark, the source of the aggression.

'You must be Keiron. Arawn told me about you. Hand me that tie you've got there.' He frowns, confused, and I hold out my hand. 'He told me you spent weeks practising, yeah, and you still can't get the bloody knot right.'

I sling the tie round my neck like it's something I do every morning.

I look around the room, give everyone a microsecond of attention, make sure I look confident. You learn to walk with your chin up and shoulders square on the estate. Any sign of weakness and the big bad wolves are lining up huffing and puffing outside your straw house. In time the kiln hardens you, till you're solid or you burn out. Either or, nothing in between. Quick glance at the pics shows me the peroxide blonde in the armchair is Arawn's wife, Katriona. I might not be in school, but the streets will learn you the sort of smarts no PhD can.

Wide end of the tie close to my belt, leaving the thin end longer. Cross the thin end over the right and back to the left. Loop it through the centre. Tough crowd's watching, but I've been to Easter Road with my departed gramps to watch Hibs play footie; you can't faze me that easily. Down the left, no, that's meant to go right and across – switch. Through the neck loop from below and down to the right. Round the back and across to the left. I must have been a gentleman in a former life. Across the front and through the loop that went round the back, then down to the left-hand side again. Finally, I thread through the neck loop, do the same for the right-hand side and then loop over to the right side and tuck the remainder around my neck. And that's how you tie a perfect Eldredge knot.

'Arawn told me I might have to help you with this.'

'No,' Katriona says, covering her mouth with both hands.

Keiron staggers back and falls into his chair. Tears swell up in his eyes. He's barely twenty, frugal tash above his lip. Them lot in here are looking at one another like they've just seen Lazarus.

'Arawn says he paid a kidney for this "bloody wedding" and he'll be damned if it doesn't go ahead,' I say.

'Aye, sounds like him, right enough. Tight tadger,' says Katriona, and she laughs. The whole room follows, and the mercury rises a notch. 'Someone make this lass a cuppa. Tell Cheryl to get dressed, and someone let Beiste know the wedding's back on. He's not getting out of it that easy.'

I breathe a sigh of relief as I'm ushered to the free dining chair at the table. A skinhead with tattoos of flames and 88s who's been sat quietly, watching, comes across the room to sit next to me. Funky. He's Arawn's brother, Walter. We talk money and he ponies up.

'You'll be coming to the wedding, right?' he says.

It doesn't sound like a request to me.

Yawn-fest wholesalers at St John Ogilvie, the Catholic shoebox-style church down in Sighthill. It's a short distance away and our party walked down here, the bride in her heels, hitching up her dress with the rest of the ladies fussing around her. The groom, Beiste, and his people are already at the church waiting. I've got a different tie on; it was Walter's grotesque idea that I wear Arawn's oversized jacket, so I resemble a scarecrow as I go up the aisle and give the bride away. He who pays the mbira player and all that – this is bonnie Scotland after all.

After I do my bit, I hang out with the ned faction on the pews. Lots of ahs and sniffling, bittersweet joy mixed in with unbearable loss. Soon they'll be back in the same church with the same priest for the funeral. Life's relentless like that. The world don't stop for a minute, not for the worst grief, not for the worst tragedy. The sun rises on cue every morning. The wind blows on her course. Rivers flow and rain falls. Vows are taken and later broken.

I am bloody moved by it all.

After, we hit the Westsyder for the reception. I'd politely declined, seeing as how I felt I'd gone above and beyond in discharging my duties, but Walter wasn't having none of it. In any case, scribbled in my notebook is a transcript of Arawn's speech. I caught his form hovering outside the stained-glass windows of the church as the couple were taking their vows. Gave him the thumbs up as he ascended to the land of the tall grass knowing his daughter was happily married.

The Westsyder's a pretty grungy pub. Katriona pulls pints here and it's a free venue. The publican's given us one half of the place, and punters nurse pints on the other side. Occasionally someone raises a glass to the newly-weds. There's a pool table and some of our party are already jamming, a few dancing along to pop coming from the speakers around the pub.

It's not a big wedding, just forty or so of us. Beiste and Cheryl are both on the wrong side of thirty and they seem happy, save for the moments Cheryl looks at the door like she's expecting someone to walk in. I've seen that look of loss and longing so many times I know that she's secretly hoping it's all been one big misunderstanding – that any moment now her dad will walk in, smile upon his face, wondering what all the fuss is about.

Sigh.

Them kinds of hopes are inevitable, but that's simply not how this works. Dead is dead, and the great magician from Galilee never told anyone his secret spell for reversing it. There's no monkey's paw either, otherwise I know a few who'd make that bargain. All these beautiful people; we're all just worm food in the end. But my thoughts are way too grim for a wedding, so I concentrate on the stuffed Yorkshires and fries I've been given instead.

After we've had our meal, I'm asked to read out Arawn's speech. It starts:

'Sorry I'm pan breed . . .'

That gets them laughing. I'd told Arawn that was a bit morbid, waaaay too soon, but he seemed to know his crowd, seeing how they cackle. It's the only thing any of us can throw back at the void. I think of death as a dark cave sometimes, and the only thing you can hear in there is the sound of human laughter bouncing off the walls. We marry. We live on, goddamn it. I read out Arawn's words to the future he authored, the relentless future that will happen without him. It's an ode to joy, and when I'm done there isn't a dry eye in the pub.

Even the bar staff weep as they pull pints.

When the dancing starts, I sneak off. Gopher-rock ain't my cup of Horlicks. I go out the door and round the back, where I find Walter leaning against the wall, having a fag.

'Yous off the now?'

'You lot want me to do the honeymoon too?' I say, and he bursts out laughing.

'Listen, I dinnae believe in all that mumbo jumbo about the afterlife, but you did alright by us today. A few folk in there're happier than they were this morn, and I cannae fault that one bit.'

'You can come back and tell me that when you cross over.'

'Aye, if that be true, I'll drop in on you.'

Some folks still think the earth is flat and the sun shines out of their backsides, so I don't usually waste no time trying to dissuade them 'cause it's pointless. I've done my job and that's all that matters. Walter's happy to let me go, but not before he takes his brother's jacket and tie back. Fair enough; I've got places to be and people to see.

VIII

Eleven-ish and I'm running a bit later than I thought, but, hey, I feel like I've just come out of a Hugh Grant romcom so that's okay. My steel-toecap boots are falling apart, making it hard to cycle. I have to pause on Hermitage Drive to do a bit of cobblering. Park my bike on the kerb and sit my booty down on the pavement. Then I grab some silver duct tape from my backpack and get to it. The left boot's coming apart from where the toecap joins the sole. I cut out some tape to cover the fraying seam, creating a silver curve running to the sole of the shoe. Then I stick another bit across the midfoot, tracing an arc just below the laces.

Looks decent, that.

My Spidey senses are tingling. Feels like I'm being watched, but when I scan the street, not a soul in sight. Hmm. Happens sometimes when you step into these sorts of neighbourhoods, coming in from the slums like I do. Douches watching you in case you steal something . . . which in my case is true since I did a spot of burglaring back in the day. So I don't have a leg to stand on.

Fuck it – where was I?

They say duct tape was used to fix aircraft wings and stuff

in a jiffy back when folks were flying around the world like it was their oyster, so it's good enough for my leather boots. The right don't need fixing, but I figure I might as well tape it up for symmetry. Anyway, it'll make 'em last a wee while longer, I reckon.

And it'll look nice with my swanky new lab coat.

When I'm done cobblering, I put on my boots and make the short ride down to Corrennie Gardens, where Lewis Wharncliffe lives. Nice little neighbourhood that invites the term *leafy*. Pretty colourful this summer with flowers in full bloom along the front gardens lining the street. It's the Braid Hills end of town, a stone's throw from the Wus'. Reckon Max and Lewis would have seen each other plenty over the years. I knock on the door and put on my most officious face. When no one answers, I knock a second time before I hear footsteps thumping down the stairs.

A lanky teenager opens the door and yawns. He's in blue-and-white-striped pyjamas, has a shiny, acne-riddled face. I reckon there's enough sebum in those pores to light half of Edinburgh. Dishevelled hair cut in a mullet – I'm down with that retro look.

'You Lewis Wharncliffe?' I ask.

'The one and only.' His voice is screechy and high pitched, but not like it's breaking.

'I need to talk to you about your friend Max Wu,' I say, hoping to sound authoritative. 'Don't worry, you're not in any trouble.'

Lewis looks me up and down with his droopy eyes and holds the door open for me. Despite his nonchalant look, this kid is electric guitars and mosh pits – there's that angsty, existential fizz bubbling beneath those blocked pores.

'Josh, get off him and play nice,' Lewis says to his little brothers tumbling in the living room. 'Sorry, babysitting duties. My parents won't even pay me for it. They just expect me to do it for free, like.'

'Bummer, man.'

'Let's go up to my room, away from this racket,' he says.

I'm not gonna turn down the opportunity to do a bit of snooping like that. Old habits die hard, and I spot juicy pickings worth nicking in this property. Have to remind myself to keep my mind on the job.

Lewis's room is an absolute tip. Clothes strewn across the bed and on the floor. Megadeth poster on one wall and Queens of the Stone Age on the other. Video game and film posters too. An upside-down crucifix – I guess that's supposed to be subversive. Prints of some Vettrianos, oozing sex and old-world charm. And books galore, magic texts mostly, but a hell of a lot more than I saw in Max's room. I notice Lewis is also into his Aleister Crowley, with several thelemic texts by the guy, plus he's got a copy of George Sinclair's 1685 *Satan's Invisible World Discovered*, which is more occult than the scientific magic he ought to be studying at the Edinburgh School. Reading this kind of stuff would be the equivalent of a surgeon getting deep into seventeenth-century quackery manuals. Just wouldn't fly.

So I ask him, 'What are you studying?'

'I major in sonicology. You know, the magic of sound, vibrations and their effects.'

Makes sense to me, seeing as I use a mbira to talk to ghosts, so I whip it out of my bag and show it to him.

'Ace – there's powerful waves you can get from this artefact,' he says. 'See, lots of people are into digital sounds and all that, but when you look at ancient, tribal ceremonial instruments, drums, didgeridoos, that kind of stuff, they really tap into the cosmic harmonics in deep and meaningful ways, sonically. You couldn't do that on a synth.'

I mirror his enthusiasm to build rapport.

'Can I buy it off you?' he asks.

'My granda made it.'

'Family heirloom, cool.'

'Some of your books aren't exactly the stuff of magical science.' Better start digging.

'At my school they call Crowley a fraud. Sinclair wasn't even on the syllabus. They've taken spirituality out of magic. They've stripped it of its soul,' he says, reaching for a bong on the table. He sets about filling it, and I recall the weed in Max's room. Two stoners veering off the beaten path. Makes sense.

'I take it you don't much like the Edinburgh School, then,' I say.

He shrugs and launches into a tirade about regulations and restrictions impeding the practice of modern magic. Some stuff about how rediscovering the old ways will 'shift the paradigm' and open up a new age of magic not just for the elites but for the masses as well. It's pretty hazy and utopian.

Misfit? I wonder. But this guy's an open book, it seems.

Doesn't even know who I am yet he's yammering already. Talkers are a godsend, so long as they aren't attempting to fill time to avoid certain subjects. But Lewis gives off the vibe that he doesn't think he's got anything to hide from me, which makes my life that little bit easier. He opens the window, fires up his bong, takes a hit, and the room's filled with notes of lemongrass and an earthy herbal smell. That's when I notice a slight tremor in his hands as I take a seat on the window-sill. The back garden's huge out here.

'You said you wanna talk about Max, yeah?' he says, holding smoke in his lungs. 'How's he holding up? You from the clinic, right?'

'I was commissioned by the clinic,' I say. Keeps it ambiguous enough. 'Max's parents said you were the last person to see him before he came down with something. Is that right?'

Lewis doesn't reply. Stares off into space with his mouth slightly agape. He wants to talk, but he's afeard like.

'Anything you say to me is strictly between us. No one else will know,' I say, hoping my white coat will signal some aura of medical confidentiality.

He blows out smoke.

There's a loud bang from downstairs.

'If you monkeys don't behave I'm coming down there!' Lewis shouts. 'Sorry, my siblings aren't house-trained. Fancy a drag?' He offers the bong and I decline.

'I have a little sister who's just as wild,' I reply. 'Max Wu came to see you before he got sick – is that correct?'

'I ain't seen Max all through the holidays.'

'But his parents said . . .'

'A load of bollocks. We ain't really been pally for near enough a year now, maybe even longer. Max is full of shit.'

Lewis takes a drag, and the bitterness in his tone is evident. Seems to me like someone got jilted. I'm not entirely sure how this would be relevant to some unknown pathogen, but in the absence of real, specific instructions as to what I'm meant to report back to Our Lady, I chuck that in the net along with everything else.

'The Wus told me you guys have been tight since you were kids.'

'Max was alright until he got a call-up from the Monks . . . At least, I think that's what happened. It's all rumours at the school, you see. No one really knows whether they exist or not. It's super secret. But why would they take Max and not me? I'm a better magician and more learned in the mysterious ways than Max.'

'Back up a second. Who are these Monks?'

'I told you, it's a rumour, so I can't say for certain,' Lewis says, agitated. 'There's all sorts of weirdness at the Edinburgh School – clubs, fraternities – but there's one in particular that's said to date back to its founding. They call themselves the Monks of the Misty Order for some reason, and it's super exclusive. They're not real monks though. Obviously.'

So I made a mistake. The hooded Grim Reaper I thought I saw on Max's wallet is actually a Monk.

'How do you join?'

'Some say you get a tap on the shoulder and a passcode whispered in your ear when you're walking through the halls. I've also heard it can be a note slipped onto your desk asking you to attend a meeting. Or you corporeally cross over into an unknown dimension beyond conventional magic. Then there's some that say certain teachers are involved in selecting the students and they're the ones that actually pick the Monks. They practise forbidden magic. At least, that's what I think. It's all speculation, because they say you don't know until you know.'

'Hmm.'

'I've been hunting them since forever, but I've always come up short. It's like trying to find a unicorn in the middle of Edinburgh. There's lots of rumours, some dark, forbidden occultish shit, but nothing I can say for certain. Max had a theory that you don't wait for the Monks to invite you in – you find them yourself. I didn't believe it at the time, but I think he got in.'

'What makes you certain of that? If he did get into the fraternity, why wouldn't he bring you along?'

'I just know, okay? Something's well shady about him. Max and me used to link up to play *Froidberg's War*, and then suddenly he stopped, just like that. We were thick as thieves and then, with no explanation, he wasn't hanging out with me no more. Naturally, I'm like, WTF? But he wouldn't even give me a straight answer. Just kept saying he was busy with something big he was working on. We used to do *everything* together. Then there were days he wasn't home at night, and the next thing I hear is his mum asking if he'd slept over here and so, of course, I lied to cover his behind, but it never stopped, kept happening . . . and before I knew it, it was too late for me to tell the truth, to say hey, I don't know where he's at.'

'Did Max ever tell you where he'd been or what he was up to?'

'Seriously? Are you even listening to anything I've been saying?' Lewis throws a strop. Takes a drag from his bong and blows it past me out the window.

'I had to double-check.'

'Whatever it is, I knew it was gonna end badly. I've been to the clinic, and it can't be good when they have Max in a freezer like that. Might as well be in the morgue already. I'm gonna find those bawbags and make them pay for what they did to my pal.'

Not while you're out here babysitting and getting stoned, my friend, I think. It's gonna be up to me. But at least I have an ally of sorts. Maybe this intel's square, or Lewis is a paranoid jakey, bum out the window. I'm not sure yet. At the very least I can make out that there was a change in behaviour prior to Max getting sick, so that counts for something. Then again, who knows how friendships shift between lads like this. It's not exactly like outgrowing *Froidberg's War* is a bad thing.

'You know what the kicker is?' Lewis says, all mellow and philosophical.

'Go on.'

'They used Max to pinch my research. Can you believe it? I wasn't worthy to join the Monks, but I'm a complete tube, so they stole my best mate and then used him to dig out the work I'd done on esoterica. Max lifted my notes. I've got nothing left.'

'What sort of arcane knowledge are we talking about?'

'I've been trying to crack the *Daemonologie*,' he says, staring intensely, dilated pupils in his grey eyes. Bingo.

Fireworks are popping off in my noggin when something whizzes through the open window and lands on the carpet with a dull thud. A green package.

'Skellypog! Get on the ground,' Lewis shouts.

I don't need to be told twice. The package goes bonkers, springing into the air and breaking the lightbulb before pinging under his desk, where it bangs against the woodwork. All while making weird croaking sounds like a toad on heat as it knocks stuff over, zipping across the room at incredible speeds. I'm curled up in the foetal position when I feel my scarf move out of my pocket and extend itself over me. The skellypog or whatever the fuck that is must have come my way 'cause the scarf flicks faster than a cobra striking. Suddenly the croaking grows muffled before winding down. It farts one last time, releasing a vile plume of gas.

All that's left is my vibrating ninja scarf holding the so-called skellypog. It's made of cashmere but grips hard as a vice. Never have I been happier seeing its moth-eaten colourful squares so proudly on display.

'Bastards,' says Lewis, getting up from the floor. 'Look at the state of my room.'

'What was that about?'

'A message from the Monks, I think,' he replies soberly. 'You pop up asking questions and my place gets bombed.'

I did feel I was being watched earlier. Maybe someone was following me.

I get up slowly, and by now the thing in the scarf is proper dead. I ain't sure if it's safe to let it out, given the dents on the plastering, the broken mirror and the trail of disaster left in Lewis's room. Stinks like a skunk's let one rip in here. I peek outside, but there's no one in the back garden. Whoever lobbed this flying turd must have bailed while we were taking cover. Coward.

'That is one epic artefact,' he says.

'What?'

'Your scarf. May I?'

He holds out his hand, and I move my ninja scarf his way. It unfurls and drops a camouflage-painted block of wood roughly the size of my fist. It's got eyes and a toothy smile carved in front.

'We make these in school for the kicks, kind of like a prank type thing. It mashes your stuff up if you're not careful. Broken a few noses, and teeth too. This means the Monks are watching me. They know that I know.'

'At least no one's hurt,' I say.

'Look at this mess . . . My mum's going to kill me.'

I close the window slightly, but not all the way because it's pure rank in here. Now, I don't know if this is just some kind of prank the boys at magic school play or if it's really a message from some secret fraternity, but either way, it ain't funny. Worst-case scenario is these padres are watching Lewis, which means they know about me. That must mean I'm already onto something, but what exactly? There's only one thing for it. I gotta arrange a meet at the Library.

IX

The glow of the evening sun casts long shadows from the pillars of the unfinished replica of the Parthenon atop Calton Hill. The shadows stretch along the undulating terrain, hiding me while I try to find the hairline fracture running along the third pillar from the left. Once I step into it, I stumble like you do when you're going down stairs and you hit the landing but still expect another step below you. A blur of colour, a hum that rattles my bones. My stomach plummets. When I regain my footing, I find myself in a cavernous room, roughly hewn walls slick with condensation. There's an old bellhop in a cap and maroon uniform dozing on a chair. He's startled awake by my entrance, and he clears his throat.

'Library card,' he says morosely.

I hand him the desiccated human ear I keep in a pouch in my backpack. He punches a hole in the earlobe and hands it back to me, saying, 'Bicycles in the racks provided within the anteroom,' before promptly falling asleep once more.

I still get the heebie-jeebies every time I come into this place 'cause the first time I was nearly hung by the neck until I expired by its psycho librarians. One of them is my day-one-super-duper bestie for life and beyond, but still, them folks run a tight ship and this place is more exclusive than the Royal & Ancient in St Andrews. Not that I'm into golf or any of that malarkey, but unless you're a magician you ain't getting the ear that marks you as a member. I've even met a celebrity here, though that didn't end well . . . for them.

It's a cool spot to hit the books, especially since I want some business-type texts to guide my practice. Whether I'm sleuthing or ghostalking, I need to be running my shit like a pro if I'm gonna make it in the magicking world, especially since I'm starting with the major handicap of not going to one of them fancy magic schools. I gotta work twice as hard and be ten times as good.

But today I'm here to meet Priya, Jomo and Lewis. Gotta make sense of this mess, and four heads are better than one. Lewis doesn't know how lucky he's got it, having direct access to the Library thanks to the Edinburgh School. Bet he never got threatened with hanging by the neck till expiry.

I make my way down the stone stairs with my BMX slung upon my shoulder, deeper into the heart of the gallery. They pretty much carved out the insides of Calton Hill, so the Library is less of a building and more of a sculpture. Or maybe that should be Libraries in the plural 'cause it's officially named 'Calton Hill Library, incorporating the Library of the Dead'.

Same difference, as far as I'm concerned.

I get down to the front desk, where Mr Sneddon is doing paperwork.

'Hey there,' I say.

'Please keep your voice down, Miss Moyo. This is a library, not a pub,' he replies in a hushed tone.

'Nice to see you too,' I whisper, which earns me a half-smile in return. 'I need your help, Mr Sneddon. I'm looking for books on how to improve my business skills. It's not going all that well at the moment.'

'Magipreneurship?'

'Something like that,' I reply.

'Come with me.'

We're in the reception area three storeys down the orb-like structure of the main section of the Library. I've been here enough times to know it's labyrinthian and there's still many sections I haven't explored. They didn't give me no induction or nothing like that when I started. I stay close behind Sneddon, who wears his flowing dark green cassock that makes him look like a priest. He walks with hunched shoulders and a shuffling gait, struggling up the stairs to the balcony one floor up. Burning candles on the hewn black rock illuminate the way. We pass by a white marble statue of Heracles slaying the many-headed hydra. He's depicted wearing a lion's skull for his helmet, and in the shifting candlelight he seems to come alive, shadows flickering as we pass.

Him and that hydra will be at it forever.

Sneddon veers suddenly left, and we find ourselves walking through a row of stone bookshelves carved up and out of the floor. One of them has a broken middle shelf that lies slanted on the shelf below. Books of decreasing size line the shelf at an angle that matches the damage. The smallest book there is no larger than my thumb.

The set-up makes me wonder what would happen if this

whole hill collapsed atop our heads. Should have brought a hard hat with me.

'In here,' Sneddon says, walking through a bead curtain doorway into a branching cavern. It's like stepping into an animal's lair. The floor here is uneven, sloping upwards, while the ceiling presses down until they meet in the distance.

More books, thousands upon thousands of them all on the shelves. It's a hodgepodge of paperbacks, hardbacks, cloth-bound, leatherbound – all sorts of material out there. One immediately catches my eye, and I pull it off the bookshelf.

The Wealth of Magicians.

I might take a gander 'cause it sounds alright.

'I don't think so,' Sneddon says, snatching the book from my hand and replacing it on the shelf. 'Dated, obtuse, highly theoretical, not the sort of contemporary practical knowledge you need. I was thinking more of Bannatyne or Rupini. This way.' We go past three more shelves before turning into one on the right. Sneddon plucks a red book from the top shelf. 'That's more like it.'

Rich Sorcerer, Poor Sorcerer: A Practical Guide to the Sound Management of Your Magical Career by Rossworth Rupini. The author is a middle-aged guy on the front cover with a Hollywood smile exuding confidence, good genes and success.

What do I know? Let's do a first-page test, go through the introduction and see what this is all about:

'It's a little acknowledged fact that money is the invisible hand that guides magic. Indeed, talk of the subject is considered unrefined or even shameful in certain circles. The truth is that ever since the first shaman accepted a goat or chicken in exchange for a prayer, a charm or a hex, the path for magical enterprise was set. Ask yourself, how does Gandalf pay his mortgage? Does Glinda the Good Witch turn bailiffs into frogs when they visit about her credit card debts? No, here in the real world, practical management of one's business affairs is crucial for success, happiness and respect in the magicking world and in your personal life. Drawing from over three decades of personal experience and using countless examples taken from top-echelon busigicians, I will show you the pathway to prosperity . . .'

This guy's speaking my lingo and I'm lapping up every word, so I look up and wink at Sneddon, who has his arms folded, hidden within the long sleeves of his robes.

Then I have an idea.

'Mr Sneddon, I'm on the go a lot, so I was wondering if you had, like, an audio version of this book.'

A pained look passes over Sneddon's face. I assume he's one of those dead-tree fundamentalists, the sort who'd stick the head of every e-book reader upon a pike if they were king.

'It so happens we do for some texts,' he says reluctantly.

Just then I recall the jargon of this place. The librarians call everything in this section 'texts' for some reason, even though it's the normal stuff, you know, hardbacks, scrolls, pamphlets, palimpsests, paperbacks, et cetera. Makes you wonder where the 'books' are then. But what do I know, I'm only an associate member of the Library with 'limited privileges'. Long story.

Sneddon holds his hand out, and I give him the *text*.

'Lift the jacket and check under the spine. If you find an

earworm there, that's your audio file,' he says, displaying a grey wriggler snug against the spine of the book. 'Most of the contemporary texts have them – thankfully, not so much the older material. These rare creatures are only found in the soils on the Isle of Rùm in the Inner Hebrides.'

'Ha?' I'm totally lost.

Sneddon sighs. He pulls the earworm from the book, and it squirms between his fingers. Before I can react, he sticks the damned thing in my ear. I'm about to front on account I feel violated, when I hear, very clearly, a ballsy Midwestern salesman's accent: Rossworth Rupini, presenting his book. It's directly in my head, as close and as intimate as my own thoughts. I've listened to lots of books and podcasts and stuff like that, but nothing that feels like this. I can still hear the ambient noise of what's going on around me. Must look awkward though, with half the wriggler in my ear canal, tail dangling out. Then again, how else would I remove it? It's like an ear tampon, I think, drawing it out painlessly.

'I've seen it all now,' I say.

'Not even the half, Miss Moyo,' Sneddon replies dryly.

'But why didn't you call them bookworms?'

'Don't be tedious.'

'Whatever. I think I'm going to be best friends with them earworms of yours.'

'Good, seeing as they have an affinity for readers with nothing in between their ears.'

I feel the third-degree burn across seventy percent of my skin right there. Still, I'm sorted and pleased for it 'cause I can read on the go now. The only proviso, Sneddon warns, is that the earworm has to be within three feet of the text to work, so I still have to take the book with me. Guess digital file transfers, streaming, the cloud, that sort of thing is out of the question in this place. Still, I'm happy, and I make sure to let Sneddon know.

'I'm glad to have been of some use,' he says. 'Is there anything else, Miss Moyo?'

'Just one thing, where is Jomo?' I ask.

'Your friend Mr Maige Junior is on candle wax–cleaning duties. If you want to find him, I suggest you follow the sound of scraping. Have a nice day.'

'You too, Mr Sneddon,' I say as he walks off. Still can't get over the fact that you have to call everyone in here Mr or Ms or whatever. It's a posh wank, but when in Rome don't forget your laurel wreath.

At least that's one thing I can strike off my list. From now on I shall engage in the 'sound, practical management' of my 'business affairs'.

Got a bit of time to kill before Priya and Lewis get here, so I might as well sort out issue number two, which is practising my spellcraft. If the skellypog bomb earlier today taught me anything, it's that I have to be better prepared for nasty surprises. Whether that was a prank or no, I have to up my game in this hustle if I'm to get my goats and chickens.

X

God, the stairs in this place are brutal. And they ain't got no lifts either, so you just have to go till your knees and hips give in. I suppose it's 'cause they haven't yet heard of this new invention called electricity. I swear, it's ridiculous, all you can smell is wax and old books in here. I'm digging the dope marble statues, though. They stand out against the dour walls of the Library, their smoothness a counterpoint to the roughly chiselled walls.

I get to the bottom floor, and from down here you can see the immense scale of the Library. The arcing walls travel up, bulging at their widest on the third balcony, before tapering off again as they ascend to the top. There's walkways across certain sections, and from below the candles look like stars shining against the black night. It's huge, beautiful and a wee bit scary.

Jomo is knelt on the floor, scraping wax off the white sarcophagus they say holds the remains of David Hume, the famous philosopher dude from back in the Enlightenment days. Jomo's hard at it, but when he looks up and sees me, his face brightens like Christmas lights.

'Ropantabulous!' he says.

A furious *shhh* comes from some nook around us.

'Hey, man,' I whisper, leaning in for a hug. He smells of cheap Brut and his unruly afro's in my face.

'Fancy having a go?' Jomo says, offering his scraper.

'Nae chance, pal.'

'It was worth a try.'

Jomo's my bestie, but I don't get to see him as often on the outside as we used to before I started working. But that's alright 'cause since he got an acolyte gig in this place we'll keep bumping into each other. In many ways the Library's taken the place of school as far as our friendship goes. He's capital A awesome and I love him to bits, though I can't help but point out the flakes of white in his hair look like a serious case of dandruff.

'That's wax,' he protests.

'Then I wonder what you look like when they have you clean the toilets.'

'Funny.'

'We need a powwow,' I say. 'Something's going down.'

Jomo gives me the side-eye, wary from our last adventure. But then he relents, as he always does when I ask him for something.

'Whatever.'

A bit dumb considering he doesn't even know the score, but that's Jomo for you. He's always been booksmart, not streetsmart. But we look out for one another, and that's the most important thing. The Library is training him to be a proper librarian, which seems to involve loads of manual labour. But being surrounded by hundreds of thousands of books is practically a wet dream for Jomo. We agree to meet when he sees Priya, who's due in a bit.

Leaving Jomo, I head below to the underHume, which is literally under David Hume's final resting place. Down here, the Library seems more like a dungeon than anything. The lighting is more frugal, but it's the only place where you're allowed to practise magic. Upstairs, the librarians are likely to catch a fit, and they're not averse to disproportionate sanctions for any infractions.

I find myself an empty practice room. Low ceiling, coarse floor and walls. If there were a few bones on the ground and maybe some charcoal drawings, it might have made a great home for the Cro-Magnon geezers.

Now Edinburgh's a dangerous city at the best of times. That's why I carry my dagger with me, always. Never leave home without it. My katty, too, 'cause screw hand-to-hand – it's no good playing fair from six feet under. I'd rather live to fight another day, or preferably not fight at all if I can help it, but that's not a choice you get to make sometimes. When some bampot comes at you, you gotta be ready.

And being ready starts with yourself. Miyamoto Musashi says, 'You can only fight the way you practise,' and that means by the time you get into something, you better be prepared. He was the real deal back in Japan – greatest swordsman who ever lived. Never lost a battle, and that's 'cause he first won the greatest fight of all, the one against himself. You have to master yourself before you can take on the world. At least, that's what I think he means in his book.

Now, I don't fight with no swords, but I've got my katty,

77

dagger and, crucially, my ninja scarf, which Sir Callander gave to me a while back. Brother Musashi also teaches us: 'Do not collect weapons or practise with weapons beyond what is useful.' I'm with him on that 'cause if you practise with loads you end up not really mastering anything at all. Now, I'm an ace with the katty, I slice and dice with my dagger as well as the next lass, but the scarf kinda does its own thing. It comes to life whenever it feels like, like a reflex action when I'm in danger, but I want to learn to control it so I can actually use it to my advantage instead of hoping it wakes up. That's peak Musashi: you've got to be in full control or else you've lost before the fight's begun.

I'm no badass samurai dude, though, and I've taken my fair share of licks over the years. So I know I have a long way to go yet.

Here goes. I take the scarf from my lab coat pocket, hold either end in my hands and give it a good tug to wake it up.

'Right, ninja scarf, you and me are going to practise some moves together, okay?' I say.

Doesn't answer, of course. But if it can sense when I'm in danger, that means it sure as hell knows what's going on.

'Come on, show us what you've got. Punch up in front of me,' I say, flicking one end of the scarf. It flies out impressively enough, but then falls limp to the ground.

I pull it back and twirl the ends – there's something in there, something more than just mere cashmere, but when I flick it out again, I'm met with failure. Knapf. I need the ninja scarf to do three things for me in a fight scenario. It should be able to attack an opponent at range, block and tangle up my adversary, which would leave me free to strike. The last one I pinched straight out of the Diana Prince S&M handbook, though I doubt my scarf can compel anyone to tell the truth. Still, if I nail this then fighting me should be like fighting an opponent with four arms.

Nothing for it but to have another go. I even pretend to be scared to see if the scarf will come to life but get nothing for my acting skills. Without the scarf's cooperation, it looks like I'm attempting rhythmic gymnastics, the routine they do with a ribbon. That's the sort of look that's like to get your behind kicked in EH1, rather than striking fear into your enemies.

Come to think of it, what are the odds Miyamoto Musashi had a magic sword? I've watched movies from Japan where there's supposed to be swords that trapped the souls of opponents, making their wielder invincible. Hmm, I'll have to figure this all out, maybe even ask Sir Callander for some tips . . . Then again, I'm not even a real apprentice, just an intern, so he probably won't be bothered to help. Old-school apprentices had a master who was actually expected to teach them stuff. That was part of the deal. Fuck knows what interns can expect; they are completely at the mercy of whoever takes them on.

Priya and Jomo come into the room just as I attempt another attack. Priya watches me with no small amount of bemusement, before I stop.

'Looking a bit limp there, sister. Performance anxiety?' she says with a giggle.

'A bit of help would be nice, since you're the only one here who actually went to magic school.'

'I'm not an expert in artefacts, Ropa. Healing and herbology is more my thing,' she says, 'but, and this is such a big but you might wanna twerk with it, have you named the scarf?'

'What's that got to do with the price of tea?'

Jomo cringes, and I realize I've missed something rather obvious. What can I say, it's been a long day.

'To name something is to own it, to have mastery over it. The magic we do is rooted in language,' Priya explains. Then she laughs. 'And I'll have you know I prefer Brodies tea.' That joke goes over my head too.

Defeated, I put the scarf away, right as Lewis walks in, rigged up in the sort of black that proudly declares him a child of the night. His monstrous platform boots have four buckles running along the side with metal studs galore, and he's wearing ripped jeans and a black vest splattered with paint. He wears indigo matte lipstick and looks like a porcelain doll 'cause of the white foundation that covers the acne. With his eyebrows and lashes done up too, he's rocking out like the catastrophe never happened.

He stands in the doorway, watching us with a bit of a smirk. There's more fizz about him, and I'm sure he's on an upper. I've been around users at my slum long enough to know what that looks like.

'Looks like the Elgin's the place to be these days – even Lord Kelvin's finest is in attendance,' he says, giving Priya a wink.

Must be something up 'cause she doesn't respond. Is there some kind of rivalry between the Edinburgh School and the Kelvin Institute?

'Come on, it's still a magic school – maybe the worst of the four, but half a loaf . . . which leads to my next point,' he says, turning to me. 'See, I've been doing a bit of digging myself, and it looks like no one from the four schools has heard of you. Practising without accreditation, that's a serious offence.'

I think I liked him better this morning. Now he's got that full-on toff arrogance that's *so* not punk.

'She's Callander's apprentice, so I'd watch it if I were you,' Priya says. 'And save that Edinburgh School BS for someone who actually cares.'

Lewis raises his eyebrows and snorts. Yep, he's got the swagger of a lad whose confidence was shipped in from South America.

'Geez, I was just kidding. Priyanka Kapoor, I used to love watching you play rugby when I was a junior. Let's do this for Max. That's why you brought us here, right, Ropa?'

It's easier to focus on work when folks stop trying to measure the length of their twallies in your face. So I make quick intros, more for Priya's and Jomo's benefit, 'cause I didn't get the chance to tell them about Lewis. Then I give everyone a rundown of the case: the mysterious illness, the *Daemonologie* book and the Monks of the Misty Order.

'See, Max had gotten weird on me ages ago, right?' Lewis says. 'Then he came back all of a sudden asking for my help with esoterica. I knew him, and he wasn't into that kind of stuff anyway.'

'What did he major in?' Jomo asks.

'Meteorological manipulation and the illusionary. He was going to join his dad in the film industry,' says Priya.

'Spot on,' Lewis says, 'except he was secretly going deep into the occult.'

'Forbidden deep?' Priya asks.

'Pre-scientific magic, like, before the Enlightenment, up to and including ancient Pictish wicca, you know, witchcraft,' Lewis replies. 'Rector Wedderburn would catch a fit if he knew. But since my minor is the history of the crafts – that's why they haven't done me for half the stuff I've read – Max said he wanted me to help. He was asking stuff about opening portals and doorways to other realms.'

So that explains the astral tourism card in his wallet. Who better to lead you off to other realms than a magician who works in that field. And this is something that I actually know about – astral realms are the bread and butter of a ghostalker.

The Society looks down on practitioners of the extranatural like me because the highest magicians are considered to be those who scientifically manipulate the natural world. A ghostalker isn't really considered a magician. This is a blind spot, 'cause now you have kids like Max trying to get into it themselves without proper instruction. I learnt my trade from my gran, and she's not a 'real magician' either. She doesn't have the sort of book learning required to be in the Society of Sceptical Enquirers.

'Good thing we have an expert in projection here with us,' Priya says, gesturing at me.

'I should have figured,' says Lewis.

'You don't wanna mess with astral projection. There's a lot of people who are not in the light, and if Max was fooling around with this stuff then who knows what he unlocked,'

I say. 'Is there a possibility he went to some realm and came back sick because of it?'

'Which realm, and causing what illness? Unless we know for definite then there's still nothing I can do in terms of Max's cure,' Priya replies.

Bugger that, I knew it couldn't have been so easy. Otherwise this would have been a good pay day. The astral plane is infinite, realms upon realms. It's too unwieldy, and finding out where Max went would be impossible. I've been out there and never got sick, though. Touch wood.

I can take care of the astral stuff, but I also need to make use of the labour I've got. Many hands and all that.

'Lewis and Jomo, I want you both to find out why Max was trying to project. See if you can come up with why these Monks want this info. Maybe it'll point us to a specific realm.'

'I'll speak with Lethington and see if he knows anything too,' Priya says.

'You do that, but I'll need you with me tomorrow night to follow up on the lead I've got in my back pocket,' I say. Maybe Max projected on his own . . . or perhaps he had help from a certain Bo Bumblebeam, astral tour guide. 'Lewis, Jomo, you guys find anything at all, ring me straight away.'

I don't give anyone a get-out clause because the clock's ticking and I can't do everything myself. I reckon me and Priya could do with a little tour tomorrow, but first thing in the morning, I gotta hit the bank.

XI

Dreich day cramping my style as I cycle onto the grounds of 36 St Andrew Square, the bank looming ahead. Scottish summers leave a lot to be desired at the best of times, but this takes the piss. Grey clouds and gloom from horizon to horizon. Can't afford to be late, though, seeing as this is my first proper day interning with the Society of Sceptical Enquirers. I might not be getting paid for it, but it's a start, and once I become a great magician myself, I'll be proper minted. I've made my peace with it seeing as I'm due good dosh from the Wus.

Funny how things work out like that sometimes. Almost feels like the universe has a plan for me. Yay.

I'm not sure where to park my bike, though. It's a pain in the arse, but bikes are like gold out here in Edinburgh. Chain yours to the wrong railing, they might take your wheels and leave you the frame. Having said that, I'm gonna need new tyres soon. My threads have had it. Screw this, I'll take my bike in with me, I think, but the black doors of 36 St Andrew Square are shut and bolted. Bugger.

I'm well drookit from riding through the drizzle earlier, so I could do with the warmth inside. Sign on the door says they are open 08:30 to 17:30 Mon to Fri, with a 16:00 finish on a Saturday. Means I have an hour's wait.

'Ah, the new *intern*,' Cockburn says, walking up the drive.

Startles me, 'cause I wasn't expecting her to sneak up like that. I would rather it were Callander I was seeing instead. He's my plug in this joint, and I'm not feeling Cockburn despite her plastic smile. She wears a dull business suit with exaggerated shoulder pads, and she looks me over disapprovingly. I'm in my lab coat, a Rajinikanth T-shirt, faded blue jeans and my boots, not the corporate shit I wore last time. I figure they ain't paying me enough to endure corns from ill-fitting borrowed shoes.

'Hit the ground running, that's the best way,' she says in a tone that suggests she expects me to fall straight on my face.

'I look forward to it,' I reply.

She stands in front of the door and I hear the lock mechanism, then the handle turns and it swings open all by itself.

'Come on then,' Cockburn says, going inside. Only now do I notice that her clothes are dry, despite the lack of umbrella. Not a hair out of place either. I could do with some of that voodoo.

I recall Callander's technique, make sure I brush my left shoulder against the door frame and do the finger-palm-facing-outward thing with my right hand. No mean feat since I'm also having to wheel the bike in. Either way, I make it into the parallel zone that sits within the bank, just in time to see Cockburn going up the wooden staircase to the first floor. She walks purposefully, as though nothing can stand in her way. It's that dung beetle work ethic I sense from her – the ability to get the job done regardless. Methinks I should make friends, but that seems easier said than done, since through no fault of my own she's taken a disliking to me.

I'm still struggling up the stairs and keep close to the banister. It's that crossed-wires thing of your left moving when in your head it should be the right, so I'm extra careful.

'I heard you are Melsie Mhondoro's granddaughter – is this true?' Cockburn asks when I'm halfway up the stairs, my bike hoisted on my shoulder.

'Yeah, what's she—'

'Don't think that will grant you any favours here. You will start from the bottom and leave at the bottom if I have anything to do with it. This opportunity you've stolen from a more deserving young magician is something you ought to be ashamed of. If you had half an ounce of decency, you would go back to the hole you crawled out of.'

Screw being friends. Now she's got my piss boiling.

'I don't know what your beef is, lady, and, frankly, I don't give a rat's arse. I'm here 'cause Sir Callander wants me here, and that's the long and short of it. You don't like it, take it up with him.'

I've just made it onto the landing when Cockburn stops in the corridor ahead of me. She swivels effortlessly, almost like a ballerina in a music box, blocking my path. She draws her lips into something resembling a smile, but her eyes are fixed on me with pure malice.

'I've been doing this for far too long, little girl. You don't want to mess with me.'

If I was Brother Musashi I'd challenge her to a duel on

the front lawn and that'd be the end of it. As things stand, I'm gonna have to find another way round this problem, 'cause that's all it is, a problem. See, you can either blame someone else for the shit that's going down, like, boohoo, they don't like me. That's all fair and good, but it means you've handed the power over to them – you have no control over the situation. Or you figure them out and find a way to neuter them. For me, that means becoming indispensable to the Society.

Whether she likes it or not, we're wearing the same strip. I give Cockburn my sweetest smile, the one with too many teeth showing.

She draws back.

'Follow me,' she barks, and continues down the corridor.

The lights are off and the corridor is dim. The only sunlight comes in via the open doors. Still, in this poor illumination I can see the portraits of various men lining the corridors. Must be old bankers or Society men from the 1700s onwards. There ain't one woman among them by the time we reach Callander at the far end. Can't say I'm surprised. It is what it is.

We wind up in a large office with ten small desks, six by the walls and four in the middle. It's got oak-panelled walls polished to a shine, a royal-purple carpet and a massive chandelier. I can only imagine what it was like before it became an office. There's computers on the desks, stacks of paperwork, pens, stationery. The air's stale, but fairer than the reek permeating the streets of Edinburgh.

'That desk in the corner is yours.' Cockburn points to one furthest from the window with mounds of papers on it and no computer. The legs of the desk have claw marks. 'You have three piles of circulars and envelopes. Staple the three sheets together, place them in the envelopes provided and address them according to my list. You will be asked to make teas, do tidying, photocopying and other small tasks as I see fit in between. This should keep you nicely occupied until your internship comes to an end, which I hope should be soon.'

'Thank you, but I have other plans for Miss Moyo,' Callander says, appearing in the doorway.

'I thought you'd not want to occupy yourself with such trivial matters,' Cockburn says.

'The role in question is the secretary's intern,' Callander replies. 'And as secretary, I very much take a keen interest in my intern's activities. I intend to beef up the General Discoveries Directorate with Ropa Moyo at its heart.'

Cockburn jerks back suddenly and places her hand on her breast. Now, I'm not sure what this directorate's about, but the shock on her face tells the whole story.

'This young lady has no training, no experience whatsoever. She's not even a proper magician. She's a mere *ghostalker*,' she says.

'My role as secretary for the Society also makes me the Discoverer General, charged with seeking magical potential, and I fully intend to make use of that power, Frances. Also, it is time for the Society to once again deal sternly with the illicit practice of magic in Scotland. Don't worry, there'll be no pricking or dunking of "witches" or any such excess: this is the modern age, after all. But Ms Moyo will be most useful in our enquiries.'

'Well, if you intend to do that, then you must start by

investigating Siobhan Kavanagh, a prominent and beloved member of this Society. She's been missing for months.'

'Missing persons is a police matter, not one of magic.'

'Sir Callander, I strongly counsel against this course of action.'

'If we continue to tolerate malfeasance in magic then we are bound to attract the attention of London. Would you have the independence of this institution put at further risk, Frances?'

'I . . . well, I suppose not . . .'

'Then I should be most grateful if you could please establish an office for Miss Moyo close to my own. She will be reporting directly to me and no one else.'

Callander steps away from the door and gestures for Cockburn to leave. Her face has turned beet red, and I resist the urge to smirk. Seriously, I wanna moon her, but I keep my trousers on. Gotta be professional. As she walks out with her tail between her legs, she pauses at the door.

'Cornelius Lethington from Our Lady's clinic was in touch over the weekend,' she says.

'What of it?' Callander replies.

'It seems *your* intern has secured a commission with the clinic, using the internship credentials since she is not an accredited practitioner. Naturally, Lethington couldn't believe you'd actually chosen her over the dozens of bright scholars that leave the four schools every year. Be that as it may, I have informed the clinic that Miss Moyo cannot expect to profit from any of the magical investigations she's undertaking for them or their patients, since she is in the employ of the Society.'

Arsewipe.

Feels like I've been slapped in the face with a wet fish. My heart sinks into my boots.

'Your interpretation of the rules on that count is accurate, Frances,' Callander says softly. 'Miss Moyo will not be remunerated for any services she discharges under her internship.'

Cockburn looks over my way, smiles and walks away.

I was counting on the dosh from the Wus to see me through. But if they ain't paying and it's been rolled into my *unpaid* internship, then how the hell am I supposed to make ends point in the same general direction, let alone meet? This is really messed up. I feel like quitting this gig on the spot. Then again, I'm going full Mick Jagger, and I ain't about to give Cockburn no satisfaction.

'Maybe you should tell me about this commission of yours from the clinic, Ms Moyo,' Sir Callander says, waving his finger, causing the door to shut itself.

XII

The smog descends upon Edinburgh as the day progresses until you can barely see what's in front of you. The city stinks so much folks are walking with masks on. My scarf covers my mouth and nose, but the stench gets in all the same. Asthmatics be damned. It's all because of the sewage in the New Loch, where the Princes Street Gardens used to be. The miasma courses its way through streets, wynds and closes, before slipping into homes and offices through windows and chimneys like a burglar. There's no respite anywhere within a mile's radius of the city centre.

The castle looms on the rock above the loch. You can barely make out its outline in the haze. The power's off, so chimneys across Edinburgh spew out woodsmoke into the air.

Somewhere in this grim atmosphere drifts a shadow unseen to most, for the city has a fair few resident ghouls that refuse to move on. These are the suicides who leapt from the Gothic spires of the Scott Monument which leans at an angle in the murky waters of the New Loch. The older ones might have got splatted by Lothian buses back when the city had a regular transport network. Or maybe they were just shoppers who keeled over bargain-hunting in the Jenners concessions back when there was still a shop by that name.

The very oldest lurk as spectral wraiths in the New Calton Burial Grounds, Greyfriars Kirkyard, Grange Cemetery. The newer ones would have been had by cut-throats and robbers in the numberless dark alleyways around the city. It don't matter. Edinburgh has changed, time has passed, yet still they remain, desperately mingling amidst the living before the tug of the everyThere yanks them back to the realm of the dead.

Ghosts wax and wane with the seasons. Summer is low tide, and I see far less of them on the streets, almost as though the season's bustling life lessens the hold of the world of the dead that is eternally coiled to our own. They move less freely, and the ones that appear are usually confined to cemeteries or the sites where they died, places with a lower natural resistance to the extranatural. Then autumn comes along and they roll in, gradually peaking in the depths of winter before ebbing with the spring like a vanquished army rolling up its tents and retreating.

Always they plot their return in this eternal dance.

I've got the worm in my ear, listening to Rupini going on about how to distinguish oneself in a crowded marketplace. Must admit, *Rich Sorcerer, Poor Sorcerer* is quite the read, and I've already picked up on a couple of things that should help sharpen my business acumen. Problem is, I'm not allowed to make any money off my work due to Cockburn cockblocking my every move in the Society. She wants me out, and that's just made me even more determined to stay in. But someone's got to pay the piper or there ain't gonna be no tune for no one to jig off. Unless I get that sorted, I'm gonna be in the 'poor sorcerer' camp, and Rupini says that makes me a chump.

Callander insisted I've still got to do the job for the Wus. It's now officially Society business, and I can't get paid a mini-penny off that. Sucks major arse. I like what I do, and it's not like I'm asking for any more than I'm due. An honest wage for an honest day's work, that's all. I'm not T'Challa or Bruce Wayne, swimming in it and only doing this hero business as a side hustle.

Majorly hacked off and stressed out now.

I take a left after the National Records building and head down Leith Street. Meeting up with Priya in a coffee shop on Elm Row, but running a bit early, so I take my time and wheel my BMX down the slope nice and slow, going by the giant jobby on the St Mary's end. A hand grabs my arm. Immediately, I let my bike fall to the ground and reach for my dagger. But a sharp blade pricks the skin over my carotid artery before I can even make a move.

'That maggot in yer ear's mingin',' a familiar voice says. That's why my scarf didn't bother reacting.

'It's not a maggot, it's an earworm,' I reply.

'Aye, is that right?' He lets my arm go. 'Must be sucking out your brains, 'cause yous ken better than to be seagulling in these parts, lassie.'

Rooster Rob's got a point, I think, looking at him and smiling, though he can't see that on account of my masked face. He's quite a way off his perch on Camelot atop Arthur's Seat, and I wonder what's made him come down to the streets. There's two heavies in leather gear lingering nearby, and I figure this welcome party ain't just for me alone.

But a chance encounter? Nah, never with the Rooster.

'You're a sore for sighted eyes,' I say, taking out my audio-book worm and pocketing it.

He laughs heartily as he towers over me, red mohawk jiggling with the rest of him. Then he stops abruptly.

'And you look like an aubergine with that hair of yours.' Instantaneously Rob turns cold. 'If I recall correctly, you owe us, Ropa Moyo.'

Small matter of owing favours to one of Edinburgh's most powerful criminal enterprises, the Clan. I used to be a member and all, maybe still am . . . It gets a bit confusing, but they run the city centre, all the way down to Leith, looping round to Lochend then across the city again and back up as far as Gorgie. Favours mean cash, and that's the one thing I ain't got none of, but knowing Rob, that's my problem, not his.

'You'll be wanting to square this debt, else you'll lose your city pass.'

Knowing these guys, that's a pretty mild penalty. Then again, how am I supposed to use the bank or the Library if I'm not allowed in the city centre? Knapfery. Not good at all, this. Universe, you really seem hell-bent on screwing me over seven ways till Sunday.

'I'm working on it,' I say.

Sheesh, these mutts don't ever let the bone go. They helped me save a bunch of kids a while back, and we were copacetic for a while until I got a random invoice demanding payment for services rendered. Dick move, but that's how the Clan gets you to work for 'em. If I don't sort it, they'll drag me back into doing jobs burglarizing God-fearing folks, and I ain't wearing the skis to go down that slippery slope.

'Dinnae let me see yous on this patch again before we're square,' Rob says, walking off towards York Place, past the ruins of Edinburgh's Jobby. The grand old hotel was built back when and opened to general derision because it resembled a poop emoji. It went out of business after the catastrophe, when foreign tourists dried up.

The heavies go past me, giving me hard stares that must make them feel super tough. But it's okay – I give the Rooster the finger behind his back before picking up my bike and heading off again.

XIII

Priya's already waiting for me outside Jasper's Coffeelation on Elm Row, and she hands me a styrofoam cup as soon as I arrive. The bangles on her wrist jingle when she takes back her hand. My mocha's lukewarm, but there's enough sugar in there to perk up a sloth and I'm grateful for the kick as I take a swig. She knows just what I need.

'How's Max holding up?'

'Still stable, but that won't last much longer. His body's not loaded up with any pathogen we can detect, but he's frying himself. You got anything else for us?' she says.

'Not yet,' I reply, taking another sip. 'And why's your guy Lethington ratting me out to the Society, anyways? Thanks to him, I ain't getting paid for this gig no more.'

Priya furrows her brow and sighs.

'Must be something to do with one lab coat stolen from our staffroom.' She touches my coat, playing with the hem.

'I have no idea what you're on about. This coat's been in my family for a couple of generations.'

'Then there's Lethington's Jammie Dodgers . . .'

'An honest mistake anyone could have made.'

'And that, dear Ropa, is why he contacted the Society to verify your credentials.'

Goddamn. *All that for a couple of biscuits?* Then again, I suppose it's the principle of it. A horse passing by takes a dump on the road in front of us, and I decide it's time to move. The long days of summer are in our favour, but I still have to get back to Gran and Izwi before bedtime so I can hang with them for a bit. Work-life balance – the struggle is very real.

I unfold the flyer for Bo Bumblebeam's astral tours, which I got from Max's wallet. Although the front side's filled with advertisements, the back is blank, but it does something peculiar if you run your finger over it. Almost like an invisible ink trick, a compass needle appears in the middle, pointing to the north, where a blinking black dot appears.

'Tracking paper, nice,' says Priya. 'We would set up secret raves at the Institute and use it to guide the folks who were invited. It homes in on the master paper. Only problem is it doesn't tell you the distance, so you better hope it's not directing us to Inverness.'

'I figured it would take us to Bo Bumblebeam so we can ask him some questions.'

'That should be fun,' says Priya as we make our way down Leith Walk. 'Low-end busigicians are always a lot more fun to hang with than the toffs.'

'I wonder how many of the working-class magicians are from the Edinburgh School.'

'A select few, scholarship boys, certainly not the likes of Bo Bumblebeam . . . I'm afraid to admit he's from my alma mater.' She shakes her head. 'Wish I could've gone somewhere better.'

'At least you're not homeschooled like me, Priya.'

'Aye, suppose it could be worse,' she says with a laugh.

The smog eases somewhat the further we go from the city centre as we make quick progress to The Foot of the Walk, following the paper compass. It's all downhill, and this stretch of road's in pretty good nick. There's a whole bunch of hawkers tryna make a buck, street food sellers doing the same, hustlers shooting street craps just outside Spoonies, a couple of beggars and some street preachers yakking on about the end times like it's the catastrophe all over again. Been a min since I been down these ends. Business being what it is, I try to stay south of the city as much as I can.

Graffiti declaring 'The Republik of Leith' runs along the walls, as well as some stock denunciations of the Sandhurst Club as we get to the kirk. We weave our way through the tenements till we go over Commercial Street to the shore, where the Water of Leith meets the armpit of Scotland.

Nothing but ultra-rough pubs down here. The boats anchored in the water, though far from seaworthy, have been taken over by squatters. The litter on the cobbled streets and in the river makes the place the ultimate refuse tip. Still, you get your happy drunks – the booze here's the cheapest in the city, mainly 'cause they sell moonshine and homebrews, so I've heard. Working ladies and rent boys look me and Priya up and down, before evaluating we're neither punters nor competition and turning their attention to more lucrative enterprise.

There's wagons and caravans hitched up at intervals, all along the river to the docks beyond. Travellers like to pitch here for some reason, and when they do, no one messes with them. Even the Clan knows well enough to leave this lot alone. The big men with shitty tattoos are hard bare-knuckle fighters, and they have fiery tempers, especially when stoked by cheap whisky. The results are there for all to see, broken windows and missing teeth. Half-naked bairns run down the streets, but the adults pay them no heed at all.

The air from the sea's crisp and fresh these ends, so Leith at least has that.

'Lookie here, if it ain't young Ropa. Ye was only a bairn, waist high, last I saw ye, lassie,' says a big man with an eyepatch, who I don't recognize.

'Hello,' I say with a smile, pretending to know him. 'It's been a long time.'

'Nonsense, ye dinnae even ken who I be. Artchival Fleckie at yer service. And who's this bonnie critter ye brings with?'

'That's my pal, Priya.'

Artchival takes Priya's hand in his giant paw, bows low and kisses it. 'I'll make ye queen of the Gypsies if ye agree tae be mine,' he says.

'Just my luck, a proposal already. You do that to all the girls, Artchival?'

'Only the special ones.'

'Well, good luck with that,' Priya replies.

Artchival roars with laughter and then shrugs as if to say a man can only try. He might look like a bear, but there's a gentleness in his eye.

A busker with a guitar sings bawdy songs for a few shillings, and his voice cuts through the carnivalesque atmosphere. Gran used to have friends amongst the Travelling Folk back in the day, including a fair few fortune tellers, if my memory serves me right. She'd spend ages having a chinwag and reading cards.

'You know a fella by the name of Bo Bumblebeam?' I ask. 'We heard he was pitched out here.' The tracking paper says he's here somewhere but isn't any more specific, because the arrow has met the dot.

Artchival huffs and shakes his head. 'There's more exciting ways of getting fleeced than his bloody astral tours, lassies. Why not see Theodosia Lovell, who'll tell yer fortunes fer half the price?' Then he turns to Priya. 'Might even tell ye who yer future husband be while she's at it.'

'I doubt he's pushing fifty and makes a habit of accosting girls young enough to be his granddaughters,' Priya replies sharply.

'Well, that's me telt,' Artchival replies with a laugh. He plays with his braces and turns to me. 'Bumblebeam's nae one of us, so whatever business yer have with him's up tae ye. Find him parked on that bridge yonder . . . and when ye get home after ye've been well swicked, kindly tell Melsie Mhondoro that the Travelling Folk miss her company. She's welcome by our hearths anytime . . . and so is her grand-daughter, as long as she brings her bonnie pal along.'

To get to Bo Bumblebeam's, me and Priya go past an old harpoon swarming with kids, a relic of Edinburgh's whaling history. The hulking concrete mass of the great Edinburgh seawall looms over everything, keeping us safe from the waters of the Forth that threaten to overwhelm the capital. It was the last major project constructed in Scotland before the catastrophe. Fifers across the sea who got flooded hate it because to them it is a symbol of how Edinburgh got favoured, as always, at their expense.

We walk by the blocks of flats overlooking the revellers to a narrow wood-decked bridge with rail tracks running nowhere. Maybe somewhere once, but it's long been super-seded by a modern tarmacked one leading to Ocean Terminal. The bridge is supported by rusted arches on either side and held together by sturdy railings. Bumblebeam's name is adver-tised in bold golden lettering against a star-strewn causeway depicted on a banner strung across the bridge.

My footsteps clank on the decking as me and Priya make our way over.

Bang in the middle of the bridge is an old-school wagon. It sits high on wooden wheels with steel banding. Priya seems as taken as I am by the striking bohemian painting on the carriage: lime with vivid hues of blue and red, and images of peacock feathers, their eyes giving off a mystical vibe. It has shuttered windows and a red lantern burns on the corner above the driver's seat.

Four white Clydesdale horses are tied to the railings of the bridge. They have flowing manes and fine silky feathers on their legs. These beasts are nearly twice as tall as I am, exuding raw strength. Bumblebeam must be breaking the bank to keep these fellas fed, watered and shoed.

'Shall we go in?' I ask.

'In case you haven't noticed, the wagon's a bit eighteenth-century for my wheelchair. I'll wait out here for you, biped,' Priya says, going over to one of the horses and stroking its foreleg.

'I'll give you a shout if there's any problems.'

'In the event of which I'll blow that wagon apart like it was made of matchsticks,' she replies.

That's exactly what I need to hear, 'cause according to Callander, Bo Bumblebeam was on the Society register early on in his career, but he's been off it for at least a decade. This is fine when a magician retires or relocates, but sometimes, rarely though, they go rogue. He shouldn't be practising without a licence. I'm thinking I can leverage this to get the intel I need off him. Ropa Moyo's gone full-on official. Interning for the Society has its pluses after all, if one discounts the lack of wages.

I climb up the stairs and knock on the door. After a couple of 'hellos' without reply, I open the damn thing anyway and catch sight of three people. They're holding hands, slumped across a decorated satin duvet atop the bed on the left side of the carriage. I leave the door ajar so Priya can see what's going on inside. This wagon's probably the only place I've been that's smaller than our cara. There's a very narrow carpeted gap leading to a cabinet with a mirror and cosmetics. A painting of the sea sits on one wall, and on the other is that of a Labrador. Incense sticks burn in a holder on the cabinet, filling the air with an exotic scent.

The people on the bed don't stir as I enter.

In the middle is a rotund geezer in his forties with a Dalí moustache. His extravagant velvet suit and bow tie identify him as Bo Bumblebeam. The other two, a man and woman in their twenties, lie peacefully as though dreaming, a stark contrast to the marked concentration stencilled on Bumblebeam's face.

Must be how he does his astral tours.

Seems like the grift here's taking souls for a wee break to the astral plane and bringing them back for a quick buck, kinda like a safari. Not a bad hustle, I suppose. If I had a licence it'd be something I wouldn't mind exploring, though I ain't too sure about that *Doctor Strange* stuff of knocking people's souls out of their bodies and all that jazz. Bumblebeam must have a way of taking these guys across to tour the astral realm, and 'cause time works a bit different out there compared to this side of reality, he can easily make a short spin here feel like a couple of days there, depending on the realm he chooses. Some places I've been to make a few seconds feel like eternity.

I'm thinking of going in and surprising Bumblebeam before he gets back. It's a bit risky, sure, but catching folks off balance helps elicit truthful answers, or else the lies are so ridiculous they're easier to catch. But the astral realm's infinite, so how will I find out where exactly he is?

See, back when I was still learning kitchen table magic from Gran, I used to believe that there was this invisible thread that tied the soul to the body so it could always be reeled back in like a trout on a line. Now I know that's old fishwives' bollocks. Scientifically, the soul and the body are 'entangled' in a manner analogous to the quantum entanglement of sub-atomic particles. As such, no matter how far apart they may be, there's an instantaneous communication going. If the body dies, the soul's stuck out there drifting with no way back, but if the soul dies, well, it's kaput for the body too.

Now, looking at this ménage à trois, I reckon Bumblebeam's got some way of entangling hisself with them two, and that's how he can take them frolicking through the delights of the astral plane. Ergo, if I hold one of their hands and project out, I should land right where they are. QED.

Priya's quit horsing around, and she's watching me intently from outside, making sure it's all halal in here.

I sit on the bed – bit of a squeeze with all these people already on it, but hey ho – take the woman's hand and lie back, my backpack still under me. Then I close my eyes and relax my body from head to toe. My mind drifts, until I'm lifted out of my flesh, up through the ceiling towards the palette of colourful stars, and threaded into a very different realm. Normally, I'd have to guide myself through the innumerable planes, but this time it's different. Feels like I'm being pulled out by a gentle tide through the vastness of infinity.

I land in a desert city whose white sands feel strangely like moss underfoot. All around me are half-formed buildings, hollowed out like life-size models of something intended but never built. Narrow dirt tracks suddenly give way to multi-lane highways. A jumble of architectural forms: horizontal skyscrapers glued atop pyramids, brutalist concrete apartments running along till they give way to bamboo scaffolding that in turn morphs into Chinese temples, standing on their roofs like ships of the line. It's like Szukalski, Gaudí and Piranesi got stoned together and threw their ideas in a mosh pit.

I've never been in this realm before. The chaos and romance written in the buildings atop the white dunes suggest to me that this must be a place of unfinished or maybe unfulfilled dreams from our own realm or one similar to it. There's an air of nostalgia, the remembrance of something pleasant, maybe from childhood when possibilities were endless.

Voices drift from nearby, and through the window of an unfinished Mughal palace, I spot three figures wandering along an open courtyard.

'I thought you said there'd be no one else here, Bo,' the man says as I walk up to them.

Bumblebeam turns to me with astonishment.

'This is a realm of things, not of beings. Things that were meant to be but never became and those that are intended but destined never to materialize,' he says in a phoney Asian accent. 'But it seems a fellow traveller has wandered in. Namaste, there is room for all here.'

Above us in the sky, a mud mosque sails past, casting a shadow that blots out the sun briefly like an eclipse. I go straight in while I still have the element of surprise.

'I'm here by order of the secretary of the Society of Sceptical Enquirers, Mr Bumblebeam.' Keep it formal. Make him aware I know he's running an illicit business and he'll be forced to cooperate, I'm sure. 'What happened to Max Wu?'

His Dalí tash quivers. Now, fear is an emotion that can tip things one way or the other. You either get acquiescence or the fight of your life. But I come with the full authority of Scotland's ancient magical society, so I'm banking on cooperation here.

'I told those boys I didn't want to have anything to do with it, but what can a small busigician like me do against the Monks of the Misty Order?' he says. 'It's not as if I could turn to the Society for help now, could I?'

Odd that he's afraid of the Monks. They're just a group of schoolboys playing fancy pretend . . . aren't they?

'What did you do for them?'

'It wasn't my fault, I tell you. I don't mess with that kind of stuff, never have, licence or no. They went too far and opened the door. Now we're all tainted.'

'What do you mean by that? Explain,' I demand.

Bumblebeam murmurs and steps back, holding his hands to his chest. There's a wild, desperate look in his eyes.

'What's going on here?' the woman asks.

'I can't, he'll kill us all. Forgive me,' he wails, waving his right hand across in a sweeping motion.

I detect a radical entropic shift. The desert sands ripple as if the earth is churning deep beneath our feet. And when Bo Bumblebeam vanishes into thin air, I realize just how screwed we are. There's a roar unlike anything I've ever heard before in my life. And the mother of all sandstorms blasts everything to fuck.

Maybe throwing my weight around wasn't such a good idea on this guy's turf. He's an astral master, after all. Musashi teaches, 'Know your enemy, know his sword', and here I am going in like a knob all because I've got some unpaid internship.

I'm flung into the air, pelted by sand that blots out the sun, sweeping through half-finished alleyways and boulevards. I'm about to bail from this realm to the real world when somewhere in the howling sandstorm I hear the woman's panicked cry. Amateurs have no business projecting. I can't just leave her here. Even the safest-looking realm contains its own hazards for the uninitiated, so without their tour guide, these two adventurers are done for.

For a split second, I wonder how Bumblebeam even managed to set this all off, but my instinct for self-preservation takes over and I focus on the here and now. That's all that matters.

The noise is like being in the middle of a raging tempest. I hear the shriek of metal beams twisted, the snap of wood beams and tiles, but those are minor notes beneath the intense howl of wind sweeping through. Buildings shake and quiver and sway. Windows are broken by the hail of stones flying in the air. A good few get me, and it's bloody painful.

I can't stay here for long. Die here, die out there.

I do all I can to steer myself through the air, twisting to avoid slamming into the walls and shit. Bit of a bugger doing it through squinty eyes, but the sand's brutal and the churning currents make this more whitewater rafting than surfing. It's dizzying, but I'm stunned when the first building, a grotesque shopping mall, is lifted from its foundations and flung up as though it were a leaf. I don't even get a chance to yell 'bloody hell' before other buildings unmoor, tumbling as they go.

A pyramid slams into a hulking stone keep castle with a deafening crunch that sends monster-sized boulders hurtling towards me. I need to get out of this bitch pronto. With each collision the air turns into a soup filled with the debris of broken things that never were, making it harder to navigate.

Give me the everyThere any day compared to this.

Somewhere in this churning madness, I sense the panicked woman and fly out towards her. It's 'cause I'm holding her hand in the real world and she is the beacon that led me here.

I'm Clark Kenting my arse like an eaglet bailed from the nest for the first time. And then I see her spinning like an out-of-control skydiver below me, sandwiched between two incredible steel-and-glass skyscrapers crashing towards one another.

I neither see nor sense her partner at all.

Positioning my arms to the side, I swoop down like an arrow. Those bloody skyscrapers are gaining. Keep having to adjust my course 'cause my target is in a super-erratic tailspin.

Whatever happens, I gotta get there before those bloody buildings hit us.

A massive plasterboard wall strikes my left shoulder, causing me to tumble and lose my bearings, before I reacquire the woman some fifty feet below me. Bloody terrified to the nth degree, but I'm committed now, so here goes. I dip down head first into the wind, losing altitude, gaining speed, the rushing walls of glass pressing in on either side as the skyscrapers come in to collide. I throw my hands forward as I slam into the woman and embrace her, holding tight.

There's an incredible crunch and screech. A plane of cold glass and steel shoves us inexorably towards its counterpart, where we will be squished into non-existence.

I close my eyes and squeeze myself in the narrowing gap, like a thread through the eye of the most messed-up needle that leads home.

XIV

I'm hit by an electric-lime strobe light before I can even get my bearings. The lassie next to me is screaming her head off and flailing about like she's still falling. Her arm catches me on the nose and I yell in pain, 'Cut it out, man. You're safe now.' She's babbling like it's the Pentecost, and I can't get no sense from her. When I sit up, I notice Priya, hair standing on end like she's had a ride on Old Sparky, an almighty scowl on her face.

The air has an acrid chemical scent that overpowers the incense burning in the carriage.

I spit out splinters of wood from my mouth and brush chips off my face and out of my hair. Absolutely covered in it. Sore back. Lying on my backpack was a dumb idea.

'You guys okay in there?' Priya asks. ''Cause it was one hell of a fight out here.'

'What's going on? This isn't what Nat and me paid for,' the woman shouts in my face.

'What's your name?' I ask her.

'Nat is still in that place. You've got to get him out,' she says. 'What kind of service is this? Tonight was supposed to be our first holiday together.'

Oh no.

Outside, green and red flames burn atop the black waters of the river. The fire reaches back upstream, all the way to the bridge running across Commercial Street, consuming the floating litter. Revellers crowd the far bank, engrossed in the spectacle.

I look up and see stars. The roof of the wagon's been blown clean off. I guess that explains the wood splinters.

'Your fella Bo woke up in a right old temper,' Priya says. 'He was gonna off you lot if I hadn't stopped him. Epic nippleskimpel out here, I can tell you that.'

'Where is he?' I ask.

'Scampered off into the night. I couldn't follow, had to make sure you lot were alright.'

'For heaven's sake, you've got to go back and help Nat!' the woman screams. She's going nuts, standing over the limp body of her partner, shaking him as though this would coax his soul back.

The reason I couldn't sense Nat was 'cause I was holding this woman's hand, and she was holding on to Bumblebeam, who was holding on to him. When Bumblebeam broke the connection, that left her as the only person I could find in that place. Still, I reckon if I establish a connection, I might just be able to extricate him.

Plan? Kinda.

Ain't exactly swimming in options the now.

Truth be told, I'm not wanting to go back to the realm we've just bailed from. And now the guy with the power to stop all this has got away. Top that off with my headache and you've got the dream holiday from hell maxi-combo served with your humble pie and a dollop of brown sauce. Still, it was my decision to confront Bo Bumblebeam, so this mess is on me.

I've got to fix this.

'Cover me, Priya. I'm going back in,' I say.

But as soon as I take Nat's hand, I can tell straight away everything ain't as it should be. Even with his partner shaking him like a rag doll, it's easy to see no one's home. I lay my hand on her shoulder to stop her, then reach out to feel for a pulse on Nat's neck.

He's warm enough still, but I don't get a pulse. I press even harder and still get nothing. Drool runs down the side of his face. No longer serene, it's contorted in fear.

'You need to check him,' I say urgently to Priya.

In the blink of an eye, she wheels herself over to the stairs and hoists herself onto the second step. Using her arms, she levers herself onto the third step and into the wagon. Then Priya adjusts her trailing legs, grabs the edge of the bed and lifts herself up onto it beside Nat, leaving me and the lassie huddling in the corner.

Priya does a quick check for vitals, finds none and begins administering CPR, working chest compressions with her powerful arms. It's enough to rock the carriage side to side. There's an intense look of concentration on her face that I've never seen before.

'There's a black bag under my chair. Get it, now!' Priya commands.

I'm out like a bolt, jumping down the steps onto the bridge.

Under the wheelchair's seat, I find a black canvas bag adorned with the Rod of Asclepius, a serpent twined around a staff.

'Hurry up already.'

I rush back into the wagon and unzip the bag next to Priya.

'Pass me the EpiPen,' she says. I draw a blank. 'Adrenaline, it's in the yellow box, Ropa.'

I'm frantically searching the bag. It's got herbs, several vials, some syringes, tubes, sachets and pills and bandages, and a whole heap of stuff I know nothing about.

'Is he going to be okay?' the woman says in tears.

'Which one is it?' I ask.

'Here, keep up with these chest compressions,' Priya says to her. 'I'll get it myself.'

The woman does as she is told immediately. I stand there like a dick, watching Priya go through the kit, in a flash finding the right needle. She unsheathes the EpiPen and jabs it into Nat's thigh straight through his clothes. I flinch, 'cause that looks proper sore.

Nothing happens.

'We need an ambulance,' the lassie says . . . but everyone knows the emergency services won't come to Leith at night, especially not to the shore.

Artchival and a woman wearing a headscarf and a long pleated skirt arrive at the bottom of the steps. She has a shawl on, brilliant colours contrasting with her curly black hair. Could be anything between forty and seventy. And that's what I get from her, the vortex of time before ticking clocks were born and long after batteries run out on digital watches. It's a time measured by births and deaths of lambs and sheep, the turning of the seasons, of one immersed in the natural rhythms of the world itself. She wears many rings, a couple on every finger, a gold one for each thumb.

'Ye cannae save he, wee healer. I've felt his immortal soul ground tae emptiness – he's beyond yer power now.' Her voice is raspy and harsh. 'Artchival telt me ye was aboot, Ropa Moyo, but ye wouldnae ask tae see Theodosia Lovell, who slit her hand an' mixed blood with yer nanna. Instead ye bring the Riper hissel upon this tender night.'

Priya stops Nat's partner and the carriage ceases to rock. The woman's sobbing breaks my heart. I shouldn't have gone into that plane.

I wilt under Artchival's angry stare. Where before he was jovial, now he's grim as granite. For some reason he holds an antique black kettle in one hand and a china teacup in the other. Hardly the time for a cuppa, but I guess the Travelling Folk have their own ways.

'I'm sorry, we were doing work for the Society,' I say.

Theodosia Lovell hocks and spits on the ground at the mention of *the Society*. I remind myself that outside the straight streets of the New Town, it may mean something completely different in the same way the police aren't friends to the folks in my slum. Lesson learnt – twice in one day.

'I apologize,' I say, putting my hand to my heart.

'Come here.' She beckons with a finger, and I'm compelled down the steps.

The fires on the river are abating gradually. Foul smoke hangs in the air, making me cough. Theodosia Lovell grabs my chin, pushes my head back and stares me in the eye. I notice she's got that heterochromia thing going on, one hazel-coloured eye and one blue. Her gaze is piercing, as though she's searching for something through the windows to my soul. Her grip is tight, strong, rough fingers and long nails digging into my skin, and I wither against those eyes that have seen a lot. Purple eyeliner does nothing to taper their intensity.

She lets go gently after a while.

'I see plenty o' pain an' misery tae keep ye constant companionship upon this yer path. Cannae be helped, lassie. If yer shoulders werenae half as broad, it'd only pass to yer nearest kin. Bear it well an' the Travelling Folk'll always be there tae lend a hand, sure as Simon did fer Chriss hissel.'

Artchival grimly nods.

I'm not sure what this is all about, but I thank Theodosia Lovell anyway. The fact that there's a weeping woman and a dead body in the carriage doesn't seem to interest her much at this stage. Across the bridge, a fiddler's struck up a tune and the revellers are already getting back to their partying. Sunshine on Leith always, no matter the hour or the circumstances.

'This way, lads,' Artchival says to two young men dressed like him. 'Help the woman get her man intae their car and drive her home or wherever she wants. This isnae our business; it's that scoundrel Bumblebeam's, and we cannae have our good names tacked tae it.'

I stand aside as the two men help Priya out of the wagon, back into her chair. She seems pissed, frosty even, and I think for a healer to lose someone like that must be a painful thing. But how could she have saved a body when the soul was as dead as any on Chichikov's list? I place a hand on her shoulder, watching the two men quietly coax Nat's weeping partner out under Artchival's watchful eye. They wrap the body in Bumblebeam's sheets and carry it out with such gentleness.

The men move off into the night with the weeping woman trailing behind, and I'm kicking myself harder than Priya for failing to save him.

In *The Book of Five Rings*, Brother Musashi cautions, 'Do not regret what you have done,' but this still sucks arse, royally. Bumblebeam's actions aren't my fault, but the outcome is my responsibility regardless. I shouldn't have gone in there with vulnerable people. Wish I hadn't. And maybe then Nat would still be alive.

Didn't even get the info I needed from Bo.

I'll report him to Sir Callander in the morn. Now, all I can do is focus on salvaging what I can from this debacle, because that's the warrior's way. I can't walk away empty-handed, like the man died for nothing.

'We'll take the horses and you can keep the wagon,' I say to the Travelling Folk by way of an opening gambit.

Artchival glances at Theodosia Lovell, and the corners of her lips go up ever so slightly.

'Aye, make us clean up after yous and leave us that pile of tinder,' he says, back to his jovial self. 'Priya who wouldnae be my queen, 'twas quite the firework display ye put on fer us. An impressive duel much as I've ever seen magicians go at it before, and I say this as an old bare-knuckle boxer who kens what it is tae be tested nae holds barred. Bumblebeam was nae match fer ye. For that, yous get one horse, not a whisker more.'

'Two horses. I pick first, and you still get to keep the wagon all the same,' I counter. This will be more than enough to pay off the Rooster and cover my expenses.

'Bumblebeam isn't just some villainous villain, he's a working man. Yeah, he messed up, but that doesn't entitle you to his stuff, Ropa. This wreck is his home,' says Priya angrily.

'Such magnanimity towards a vanquished foe, my queen!' Artchival exclaims.

'He tried to kill us, so we're taking his stuff,' I say.

'Not if I have anything to do with it.' Priya pushes my hand off her shoulder. Frown on her face like the spring's loaded to take a swing.

'This is my call, Priyanka,' I say, pulling rank. She can afford to be all moral and righteous and shit, 'cause she's got a job, a good wage and a cosy flat to go back to after all this. I ain't got none of that. I'm going back to a caravan, debt and hungry mouths to feed. So, yeah, I'm gonna be like Genghis Khan's armies marching westwards from the east, feeding off the land, if I have to go all the way to the banks of the Sajo River.

I'll salvage what I can from these jobs.

Priya opens her mouth to speak, but Theodosia Lovell steps in.

'The healer speaks true, as ye do the same, Ropa Moyo. But when the Travelling Folk are abroad, that decision rests with me,' she says. 'Artchival will give ye neither beast nor lowy for the spoils are nae fer yer. Let yer scruples be eased, wee healer, fer I've seen Boniface Bumblebeam sow the wind an' the whirlwind is coming tae reap him. He'll have nae use fer these trinkets now. Mark this well, Ropa Moyo. Might be a time in a future nae far off when this healer's voice'll be yer conscience as ye be tippin' towards darkness, so heed her well fer she loves ye true an' likewise. Ye have an outsized orenda, bending the warld as ye go, but it disnae mean ye always get yer own way oot of it. Oft times it'll push against ye. And in those moments ye will either bend, break or stand yer ground.'

She turns to Artchival and instructs him to pour from the kettle. He holds the cup out, and the steaming black liquid hitting it sounds like piss. The brew's pungent even with smoke in the air. Theodosia Lovell offers the cup to me, using both hands. I reach for it and our fingers touch, but she doesn't let go. This brew's made the old way, with tea leaves, and a couple float on top.

I'm not sure if she wants me to drink it or what.

'Yer nanna's third eye disnae see half as well as it used tae, which is still further than most, mind ye. Tell her Theodosia Lovell says when all this is over, oor paths shall cross once more, but nae before.' She lets go of the teacup, and I'm thinking, how the hell am I supposed to cycle back home with this?

As if reading my mind, she says, 'Put it in yer bag, lassie. Nothing can spill that brewed by mine hand till it's served.'

XV

Shattered and stinking of smoke by the time I get home to
Hermiston Slum. My lab coat is covered in soot and grime, but
I doubt I'll be washing it anytime soon. I'm still radging at
Priya, and she's just as sore with me. She means well and all,
but it's food out of my mouth. Can't be helped now, even though
the fat lady ain't even warmed up her vocal cords as far as this
gig's concerned. Still, being stiffed by the Travellers has put
plenty of lead in my zeppelin, and I ain't too buoyant right now.

It's late but the summer sun's hanging someplace just
beyond the horizon. The speakeasy nearby's booming indie
hits from the noughties and the bass is annoying.

River ain't in her burrow when I peek in to say hello. Must
be on the prowl, but at least Gran and Izwi are still up watching
telly when I enter the caravan.

'Ropa, can I have your phone?' Izwi says before I can even
shut the door.

'Nice to see you too, sis,' I say, putting down my backpack.
I fish my mobile out of my pocket and toss it her way. 'How's
tricks, Gran?'

'The usual aches and pains. If it's not one thing, it's the
other. The body betrays you in the end. That's why you have
to take good care of yours. How was your day, child?'

'Same old.'

'Is that right?'

What else can I say? I got a man killed and kicked off a magical duel in Leith?

There's a vase with wildflowers sat on the counter. The vase is actually a repurposed clip top jar which makes the yarrow, fireweed and lady's bedstraw arrangement look charming.

'Where did these come from?' I ask.

'Gran's got a boyfriend,' Izwi says.

'I do not,' she replies, embarrassed. 'Gary O'Donohue had them sent over. He is very kind.'

'Why didn't he bring them over himself? Only lives down the lane.'

'How am I supposed to know what's going on in that man's head?' Gran says, straightening the doek over her head.

'He's got the hots for you.'

'What you mean to say is that he's a very thoughtful and considerate gentleman. Now stop pestering me and fetch yourself a plate off the hob.'

Don't need to be asked twice, especially since it's pumpkin mash and peas with red kidney beans. Gran says she used to have this mash a lot as a little girl. Calls it nhopi or something like that, and even though it ain't Halloween yet, this is still a treat.

Plonk myself on the berth opposite and sloch my chow like a hog on the trough. It's well nice. But it don't take me long to hoover it down before I start thinking about Max Wu, the Monks, Bumblebeam, Lewis and the fine mess tonight. It's not stuff I want to be coming at me when I'm chilling with my family, but I have this nagging feeling I'm missing something. Whatever happens, I have to find Bumblebeam and extract whatever info I can about what he and 'those boys' did that's got him so spooked.

Where did they go? What did they do? What could he be so frightened of that he could react like that? They're just kids, after all.

Weird though, being here with my family and behaving like everything's normal after what happened tonight. Pretty disorientating. One minute I'm watching Priya try to save a dead man; next here I am watching reruns of *Taggart* and eating pumpkin mash. But I'll take this mundane shit over what I just went through any day.

'Penny for your thoughts,' says Gran.

'You should offer a princeling at least,' I reply, and chuckle. 'Nothing on my mind really. How come you're not knitting today? Ran out of wool?'

'My wrist hurts a little, so I thought I'd rest it, but only for a short while.'

'Phew, 'cause I think a fair few sheep farmers would visit with pitchforks if you stopped completely.'

Our caravan feels like a haberdashery at times. Gran's always knitting stuff, and she gives most of it away to our neighbours. Some gear she sells for a modest fee, and that's the dosh which helps with her meds, et cetera. But usually there's paper bags of wool all round her berth, buttons in jars, zippers, half-done outfits, knitting needles and all sorts poking about. Keeps her occupied and that's a good thing.

My folks died ages ago. I don't like to think about it. Kinda ironic since all I do is see dead people. But I started doing that long after they were gone, and I ain't never seen them here or in the everyThere where the dead go after they pass either. When I started moving between realms, I hoped I'd get to bump into them. But it ain't happened yet. Maybe one day, but I ain't holding my breath on that one.

Funny thing is, death still sucks royally even though I know, objectively, like, it's merely a transition from one world to the other. Must be something about being human that means no matter what, the idea of leaving this world is just so horrible nothing can assuage the terror of it. Maybe that's why some ghosts linger like they do. Don't get me wrong, the other realms of existence are pretty dope and all, with psychedelic shit you don't get to experience here. But in this realm, you truly feel *alive* in ways you don't anywhere else.

I've got a couple of pics of my mom on my phone. She was beautiful. Can't bear looking at them half the time. Weird thing is, I ain't got none of my dad even though he died after her. He's all fuzzy in my recollections. Gran says she ain't got none neither, that he didn't like getting his picture taken. That's alright though; wouldn't do me much good anyways. I'd rather be grateful for what I got. Izwi, Gran, that's all I need, and them two keep me busy enough, like. Some folks out there ain't got no one at all, and that's pretty scary. Others can't stand their own, and that's a major baw ache. Me, I got the best two in the world and great friends, so as far as I can see, I'm winning at this life thing.

I polish off my chow and make for the sink to do the dishes. It's supposed to be Izwi's day to do 'em, but I ain't about to dish out a bollocking 'cause Gran's pumpkin mash is settling nicely in my stomach. Anyway, I've had more than my share of confrontation today. And so I'm at the sink about to get washing when I remember something.

'Gran, you know a woman called Theodosia Lovell?'

She gasps, and her face lights up with pure joy, bringing out all the beautiful wrinkles. It's about the most excited I've seen Gran in ages. Come to think of it, Gran in her doek and Theodosia in her headscarf have that sister from another mother vibe.

'You've met her? Is she in town? Will she come to see us?'

'I was at the shore down in Leith, but she said nothing about coming down these ends. Didn't even ask where we live or anything. Maybe we can go there tomorrow if you really want to see her.'

The excitement drains from her face. Disappointment.

'Travelling Folk seldom stay long. We could go there right now and find them gone. Few ever see Theodosia Lovell twice in the same place.'

'Who's Theodore Lover?' Izwi asks, eyes glued to my phone.

'Theodosia is a very dear friend of mine. I've not seen her in years, but for her to come to Edinburgh and leave without seeing me breaks my heart,' Gran says with much sorrow in her voice.

'I nearly forgot. She wanted me to give you something,' I say.

Gran's face lights up again like it's the fifth of November. But with my backpack lying on its side, I'm sure all I'm getting out of there's egg on my face. Stupid idea for me to cycle round Edinburgh with a cup of tea in my bag. Probably them

Travellers are having a good laugh at my expense. I hope my books didn't get ruined, 'cause Sneddon will have a fit.

Never mind, I'll just have to tell Gran Theodosia Lovell gave her the cup as a gift.

I open my backpack, take out a couple of books and my mbira, then in the bottom corner is the teacup sat upright. Oddly still piping hot when I take it out and not a single drop spilt. Damn. I'll take ghouls over this kind of strangeness any day. When I finally manage to unstick my eyebrows from the ceiling, I take the cup to Gran. It's a vintage teacup with a black rose floral design and gold trim. The handle is also gold, shining in the light.

'Eww. That smells,' Izwi says.

Gran receives the cup with both hands. She smells the tea, which has lost none of its pungency, and brings it to her lips. Then she drinks every drop in one go, her throat moving up and down.

Afterwards she brings the cup down near her breast and peers inside it. The milky cataracts clouding her irises move quickly back and forth as though she's reading a script and not staring at dregs.

Suddenly she cries out in terror and drops the cup to the floor.

'You okay?' I ask, touching her arm.

Her mouth is open, hand to her heart, eyes wide in shock like she's seen Auld Nick himself.

'What is it, Gran?' I ask.

'Nothing that concerns you, child. Not yet anyway,' she says, fighting to regain her composure. Gently, she adds, 'Get back to your dishes and let an old woman cogitate.'

   'You sure, Gran?' I ask, but she's far, far away now.

   The teacup lies shattered, fragments of china on the floor.

I pick them up, one by one, and throw them in the bin.

XVI

Thank Krishna for the holidays. At least I can get up later and not worry about taking Izwi to school. I'm still frazzled after last night. Sent Priya and Jomo a couple of texts this morning, but no one's replied to me yet. Still, the grind don't stop, and I have to go to the office . . . 'The office', I like the sound of that. Makes me sound legit and all. Gran still ain't told me the score from last night, but I don't ask and she don't push me on stuff. Works best like that.

Cycling through Dalry, headed towards Haymarket. Bit of a nip in the air, but I've worked up a sweat. Scottish summer can be crap like that sometimes. Each day's a spin of the meteorological roulette wheel. Got the earworm in, listening to Rossworth Rupini yak on about the difference between wealth creators and moochers, and I'm totally feeling his vibe. I've listened to loads of audiobooks, but tuning in to the worm's a whole 'nother level in this reading game. With audio, you plug in and listen, but I swear with the worm it's like the info's being downloaded straight into your head, becoming your thoughts and memories.

I better keep my eyes on the road since an ox-drawn cart's broken down on Shandwick Place and we're all having to go round the pissed-off bullocks. Town's packed today, and I wonder what's up 'cause this ain't no bank holiday. Then I see dozens of hot air balloons emblazoned with the Union Jack drifting across the sky and remember it's the King's Market Week.

For the next seven days you don't need no licence or nothing, you can just set up a stall and sell your wares as long as you're a resident of this town. But folks from Musselburgh and Fife sneak in, pretending to be local. Lots of kids of all ages working to help their families. I ain't never seen this myself, only heard about it, but there used to be a time when Edinburgh had some kind of festival and people would stream in from all over the world. This was before the catastrophe, mind you. Even heard them claim the city's population would double or something, which sounds like bollocks if you ask me. Like, where would you put all them extra people? The King's Market Week is hectic enough, thank you very much.

I avoid the madness of Princes Street by going up South Charlotte Street onto George Street.

From there it's the home straight to the bank. Despite yesterday, I'm feeling great 'cause I'm getting my own office and I can't wait to see it. I'll sit there with my feet on the desk and yell, 'You may enter,' whenever someone knocks.

I can even picture a brass sign with my name on the door. Ropa Moyo's gone corporate, baby.

As soon as I stop, I take the worm out of my ear and put it back in the copy of Rupini. Sneddon warned me they can die if they aren't returned to the book within a couple of hours after use and there's a fine for wasting the worm. Something about the costs and time needed to train a new one. Don't know much about it, but I really can't afford to scrounge for extra cash right now.

Hoist my bike onto my shoulder, spring in my step as I enter the bank. I make it all the way up the stairs before bloody Cockburn catches me at the landing.

'You really should stop bringing that bicycle upstairs, Miss Moyo,' she says.

'I can't leave it outside.'

'There's a secure storage facility on the ground floor, round the back of the building.'

'That meeting's in five,' says a dapper fella I ain't met before, passing us.

'I'll be with you in a minute. Just have to see the new girl to her office,' Cockburn replies. 'Come along then.'

We go up the stairs to the second floor, and I'm ecstatic. Ha, right to the top and I've only been here a minute. I love my life. The floor is tastefully carpeted, and there are black-and-white pictures of gentlemen on the walls. We pass shadows of bank staff moving in the normal dimension. Round a corner, Cockburn shows me the door at the end and informs me that's the secretary's office. Then we get to mine.

It has a small white door with a sign that says *General Discoveries*. Cockburn turns the silver knob, swings the door open and tugs the pull-cord light switch. An old-school incandescent bulb flickers to life, and Cockburn invites me inside.

There's barely enough room in here for a coffin! This is, like, a walk-in cupboard. No windows neither. I see the smirk on Cockburn's face and know this is a total piss-take. The only furniture in here's a wooden school desk, the type with an inkwell hole and a lid to put stuff inside. It's got a little chair too, meant for primary school kids.

'How do you like your new office, Miss Moyo?'

'Perfectly sufficient. Thank you, Ms Cockburn,' I reply, all neutral. I won't give her the satisfaction.

'When you're done settling in, be sure to see the secretary. Now if you'll excuse me, I have meetings to attend.' She starts to make her way down the hall but stops for a parting shot: 'And next time, please dress more appropriately for the office.'

I survey my new domain, peeved as anything. Suppose an oak desk and ergonomic swivel chair would have been too much to ask for, hey. I park my bike outside 'cause there's no way it'll fit in here. Then I chuck my backpack on the desk and lean against the wall. A window really would have been nice . . .

Either way, this is my office now and I better make the best of it. No use moaning and moping about.

First things first, turn this desk around so I face the door and have my back to the wall. Easier said than done, 'cause the room's too narrow to turn it one-eighty, so I have to drag it out, turn it in the corridor and drag it back inside. It rests against the right wall, giving me a narrow gap to squeeze through and get behind it. Keeping the chair for now, but that situation's solvable 'cause I can just pinch one from someone else's office.

Things are taking shape when there's a knock on my door.

'Come on in,' I say.

Sir Callander's tall frame fills the tight doorway, and a massive ginger tabby paces at his feet. It's a right minger and oozes feline arrogance. Sir Callander tsks at the sight of my office with its cobwebs running along the cornices.

'That's one big cat you've got there, Sir Callander,' I say.

'Oh, this is Petals, and she's part of the furniture. If you look at the pictures you'll find she's been with the last three secretaries.'

'They live that long?'

'Cats, yes. Secretaries, not so much. A few too many, er, *unfortunate* accidents over the years. I see Frances has gone out of her way to ensure you're well settled.'

'I imagine your office is like this too.'

'Somewhat.' Callander shuts the door, and the Office of General Discoveries takes on the appearance of an interrogation room under the harsh light of the unshaded bulb. He's not fat, but he takes up a lot of room with his presence, and the cat doesn't help either. But at least now I know she's responsible for the scratch marks on the furniture.

'I would offer you a seat, but . . .' I gesture to show there isn't one.

'Update me on the Max Wu situation. Have you made any progress? In future I shall be expecting written reports for my eyes only. The role you find yourself in demands discretion.'

'Loose lips.'

'Precisely.'

His brow is knitted in concentration as I debrief on the misadventure with Bumblebeam and his astral tourists, and how Priya saved my hide. Occasionally Callander grunts, but in the main he just listens. When I mention Theodosia Lovell he frowns, so I omit the story of Gran's cuppa. Yikes.

'Is Lovell still here, in the city?'

'Last night she was.'

'I should have been informed as soon as she was spotted.'

'We can go to Leith right now. Why do you want to see her, though?'

'It would be too late. Lovell is an enemy of the Society, but we've not been able to neuter her. She runs like sand in an hourglass. But she is of no concern to you going forward. Your focus should be on finding Bo Bumblebeam. He sounds desperate, so you shouldn't confront him. Rather, call me and I will handle it. Unlicensed practitioners of any stripe are an affront to everything this Society stands for, and their presence will no longer be tolerated during my tenure. But officially, none exist since we cannot afford to attract London's attention. These are internal matters,' he says sternly. 'I am counting on your intelligence, but you must learn to avoid trouble and defend yourself if necessary, understood?'

He's teaching Granny to suck eggs, but I nod anyway.

'What are you reading now to improve your spellcraft?'

'Well, it's not exactly spellcraft, but Rossworth Rupini's *Rich Sorcerer*,' I say.

'That mountebank will teach you nothing of substance; you'd best desist and occupy yourself with something more useful. The Elgin has many great resources on our craft, which you must use to work on your fundamentals, Miss Moyo. Remember that to secure your place in the Society you will get tested, and this time you *must* pass. Be ever mindful that your failures reflect on me. Now, here's a text you'll find more rewarding. It is from my personal collection here in my office, so I expect it to be returned as is when you're done with it.'

Callander holds his left hand in the air, and in the space of a blink a white book appears. He passes it to me: *The Able Practitioner's Handbook of Self-Defence* by Barrington Clifford. The cover has what I initially think is a fencer in an elegant position with one hand extended, until I see that instead of an épée sword, he's actually holding a wand.

'Thanks,' I say. 'When am I taking the test again so I can become a proper apprentice instead of an unpaid intern?'

'When you're ready. Now, if you will excuse me, I have matters to attend to. Stay vigilant and keep me informed.'

'I need your mobile,' I say as he makes to leave.

He snaps his fingers and a business card drops from the ceiling onto my desk. 'Have a nice day, Miss Moyo.'

Once the gaffer leaves, I linger for a bit, but I really have no work in this place. It's not exactly like I have photocopying and teas to make as Cockburn originally intended. And Callander's thrown me into his own private department without really telling me what else I'm expected to do, so I figure I'll take my investigation where the grind works best for me, and that's the streets. I'm happy enough taking initiative, but before I go, I'll have a nosey . . . and then sarnies.

I grab my gear and leave my office, only now noticing the door doesn't even have a keyhole; it can't be locked. Maybe that's a move by Cockburn so she can snoop on me or my stuff. Funny that, being inside of a bank but not feeling secure.

I greet a short man in work trousers and a blue T-shirt lugging two full bin liners. He wears a beanie hat and has a long goatee.

'So you're the new girl, eh,' he says, and holds out his hand. 'Name's Darragh, and I'm the general dogsbody around here.'

'Ropa,' I reply, shaking his hand.

'Good to see you're not one of those uptight tossers who come in here thinking they're the bee's knees, 'cause I don't give a rat's arse about any of it. The only one I'll say "m'lord, three bags full" to is the gaffer himself. The rest of yous can stuff it for all I care.'

'I'm totally fine with that.' I hold my hands up in peace.

'Then we'll get on swimmingly. You need anything, Darragh's your man. Stay away from the dragon lady – I'm sure you've met her already.'

'Cockburn.'

'She's a ball-breaker, that one. Don't let none of them stick their fingers up your bumhole and you should be fine. Any problems, you come to me. I've got the gaffer's ear, and that's why they don't try nothing with me. Now I'd appreciate it if you got that bike of yours out of my corridor and downstairs, thank you very much.'

I reckon Darragh's alright, the cheeky bugger. His nose is flushed red and the reek of Buckfast Tonic Wine on his breath is overwhelming, but to see the steadiness of his gait, you know he's a pro. My granda was like that too, rest his soul.

I pick up my bike and head down to the first floor, towards the general office Cockburn had meant for me to work in. In the corridors I pass by men in suits who don't greet me.

Reckon in time I'll get to know who's who, but for now it's all so cold and alien to me.

'We were wondering when you'd turn up,' a woman sat near the door says.

'Why on earth would she hang out with us plebs when she's up on the top floor with the lord of the manor himself, Carrie?' a random guy says.

Another woman scrutinizes me with suspicion. 'I've been here for how many years now, and Sir Callander's never said a word to me. Not one word.'

'Don't mind them, welcome to the party room,' Carrie says.

'The only song the DJ plays is "Forty Hour Week". Keeps the hamsters turning their wheels.'

'The Hamster Squad, magical society's finest paper-pushers at your service, mademoiselle,' Carrie says with a flourish. 'You have no idea how much paperwork Scottish magic generates: reports, permits, applications, enquiries, standards, newsletters, finance, finance, more finance, insurance, complaints, investigations and enquiries, recommendations, then you have all the paperwork from the four schools plus partner organizations such as the Allied Esoteric Professions Council—'

'Emails, we're drowning in them.'

'This is literally Dante's eighth circle of hell.'

'I thought this was the second circle.'

'You wish.'

They bounce back and forth like that for a good time, while I stand about like a knob with my bike on my shoulder. Seems like I've stumbled into geek central, and I like it. Almost regret not being placed in here, 'cause this lot seem alright.

When they finally get round to the intros, and there's eight of them working in here, I recall Carrie, the girl by the door, Abdul, formerly known as random guy, Sin, short for Sinéad, and Aurora 'cause that's always a funky name. The other guys I'll have to pick up later 'cause even though I'm told their names, they don't stick out for me.

'Bikes aren't allowed up here, pal,' says Carrie.

'Whatever you do, don't mess with Darragh,' Abdul adds.

'I know, I know,' I reply.

'What's Sir Callander got you doing on the third floor anyways?' Carrie asks.

I hesitate 'cause I'm sure I'm only reporting to him. Sunken ships and all that.

'What happens upstairs stays upstairs,' Abdul says, rescuing me.

'It's got to be more exciting than this,' Carrie replies.

'Speak for yourself. I'm having a blast copy-editing the latest guidelines on managing preternatural metacognitive manifestations in students across the four schools.'

'I'll take that and raise you the budget for the next annual conference in Dunvegan. It's hectic.'

'Yeah, right, all you have to do is copy and paste last year's figures.'

'All those years we spent at magic school,' Carrie says, shaking her head. 'Who'd have thought we'd wind up here?'

The room explodes in good-natured laughter, like this is the funniest stuff ever. Bit of a relief I ain't on this hamster wheel then. These guys are trained magicians, yet here they are doing dreary admin work. But I like their self-deprecating style, and I definitely get a sense there's a real bond between the team here.

'If you need anything, Ropa Moyo, you just let us know,' says Carrie.

'Like, how to survive the day-to-day grind of the Society,' says Aurora.

'Self-medicating on alcohol at the best oyster bar in Edinburgh is our preferred method. It's cheaper than visiting a therapist. You should join us sometime.'

'I think she's a bit underage for that, Abdul.'

'We also provide psychic paper if you need an ID,' he says with a wink.

'Really?' I ask.

'Don't believe everything Mr Sleekit says,' Sinéad replies.

Feels like being back in high school when the teacher's out. But much as I like the Hamster Squad, my wheel's allowed to roll out into the sunshine, and I make them aware of this fact as I leave.

'Well done, you dorks,' Sin hisses. 'Now she's never coming back here. Would it hurt you to dial it down and, like, be normal for a change?'

'She'll be back,' Abdul says knowingly.

I chuckle, heading down to have my brunch. Seems like at least I've found my tribe inside this cold bureaucracy.

In the banking hall, I sit myself on a desk and grab my sarnies and apple juice. It's nice out here, with natural light pouring in through the glass stars in the dome above. Not nearly so dour as the corridors with portraits of Sir This and Lord That plastered across the walls. I check out the shadows of customers and bankers in the real world going about their business while I'm chilling here on the *inside*. If I concentrate hard enough, I even catch snippets of their conversations, coming in like fading echoes.

Soon I tire of that and take out my copy of *The Able Practitioner's Handbook* to see what Barrington Clifford's got to say about it all. Earworm in the spine? No such luck. There's an intimidating pic of the author in military dress, with medals on his chest, and the bio says something about him serving the empire during World War Two. A gushing, patriotic foreword says this text is essential reading for serving magicians in the British Army, blah blah. I skip ahead and dive into the first chapter:

'I have served my country honourably under some of the toughest conditions imaginable, and this book contains suggestions on how to conduct oneself in dire circumstances. Indeed, there are a great many texts written on the subject, but while such books are impressive in theory, they quickly prove false when tested under real-world conditions. Therefore, my text seeks only to teach the simplest and most practical skills which any practitioner of the second science can rely upon in danger. In any confrontation, the aim is to neutralize your opponent while ensuring your opponent does you no harm. The former we term "attack" and the latter "defence". These form the fundamentals of any conflict situation. Fighting using magic, stripped down to its essence, primarily consists of the radical transference or deflection of energy. It is fundamentally no different from fighting with fists, clubs, swords or indeed the most sophisticated weapons of war. And so the serviceman need only concentrate on magic dealing with the most basic forces when fighting: air, fire and electricity.

'While later sections of my book deal with the options available for the magician practising outside the line of fire, most of the text deals with in-action scenarios for which there is little time for elaborate casting. These actions require base-level craft accessible even to the earliest students of the second science . . .'

Really digging the modesty with which Clifford sells his book, and how refreshingly direct he is, when I'm disturbed by movements in the normal world. A scuffle is occurring. Having finished my chow, I mark my page and pack the book. Reckon I might as well take a look-see, seeing as I'm due to hit the road anyways.

Someone's being dragged out of the non-magical banking hall. A man is unceremoniously dumped onto the driveway by the security guard. In the daylight outside, they're no longer shadows.

'Look, we're going to have to call the police if you persist, and that won't go too well for you,' the guard says. 'Get out of here.'

I can hear them easily too. Must be 'cause I'm right on the threshold.

'I haven't got a problem with you guys. It's the ones inside I want to talk to,' the man says from the ground. He's one of them hipsters with a manicured beard and lumberjack shirt with the sleeves rolled up. Though you can just tell by his pale skin he ain't done no hard day's labouring under the sun. A bit unusual for someone like this to kick up a racket at a bank of all places. Almost like he wants attention. The Society of Sceptical Enquirers is about as obscure as the Institute and Faculty of Actuaries or the College of Podiatry. It's just one of many professional bodies like the Chartered Institute of Loss Adjusters, or Institute of Refrigeration, or Society of Dyers and Colourists, or Society of Indexers, which are all rather useful but known only to people with a specialist interest. Hell, even I wasn't aware of the Society until I blundered into it.

Another official from the bank comes out with a brown trunk suitcase and a leather briefcase. He tosses them onto the ground beside the man.

'I don't know what you've been taking, pal, but this is just a bank, nothing more. There's no secret societies or the Illuminati hidden behind pillars. Take my advice, go home and sleep it off if you don't fancy a stint in the cells.'

'Tell *them*, the ones behind this entire facade, that I won't let them get away with it. They owe my family and I refuse to be bullied. I'll not be scared off. Make sure you tell them that.'

'Aye, whatever,' says the guard with a weary wave of his hand.

The man gets up, dusts himself off and gathers his belongings. He heads out, turning now and again as if expecting something. When he is round the corner, I slip out and follow discreetly. I am the General Discoveries Department, after all.

XVII

It's easy to blend into the crowds of the King's Market Week. So many people about, I don't even need to make an effort as I follow the man lugging his cases through the crowd. Once or twice he is forced to put the large trunk case down and swap hands. I wonder why he simply didn't use one with wheels.

He crosses Princes Street onto North Bridge, going past the Balmoral, and I stay on his trail. If he was shouting about secret societies at the bank, I reckon he's talkin' about the Society, so I wonder what his beef is. Could be a nutjob. And he's got an American accent too, which for me is straight out of the telly. Gran says there was a time you couldn't move on the pavements in Edinburgh 'cause of tourists blocking the way, taking selfies and up to all kinds of nuisance. Them pavements are heavin' today with or without them, so there.

My quarry glances across the New Loch stretching out all the way to the foot of Castlehill. His jeans make you wanna ask if his cat's died, ankles and calves showing like that. Fella like him's gonna be easy pickings for the chories thieving and robbing about the city centre.

Past the Scotsman Hotel, the hipster slows down and I'm

forced to do the same. Folks brush past me, and I crawl along until he picks up pace again. Don't wanna lose him in the bustling Mile, but I realize my error seeing him stood a few feet ahead by the window of a newsagent. I can't stop inconspicuously – not without him noticing. I carry on as though I'm minding my own business, but when I make to pass, the hipster blocks me with his briefcase. I place my hand on my dagger's hilt.

'I know you're following me,' he says.

'Don't know what you on about, pal. Get out of my face.'

He narrows his eyes at me. 'You're Ropa Moyo, aren't you?' He lowers his voice. 'Friend of a friend told me how you saved those sick kids. Tracked down the rogue magician and everything.'

Whoa. Never figured I'd be a celebrity. Gotta play it cool, though.

'Bit too early to be on the Bucky,' I tell him.

He winces and bows his head. There's burns on his forearms I hadn't seen at the bank.

'I'm not looking for trouble. I'm only here to ask for what's mine, and I heard you can help me. Last night your people sent thugs after me, and I barely made it out in one piece. But I'm not leaving this country until the Society of Sceptical Enquirers gives me what I'm owed.' There's a look of fierce determination in his eyes. Stubbornness too. Despite the beard, he's just some dude in his mid-twenties, and I'm even more certain he can't handle himself.

'I'll pay for your time,' he adds.

The way to a girl's heart.

'How about you buy me a cuppa and you can tell me about your beef?'

'Thank you. You're the first person from that blasted organization that's even agreed to talk to me. I've tried everything—'

'Yeah, yeah, drink first.' I'm always one for squeezing 'em if I can. It's dog eat dog out here.

Soon enough we find a Beanie Roasters which smells like a caffeine junkie's paradise, and I think, why not – order an iced mintoffeecial special, carrot cake, a flapjack and a bag of nuts for later. I know I ate already, but my belly's always got room. Hipster boy goes for a macchiato, and I inform the barista that he's paying. You don't wanna leave room for confusion, and I reckon Uncle Sam still owes us for bailing on us during the catastrophe. Ain't reparations a bitch?

He pays without hesitation, and I tell him to find us a table near the window, since he's got them bags. I've chosen this cafe 'cause it's down the bottom of the Royal Mile near Holyrood, and so I'm deep in the Clan's postcode. They may be pissed with me, but if anything kicks off with this guy I can count on them to bail me out . . . which would add to my debt, of course.

'Let's start with your name,' I say, taking the first bite of cake.

'Thomas Mounsey. Tom.'

'Ropa.' I shake his hand across the table. 'Which part of America you from?' His accent sounds slightly odd, by the telly's standards.

'I'm Canadian, from Vancouver.'

I quickly move on. 'Your arms. You said you got into a scuffle last night?'

141

'Some guy and a kid came after me as I was arriving at my hotel. They must have been waiting for me, which means they knew where I was staying.'

'You know their names, seen them before, that kind of thing?'

'No. But they were magicians.'

'How'd you know?'

'The kid threw a fireball at me,' Tom replies stoically.

There's no disputing that one, I suppose. Now I can make fire, but I don't do barbecues like he's described. And having seen the aftermath of Priya's fight at the shore, I can tell they ain't no laughing matter. The magico-scientific name for them is thermospheres, but Joe Public wouldn't know that.

'My coat caught alight,' he adds.

'Did you get a good look at them?'

'The kid's a bit taller than you are. He was wearing chinos and a pink T-shirt. Posh-boy weekend wear. I think he had a gold watch on too: old-fashioned, expensive looking. And he had a big nose, and a moptop haircut like he was auditioning for the Beatles. The old guy was strange. He had a silly moustache, a bow tie and suit. He looked like he'd stepped out of the circus.'

I don't recognize the kid's description, but the guy sounds right familiar.

'You mean a Dalí tash?'

'The kind of moustache that curls upwards like Hercule Poirot's.'

Now what on earth would Bumblebeam have to do with the last foreigner in Scotland? He flees his wagon and leaves

everything, all his worldly possessions, to go after this guy?
I think of the posh kid with him, hurling that fireball. I'd bet
all my life savings the Monks are involved. Maybe with this
guy I can kill two birds with one stone – find out more about
the Monks and cash in besides.

'I'm sorry to say you've mixed yourself up with someone
pretty messed up, but this ain't the Society's doing.'

'It's to do with the money your people owe me, isn't it?'

'Look, I'll level with you. I'm just an unpaid intern, so
don't blame me for nothing. Maybe you can give me your
invoice and I'll look into this for you. How about that?'

Tom laughs bitterly and buries his face in his hands. The
burns look red and angry even with the cream he's got on
them. He shakes his head, and I know I've kinda blown it.

'I know you mean well, but what good is an intern to me?
This is a waste of my time.'

Okay, Ropa, reel him back in. You can do this.

'Like it or not, I'm all you've got, pal. I know this city like
the back of my hand and have a few friends who might even
help keep you safe. And as an intern, you know I ain't no
lackey of the Society. Would you rather have me on your side
or keep banging your head against a brick wall?'

He considers this for a second while I finish off my carrot
cake. The mintoffeecial hits the bullseye for fifty points, and
I let it linger on my tongue before I swallow. If Tom don't
need me then this drink was almost worth it anyhows.

'You make a valid point,' he admits.

'I don't come free, mind. I'll need a lord's handshake for
my retainer, and my cut's twenty percent of what the Society

owes you.' Place my cup back on the table hard enough to make a noise. All in or out, I'm about the bacon.

'Ten percent.' He nods.

'Fifteen.'

'Even if I gave you one half of one percent, you'd still have enough to buy your own island with change to spare,' he says, lowering his voice and looking me in the eye, mondo serious now. 'It's my family's money, and as the sole heir, I consent to your offer of a fifteen percent cut if you can help me get it back.'

Bless Allah, sounds like big money. I hand Tom a napkin and grab a pen from my bag. I ain't no mug. Nothing means anything unless it's on paper. He smiles and scribbles our agreement down, dates it and signs, before handing it over. I slip it in my bag.

'Give me my pen back,' I say.

Tom holds up his hands, laughs and then slides it back to me. There's something charmingly innocent about his demeanour. Edinburgh will chew him up and spit him out if I don't look after him.

'Have you heard of the Paterson fortune?' he asks.

Means nothing to me, so I shrug.

'I'll have to start all the way back in 1698, when it all began. You've heard of the Darien Scheme?'

That's an easy one, all Scots know about that. But I don't respond to his question, merely gesture with an open palm, telling him to proceed. It's always best if you let them talk. You can be a smart-arse showing off this and that, but in the process get them to skip on the relevant bits. And if this damned thing's starting before the advent of emojis then I might even bag myself a second mintoffeecial in the process.

Tom starts with some basics, from back in the seventeenth century when Escocia was a wee shithole, much as it is now, but at least an independent Scottish kingdom. Now, in the 1690s some cold weather caused a famine, killing off fifteen percent of the population – same as my cut, oddly enough – and the economy was in shambles.

This is where Thomas Mounsey's great-great-great-you-get-the-gist comes in. See, William Paterson from Tinwald in Dumfriesshire was an adventurer in the Caribbean, checking out the new English Empire. It's the sort of thing that can give a man notions, and so Paterson came back with a tan and a dream that Scotland should also carve out its own empire. That was en vogue at the time. A wee bit of coloni-alism, sprinkle in some raping, nice chunk of murdering, maybe a dash of slaving, and you have your basic ingredients to make a shit-ton of wealth. What could possibly go wrong?

'In his spare time he also co-founded the Bank of England,' Mounsey adds an ancestral humble brag.

Paterson's big dream was to colonize the Isthmus of Darien, better known as Panama.

The guy was a visionary, grant him that. Way back in the seventeenth century, when everyone else was dreaming of grabbing as much land as they could, Paterson understood Panama's strategic position for the shipping industry. If Scotland set up a free-trade zone there, they could just kick back and watch the dosh roll in while everyone else did the heavy lifting. It was a smart plan, but colonization ain't cheap.

Like any enterprise, you gotta put your own wonga on the table long before the profits start rolling in.

'I want to give you the full picture, so you know exactly what happened,' Tom says.

'I'll have another one of these,' I say, waving my empty mintoffeecial and starting on my flapjack. Tom obliges, and soon enough he's back on his tale.

So the Scots set about raising the cash, and they sought subscriptions from the English and Dutch to help finance the project. Money flowed in fair enough, but soon as things started looking real, the auld enemy set about cockblocking. They wanted a monopoly on trade, and so they told King William to put a stop to this Scottish nonsense, and right enough the English and Dutch investors pulled out, leaving our lot standing there with their cocks in their hands. Naturally, a wave of righteous patriotic fervour swept across the country and the Scots went proper *Braveheart*, girded their kilts and sought to raise the cash themselves. Lots of folks chipped in, from housewives to lairds and everyone else in between, so by the time the nationwide whip-round was through, they'd raised a hefty sum equivalent to one-fifth of the nation's wealth – a big middle finger to the wankers south of the border.

So far so good. The next step was buying ships and outfitting them. Now, the Scots weren't too experienced on this front, but who cares? Five ships with 1,200 souls set sail from the Port of Leith with the hopes of the entire nation behind them.

'It was a time of great optimism,' Tom says.

'Yep, I'm sure the natives in Panama were waiting with open arms,' I reply.

'Erm, yeah, anyway . . .'

The Scots arrived in the Promised Land in November 1698, ready to make serious hay. But between the locals, malaria and a whole run of other bad luck, the colony went kaput. Of the 1,200 who set off from Leith, only three hundred remained. The rest had died gruesome tropical deaths and become fertilizer for the rainforest.

So what d'you do when you're in the casino and you've played a bad hand?

You double down, and that's exactly what the Scots did in 1699, sending another thousand odd souls from the Clyde. I think someone once said, 'Insanity is doing the same thing over and over again and expecting different results,' or some such jazz, so the new settlers pretty much suffered the same fate. Shipping monopoly, colonial ambitions, cash – all gone.

'No offence, Tom,' I say, 'but I don't exactly see what any of this has to do with you.'

By now I've finished my second drink and there's no room in my belly for nothing else. Pity, 'cause I was enjoying milking this hipster, though my bladder's not thanking me for the privilege just now.

'We're getting there,' Tom replies.

'Hold that thought. I need to see a man about a dog,' I say.

XVIII

I'm leaving the bog seven stone lighter when my phone pings. Message from Priya. Says they have another kid at the clinic with Max Wu's symptoms. I ping back with an ETA and move to wind things up here. Gotta get back to my grind.

Tom's melancholic now, staring outside the window and watching the crowds go by. There's a man carrying a pig across his shoulders, closely followed by a juggler. A busker with a guitar's setting up. Thank God it ain't bagpipes again.

'Where were we?' I say, settling down.

'The Darien Scheme burned a massive hole in Scotland's finances. Lots of people lost out,' Tom says. 'The aristocrats and the merchant classes saw only one possible way to claw their money back.'

'Union with England.'

The fine irony of it all. Scotland had been independent all along – hell, even survived the Roman invasions. And then she set out to colonize and got herself colonized in the process. All because Scotland desperately needed finance, which meant ready access to those new English markets. The union was a more polite absorption into the burgeoning English Empire than most got.

Still, that was the bargain made. Give up our parliament and sovereignty and get a slice of that almighty pie the English were carving out around the globe. A bit more than thirty pieces of silver, but still substantially less than what Mel Gibson bled for.

'The last act passed by the Scots Parliament was the key point here,' Tom finally said, and I pricked up my ears. 'They directed that just over £398,000 in compensation should be paid to the subscribers of the Darien Scheme. And a group was set up to receive and allocate these funds, which later became the Equivalent Company. This was the precursor to Scotland's second bank.'

'They formed the Royal Bank of Scotland?'

'Bingo.'

'So everyone gets their dosh back and they all lived happily ever after.'

'Not quite everyone. Your magical Society did the dirty after my ancestor William Paterson died. They took his funds and buried them. The Society of Sceptical Enquirers – its wealth, prestige and power, all were built on money stolen from my family. Without it, Scottish magic would be nothing.'

According to Tom, most Darien subscribers received the funds they were due in cash and stock options. But Paterson died before his payout. Then the executor of his will swapped £8,000 of Paterson's stocks for equity in the Royal Bank of Scotland. And this, crucially to Tom, it seems, was one half of the problem.

This is getting rather convoluted for me. But I can still imagine how that initial eight grand in shares would have grown and grown over time, and then there'd have been all the dividends over that period. The Royal Bank of Scotland pulled off some Ferengi shit, expanding from a tiny one-office affair in Edinburgh to being a multi-billion-pound operation, back when we still had the sterling, making it one of the biggest banks in the world, with tentacles around the globe, a web of subsidiaries roped in via mergers and acquisitions. Unfathomable amounts of money flowing in and out of its accounts. Adjusted for inflation over three hundred years, that initial investment would be astronomical.

'William Paterson's sister Janet had two daughters and a son, John Mounsey, in Kirkcudbrightshire, and I am descended from him.'

'So why's your family only bringing this up now?' I ask.

'There is no family anymore. Just me. But this isn't the first time we've demanded what is rightfully ours.' Tom's sour now, hands balled into fists, a frown on his face like he'd have a go with anyone. 'In 1843, Alexander Mounsey left William Paterson's ancestral farm, Skipmyres, moved to Canada and died there. And in 1861, his grandchildren, through lawyers based in Toronto, pressed the Bank of England and the Royal Bank for restitution.'

'Since you're here today I can only guess the outcome.'

'Obfuscation, prevarication, stonewalling and downright lies was all they got for the millions owed at the time. In 1874, the family tried through a different law firm, but once again they got the same result. More lies. The paper trail led to a dead end.'

I think on this for a wee while. Reckon I'd be just as pissed if my family had been stiffed like that.

'My father spent his whole life on this, seeking documents to prove our claim. But get this . . . the second blow to my claim. The RBS transferred my family's equity in the bank to the Society of Sceptical Enquirers, right near the beginning. As the bank has grown, so too have those shares. That's why my family hadn't been given it and couldn't trace it. And the Society is easily the most opaque organization in the world of finance, after the Vatican. They became a hidden part of the bank, pulling strings from the shadows.'

'Why didn't he press it then, if he had all this information?' I ask.

'He ran out of time to make his case. And if the proof wasn't watertight, he knew he'd get nothing. You know how powerful these people are.'

'So what's changed now then?'

'The catastrophe. My father heard the king wasn't happy the Society stood in the way of the Second Restoration. And after the Sandhurst Club had helped him consolidate his position, he froze the Society out of the bank to weaken them, but he hasn't broken them yet. Their endowment remains, also frozen, forcing them to rely on their other resources, which, while substantial, are dwarfed by their share in the bank. Their offices and stuff are still on the bank's territory, but Dad heard the secretary of the Society no longer sits on the board of the bank. This has given us hope, because while I have a lot of research Dad did, I need hard proof of the Society's fraud. If I were then to petition the king with that in hand, I'm sure he'd seize the opportunity to deliver the final blow. That's the plan, but we had to wait for the dust to settle because things were so chaotic in Britain. My father died last month. It was his final wish for our family's fortune to be restored.' Tom's voice is hoarse with grief and passion.

He has the look of a martyr, and I for one believe him. Dodgy fortunes made the empire, and if he can get just an ounce of this cheese then I'm gonna be right there nibbling it with him. Universe, are you back on my side now?

I can't see how a grifter like Bumblebeam would fit into this picture. But the Monks are clearly involved, and you can trust a bunch of rich kids to go fortune-hunting. Adds up in my ledger.

Tom Mounsey is my golden goose and I have to keep him safe. No way I'm letting them lot get a piece of him.

Right on cue, the atmosphere in the cafe changes as some rough-looking types wander in. The customers hush and the staff of the Beanie Roasters stand uncomfortably behind the counter. Three ruffians come to our table.

'Rooster Rob, I figured I'd scamper before you caught wind of me,' I say.

'I told yous tae stay off our turf until you paid what you owed,' Rob says, hovering over us.

'Looks like fate has an opportunity for us both, so let's talk business. Please join us.' I offer him a seat. He stands there for a few seconds too long, then deigns to humour me.

'Tom Mounsey, meet the king of Camelot, Rooster Rob. The Rooster and his associates will be your security for the duration of your stay. You will find Camelot is a delightful place.'

'This be some kind of prank, Ropa Moyo?'

'Only if you find cash funny, Rob. Some bastards are after this man's hide, and if you keep him safe there's a payday at the end of it for all of us.'

'In case you didnae ken, we're in the middle of a war with the Pilton Crew, who, as we speak, are trying tae take over Stockbridge. Now why would I waste time and men babysitting this pillock?'

I didn't know there was a war on. A handful of gangs work in Edinburgh, but few have the might to challenge the Clan. Last major conflict I know of was the Battle of the Meadows, when the Clan took on the Tollcross Terror Tots, who wore dungarees and bowler hats. It was a fight for dominance over the city, but that was yonks ago. Ain't been no war since then. Most of the gangs are content operating on estates away from the city centre, which the Clan holds exclusively. You got the Niddrie Marshalls, Young Drylaw Team, Oxgangs Woodpeckers, Broomhouse Bombers, the Wester Hailes Ambulance Squad, Clermiston Choirboys, and quite a few more whose range is less than a couple of post-codes wide. None of them would dare take on the Clan unless they were feeling suicidal. Someone's obviously gotten way too big for their boots.

'Will this be sufficient to retain your services?' Tom asks, handing Rob a wad of notes.

Rob's expression changes when he sees the money. He counts it note by note, then gives the barest of nods. The Rooster's word is his bond, and I'd take that nod over a signed contract any day of the week.

'Hey, what about my retainer?' I ask Tom.

He counts a bit more money and makes to hand it to me, but Rob snatches it from him.

'Dick move,' I protest. 'You don't have to do me like that.'

'Ropa Moyo, yous have your visa back till the end of this business. But we still want the remainder you owe,' Rob says.

I can read the Rooster's tone and know when to push and when not to. In the middle of a war might not be the best time. With fifteen percent of the Paterson fortune under my belt, the remainder shouldn't be a problem. But I'll get my own back.

'One more thing, Rob,' I add quietly, out of Tom's earshot. 'I need your ears and eyes on the street. Working busigician, goes by the name Bo Bumblebeam. If he's spotted anywhere in the city, I need to know right away.'

The Rooster doesn't respond. Just slowly gets up, then instructs one of his goons to help with Tom's suitcase trunk. Five-star-hotel service complete with bellhops and the best concierge in Edinburgh. I hope Tom's gonna enjoy the comforts Camelot has to offer. It's the safest spot in the city for him. Meanwhile, I'm all fuelled up. Time to don my deerstalker hat, grab my magnifying glass and find out what's really going on.

XIX

I nearly get knocked over by a mule-drawn wagon while messaging Lewis and Jomo, asking them to meet up at Our Lady. 'Watch yersel, hen,' the driver shouts, waving his fist at me. The sun's proper blazing, and I'm roasting on this bike for the final straight to the clinic. Got a lot on my mind. I'm still spinning at the prospect of hitting the jackpot by potentially screwing over my employer . . . but, hey, I'm just an unpaid intern. Wasn't my job supposed to be womanning the photocopier and making teas?

Callander, though. Don't like the thought of seeing his disappointment.

I'm hit by the delightful fragrance of what money can buy coming into Our Lady of Mysterious Ailments. The herbs they grow attract butterflies and bumblebees, and the air's filled with life. A skateboard rumbles behind me just as I park, and I spot Jomo rolling onto the grounds. At least he's dressed normal in shorts and tee, rather than the altar-boy fashion he wears at the Library.

He lifts up the front wheels of his board, dismounts, then kicks up his board, catching it in one fluid motion. If it was anyone else but this dork, it would look kinda cool.

'Ropamatronic,' he says. 'I was calling out to you from behind, but you obvs didn't hear me.'

'Hey, man. I must be deaf or something.'

'I was half expecting to see you with an earworm plugged in.' He puts his arm around me and leans in, brushing his massive afro against my chin. I throw my arm around his shoulder and we enter the clinic linked up like Tweedledum and Tweedledee. 'I've been loving the research on King James you asked me to do. Like, seriously, he was full of it, but also the sort of nerd the Library would have gladly taken on. Shame about all the witch burnings, man.'

'Great, you guys are right on time,' says Priya as we enter the staffroom. She doesn't look at me. Awkward. 'I have to do this on my break. No rest for the wicked – today's been an absolute killer. I can't wait to get home and soak in my tub.'

'Hey, Priya, looking dapper in that coat. Can I have one too, seeing as Ropa's got hers?' Jomo says.

I'm kicking myself. Forgot to take the damned thing off. But Priya plays it cool. Maybe not that – frosty.

'Only if you give me one of those funky dresses you all wear at the Library.'

'We're book surgeons,' Jomo replies, and laughs.

I spy a new packet of Jammie Dodgers and scuttle over to nick a few. Tradition.

'Oy, Lethington's gonna have my hide for that,' Priya protests.

I blow her a kiss.

'You still miffed with me?' I ask.

'Sorry I'm late,' says Lewis, rushing in. 'Traffic's mad, innit?'

That's all of us.

'Now everyone's here, you lot come with me,' Priya says. I can't help but notice she ignores my question. Fuck it.

'Damn. That's the D-Man, Doug Duffie. There's no way he's mixed up in all this,' says Lewis. 'Sport is more his thing. We're on the same rugby team.'

The D-Man's a sixteen-year-old passed out on a bed in the middle of the room, surrounded by strategically placed rock crystals of all colours and shades. It's proper Baltic in here, same as Max's room, but you wouldn't know it from the intense heat radiating off the D-Man. On the bedside table is a copy of King James's *Daemonologie*, along with some of the lad's gear.

'Exactly the same symptoms as Max, down to a tee. And after last night's events, Ropa, I think I know why. I hypothesize that something's interfering with the soul-body entanglement in these patients, and the psychic friction's setting off the fever. Lethington thinks it's plausible, and we've adjusted the treatment field accordingly.'

French to me. Priya takes a familiar flyer and hands it to me. It's the same as the one Max had in his wallet.

'You found this on Doug Duffie, too? That means they both went on Bo Bumblebeam's astral tours and came out with this condition. What about his other clients?' I ask, a bit worried given that I'd been out in the astral realm with him as well. Rather not catch whatever these boys have.

The tense look on Priya's face tells me she shares my concerns.

'I've thought of that, but no one else in any of the hospitals in the city has come in with these symptoms,' says Priya.

'Right, otherwise we should be seeing dozens of people with this condition,' Lewis chips in. 'This looks to me like they went searching for something specific.'

'You mean to say they weren't visiting a realm, but were actually trying to bring something back in?' Jomo asks.

I've been out there many times, and I've not once been able to bring back anything. It's impossible. I've seen all sorts of things in different realms, precious stones and wealth beyond imagining, but you can't take it with you. Gran says that our world is the only material realm there is.

'Lewis, explain,' I say.

'What if the Monks of the Misty Order succeeded in bringing something back? Something bad. That's why they needed to crack *Daemonologie*. Chapter four is about the method of transportation and the illusions of Satan, and five is about the curse and remedy of diseases.'

'It was believed witchcraft could be used to cure or cause disease hundreds of years ago,' says Priya.

'Exactly. So in this text, there's talk of Satan giving them magical stones from another realm. And ancient magicians did at least believe that it was once possible to transport things from the astral plane.'

'But according to them, it stopped when Clan MacLeod seized the Fairy Flag, right?' she asks.

'The timelines are off, but yes.'

'Wow, wait a minute, what are you guys talking about?' I ask.

I wish I'd had some of that fancy magic schooling. Feel tired sometimes of trying to parse through all their mumbo jumbo.

'It used to be possible to bring things into this world from other realms, Ropa,' says Lewis. 'That's why Max pinched my research. I didn't think it was useful, but the Monks may have figured out how to do it, using Bo Bumblebeam to help them cross over.'

'And whatever they brought back is making them ill,' I finish.

Jomo lets out a long, low whistle, and Priya looks equally horrified.

Now, I've dealt with the extranatural for a living, and you don't wanna mess with that stuff if you don't know what you're doing. Took years for Gran to drill the right etiquette in my skull, and I still don't feel like I've got it all down. This is orders of magnitudes worse than simply visiting the wrong part of the astral plane. What are these kids playing at? Anyone who's watched *The Mummy* knows it's best to leave that shit where you find it.

'Edinburgh School brats,' Priya says exasperatedly.

'Look, the school doesn't teach us this stuff. They make us aware it's there and forbidden, but you don't get how-to classes. Never,' Lewis replies defensively.

'This changes everything. I need to talk to Lethington. We can't recentre these boys unless we find out what they brought here. This is a mess,' she says. Then she snaps at me, 'I need that information, Ropa.'

I rack my brain to see if there's anything or anyone that fits from over the last few days. Brother Musashi talks about the difference between seeing and perceiving. 'Perception is strong and sight weak. In strategy it is important to see distant things as if they were close and to take a distanced view of close things.' Join those dots.

'Lewis, who's the posh kid from your school, the one with the mop haircut?' I ask, thinking of Bo Bumblebeam's mysterious accomplice.

He narrows his eyes.

'Rory MacCulloch?' He takes out his phone, scrolls through some photos and shows me.

Weird-looking kid with an intense stare. It's a group photo but he has this loner vibe, like he doesn't quite fit in. Lewis flips to the next pic, and this one's Rory taken unawares. A bucket of water, blurry in the shot, is coming at him while he's sat behind a desk somewhere.

'Send me both of those,' I say. 'I think Rory and I need to have a chat.'

'Done. There's just one itsy-bitsy niggle,' Lewis says. 'Rory's a boarder. There's no way he'd be in Edinburgh for the summer. He should be at his family's estate in Clackmannanshire.'

XX

By the time I leave the clinic I've given the crew their assign-
ments. Lewis is to get Rory's number for me, which he didn't
have, Jomo is digging into the extranatural transportation of
objects between realms, and Priya is to keep me posted on
the latest developments with the patients. Feels like that's
what the General Discoveries Directorate would want to
happen, and I am the directorate, so . . .

All this juggling's got my engine revving on my ride home
through Craiglockhart. I veer down Chesser to the Slateford
Bowling Club, near the Water of Leith. The bowling club
happens to have a plum tree on its grounds, and I've been
checking its progress from time to time on forays, so I know
the plums should be ripe now.

I bag myself a nice punnet. Well, I really just pick a few
and chuck 'em in my backpack, but I reckon it should be a
treat for my peeps. I only ever harvest what I need and leave
the rest for whoever comes through next. Otherwise, they'd
only rot, which is a waste. Gotta be savvy, know where the
orchards are, the random fruit trees on roadsides, the fields
where edible mushrooms pop up in season, paths to visit for
berries and all that. In a couple of weeks I have a date with

some crab-apple trees on the old industrial estate near Hermiston Gait. No one need ever starve in Edinburgh during the summer.

It's a step up from what I've heard of back in the day when folks were chopping up their dogs and eating them. I try to keep my eyes peeled when I'm out and about. It's the kind of thing country folk do which city dwellers have long since forgotten. I hope the good patrons of Slateford Bowling Club don't take no offence as I make my quick getaway.

Soon enough I'm back at the slum with plenty of daylight to spare. I meet old Gary hard at it on his allotment. His hours seem to coincide nicely with my arrival, and I get the feeling he's been waiting for me.

'Alright, pal,' I say.

He straightens up and makes a nice 'ooh', holding his back with one hand.

'Ropa, I've got something for your nanna,' he says, picking up a plastic bag from the ground and hobbling towards me. His gait improves with each step, almost as though it takes a while for the old joints to click into place.

'And I've got something for you,' I say, handing over a couple of plums.

'You're a belter, Ropa.' Gary takes one with his dirty fingers and bites into it straight away. 'That's delicious.'

'There's more where they came from,' I say.

He hands me the plastic bag and I take a peek. The smell hits me, and I know someone's been fishing.

'What kind?' The fish are wrapped in a second bag, so I can't see them proper.

'Oor very own brown trout,' he says proudly. 'Caught them myself.'

'That's so cool.'

There's an awkward silence that falls between us. Gary's drawn his lips like there's something he wants to say but can't quite find the words for. I give him a little smile to encourage him.

'See, Ropa, I was wondering . . .'

'Yes.'

'I got to thinking. Well. I don't know, it's silly, of course . . . but I was wondering if maybe your nanna would fancy picnicking sometime? I mean, it would be a waste of this fine weather to stay cooped up all the time in that caravan, ken what I mean? Just a picnic, that's all, nothing too fancy or anything like that. I'm a simple fellow—'

'Yes.'

'Ha? But you havenae asked her.'

'The answer is still yes. I'll make sure of it.'

'Gee.' He breaks out into a gap-toothed smile, beaming brighter than the summer sun, and I can be glad I've at least made one person happy today. Now all I have to do is get Gran on board.

When I get to our caravan I see what's panicked Gary enough to make his move now. Parked outside is a swanky vintage Bentley straight out of a black-and-white movie from the 1920s. It's a stunning red two-seater sports car, probably some aristocrat's midlife crisis back when. The chrome shines so bright it almost blinds me, spare wheel on the side, leather seats, decadence in overdrive. Never mind the cost of this thing. It's a guzzler, and a civilian car. Whoever drives this has access to fuel, which, unless they are a minted farmer or haulier of some sort, means they are connected.

It don't belong in Hermiston Slum. I'm wondering who even has the balls to bring it here and why no one's attempted to snatch the stuff inside in plain sight. But when I reach for the door, I'm zapped by black lightning leaping from the body of the car. Ouch. Static? No way. I nearly fall off my bike scrambling to get away.

The sting's pretty damn bad.

Lesson learnt, I leave well enough alone and make a beeline for the cara.

I hear voices inside so I put my ear to the door. Spying on Gran's never been a thing for me, but neither have we ever had Bentleys park so boldly in our slum.

'Events are moving faster than I'd foreseen, Ian. Something's coming that will make the catastrophe seem like a walk in the park.' That's Gran's voice.

'Curious. Theodosia Lovell visits the city and now here you are portending doom. How long have we got?'

'A few months, perhaps. Maybe less.'

'I need more than that, Melsie.'

'My sight isn't quite what it used to be. I can just about smell the coming storm.'

'It's hard enough for me to deal with the here and now without these distractions. As always, it will be up to me to batten down the hatches using the full weight of the Society. I can only hope that will be enough. You've been out too long indulging yourself amongst the riff-raff while we've held things together.'

This is news to me. Gran used to be one of the Society? That can't be right. Can it?

'That's not fair.'

'You *abandoned* us, Melsie.'

'I have my reasons.'

'Which you never explained. Now suddenly you call, asking to see me after all these years.' Surely it can't be . . . That voice is all too familiar. 'You failed to impart your so-called chivanhu craft to Ropa – except for some of the basics. Now I must ensure her sister at least has an opportunity to develop her family's talents. I've made arrangements with the Doric School. She will be safe there whenever whatever you have glimpsed comes.'

'I don't want to go to Aberdeen!' Izwi says. 'I don't want to study magic.'

'Ian, these girls are all I have.' Gran's voice breaks.

'This is no time for sentiment, Melsie. It's about what's best for the girls and their future . . . everyone's future. You may come inside now, Miss Moyo. We can't have you standing there with your ear to the door all day,' the man says.

Busted.

I open the door to see Sir Callander sat on my berth opposite Gran. His presence fills the tiny caravan, and it almost seems inappropriate that he's in such a shabby space. Why would he even come here? It's not exactly like he's ever taken an interest in where I live before. I place the fish and my bag on the counter.

'Sir Callander, what are you doing here?'

'Securing your little sister's future. We've heard she is very bright, diligent, and, given the right opportunity, we believe she can go on to become a first-class practitioner. I've secured a scholarship for her with the Doric School. They have wonderful boarding facilities, and while she is older than the year group we have enrolled her in, I believe with extra support she should catch up with her peers. The head teacher, Calista Featherstone, is a good friend of mine and will ensure her success.'

'I don't want to go to *Aberdeen*,' Izwi shouts, flinging a pillow against the window. She falls back onto the berth and thrashes about, throwing the mother of all tantrums.

I think of all the times I've wished for something better for her. Dropped out of school myself so I could take care of her and Gran. But this, a scholarship, boarding, regular meals. Can't bear the thought of being apart from her stubborn little arse . . . but it's better than anything I could ever give her.

'Aberdeen's far away. Can't you find something local?' I ask.

'The Edinburgh Ordinary School for Boys won't have her. My relationship with Montgomery Wedderburn is not enough to surmount the question of her gender. The Kelvin Institute in Glasgow won't take students this young. And St Andrews will not hear of it, so Aberdeen it must be. You cannot even begin to imagine the strings I've had to pull to make this happen.'

'Ian,' says Gran.

'Melsie, I have a million and one responsibilities on my plate. I consider this matter settled.' Callander gets up abruptly and bangs his head against the ceiling. He grimaces, bows his head and makes for the door.

I get out of his way.

'I suppose this is goodbye, then, old friend,' says Gran, choking with emotion.

Callander stops with his hand on the door handle. A pained look passes across his face and he freezes for a moment. Then he takes a deep breath and composes himself.

'This is the right thing to do,' he says softly. He opens the door and steps outside. 'With me, Miss Moyo.'

I go back outdoors and stand with Callander as he surveys the chaos of the slum. Pirate wires running from the power lines to feed the caravans, sheds and makeshift shelters all around. I feel embarrassed for living here. It was simple enough when I met Callander in town, but for him to come out here and see my ends sucks.

I don't want no one's pity or their charity, just a fair shot of making my way.

We walk to his ride behind the cara.

'I don't need to explain to you what the benefits of a proper education in scientific magic are,' he says. 'Can I trust you to get your little sister on board? She appears wilful, an admirable quality if channelled in the right direction. But the other way lies disaster.'

'Is that the only reason you want Izwi elsewhere? I heard you and Gran talk about something bad coming t—'

'It is for her own good,' Callander replies sharply. 'That is all you need to know. Now, what's the latest news on Max Wu?'

He is a prickly bastard, but what more can I say – he's the boss. I break it down for him: Doug Duffie, Bumblebeam, the Rory lead, every relevant thing except for my Canadian goose Tom Mounsey. Callander listens attentively, now and again querying some aspect of my reasoning, but generally he seems content with my progress.

'Proceed with caution and wrap it up,' he says, getting into his Bentley. When it starts up, the noise from the engine's the rumble of an eight-litre storm.

'One more thing,' I say as Callander shifts into gear.

'Go on.'

'I'd like access to the Society's archives.'

He raises an eyebrow.

'It's for my studies,' I hastily add.

That's all *he* needs to know. No need to tell him my research is on the Paterson fortune.

'The Society's records are synonymous with the bank's, and you will find them stored in the Gyle. I'll arrange that for you.'

As soon as Callander leaves, I rush back to the caravan and find Gran sat with Izwi on her lap. Little sis has her arms thrown around Gran's neck and her face buried in her bosom. I sit on my berth, the same spot Callander was in. It's odd that he was here so soon after I told him about Theodosia Lovell. He called her an enemy of the Society, but she is Gran's friend. Now all of a sudden Callander wants Izwi shunted away to Aberdeen 'for her own good'? I can't help but ask the question:

'So, you gonna tell me how you know Sir Callander, Gran?'

'We go back a long way,' she replies, stroking Izwi's hair. 'Another lifetime ago.'

And that's all I get from her. Just those two lines. It's pretty worthless as far as explanations go. I know Gran used to go round doing a bit of ghostbusting and stuff, so maybe it's from that. But I'm speculating when the horse is right beside me, and I need the words from its mouth.

'I don't like that man,' Izwi says.

'Gran?' I persist.

'So this job of yours is with the magicians, Ropa?' Gran says.

'That doesn't answer my question,' I reply. 'Were you in the Society?'

She sighs. 'The Society doesn't have all the answers, though they may pretend otherwise. I can teach you a different kind of magic if only you will let me try, child.'

'Gran, look at us. Have you seen the state of this place?' I shake my head. 'We're broke, living hand to mouth. We wouldn't be here if we were proper magicians, with the right certificates and accreditation. We wouldn't be scrambling for jobs that pay peanuts. I don't want to be in this slum for the rest of my life. I want out.'

Can't really say it outright, but Shona magic is so lame. The Society doesn't even consider it proper magic anyway, so I'd just be wasting my time practising it. Only scientific magic makes the cut out here.

I'm learning real, actual magic now. I can't go back to the ancestors and all that mystical stuff.

'There are a lot of things you do not understand, child. You are mature but still very young. The Society isn't all it appears to be,' she says finally. 'There are things I still wish to teach you, ancient things you will not find anywhere else.'

'You practised magic without a licence, and look how far it got us.'

There's a pained expression on Gran's face. I don't want to be saying these things, but it's the truth.

'I feel you drifting away from me, child.'

'Don't be silly, Gran.'

She pauses for a long moment weighing her words. 'Okay. Is this the future you want then?' she asks at last.

'It's the right thing to do,' I reply, echoing Callander's words.

Hard as it is for me to imagine, 'cause she's always just been Gran to me, I see there was a whole 'nother life she lived long before I was even a tadpole in my dad's balls. I appreciate my gran, and everything she's taught me and tried to teach me, but there's no way I'd give up scientific magic for mysticism. I guess the only silver lining of all this is that Gary O'Donohue don't have no competition. I'd take him as a step-granda over Callander any day.

'Gran, your admirer's finally asking for a date,' I say, to change the subject.

XXI

Wake up late to a sweet scent coming off the hob. Sunshine flowing through the windows and birdsong coming from yonder. Gotta look on the bright side – I might not get paid a mini-penny but my office hours are mine to make as I see fit. Hell, I count Callander's visit last night as overtime.

I yawn and swing my legs off the berth.

Check my phone for messages. I've got Rory's number off Lewis, so that's a good start. If he was seen with Bo Bumblebeam, he needs investigating. Jomo's sent me a video of a singing dinosaur for some reason. Nothing off Priya. I send her a heart-kiss emoji. We might not think the same, but I see no reason in letting this stew on. There's work for us to do still.

Gran's at the hob stirring the pot, with Izwi standing by as her trusty sous-chef. I amble over before peering across Gran's shoulder.

'Did you sleep well, child?'

'Like a baby.'

'I don't know why everyone says that. Babies wake up in the middle of the night crying and pooping,' Izwi says.

'And what do you know of it?' I ask.

'I was a baby once,' she replies.

Gran laughs, her joy rolling through the tiny caravan until we all catch it and join in her mirth. At least she ain't sour with me like she was last night. She takes out the wooden spoon from the saucepan and holds it to my lips. I blow and have a taste of bramble jam. Wow.

'Izwi picked berries for us along the canal,' she says.

'I can see that.'

A small woven basket on the counter still has leftover berries, and next to it are empty jars for the jam when it's done. For me, the jam's a great compote substitute to have with my porridge in the morning. Same difference really, as far as I'm concerned. But if it's jam-making day, then I reckon them two'll be at it a while this morn. Gran likes to give some jars away to the neighbours, and I make certain Gary O'Donohue's at the top of that list. Cupiding is sooo much fun.

I get back to my berth and try Rory's number. Don't even ring or nothing. All I get's the lady telling me, 'The number you have dialled is not recognized'. Stuff that. I send Lewis a message asking him to double-check it. Then I surf various socials, looking for Rory, but all his profiles are private and I can't see what he's been up to or message him. I send Lewis a request to screenshot the most recent entries along with a new number. They must be friends online – they go to school together.

Phone pings. It's Priya, saying she's off today and willing to tag along if I'll have her with. And, *yay*, I get a fist bump back. It's not a kiss, though. Still, that gives me a wee surge of energy, and soon enough I'm up, lab coat on, backpack –

check – ready to hit the road. Scarf – never leave home without it, summer be damned.

'Are you leaving, Ropa? I'd like us to spend some time together,' Gran says.

'Sorry, Gran, work calls. You know how it goes.'

'You're never here,' Izwi says sulkily.

'I have to work, sis.'

'I wanna come with you,' she replies, blocking my path. I have to stand back 'cause she's covered in sugar and jam, and I don't want none of that on my doctoring coat.

'I'll bring back something nice for you.'

Bribery always works with Izwi. She carries on like this and I can guarantee a bright future for her in Police Scotland. There's turmoil written all over her face as she considers my offer.

'No.'

I'm a bit taken aback. What could possibly beat sweet treats in her little head? I'm losing my touch.

'I can't take you with me. It can be dange— Sometimes my work is . . . There's long distances involved and you don't have a bike, sis. How about you walk me up to Calder then, and I'll still bring something special for you when I come back?'

The corners of her mouth turn downwards, but she agrees all the same. It's a fair compromise. Making time for my family ain't so easy with everything I've got going on. But once this is all done, I'll be able to. Hell, with my cut of the fortune we'll be swimming in it and we can do whatever we want. It's worth a bit of pain to get that long-term gain. Just a little bit longer, that's all.

We make our way out, leaving Gran to her work. I grab my bike and River comes out from under the cara to join us. She nuzzles my leg before settling in the space between me and Izwi as we make our way out the slum. Noisy this morn with folks about their industry. There's dosh to be made at the King's Market, and the hawkers are pushing carts filled with wares. An electric scooter passes us by. Someone's hammering away at their sheet-metal roof and the sound bores right through my eardrums. Hectic on a braw day like this, and that convinces me I need to get going too as we cross over the bypass.

I wanna talk to Izwi about the offer Callander's made to get her through magic school. Not that I'd ever want us separated, but it's a great opportunity, so I have to lay it out to her straight. She's a smart kid – I think she'll get it eventually. I'm about to start when I think, hang on a minute, if the Paterson fortune comes through, we'll be proper minted and so all this won't be necessary at all.

'What you smiling about?' Izwi asks.

'Nothing,' I say, but I can't stop all the same.

'Whatever.'

Not going to break it to the kid yet, but that's definitely why I've got to link up with Tom later on and see if a visit to the archives will yield anything new in his quest. His family fortune might well keep my family together. I could send Izwi to a top-notch school in Edinburgh if money's taken care of. Not to mention a proper house with indoor plumbing for Gran.

By the time we reach the big roundabout near Broomhouse, I'm filled with so much optimism I could burst. I send

Izwi back with River, mount my bike and shoot off down Longstone way, which will take me across to Craiglockhart. From there I can get to Merchiston peasy, and to the Edinburgh School of magic.

Priya's waiting for me at the corner of Gillsland Road, a stone's throw from the clinic. She's looking like the stuff of the season in a saffron crinkle dress that flows to just below her knees.

'You're quite the lass about town,' I say.

'And I take it you're the Doctor?'

'Number thirteen, baby.'

'A very unlucky number.'

'Numerology was never my strong point. Shall we head up?'

Priya bites her lower lip and looks pensive. Then she clenches her jaw and gives me a long look.

'I accept your apology,' she says after a while.

'I don't remember giving one,' I reply.

'You've sent me two kisses today.'

'So what, Judas kissed Jesus. It don't mean nothing,' I say. 'I didn't see you send me any kisses back. What's that about?'

'Don't make this any more awkward than it has to be. I'm sorry too, alright.' She raises her fist and I bump it. 'Good, now are we gonna stand here rubbing clits all day or shall we get to it?'

Behind Priya's an incredible beech hedge that's taller than city ordinances allow for . . . as if anyone cares about that. Been past here loads on my runs and never cared to think what was on the other side of it. It must be at least a hundred feet tall and so dense it might as well be the rampart on some medieval castle. The leaves are eerily still, even with a good breeze blowing.

The Edinburgh School must want max privacy, but it seems a bit paranoid not to even have an entrance on Colinton Road, which is the main thoroughfare. Instead, the hedge continues uninterrupted all the way to Tipperlin Road.

'Must have been a pain for you going to school all the way in Glasgow when there's a perfectly good one in Edinburgh,' I say to help fade away the lingering awkwardness.

'Even Auld Nick himself couldn't get his daughter into this school if he tried. Nah, this place is for douches, Ropa. I'm a Kelvinite through and through, and I don't have any regrets about the length of my school run. You've met a few practitioners from the Edinburgh School. They all walk around with fingers stuck up their bumholes.'

'Lewis is alright, though.'

'You're still too new to know any better. Trust me, the Edinburgh boys are a piece of work.'

'Sir Callander?'

'Granted, there's minor exceptions.' She gestures to the line of houses across the street. 'See, the land around the school belongs to it, so they house their staff there.'

Decent perks. Costs a fair bit otherwise to live in these ends, I'd imagine. Priya halts in front of a black gate whose metal bars are the shape of serpents. The detail is so well done even their scales are individually rendered. There's a strange beauty to it, and if I move, the play of light makes the serpents look like they're writhing in some kind of vertical snake pit.

'The gate's all about representations of beithir,' says Priya. 'You know that one?'

I nod, though there's always been this ambiguity about whether beithir were serpents or dragons, dwelling in the caves and corries of the remotest parts of these isles. I go with serpent since beithir never breathed out fire or did any dragony stuff. But it was the deadliest, most poisonous snake ever, only sighted on summer nights when lightning strikes occurred. If you kill a snake in Scotland, you're supposed to cut off the head and separate it as far as you can from the body or else it returns as a beithir and you're screwed.

I'd wanted Lewis with us today, but he's babysitting his siblings and can't come out. Priya's cool though, 'cause she knows these schools.

'You've been here before, yeah?' I ask.

'A couple of times, for sports and meets, back before my res.'

'How do we get in? Is there like a bell or something?'

'The gate lets you in, Ropa,' Priya replies matter-of-factly.

Beyond the gate looks more woodland than anything, obscuring the view. The road immediately veers left and winds instead of taking the straight route to where the school buildings should be.

Priya holds out her hand, close to the tangled mass of snakes that makes up the gate, and she incants:

'Deus over the ports and the gates, let what is barred be cleared, for we are here rightfully as pupils, Portunus.'

There's loud hissing that's so startling I step back afeard, but Priya remains right where she is. The coiling snakes start to disentangle, metallic scales grating against one another as they draw back. They slither into the hedges until only their heads remain visible as their dead eyes stare into the yawning gap. This is the most unwelcoming school entrance I've ever seen. I'm kinda relieved this place ain't an option for Izwi.

'There was always someone to meet us at the gate, so I learnt the password.'

'I'm not liking the thought of walking in between them snakes, Priya.'

'Pussy,' she taunts, going in. She turns back and shrugs as if it's no big deal.

The snakes start to creep back in place to bar the entrance, and I rush in despite my gut. This is my job, after all, and I've got to get it done. Maybe I'm all wary like this since I ain't used to these sorts of schools, whereas Priya just sees it as normal. But as much as I rationalize this shit, my Spidey senses are tingling like a bad case of thrush. We make our way up the cobbled road snaking deeper into the woodland. In the distance looms a large grey building, hard to make out from within all this foliage. Each line of sight gives you the view of a wall or window, but it's impossible to see the whole.

The shade makes the place feel much cooler than the tar outside the school. From my right comes the sound of running water, maybe a fountain in the woods. There's bracken and bramble broken by hedging and shrubbery. I spot what looks like a man in the woods, but on closer inspection, it only turns out to be topiary, box hedge in the shape of a human. There's more about shaped like all sorts of fantastical animals and kelpies: Nessie, boobrie, cait sith, which looks very like a jaguar, something fish-like, maybe a morool. We walk past a demon on a horse who, if this theme is consistent, must be the nuckelavee or something similarly sexy.

This stuff's done by a proper artist. I can tell by the proportions and the choice of plants – yew, holly and box – each with leaves suited to the shape created. That's one heck of a gardener they've got here.

While the way is flat, it feels like I'm walking uphill, and I even have to lean in to walk properly. Priya's working hard in her chair too.

'How come—'

'It's a false flat, an optical illusion. Same thing you get at Electric Brae in Ayrshire. They took the concept from gravity hills and applied it to the gardenscape here. David Hume once argued that we have nothing upon this earth but our senses to depend on. The school teaches the students not to trust their assumptions but instead to question everything, to become Sceptical Enquirers.'

Turns out this is because of Hume's oversized influence on Scottish magic, which began to shift from mysticism to science around the eighteenth century. Priya explains that there's ongoing debate as to whether or not Hume himself was a magician, for which there's scant evidence. But since he lived on South St David Street just off St Andrew Square, there can be no doubt he would have known of and engaged with his neighbours at Dundas House. Hume's empiricism and scepticism created the intellectual framework for handling magic because by showing the limits of reason and logic, phenomena previously misunderstood could be legitimately explored. What was known then as 'Natural Magick' became the foundation of 'the second science'. It also allowed the early members of the Society to live with the conceptual contradictions of their work.

'Pretty neat, hey?' Priya says.

'Not so great for my calves.' I'm exaggerating. Every Edinburgher knows hillwork's part of the contract. There's strange rustling behind us. 'What's that?'

'Christ, you're a bag of nerves today. What happened to the girl with balls the size of kettlebells?' But Priya's voice doesn't sound confident at all.

The rustling picks up from all round us, coming from deep within the woodland. The old trees creak, and I get this ominous vibe just as I recall that Priya's incantation to open the gates specifically said, '. . . we are here rightfully as pupils'. Only we're not. And why would the Edinburgh boys be so confident to reveal this password with folks from elsewhere within earshot? So the gates opened, but we're not pupils. We're not even boys. I should have come on a different day with Lewis.

'Priya . . .'

'Faster, to the building,' she replies.

Then there's the low rumble, the sound of something torn out, followed by shaking and clumps of earth falling to the ground. Yep, that'll be roots leaving the soil. Oh no.

'Run,' Priya shouts.

If the beech hedge is the wall, then these woods are the moat and we've blundered in head first. I duck a swinging oak branch aimed straight for me. Before I get my bearings I spot a hedge stag galloping towards us, head down, gigantic antlers primed.

Up ahead, a lion emerges to block our path, green mane bristling with menace. It opens its mouth, and instead of a roar, out pours the sounds of leaves thrashing in heavy wind.

'This way,' Priya shouts, taking the footpath away, as if there's any other option. I'm not liking it one bit because if them plants are coming to life like that, we're only getting into the thick of it.

We veer down a gravel path to the left, and I can hear Priya right behind me, working hard to move in this uneven terrain. The entire canopy has come to life, and a hail of conkers, pine cones and acorns showers down on us. I catch some on the noggin and don't much like that, but the complaints department's shut and so I keep legging it.

A vine swipes at my legs and I stumble before regaining my balance. But the damned thing's got hold of my bike, winding itself round the spokes on the wheel. Stuff that. I let go of the bike and sprint for a clearing ahead, cursing whatever deities as soon as I hit the lawn with Priya in tow. On a sunny day like this, the garden we wind up in looks proper genteel, the sort of place to picnic in.

But before I can catch my breath, an almighty menagerie of topiary animals bursts forth from the woods. The hideous nuckelavee leads the charge, and I ain't sticking around to learn its intentions.

'To the building,' I shout, pointing to the grey school. Priya's way ahead of me on this one, racing across the lawns like it's Ladies Day at Musselburgh Racecourse.

I'm out of breath but running still, hearing the scary rustling noise of the hedges coming for us.

Priya yells Cerulean incantations, and I'm praying her herbology can get us out of this pickle. But even I know we're in trouble when she pivots to Dionysus just as we rush up the mound towards the school building. We run clear across the lawn onto the solid pavement at a world-record pace. A massive clump of earth explodes over us, showering us in dirt, but we keep going, right up to the massive white door. Sanctuary!

I try the handle, but it won't open.

The hedge creatures are gaining.

'Out of the way,' Priya yells. She quickly incants a spell I don't catch, which sends a blast of air to the door. But the wood flexes inwards, absorbing it all, and springs back in place, launching her spell right at us. I'm hit by a wind so powerful it throws me onto the ground. Priya absorbs the force by wheeling back a distance, surfing it. Smooth. But I think I landed on my tailbone, 'cause my butt hurts.

This is why I never liked school.

'Run,' she says.

'No shit, Sherlock,' I say, scrambling off the ground.

I bolt along the path that follows the length of the building. Then I reach for the shades in my breast pocket and put them on. Time for the one spell I can competently do.

I shout, 'Prometheus!'

Everything turns white in a sea of incandescent sparks that ripple out, catching the hedge creatures and singeing them.

Take that. I know plants don't like fire.

There's a sharp, whistle-like noise, maybe shrieks of pain. But still they keep coming towards us. This time with renewed vigour and aggression, burning leaves and all.

Priya looks over her shoulder.

'You've just pissed them off, Ropa,' she says.

'And you were singing them lullabies?'

'I was trying to get the earth to bind them, but this place is saturated with countermeasures. It's impossible to get anything done,' she replies as we round the corner of the main school building. 'Over there, to the rugby field.'

I don't know what she's on about, 'cause I don't see no H-shaped posts. Instead, there's a bunch of paving blocks floating in the air, like a sort of pyramid above a sandpit.

Priya heads straight towards it. Her chair vaults into the air, onto the first block, bouncing onto the next at speed until she's on the third tier.

I jump for the first one, barely make it and have to haul myself up until I'm right on it. The second tier's a doable leap over, but the third's too far for me to reach. The distance between them increases so the top one's much further up.

'You've got to jump, otherwise they'll get you, Ropa.'

'I won't make it.'

XXII

As far as grisly ends go, death by hedge creature menagerie never once factored into my calculations. Brother Musashi says stuff like 'Don't fear death', but the way my ticker's kicking, I'm likely to go down with a myocardial infarction before them plants turn me into fertilizer.

They've slowed down, surrounding the sandpit below us. Watching? They ain't got eyes, but they sure as hell know where we're at.

Their roots trail on the lawn.

Sharp thorns ready to dig into our flesh.

The badass nuckelavee's at the head of this whole thing. If I had to go up against a half-man, half-horse situation, I'd have taken my chances with a centaur; they're always seen as wise and reasonable. The nuckelavee's a whole different league of bampottary, a mashed-up horse-rider combo stripped of flesh so you can see the muscles and sinew. The rider's torso has no legs, and he's grafted onto his horse's back. His arms are long enough to reach the ground and the claws on them are sharp. They say its breath alone was enough to wilt crops and bring disease upon your livestock. And its name was only ever spoken in fearful whispers. Right now, its topiary incarnation's coming towards me, claws reaching out.

I whip out the scarf from my pocket.

'Grab the other end of Cruickshank and pull me up,' I say.

'Ha?'

'My scarf's called Cruickshank,' I yell, tossing one end up to Priya. No time to explain that I figured it was old, crooked and a bit of a mad ninja, hence the moniker.

Priya engages the brakes on her chair, precariously positioned on the floating slab. She grabs the scarf with both hands.

'Quickly, Ropa, it's right behind you.'

That rustling noise, so close.

'Come on, Cruickshank, help me out,' I say.

I leap off my slab, feeling a gust of air from the hedge creature's attempted grasp. But my scarf doesn't disappoint. It loops me in an incredible arc through the air until I land right on Priya's lap.

The floating slab wobbles but holds firm all the same.

A gruesome smile appears on the nuckelavee's face. It's a hole drawn through the leaves, and it fills me with dread. Some of the leaves are singed from the Promethean sparks, making him look like something dragged out of hell. You can sense the malice coming off him, from all of these hedge creatures. It's fucked up.

'We've got ourselves in a right nippleskimpel,' Priya says.

'I honestly hadn't noticed.' Lowest form of humour, I know. 'Seriously, I thought you did botany and stuff. Can't you do an Aquaman and talk to these guys?'

'That's fish – plants are a huge difference, involving a

central nervous system. You must not have been listening when I told you about counterspells . . . Oh oh. This is bad. Very, very bad.'

I look down and see the nuckelavee rustle an order to the menagerie. The herd parts to create a path, and from the ranks, something walks up that looks like cow parsley. It's a plant nearly two metres tall with thick, bristly stems, and crowning its head are white flowers in umbels. This is some *Day of the Triffids* bull, and I'm bricking it.

'What the hell is that, man?'

'Giant hogweed. If it touches your skin, you're going to burn and blister. It's the worst.'

The still smiling nuckelavee offers the hogweed a ride and looks straight up to us perched on our wee lifeboat. He raises the poisonous plant and slowly brings it towards us. The other plants rustle in scary anticipation as though we're militant vegans about to get our comeuppance.

'Do something,' I say desperately.

'Like what?'

'Nuke 'em. You're the only qualified magician here, for crying out loud.'

'A protogenoi spell.'

'Ha?'

'You asked for a nuke.'

'Do it already!'

The giant hogweed's an arm's length away, and I don't want it anywhere near me. I can already feel my face itching.

'In the beginning, primes and firsts, order upon chaos. In this dire need I invoke Physis for—'

'*Stop right there*,' a gravelly voice says, cutting Priya off mid-incantation.

I'm frozen with the giant hogweed virtually in my face. But at least the nuckelavee stopped, so whoever this is, I owe her a beer, fags and crisps.

'Make way, you fanny. Mick, you've left a trail of dirt all across my lawns, and you, Agnes, not one berry off you for five years, yet here you are prancing about. Burt, I gave you a good mulching yesterday and you've ruined it now. Come on, enough of this rubbish, the lot of you. Back you go to your beds and sink those roots in deep. If I catch any of you roving about, you'll be getting some hard pruning,' she says irritably. 'All these leaves on the lawns, guys. I'll be raking for days now, and it ain't even autumn.'

The nuckelavee gives us one hard final look before turning back and retreating along with the rest of the menagerie. Christ, I can breathe again. As the plants slowly retreat, they reveal a short, barrel-chested woman in grey overalls and wellies, wearing a straw hat. She holds a pair of hedge shears in her left hand.

'Mrs Guthrie, you're a sight for sore eyes,' Priya exclaims.

'And you've just undone my summer's labours, Priyanka Kapoor.' The groundskeeper gestures, and the floating slabs tumble down, us along with them. I land on my side in the sandpit next to Priya, who's somehow managed to stay upright despite the fall.

'Ouch,' I protest.

'You'd be yelling in Spanish if Mick had fed you a mouthful of hogweed, lass.' Mrs Guthrie's gravelly voice is as rich as organic compost. 'And if you girls had dared unleash a protogenoi spell in my garden, I'd have done a lot worse to you myself. Up you get, and don't moan about it.'

'Sorry,' Priya says, abashed.

'I've met you at a few botany conferences, Priyanka, and you've always struck me as the sensible sort. But if you haven't figured out that a coupling spell might have been a better ward until help arrived, then I don't know what they teach at the Lord Kelvin. Even if you'd got past my green friends, you'd have had to face those stone gargoyles on the school building, and believe you me, they don't mess about. It's the summer and there's hardly any staff about, so you and your little friend are very lucky I happened by the noo. Trespassing, here? There's stupid, then there's *stupid*, and I can't say which category you fall into.'

Mrs Guthrie inspects the landscape and groans, pissed off by the sheer mess we've left in our wake. The pristine lawn and pavements are covered in dirt, twigs and leaves.

'And which one of you thought it was a good idea to start a fire on these grounds?'

'This is Ropa Moyo and she's Sir Callander's intern,' says Priya, throwing me under the bus.

'Nonsense. That uptight bastard hasn't taken an apprentice in years.'

'He has now, Mrs Guthrie, and she is helping me attend to Max Wu at the hospital. You heard what happened to him?'

'The students ain't none of my business; this garden's all I care about, and so unless you're here to tell me he's potted up and sprouting leaves, I don't care.' It's easy to believe. Dirt in her nails. Plant material tangled up in her curly brown hair that reaches just below her shoulders.

I dust myself off and leave the sandpit in time to see some of the hedge creatures freezing back into their previous positions. Now I've stopped shaking, I offer Mrs Guthrie my hand to shake. Her palms are calloused and rough. It's like greeting a piece of bark. She leans in and brings her face close to mine.

'You ever singe my plants again, I'll kick your skinny arse from here to John o'Groats and into the North Sea. You get me?'

I gulp and nod. She lets go of my hand.

'Come on then, I'll take you to the rector. He'll decide how to deal with all of this. You've wasted enough of my time as it is.'

'Thank you, Mrs Guthrie,' Priya says like a schoolgirl.

We follow the irritable groundskeeper on the dirt-strewn pavement back to the main school building. It's a large grey Gothic construction made of uneven stone slabs and plenty of mortar. The windows are narrow, and the ones closest to the front have stained glass with depictions of old geezers who I figure were practitioners of yore. There's something haunting about this place, even in the glare of the summer sun. Up top, hideous-faced gargoyles with wings and horns adorn the roof. Amidst those are heads of real men, looking down. The whole building's got the spook factor dialled to ten.

After our epic exertions, it's an effort keeping up with Mrs Guthrie. She walks briskly through the white doors, which open without protest before she even touches them.

We wind up in a huge hall. Up ahead is a courtyard,

bracketed by ascending stone stairs. It's super chilly in here despite the heat outside. In the far-right corner, a dark corridor lies, and in that entrance, I glimpse the ghost of a young schoolboy lurking.

I didn't know this until I started on the scientific magic malarkey, but the reason ghostly presence makes an area cold is because of certain entropic principles. The transdimensional shift from the everyThere draws thermal energy from our world, stabilizing the ghost in this realm. Paradoxically, the excess light in the summer minimizes spectral activity, so their peak season is actually winter.

The ghost vanishes past sculptures of surly-looking men done in the classical Greek style.

'The old rectors of the Edinburgh School from the founder Hamish Davenant,' Mrs Guthrie explains. 'But the only one you lot have to worry about is the current one. Up the stairs now. Quickly.'

'I'll take the lift,' Priya says.

'Right and right again. You can't miss it,' Mrs Guthrie replies.

I have to bound up them stairs 'cause keeping up with Mrs Guthrie takes some doing. Nae chance I'm lingering behind in this funky house of horrors. We wait at the landing for a few moments before Priya emerges.

There's noticeboards, posters and similar shit you'd find in a normal school, but it don't make me feel any safer after the warm welcome we had.

We head left to what appears to be the admin wing, past several closed doors. Windows on the right look down at the courtyard, which has benches and two diagonal pathways that intersect in the middle like the saltire. A fountain sits in one of the triangular chunks of lawn.

Mrs Guthrie takes us to an open door at the very end of the corridor and into a room where a severe-looking secretary taps away on a typewriter. She has grey hair in a bun, a pointy nose, and wears tortoiseshell glasses. The keys make a racket as she works, and the noise is echoed back by the wood-panelled walls. To the right is a door so neatly flush you wouldn't notice it from the panels were it not for the vintage beehive door-knob sticking out.

'Is the rector still in, Gordania?' Mrs Guthrie asks.

'Occupied,' the woman replies, without looking up from her typing.

'I caught these two frolicking about on the grounds.'

'You should have left them with security, Adair. The gargoyles know what to do with bodies.'

'This one is apparently Callander's intern, and so this makes it a Society visit.'

Gordania looks up from her work and frowns. She tilts her head slightly and lowers her glasses on the bridge of her nose to appraise me.

'Standards have fallen,' she says. Then she dials the rotary telephone on her desk, mumbles something and hangs up. 'Sit,' she says, more in the style one would command a dog. I take my place on the uncomfortable pew close to the shut door, a position I imagine hundreds of anxious schoolboys must have endured through the ages.

'Right, that'll be me off then. I have lots of tidying up to do, thanks to these two,' Mrs Guthrie says pointedly.

We sit there listening to the clanking typewriter for nearly an hour, and my butt hurts. I don't know if we're allowed to speak or not, but Priya keeps schtum and I ain't about to start with Gordania. Insane, but it feels like being back in school all over again, 'cept the ones I went to were nowhere near this posh. Didn't get that scent of polish coming off oak-panel walls or them fancy record boards with names stretching back hundreds of years.

Nah. I come from different ends to this, but a visit to the head's office still sucks arse.

Suddenly, the rector's door opens and Montgomery Wedderburn emerges, crisp as new money in his tailored suit. I stand up involuntarily. Sort of a reflex action, and while I try to remind myself that I am Callander's intern and therefore rocking about with the weight of the Society behind me, that don't do nothing to allay the fact that I'm in Wedderburnland here. After Cockburn's reception, I'm not really sure where I stand with him.

'Miss Moyo, we meet again. It is, of course, a pleasure,' he says. 'I hope you're enjoying your internship.'

'Mr Wedderburn, we didn't mean to disturb you.' I find myself apologizing.

'And you, Priscilla – no, Prisca – I remember you well from the rugby. Lord Kelvin's finest player in half a century.'

'It's Priyanka,' Priya replies, but Wedderburn has already turned his attention back to me.

'Why are you young ladies trespassing on my property?' Wedderburn removes his golden monocle and places it inside the breast pocket of his suit.

He is that spider's web, tough, complex and purposeful, and we are evidently dancing on his wires. So I lay it out for him: Max Wu, Doug Duffie and the possible link to Rory MacCulloch. And, of course, I ask about the Monks of the Misty Order.

'There are many sanctioned fraternities in this school, and the so-called Monks aren't one of them. It's a myth made up by the older boys to scare the juniors. I remember it from when I was a student myself, Miss Moyo,' Wedderburn replies. 'As for Duffie, Wu and MacCulloch, the school only acts in loco parentis during term time. We are not responsible for what the boys get up to, or sadly what may befall them, during their breaks, when they should be under their guardians' care. I am sorry we cannot be of much assistance to you, but I wish you all the best in your enquiries.' He opens his door and steps back into his office. We've barely had five minutes of his time. 'You must excuse me, my time is not my own.'

'I understand that, but we'd like to check out the dormitories, all the same,' I say quickly. Seems doubtful to me that he could possibly know everything his students get up to. That's why I must check.

'Mrs Spence, if you would please oblige them,' Wedderburn says, before he adds kindly, 'And next time, notify the school before you enter our grounds, Miss Moyo. We wouldn't want anything unfortunate to happen to you. I know Sir Callander is a man of outstanding acumen, so I believe he picked you for a reason. Heed his counsel well and your future in the Society is bound to be a bright one.'

Wedderburn slams the door shut, and that's the end of

that. I realize that in this wing, his office overlooks the field we were stuck in, so he would have seen us dealing with the hedge creatures. Did he send Mrs Guthrie to our rescue? I share my speculations with Priya.

'I wouldn't be so sure,' she whispers back.

'You're wrong about that,' I say.

'Maybe. I'm not the sleuth here.'

I'll take that. Wedderburn's given me what I wanted, and my head's still on my neck. He was good to me during my induction with the Society, too, so I've got nothing but positive vibes. I really like Rector Wedderburn, and I'm glad I have another useful ally in my ledger.

XXIII

Gordania Spence is acting like someone who's been asked to take a smelly bin out, but at least she's not walking as fast as Mrs Guthrie. Her heels clank against the laminates, which soon give way to stone flooring as we make our way to the back of the building and out of the door. She jingles a large bunch of keys. Her head is held high and there's an officious efficiency to her movement.

'The Edinburgh Ordinary School for Boys was founded by Lord Hamish Davenant in 1694 for the education of poor boys and orphans. He was a forward-thinking man who believed in the value of universal education as a tool for cultivating upstanding citizens of credit to their nation.'

I look around the lush gardens, sprawling lawns, flower-beds, the self-evident opulence of the institution, and quickly come to the understanding that the education of poor kids ain't a priority no more. Can't be that many orphaned boy wizards studying here today. None of the kids from His Majesty's Slum Hermiston have ever been here, neither could they ever dream of even sniffing it.

I'm still a bit wary of all them topiary hedge animals, though. Once bitten and all that.

'The school had a lot more land, but we were forced by the city to sell many acres in the 1800s for the hospital across the way and even more for the Merchiston Campus of Napier University. The dorms used to be here in the main building, until we expanded in 1910,' she says. It sounds very much like a practised speech, one given to prospective parents or new students on tour. 'Enclosed behind the holly hedge there is the groundskeeper's house. You've met her already. Down along this path are the dormitories.'

The architecture of the dorms is Edwardian. Unlike the hulking stonework of the main building, there are straight lines, without the grotesques and other decorations. It's a more functional two-storey building with two separate entrances. Vines creeping up the lower section of the walls seem to be a new addition from an enthusiastic groundskeeper.

'The school abuts the Royal Ed,' Priya whispers. 'That's why we called the Edinburgh boys nutters when I was in school.'

It's a juvenile joke, but I get it, since the Royal Ed is the city's main mental health hospital. I'd already figured from Priya's interactions with Lewis that the two schools are rivals. Then again, it's the Edinburgh versus Glasgow thing, and for the first time in my life, I find myself rooting for the Weegies.

'We have four boarding houses in this building, two on the ground floor and the others above it.'

'Max Wu was a day scholar,' I say.

Mrs Spence unlocks the main entrance, and we walk into a clean, spare hall that smells of fresh polish and cleaning products.

196

'Rory is in Malcolm House, named for Malcolm III, King of Scotland 1031 to 1093,' she says. 'All the houses are named after kings: Duncan, whom of course you will have heard of, Cuilén and Kenneth . . . Right, here we are, in you go.'

'Thanks, Mrs Spence,' I say.

'I hope this doesn't take too long,' she replies.

Priya rolls her eyes at me.

If the school is Gothic splendour, I'm surprised by how spartan this dorm is. I'd heard posh kids in boarding schools get their own rooms and shit, but Malcolm House is more budget backpacker by the looks of things. Wood-effect tiles, metal single beds in rows against the walls. You can tell the beds have been around, the way they sag in the middle, and on top of each is the slenderest mattress imaginable. Some of the mattresses have brownish concentric rings, courtesy of bed-wetters, I presume.

There are small cabinets next to the beds, and blanket boxes at the foot of each. Zero privacy. Kinda like our caravan if I think about it, but at least I don't have to share it with twenty-odd adolescent boys. I inspect the beds with Priya beside me.

'Is there something specific you're looking for?' Mrs Spence asks.

'Anything,' I reply.

When I get to the fifth bed, I spot some dirt on the floor and make a note of it. Then I check the bin. A Cadbury Dairy Milk wrapper.

'How often do these dorms get cleaned?' Priya asks, taking the words right out of my mouth.

'Daily during term time. Holidays, we do a deep clean right after the students leave and spot cleaning before they come back, to make sure everything's just so.'

'Have you had any work done here recently?' I probe.

'Not that I'm aware of.'

I open the door that leads to the bathrooms. Rows of sinks on one side and a urinal, followed by cubicles on the other and then showers at the far end. The mirror nearest the door's got some whitish spots on it. Dried-up spray from toothpaste. The others are clean. Now the chocolate wrapper might have been something the cleaners missed, but combine that with the dirt and toothpaste, and I'm pretty sure some-one's been here.

'Looks like you have a holiday stowaway, Mrs Spence.'

'Ridiculous. How would they get in? We keep this place locked.'

'The hedge creatures, gargoyles, et cetera, wouldn't trouble Rory, since he's a student. He could walk right in. Now, you keep the dorms locked, but them windows are easy to shimmy.' I don't reveal my burglaring curriculum vitae. 'Either he's been here or he's staying here. We'll need the school to keep an eye out and notify us if he turns up.'

Mrs Spence nods reluctantly, hands on hips as she surveys the room. Bet she's plenty mad that she's missed a stray student.

Not much else we can do except to grab my bike from a dodgy bush and head back on the trail.

XXIV

It's sweltering around midday, and I'm sweating it as me and Priya make our way up the road to Morningside. She bails on me 'cause she's got a coffee date with a lassie who she swears is the incarnation of the Venus of Willendorf. Priya'd asked me to chum her to said date, but I don't fancy being a third wheel and I'm still on the clock. But I'm going to have to ask her to teach Gran some moves. To be honest, I'd rather sit out the rest of the day, but the sun waits for no one and I've got more fish to fry than a seaside chippy.

I'm back in the city centre and cutting across the Meadows headed for Holyrood Park when an old man in a butler suit impedes me. I slam the brakes on, skidding to a halt in front of him.

'That's no hello for an old colleague, sunshine,' Wilson says.

I open my jacket to reveal my dagger, instantly raging at the sight of his mug. I met Wilson in a spooky house of horrors where we were imprisoned by a psycho Brounie. And even though I saved his arse, he was bloody ungrateful about it.

He breaks into a menacing grin. 'Why all the aggression? We're on the same side, after all.'

Bollocks to that. Still as deranged as ever, then. There's lots of folks going about their business on the pavements, and that keeps me peaceable.

'What do you want?' I ask.

'I've had a long time to consider what you did to poor Arthur Lodge. I was in despair, and all I could think of was revenge.'

'You're welcome to have a go.' I tighten my grasp on my dagger.

'Oh no, no, no.' He wags a floppy glove in my face. 'See, you're on our side now. Someone on high raised me up from where you'd cast me down. He made me whole again. And when I sought to come after you, he stayed my hand.' Wilson's eyes glint with pure malevolence. 'He has a message for you.'

I frown. This gadgie ain't making sense for me. The Brounie's vanquished, so far as I'm aware.

'Is this the Tall Man you were on about the last time I kicked your arse?'

'You must do whatever it takes to stop the Monks of the Misty Order.'

Whoa. How the hell does he know about them? Brain's suddenly whirring furiously.

'We'll take care of our end at the Advocates Library. The rest is up to you,' Wilson says. Catches me by surprise, that's for sure. 'Remember, we're on the same side . . . for now.'

Advocates Library rings a bell, but I can't think where. Mind conjures up a fancy wig, disapproving frown – nah, still can't place it.

'What do you mean by this, Wilson? Who are you working for? Is the Tall Man still a thing?'

'You think you know so much. But the One Above All sees further than any of us,' he says.

The smile falls off his face, and I see pure hatred in his eyes as he slinks off, joining the crowd headed for South Clerk Street.

I want to follow him, have it out here on the street. Nah. I have work to do. There's no chance in hell him and me could ever bat for the same team anyway. Must be the rantings of a depraved lunatic. This day's just getting zanier, but I refuse to be baited.

Not today, Lucifer.

I finally make it out to Arthur's Seat, dismount and push my bike up the steepest bit of Queen's Drive until the top levels out. There's magnificent views of the east and the south, rooftops sprawling and the Pentland Hills in the far-off distance, beyond the bypass. A flock of birds flies through the air. I don't get far, though, before I meet a bunch of bawbags manning a barricade of old furniture and razor wire.

I'd forgotten there was a war on.

There's five of them, and the lads look edgy, armed with an assortment of weapons ranging from dirks, modified cricket bats stuck with deadly nails, a samurai sword. One's even got a fucking crossbow.

'You aim that thing at me and I'll cut your bawsack off,' I say, approaching the group. 'The Rooster about?'

'Alright, Ropa?' says Cameron. I've known him since way back. He's part of the furniture as far as Camelot's concerned.

'How's the war effort going?'

'We've pushed the Pilton Crew oota Stockbridge, all the way tae Drylaw, where they belong.' He hocks and swallows it.

'Well done, lads,' I reply, rounding the barricade with my bike.

The Clan can more than hold their own against upstarts from the coast. I wonder if they'll finish off the gang from Pilton or are content to hold the border. Rob's pragmatic, so I reckon the latter's likelier. Them council estates ain't got pickings worth his while, but he ain't about to give an inch of the city centre. I'm sure he'll demand vassalage as reparation for the inconvenience.

This part of the hill's got grand views of Duddingston Loch and the sea. I can see all the way up the eastern coastline to the wreck of the *Gogarmast*. The old oil tanker ran aground near Port Seton, belching out barrels of crude that turned the beaches from Edinburgh to Bo'ness black. Travelled miles and miles, all the way to Fife, before they could plug it. No cash for clean-ups or nothing like that, so you still see the slick in the sand, and the *Gogarmast* remains where she beached to this day.

I cycle round a ram and spot Rob's circus tent pitched in the prime spot near Dunsapie Loch. Camelot's heaving, as it always does in summer, and there's hundreds of colourful tents dotted about the hilltop. Lots of folks come this way, wandering bums, chancers, adventurers and all sorts. As long as you respect the law of the Rooster you can nest here, but step out of line and you'll be thrown down the crags, wings or no.

There's an old Lothian Buses double-decker, dented and

battered, in the wee car park near the loch. It's a relic from the past. Someone's spray-painted 'Shatter the Shibboleth' boldly across the side. They are the hottest band this side of the pond's seen since Iron Maiden. I'm about to pass it, headed for Rob's tent, when I spot Tom coming out of the bus, shirtless. He looks surprised to see me, though I'd texted him earlier to let him know I'd be coming through.

'I hope this lot ain't nicked the shirt off your back,' I said.

He smiles and shakes his head. 'I've had a great time.' And I believe him too, 'cause no one's gonna mess with you if you're under the Rooster's wing. No one.

Tom invites me onto the bus. His spirits are up and he seems to be having a grand old time here. I suppose for a tourist, being sat on Arthur's Seat constitutes the deluxe Edinburgh experience. Since Camelot was established, very few folks get to come up here and enjoy the views anymore.

The bottom of the bus is messy, a bit whiffy too, but there's hobos lying there so . . . We go up the narrow stairs to the top deck, where I see Tom's made himself at home. He's made the back seat his bed. But he's got his clothes in neat piles on a free seat, some books, paperwork, toiletries, and all sorts out on display.

'The wheels on the bus go round and round,' he says, and laughs. 'I never thought I'd be staying in one of these, but I've seen worse.'

'Good for you,' I reply.

'So, what have you got planned for us, Ropa, my tour guide?'

'Partner,' I say. 'Put on a shirt, we're going to the archives.'

His eyes snap to me. 'How did you manage that?'

'By not being an annoying foreigner. Hurry up, I ain't got all day.'

I leave Tom to get ready. Gotta see the Rooster, pay homage and see if he'll lend us a spare pushbike. It will save us time. The archives aren't in the bank proper. They're my side of town, and that's five miles out.

XXV

We've worked up a right ol' sweat by the time we hit the Gyle. Sun's blazing so fierce I'm cooked medium rare and Tom's a boiled lobster. He's riding awkwardly, trying to hold onto both the handlebars and his briefcase. I'd offered to put his papers in my backpack, but he flat out refused. They contain the material his father collected about the Paterson fortune. I can understand paranoia, given what they're worth and all, but this is kinda ridiculous. It's a miracle he hasn't been run over zigzagging like that.

This place used to be a proper commercial zone. You've still got the Royal Mail depot and a handful of others who've weathered the storm, but most of the units are abandoned and fallen into decay. A couple of charities use the spaces for storage, plus soup kitchens that attract folks from the surrounding neighbourhoods.

The whole area was an old marsh before they drained and developed it, but the city rot's setting in and I fear it'll go back to that soon. The law of entropy's inescapable, it seems.

'They said Scotland was bad on the news reports when you had your troubles, but I never thought it was anything like this,' Tom says, surveying the desolation. 'No offence.'

'None taken.'

'What's it like in Canada?' I ask.

'Better than this, worse than Korea.'

I was hoping for more information than that, but he doesn't say anything else.

Fences ripped up. Fallen lamp posts and disused bus shelters. A lone rowan tree growing in a pothole in the middle of the road. We come up to two hefty men in combat fatigues, balaclavas covering their faces, trigger fingers on their SA80 service weapons. They're posted at the entrance to the bank offices, which is hidden behind a tall concrete wall, razor wire bristling on top. CCTV cameras look down from every conceivable angle. Most of the banks have moved out from this area, as did the businesses that went kaput. If it weren't for Callander telling me the archives were still located here, I'd have carried on oblivious.

'Service entrance only,' says one of the men as we approach.

'Can you tell us where the main entrance is?' Tom asks.

He doesn't get a response, and I have to stop him as he looks like he might try again. Last thing I need is for the goose that lays the golden eggs to get a Glasgow kiss.

'This way,' I say, heading for the roundabout at the bottom of the street.

'That was a bit rude, don't you think?'

'You're not in America anymore, amigo.'

'Still, there's no excuse. And it's Canada.'

Statement of the bleeding obvious, but it is what it is. There's a massive, weird metal sculpture of a deconstructed man, feet on one side, head elevated at the other end. Hands but no torso or legs, pieces connected together by metal links. We reach a small gate just off the roundabout and I try the intercom. Takes a few seconds before someone answers.

'Ropa Moyo from the Society, here to see the archives,' I say in my most confident voice.

'The archives aren't housed here,' the lady on the intercom replies.

'Oh, where are they then?'

'That's not my problem.' She hangs up.

I press the buzzer again and wait. No answer. So I keep trying.

'What?' she finally answers.

'Eat my vag,' I reply, and walk away.

Tom's laughing his head off as he follows me. Must think people out here are crazy or something, but this ain't all my fault. I'm about to call Callander when I think to check for the address again on my phone.

'So this is the bank that broke Britain,' Tom says. 'I can see why.'

Turns out the rude lady was right. I read the address wrong. We're on South Gyle Crescent when we really ought to be at South Gyle Lane. Serves me right for not paying attention to detail.

'Come on, I know where it is,' I say.

'Lead the way,' Tom says.

We track back to a wee lane just opposite the Royal Mail. Not much left down this road except broken windows and overgrown hedges on the verges. Folks from nearby Hermiston Slum raid the disused buildings around here for materials from time to time, but as the years have gone by, the pickings have become much leaner.

It's a short ride to the bottom of the road, where a grey industrial unit stands surrounded by sturdy palisade fencing made of galvanized steel. There's a wide car park with nothing in it save for a few bins near an overgrown mound. Surely this can't be it? The front of the building has a large blue bay door, the colour of the RBS, that leads to what might be an office. Pipes run along the side of the building and there are vents on the roof.

'Is this it?' Tom asks, looking disappointed.

I'm even more confused because there ain't anything save for a yellow sign near the gate that reads 'WARNING: KEEP CLEAR'. Only a trimmed triangle of lawn next to a brick footpath is a sure sign the building's in use.

This is the archive, hiding in plain sight.

Before I press the intercom, two machine gun–toting security types approach us.

'God save the king,' I greet the woman.

'Long may he reign,' she replies. 'Take out any weapons, keys and metal objects you might have on you. The jacket, too, your backpack, and put them in the sack provided.'

The male guard holds out a black sack, and we hand them through the gap in the fence. I do what she asks, giving up my catapult, dagger, belt, and chuck my bag over the top. Tom's rather reluctant to give up his briefcase, but there's no getting around this.

She opens the gate to allow us in one at a time, and I'm given the sort of pat-down that qualifies as deep-tissue massage, given how rough she is at it. Tom winces when he gets his too, so I know it ain't personal; this lady's about the business.

We follow them into the building via the double doors and settle down on the sofas opposite the reception desk. The guards ain't too chatty and I don't fancy striking up a convo with someone keeping their finger so close to the trigger like that.

'Why do you guys do that? It's so weird,' Tom asks.

'Do what exactly?' I reply.

'The "God save the king" thing.'

This question's too dumb even for a foreigner, and so I choose to ignore it, concentrating on my phone instead. Reception's blazing hot. I guess air con ain't a thing here either, and I'm virtually a puddle by the time a stern-looking woman in her thirties wearing a pinstripe suit walks in.

'You're late. Eilidh Logan, archivist,' she says. 'Is he with you?'

'This is my associate Thomas Mounsey,' I reply.

'Tom,' he says, offering his hand, but she doesn't take it.

'It's been a very long time since the Society sent anyone down here. I guess that's to be expected, given the circumstances. Can I see your Library card?'

I hand over the desiccated ear in my pocket and she inspects it. She looks at Tom, who obviously doesn't have one, and says, 'Will you be vouching for him?' I nod. 'Good.'

'So are the archives part of the bank or the Society?' I ask, curiosity getting the better of me. Also helps to know where I stand with these guys, I guess.

'Neither. We are a part of the Library, but we hold collections for both the Society of Sceptical Enquirers and the Royal Bank of Scotland. Documents mainly, physical and electronic, artworks too,' Eilidh answers. 'And since you are also wondering, you may call me Eilidh, and I'll call you Ropa. The conventions are slightly different outside the walls of Calton Hill Library. Shall we go through?' There's a clipped quality to her speech. She exudes the air of someone who prefers dealing with documents and this human interaction is costing her a great deal.

Turns out she works for Dr Maige, Jomo's dad, and if I've learnt anything about librarians, they can be sticklers for rules. These guys can get medieval at times too, so I have to be on my best behaviour.

There's hardly any people in the building. It feels, well, dead. It doesn't have any of the grandeur of the Library, nor does it have the magic of the bank on St Andrew Square. But at least the archives are cooler than the reception area. And very clean too, I discover. Not a speck of dust anywhere.

The quiet and seclusion of these archives creeps me out. CCTV cameras watch our every move.

'Is it true what everyone is saying, that Sir Callander has taken on a new apprentice?' Eilidh asks.

'Intern. You're looking at her,' I reply.

'Good for you,' she says. 'You may not take anything out of this room, and any copying has to be authorized by me. It goes without saying that we take any damaging or defacing of the materials very seriously. Take a minute to read the documents on the table over there. They will tell you what is expected of you in this place.'

Tom goes up to the table in the middle of the room and checks it out. Oddly, it looks more like a pine dinner table than a workstation.

'So what is it exactly you're looking for? Our materials are extensive, going back several hundred years. We have documents on all the various subsidiaries acquired by the bank, so you may want to narrow your search.'

'Documents concerning the Darien Scheme,' Tom replies.

'You will have to be more specific than that,' the archivist says.

Tom clenches his jaw. There's tightness on his face, because he doesn't want to give the game away. But if there's one thing I know about employees of the Library, it's that they have a code of honour.

'Eilidh, we're looking into the Paterson fortune.' I figure we should be straight about it.

Immediately, her face lights up with recognition.

'Interesting . . . and who exactly is this Thomas Mounsey?'

'I am a histori—'

'I wasn't talking to you.' Eilidh sharply cuts Tom off, keeping her eyes on me.

'He's a direct descendant of William Paterson and holds a claim to the fortune if we can prove it,' I reply. That's all the cards right there on the table, I guess.

'Does Sir Callander know about this?'

'Not yet.'

'I see,' Eilidh says, nodding slowly. 'There are certain protocols involved. The Society and the bank have to be notified.'

Son of a bitch. I was counting on some discretion, gathering our chain of evidence before making any moves. By coming here I might as well have held a megaphone and announced Tom's business while there's already some pretty nasty people after him. Amateur move.

'Eilidh, the fact there are protocols about this shows how sensitive this whole thing is. Tom's already been attacked by some nasty magicians, and broadcasting his presence is only likely to get him into more trouble.'

'Generations of my family have waited for the truth,' Tom adds, desperation in his voice. He holds out his hands to show the burns.

Eilidh inhales and puckers her lips to one side, thinking.

'We need a little time. A couple of days, that's all,' I say. And I'm holding my hands together in supplication.

'The archivist's vocation is to the past and to the truth. You've got up to the end of this week. That's the best I can do for you,' she replies solemnly. Eilidh dumps a stack of hefty folders on the worktable.

'Thank you,' we say in unison.

'Don't get too excited yet. I'm not sure what you expect to find that hasn't already been unearthed in the past. This isn't exactly the first time this claim has been brought up. It was believed that the Paterson family was satisfied by the bank's responses to their enquiries a hundred years ago, and the matter has rested since. That would be a good starting point, and then perhaps you might work your way back to the beginning.'

'That sounds perfect,' Tom says, filled with relief.

I for one am glad it's working out like this, but it means the clock's ticking from both ends. I'll definitely need to keep the golden goose safe and pick the right moment to shaft the Society. There also has to be a suitable way of presenting it to Sir Callander later. The deeper we dig in the archives, the further we go back in time. Callander did say the history of the bank was the history of modern Scotland. But I fear what we'll uncover, 'cause if there's anything I know about the past, it's that there's a lot of nasty shit layered underneath history. And it sure does kick up a stink when you dredge it back up again.

XXVI

The research room in the Royal Bank of Scotland's archives is as near to the panopticon as you're ever going to get. It's the antithesis of the Library in this respect. The Library is a labyrinth: corridors, alcoves, rooms within rooms, winding stairs waiting to be explored. It's kinda inviting once you're a member. Sure, the librarians can be a bit surly, but they'll help you find books. They *want* you to read them, to explore its secrets and discover new horizons for your mind. The archives are a fortress, disguised in plain view in a nameless building in a nondescript street on a decaying estate. It looks more like a warehouse than anything. Technology is light in the Library, but this place is all about security cameras. The archivists want you to know they are watching.

Tom's sat at the table, while I'm milling about by a grand bookshelf, checking out the titles. *A Generale Hystorie of Scottish Monies*, *Minted Coins 1867–1873*, *Temples of Mammon*, *Caledonia's Last Stand*, *The Man Who Saw the Future*. It's packed with books about Scottish banking history, along with the banks the RBS devoured in the last three hundred years.

'It's Frankenstein's monster, isn't it?' Tom says, watching me.

'What?'

'The bank. It starts off as one little branch in this city, until it engulfs the globe, even reaching deep into distant places that don't even know its name. So many resources holding together the entire Scottish economy—'

'Right, I've been going through Darien, and I feel this might be a good starting point for you,' Eilidh says, walking back in the room with an armful of documents. Almost grudgingly, she places them on the table in front of Tom.

'Thank you,' he says. 'Do we get white gloves to protect the pages?'

Eilidh snorts, a condescending smile on her mug.

'You wouldn't use those unless you're handling very old photographs or vellum. Wearing gloves increases the risk of tearing pages. That's why you shouldn't believe everything they show you on television.'

That's news to me. Then again, I ain't never been in one of these places before. I wonder how much Jomo knows about the archivists. Maybe they'll give him a placement here one day. But I doubt anyone in their right mind would want to swap the Library for this soulless industrial unit.

Brrr, it's chilly in here. I was roasting outside, and when we came in it was a bit of a relief, but this is taking the piss. I figure the temperature has something to do with protecting documents or some such malarkey. When in Rome, freeze your arse off in a toga.

Eilidh sits in a chair in the corner, watching Tom's every move – though she's got no reason to be worried about a bumbling Canadian. Her eyes never leave the pile of documents.

I've seen that look, usually on new mums when they hand their wains to someone for a minute and they can't bear to take their eyes off in case something happens. Can't blame her though, 'cause I'm scanning the place for weaknesses in their security system. Force of habit from back in the day when I was Robin Hooding. Mind you, we never did anything high stakes like banks. One-way ticket to HMP Saughton, that.

The black wall at the other end of the room has one-way mirrors, and I'm certain there's others watching back there.

Tom blows away dirt on the table from the old and worn book covers.

'Red rot, can't be helped,' Eilidh says coolly. 'With time the leather begins to degrade. Most of the materials in our archives weren't looked after using modern methods for a long time, so the rot's set in. We can only slow down the process now.'

'Right on,' Tom replies, burying himself in the contents of a ledger.

I'd be geeking out too, but there's something that worries me about this whole process as I walk towards Eilidh and stand beside her, leaning against the wall. My proximity does nothing to distract her from watching Tom with hawk eyes. Thing is, though, she's the one who gets to go to the back and bring us materials to read. We don't get the opportunity, so we don't really know what's really back there and we have to rely on her beneficence, integrity and diligence. While she seems like a good egg, trust is a currency in short supply on this side of the Equator. And if the Society really are trying to cover up the inheritance . . . It would be better to go back there ourselves and check out the collection, just to make sure.

Normally, I'd be happy to let things play out and then return late at night to do my own snooping, but given the cameras and the guys with automatic weapons, I don't much fancy that option. Little chance of me forming a tribute act to the Grateful Dead anytime soon – my mbira riffs ain't rock and roll enough. I have to try a different tack. Fine lines, though, 'cause I don't wanna alienate Eilidh.

'I was thinking that since I'm an employee of the Society, it should be alright for me to see your collection. The archives work for the Library and the Library works for the Society, so we're all part of the same team,' I say.

'There are so many holes in your premise, I wouldn't even know where to begin,' she replies firmly. 'This is a private archive, not a public one, and that means who gets to use our facilities is up to our own discretion. The Library is separate and independent from the Society, so while the two institutions are functionally interdependent, we are not "part of the same team".'

'Oh.'

'And you are lucky to be here at all, since the king severed the bank from the Society years ago. But Sir Callander pulled in a favour.'

I scrunch my face up, confused by this state of affairs. There I was thinking everything – the bank, the Library and the Society – was connected, with the magicians sat at the top of the pyramid. Weird to think of the Society as separate from the bank, never mind the Library itself.

'Now I'm sure you're wondering how come the Society uses the bank's building on St Andrew Square if the two institutions are no longer tied together.' I wasn't really, but

217

since Eilidh's raised the issue, may as well find out. 'Dundas House was initially a private residence *for* . . .?'

'Sir Lawrence Dundas,' I reply.

'And so you know Sir Lawrence was a wealthy merchant with a penchant for dabbling in the esoteric, frequently hosting a circle of like-minded gentlemen who later fashioned themselves the Sceptical Enquirers. He also happened to be the governor of the Royal Bank.'

I really should have read the book on Scottish banking Callander gave me. Anyway, I nod along even though I don't know a lot of this stuff Eilidh is on about. I figure the archivists really do hold the memories of the Society.

'When Sir Lawrence died, his son allowed the Sceptical Enquirers to continue meeting there, respecting his father's last wish that they be allowed to do so in perpetuity. Eventually, he sold it, but maintained the stipulation that the Society could continue meeting there.'

Eilidh might give out her documents grudgingly, but her thoughts pour out freely like the contents of a burst main.

'So where does the bank come into all of this?'

'You have someplace else you'd rather be?' she replies, pausing. 'I didn't think so.'

A second archivist, dressed just as soberly as Eilidh, comes into the room and deposits another stack of documents on the table, then leaves without saying a word. Silent as a monk, I think. Which reminds me that I have certain monks who're into fog or some such that I have to track down.

'By the time the bank bought the building, the Sceptical Enquirers had free rein to modify certain security aspects.

And thanks to Sir Lawrence, they can never be removed, thus solidifying the union of the two hitherto separate institutions.'

That's me told then. An association that ancient can't be unpicked so easily. It sounds like a divorced couple still living under the same roof, helping with childcare. The house might still look great from the outside, but it's pretty frosty inside.

I glance over Tom's shoulder. He's frowning, cross-referencing three open documents in front of him. Pretty hard to read all this tiny cursive. Makes me wonder how they did all that by hand back in the day. My wrist gets sore if I'm forced to use a pen for more than a squiggle, but my thumbs can text till the cows come home with no problem.

'There's massive gaps and discrepancies,' says Tom. 'There's a reference here, "see cashier's ledger". The cashiers were the bank managers of the day, and it's clear to me someone kept a second set of accounts.'

I shrug, not knowing what to make of that.

'We would not keep anything from you. The archivists do not pick sides. We are merely custodians of these records,' Eilidh says dispassionately. 'What you see is what we have.'

'There was a safe in the bank's first branch on Ship Close,' Tom says. 'What happened to it?'

'The bank's original safes were secured with magical booby traps. As a result, they were never moved, even when the branch relocated. Our records show all the contents were passed on to Dundas House, and from there on to us.'

'Hmm . . . Then it's going to be worth checking. Ropa, I'm going to need your help. I can't go through all this on my own,' Tom says, stroking his chin.

He's all pinpoint focus now – no dazed look on his face. Almost seems like a different person.

'You'll have to tell me what I'm looking for, man,' I reply.

'Here.' He picks a ledger and plonks it to one side. 'I need you to go through this line by line and look for any mention of Paterson.'

'I don't suppose there's a search function?' I say, settling myself down on the chair next to Tom, dreading the prospect of this. Don't get me wrong, I like reading as much as the next lass, but it's got to be stuff I dig, and it helps if it's in Times New Roman, not this indecipherable mess. Zzz.

Would rather pick my own nose than this, but there's mega moolah riding on it and I've done harder gigs for a lot less, so I jam on it. Soon the room's pure silent, except for Tom breathing hard through his nostrils. Eilidh maintains her posture in her chair, ever watchful. It's a slog, and I won't lie, my brain gets foggy just going through page after page of the musty ledgers.

We're noses against the grindstone when suddenly the power cuts off. Eilidh is on her feet abruptly. There's a hum from somewhere as a backup generator kicks in. Hardly need the lighting as we've got daylight for ages, being summer and all, but the guard bursts into the room.

'Stop what you're doing,' he says gruffly. Total arsewipe.

'I'm sorry, visitors aren't allowed in here when we're operating on backup power. You'll have to come back the day after tomorrow,' Eilidh explains.

'Can't we do tomorrow?'

She shakes her head. 'We only allow two researchers in

at a time, and we have academics from the University of Edinburgh visiting.'

Knapf. Not exactly like we've got the smoking gun yet. Tom gets up slowly, and I almost laugh when Eilidh comes over to the table and manually checks every single document.

'I shall look forward to seeing you again, Ropa,' she says.

After we grab our bags and bikes, we head back on the road, 'cause I have to return Tom to the Clan before heading home. Sucks, but what can I do? He is the goose after all, and I need them golden eggs to come out of his bum soon.

'I don't mind the downtime. Tomorrow you can take me to Ship Close instead,' he says.

'Sure,' I reply, while racking my brain trying to figure out where that is. I know Edinburgh like I aced The Knowledge, but for the life of me, I ain't never heard of no Ship Close.

XXVII

The heat's abated somewhat, and the route down from the city centre is downhill most of the way, which helps 'cause I'm burnt. Juggling so many balls at the mo, I'm scared I'm gonna drop one and it'll land on my noggin. The Monks, Bumblebeam, Max Wu and this bloody fortune are all tangled up somehow. But unless I can find out where Bumblebeam was taking the kids, I'm staring at a dead end. Not sure what fortune-hunting has to do with frolicking around the astral realms, either.

I need my pals to do more to help, but they've all got jobs and shit going on, so it's up to me to pull some Atlas moves.

I'm by the disused Lothian Buses depot in Longstone when I spot some rabbits grazing on the verges of the road. I stop my bike far away enough not to spook 'em and whip out my katty and ammo faster than Pietro Maximoff ever could. Aim for a fraction of a second through the Y scope and let fly. The rabbits scatter in a flash, leaving behind a fat comrade twitching on the ground. There's days I go hunting, but I'm also opportunistic and I don't let chances like this go by.

Clean headshot: poor bastard would have felt nothing, I hope.

And that's the way it should be. Ain't no point making animals suffer. There's enough of that poison going round in human society, and I see no need to drag innocent creatures into our self-made hell.

I cycle over, drop my bike on the grass and kneel next to the rabbit. Then I take off my backpack and pull out some plastic bags which I carry around just in case Maw Edinburgh throws me a bone. And if you keep your eyes peeled and your ears wax free, she often will. Though in May, Izwi and me got our skulls pecked when we were out foraging seagull eggs in Cramond. You win some and take your Ls when they come too.

Very important to check the fur of the rabbit and make sure it don't have no ulcers, swelling or anything funky 'cause of myxomatosis. When I'm satisfied this one's healthy, I pull out my dagger and slice round the leg joints, then pull the skin off. It slides over easy as taking off a jumper until I get to the head, which can be a bit tricksy but nothing major. I give it a good tug, that's all. Once it's off, I have nothing but pink, healthy flesh. Literally takes seconds.

I set to slicing and dicing like a trained butcher, popping the legs, entrails and head in one bag, the skin in another for Gran to cure. The best bits of the animal's what's left, and I divide that into two portions going in a bag each. Soon enough I've cleaned my dagger by wiping it on the grass and resheathed it, packed up my kill, and am back on the road headed home.

The first place I hit is Gary O'Donohue's shack on the bottom field across the canal. It's a shabby affair. He pretty much lives in a converted garden shed. In summer you can see the woodwork, but in winter he wraps it in heavy-duty polythene sheeting for insulation, though I still don't know how he makes it through the coldest days. There's a fire pit outside where he does his cooking. A bit of ash in there and some logs stacked to one side.

I bang on the door and he opens it quickly. Not exactly like there's another room. I catch sight of a little camper bed before he comes out and shuts the door behind him, maybe a bit embarrassed since our cara's nicer.

'I'm not staying long. Just brought you some juicy rabbit, that's all,' I say.

'Bless your soul, Ropa. It'll make a tasty roast to go with my tatties,' he replies with a grin, accepting my offering. 'Any word from your nana yet?'

'I'm working on it. You'll get your date.' I wink and make sure to leave before he starts prodding me about it all. The hopeful look on his face is just too much for me right now.

Soon enough I'm over the bridge, making my way across a dirt lane before I reach our caravan. I kneel down, open my second bag and deposit the offal, feet and head of the rabbit near the wheel. River pops out of her burrow, keen nose sniffing about.

'Hey, girl. Before you complain about which cuts you got, I've thrown the heart and liver in there too, so don't tell me they're not gourmet quality.'

River don't answer 'cause she's on the grub right away, chewing and swallowing noisily. *Don't choke on it, you silly cow.* I leave her to it and get inside the cara.

'Is that you, Ropa?' says Gran.

'The one and only,' I reply, planting a smacker on her.

'Can I have your phone?' Izwi says.

'Swap you that for a kiss.'

'No, 'cause then you'll have two and I'll only have one.'

'Come here and kiss me, child, so we'll all have two,' Gran says.

If only I could work out my issues so easily, but I don't wanna think about that jazz at the mo. Nah. I'm putting on my Michelin star for my girls tonight. I go back to the kitchen area of the cara and take the rabbit out of my backpack.

'How was your day, Ropa?' Gran asks.

'Mad. I dealt with a wee gardening problem, but nothing out of the ordinary. You know how it is, lots of tramping around, that sort of thing,' I reply, pulling out utensils and pots. Then, to make sure she doesn't follow up: 'How did you get on?'

'Gareth at the speakeasy came round to ask if I could make sloe gin for them.'

'Ain't it a bit early in the year for that?'

'That's what I told him. We'll have to wait till the first frost, and that's a while away yet. I'm not the kind of person to put them in the freezer like people do these days. Only the frost does them right.'

'Where's the flour?' I ask.

'In the tin at the bottom of the cupboard,' Gran replies.

I grab that, turn on the hob and heat up a bit of butter in our stainless-steel stock pot. It's seen better days, but it ain't got no holes and still does the job. Then I chop the half of the rabbit we have left and sprinkle some flour on it. Nothing in this world I love more than cooking for my girls.

I dice up nice big chunks of onion, carrots, celery and some garlic. Thanks to Gary O'Donohue, we're well stocked up as far as veg is concerned. Wish it was summer all year long 'cause there's grub aplenty. But it don't work like that. If people were truly smart, we'd gorge ourselves silly in the summer and hibernate all winter like bears do.

That aroma makes my tummy rumble like I'm in the jungle of the Congo in 1974, when Muhammad Ali danced with the undefeated heavyweight champion George Foreman.

Right, let's get the beef broth in there before I burn my veg. About five cups should do the job. That reminds me I've got to fetch us more water before we run out, but there'll be plenty of time for that. Throw in a bunch of thyme, and I crank up the dial to get my stew to boil. I wipe my brow, 'cause it's warming up in this cara.

'Hey, Gran, I've left the pelt on the counter for you to cure when you're ready.'

'You have to feed me first,' she replies.

In a while I'll do something separate for Izwi. The kid's a vegetarian, and if you don't respect that she'll give you some lecture about the sanctity of life. Geez. Used to think it was just a phase, but my sis is headstrong and once she sets her mind on something, it's hard to change it. Which is why I have to be careful tonight. I can win friends easily, but influencing my little sister's a monster mission.

Good thing is, Izwi ain't too far gone down the rabbit hole and turned full-on vegan, so she's partial to mac and cheese, which is a doddle to make.

Gotta open the door, let some air in, 'cause I'm sweating

like the Notorious P.I.G. and it's not a great look. The view from outside my caravan door looks all the way out across the city, right up to the castle elevated above everything else. Looks amazing in the reddening sky.

Rare in this life full of care to snatch this moment where I can stand and stare.

After a while, I fling myself on the berth next to Gran.

'Gary O'Donohue's asking for a date with you, Gran,' I say.

'Is he now?' she replies, all innocent.

'Well, I think he called it "an opportunity to meet for a bit of blether", or something similar.'

'Gran's getting a boyfriend,' Izwi says.

'Don't be silly, I'm too old for all that rubbish,' she replies, giggling like a schoolgirl.

Real coy and all, but I think Gary's in with a chance. If you watch those old black-and-white movies, which is how I think of the world whenever I imagine Gran as a young woman, then they met at balls and went out on dates with chaperones trailing every move. The speakeasy on our estate's not quite the ballroom, but it'll do for them.

The stew's ready by the time I pull Izwi's mac and cheese out of the oven. Not bad at all. Reckon I missed my true calling somewhere along the way. Like, I could have been one of them TV chefs back in the day. Yep, I'd be like Marguerite Patten, who they said could make a brill meal out of nothing.

I dish out the food into bowls and serve Gran and Izwi. The stew's got bones in it 'cause I know Gran likes to gnaw on them. Waste not and all that. Her gnashers are still in good nick.

'This is delicious,' she says.

'Cheers, Gran,' I reply.

The stew's nice and warm, and goes down my gullet a treat. A bit funny the telly's playing a rerun of *Who Framed Roger Rabbit*, but at least Izwi's too into her meal to have a go at me for hunting. I figure this would be a good time to have a wee chat with Izwi about the scholarship. This isn't what I want, but I'm hedging 'cause the Paterson fortune's not looking like a sure bet anyhows. Eggs in one basket and all that. Now's the time. Get her attention while she's happy and fed.

'Sis, I was thinking, since you like learning, wouldn't you like to be in a place with *loads* of books?'

'Yeah,' Izwi replies, face in her plate.

'You'll want to learn lots of exciting new things.'

Izwi shrugs. I catch a slight frown, maybe worry, on Gran's face, but she doesn't say anything.

'Somewhere you can meet nice new friends—'

'I've already got friends,' Izwi replies.

Okay. I'm just gonna have to come out with it.

'This opportunity you've been given by Sir Callander to go to a really great school . . . I think you should try it. I mean, sis, it will change your life. Trust me.'

'I already said *no*,' she replies. 'I don't like him – he smells. I don't like his school.'

'Izwi—'

'N. O. No, no, no.' She throws her plate across the caravan, spilling mac and cheese everywhere. Then she leaps up and storms out in an almighty huff.

I sigh and get up. Didn't exactly go down how I wanted it to, and now I've got to clean up my mess. The mac and cheese is everywhere: on my berth, the windows, floor. What a waste. I don't follow Izwi out because I know if she's radge she'll be at her best friend Eddie's trailer. I can get her later once she cools off. Trying to do that now would be like handling polonium with your bare hands. That kid will be the death of me.

'I know what you're trying to do and why you think it's right,' Gran says in a sad voice. 'Don't worry, Ropa, I'll talk to Izwi.'

'No, Gran, I'll fix it. There is another way.' Truth is, I don't want sis gone to some boarding school either. She belongs here with me and Gran, but the only way I get to keep us together is if I can make serious cheddar. That means I'm gonna have to make the Paterson fortune thing work somehow, even if it kills me.

XXVIII

Feeling a bit shite to be honest. The evening hasn't gone according to plan, but the dishes still need doing. If my parents were still alive then all this wouldn't be my problem. But it is what it is. I'm sis, mum, granddaughter, provider and the arsehole round these ends. Whatever. I ping a text to Eddie's mum, Marie, to give her the rundown so she knows why Izwi's miffed when she gets there. I've just pressed send when a call comes in. Rooster Rob.

'You wanted us tae find Bumblebeam for you. Someone else got there first, Ropa, an' he isnae gonna be sniffing flowers nae more,' he says.

'Christ.'

'I've sent the location,' he says. 'You owe us, again.'

'Wait, what exactly happened to him?'

'Damned if I ken,' Rob replies, and hangs up.

Could this day possibly get any worse? At least I've got a reply from Marie saying Izwi's arrived safe.

'What's going on?' Gran asks.

'It's work, Gran. I have to go out again, sorry. Marie says she's okay with Izwi sleeping over, but I've told her to come round and pick up the leftovers if she's interested. At least Izwi can finish off her meal.'

'You do too much, child.'

'Needs must, Gran, needs must.'

I'm out of there quickly 'cause there ain't no point in lingering when a job's waiting. This shit's getting heavy and I'm not liking any of it. For this reason, I'm taking River with me. She's fuelled up, and there's no way I'm wandering about without my extra pair of teeth given everything going on. Once Rob's location comes through, I forward it to Priya and Jomo to let them know we need to meet urgently.

Straight up into town on my bike with River trotting alongside me. The streets are still packed, this time with intoxicated revellers. The pubs drop prices to counter competition from the moonshine vendors flooding town during the King's Market Week. Fights will break out, and folks will get robbed or stabbed before all this is over. I listened to a discussion a while back where some professor from Edinburgh Napier University argued that the chaos of the King's Market Week is designed to demonstrate to folks the need for the 'leviathan' who comes in at the end to restore order. Without the king's thumb pressing down upon us, we would live in continual fear, under the constant danger of violent death, and our lives would be poor, nasty, brutish and short. Scary shit, but I ain't too sure about none of it.

Doesn't take long before I cut through Fountainbridge, then up along Lauriston Place onto George IV Bridge. This end of town's too near the courts for my liking, given my previous associations. Reckon if I hadn't given up rolling with the Clan for ghostalking, I'd have wound up here eventually.

Then again, I'm back in with that gang, however tangentially. I guess that makes me a recidivist. The favours I owe the Rooster keep mounting up, and if I don't do something, he's gonna ask me to do a job for him in return.

Proactive, that's what I need to be.

Jomo and Priya are already waiting for me near the address Rob pinged over. This end's the playground of lawyers and other leeches since this lawless city has plenty of work for them. Jomo's tucked his skateboard under his arm, and their convo stops when I get there.

'Hey, River, I've not seen you in ages, you cute vixen, you,' he says, grinning and kneeling down to her level. 'I've been stuck in the Library all day long. This is the first time I've been out for fresh air.' He's looking proper sallow for this time of the year.

'I can't say I'm really surprised Bumblebeam came to a sticky ending given his activities, but having duelled him, I know it would have to be someone highly skilled to have beaten him,' Priya says.

'That or they did the dirty on him.'

'Come on, let's get over there and have a nosey if we can.'

It's a short walk past the National Library of Scotland and on to the High Street. There's tons of pigs in stab-proof vests lurking as we go by St Giles' Cathedral and even more hanging about Parliament Square. Finally, we reach the address, and my stomach sinks 'cause I swear I've heard the name before. The Advocates Library is taped off and the area's swarming with police.

It's always best to avoid encounters with the fuzz. But I haven't worked out how we're getting in yet. Fire engines are parked in the square, with a couple of firefighters lurking. They're okay – it's the pigs I ain't so keen on.

Not an ambulance in sight, though.

'How do we get past them?' Priya asks, as though reading my mind.

We slow near the statue of David Hume. He's lounging with a book, nipple hanging out 'cause he's in a toga or bedsheet for some ungodly reason. Sex sells, even for dead philosophers.

I look round, but even my burglar's eye can't spot an option. It's all grand buildings with arches, columns and statues littered about. Anything happens this end of town, the pigs are there in a jiffy – if this was the fleshmarket, forget it. They wouldn't dare go, not at night anyway. We'd have the run of the place.

'Jomo, don't you have some kind of staff access to the Advocates Library?' I ask.

'Yeah, I have automatic right of entry for me, two girls and a fox for every single library in Scotland,' he replies, the sarcasm dripping.

We're standing there, clueless, when a hand taps my shoulder and I catch a whiff of tobacco scent.

'Good, you are already here,' Sir Callander says, as though this were a planned encounter. 'Miss Kapoor, I know you aren't exactly a pathologist, but you might as well take a look with us. Young Mr Maige, shouldn't you be at the Library?'

'I'm here to help,' Jomo replies uncertainly.

'Come along, then,' Sir Callander says, striding towards the entrance of the building. 'I take it the fox is with you?'

'Yes,' I reply.

He huffs and mutters, 'Next time why don't you bring the entire village along?'

A policeman moves to block his path, and Sir Callander glowers at him.

'I'm sorry, but there's an investigation going on. No one's allowed inside at the moment,' the policeman says. He swallows hard. Never seen a pig flustered like this before.

'Your superior contacted the office of the Discoverer General, and now he is here with his assistants in front of you. Make way,' Sir Callander demands. His irritation unsettles the copper. I doubt he's used to dealing with people who refer to themselves in the third person. The copper mumbles into his radio with a shaky hand.

There's a reply from the other end, but I only catch static. It's noisy out here with all the trade on the High Street.

'I'm sorry, you may go in,' the copper says. I swear tonight's the first time I've heard one apologize to anyone for anything. Twice in two minutes! As we go past, I notice he can't quite take his eyes off River. Yeah, strange night for us all, pal.

The acrid scent of chemical fire hits me as soon as we walk into the building. Gets right up your sinuses and rubs them raw. There's smoke wafting through the building, which explains the firemen, I guess.

Plenty of fuel for a fire in here 'cause it must have been a whole forest they chopped down for these panelled walls and the floors. Not to mention the bookshelves, desks and tables. Grand. From what I know, this library's supposed to be the prime zone for legal texts and all that, so them lot hang out here sipping lattes and making a killing. An enormous portrait of the founder, Lord Advocate George MacKenzie, hangs in the centre. His stern eyes seem to track us across the room. That's the douche who had all them Covenanters killed back in the day. I don't like lawyers.

He still built an outstanding library. Mad detail on the ceiling, which has these incredible squares. It's stunning until you see the dead man pinned to it through all four limbs, blood dripping down to the floor.

Jomo bends over and pukes.

Bo Bumblebeam won't be giving no more astral tours, that's for damn sure.

My constitution ain't built for this shit either. I resolve to come clean to Sir Callander. Full debrief without leaving anything out. The stakes on this table ain't what I rolled into the casino for, and I'll be damned if I'm going to deal with Vlad the fucking Impaler.

Don't panic. Keep cool. No need to lose your head.

The grimace stencilled upon Bo Bumblebeam's pale face is utterly frightening. Why here, though? This man was no lawyer. This shit's mental, like. Must have been alive when he was mounted there, using what appears to be the brass tubings of lamps taken from the reading tables. The bases and heads of the lamps are scattered all over the floor. Their tubing pierces his arms and legs, holding him fast against the ceiling. Must have been quite a mission to get Bumblebeam up there.

Priya's jaw is on the floor. Thing is, I'm kosher with seeing the dead 'cause it is what it is, but bodies ain't my cuppa. Too next level. My hands are trembling, so I put them in my jacket pockets and try to maintain my cool like it ain't nothing. Jomo's retreated to stand near the door, looking traumatized as hell. His attention seems to have shifted to the piles of books burned, torn and scattered on the floor.

Must be doubly worse for a bibliothec like him to be in a desecrated library.

River sniffs the air, taking in the scene with Vulcan-level Zen. She's gangster like that.

'God save the king,' a man in a black suit says.

'Good evening, Detective Inspector Balfour,' Sir Callander replies.

'How many times in the last twenty years have I called you out on one of my cases? On each occasion, you've come in, then walked out saying it had nothing to do with your *directorate*. The last time I called you, about a magnesium fire that burned down Gorgie Farm, you said it was a freak occurrence. What say you now?'

Detective Balfour has greying hair and looks to be in his mid-fifties or thereabouts. He studies each of us in turn, before returning to Sir Callander, whose eyes are fixed on the figure upon the ceiling.

There's a sharp click, Priya putting on her seatbelt. Very casually, she takes herself to the nearest wall and Peter Parkers up it, wheeling to the top until she's upside down on the ceiling. It's a bumpy ride as she moves towards Bumblebeam's body because the ceiling is uneven with all its decorations.

The man widens his eyes but maintains his stoicism.

'What colour were the flames, Detective Inspector Balfour?' Callander asks.

'You mean the fire?' he asks.

Callander nods.

'Yellow, maybe a bit red too. Why?'

No explanation is forthcoming for Balfour, and he doesn't press the matter, but I understand immediately. Magicians produce different-coloured flames depending on their potential. Mine's white, Priya's is green, and I've seen Bumblebeam make a reddish flame. As for Callander, who knows?

But if this gives the gaffer any indication of whodunnit, nothing registers on his face. Callander walks around the pool of red beneath the body. Our images are reflected in the congealing blood.

'Were there any witnesses?'

'This is Edinburgh. Half the people on those streets would murder an honest copper long before they helped with our enquiries,' Balfour replies, with no small amount of annoyance.

I get it. No one wants to be a snitch. The way the pigs go about their trade don't help things neither.

'Leave us,' Callander says to Balfour.

The policeman opens his mouth, thinks better of it, then walks out without protest. When he reaches the door, he turns back and says, 'It goes without saying this is an active crime scene, so you may not touch or tamper with anything.'

'Naturally,' Callander replies. He wanders around the room, a keen eye on everything before him. Now, normally Callander's all serious and proper, but tonight he's super intense.

I'm trailing, afeard to the nth, thinking I'm not liking where this whole thing's going. Bumblebeam was frolicking about with Rory MacCulloch. Does this mean Rory MacCulloch did this? The Monks have been messing with occult magic and shit, but they're still just kids. And I can't imagine any of those posh schoolboys doing something *this* horrible. This is next-level bad.

I'm on this train when I suddenly recall my encounter with Wilson. Didn't he say something about 'taking care of our end at the Advocates Library' earlier? Is this what he meant by that? But how exactly would an old geezer like Wilson haul a body up ceilings like that? From what I know, he ain't no magician.

Nothing's adding up here.

I have to tell Callander where I'm at with this whole thing. Full disclosure: Tom, the Paterson fortune . . . all of it.

'Sir Callander, can we have a quiet word?' I say.

He looks me in the eye, and suddenly I'm more timersome than I've ever been in my entire life. But I've got to tell him everything. I mean, he is my gaffer, so . . . That means giving up the goose with the golden eggs. Which means losing any mint I was gonna get out of this gig. Meaning Izwi has to go to Aberdeen 'cause I can't do no better for her.

'Speak,' Callander says.

'I just . . . well, I was thinking. It would have to be someone real powerful who's done this to Bo Bumblebeam, and I heard you ask about the colour of the flame. Does that mean we can check out all the yellow-flame magicians?'

He takes a minute, maintaining that intense stare as though he knows I haven't said everything.

'Yellow fire in all its differing gradations is very common amongst our practitioners. It would be difficult to find out who was responsible here. But looking at that—' he points to the ceiling '—you should come to understand that the colour of the flame indicates the practitioner's potential. And it is only that – potential, nothing more. What matters in the end is practice and dedication, the mastery of magical science. A studious magician with weak potential can defeat one with superior potential in a duel. Bumblebeam was bested in this encounter.'

I *really* should tell him . . .

'I think it's all linked to the Max Wu situation.'

'I want you to be very careful and to pay full attention to this matter.' He looks up. 'Anything useful, Ms Kapoor?'

'Only the same as what you can see,' Priya replies. 'Except for this heat coming off him. Feels like a radiator. Not a singe on his clothes though. Curious.'

So Bumblebeam was killed first, then the fire was set off? Or was it collateral damage sparked by the duel? I recall him and Priya setting the Water of Leith alight.

'Mr Maige, if you have composed yourself, I need you to arrange a meeting immediately with your father. The rest of you can go now. I will meet you at the Library.'

That's me off this hook. As I walk round the pool of blood to meet up with Priya descending from the ceiling, I'm filled with no small amount of confusion. My mind's spinning. I don't like that sort of messiness clawing at me. Feeling marginally safer and saner with River brushing against my leg as we go, though.

Detective Inspector Balfour confers with Sir Callander just as we're leaving. Callander says to him, 'I've been hearing reports of a gang war in the undergrowth of this city – perhaps that would be a more fitting focus for your enquiries.'

Gang war? I'd take that over this shit any day of the week. You start off with a sick kid, and before you know it, the whole thing's gone *Texas Chainsaw Massacre* on your arse. The Monks, Tom, Bumblebeam, Paterson – it's all connected, but I don't see the full picture yet. I guess Callander's right about one thing. Even when posh folks duke it out, it's just another form of gang war. Money's what causes these things to get out of hand, and that means I've got to keep following the cheddar.

XXIX

The Mile's still heaving despite the late hour. Edinburgh doesn't sleep during King's Market. The air's filled with the bitter tinge of moonshine, body odour, smoke and the aromas from the grub made fresh by vendors on the pavements. There's dancers, buskers and performers of all sorts trying to squeeze out a shilling or two from the punters going past.

I walk behind Priya, pushing her chair. She carries Jomo's skateboard, since he's wheeling my bike. No way we could ever go through this lot abreast, like.

'That was wild,' Priya says, weirdly chirpy in the fresh air. 'Excuse me, people, wheelchair coming through . . . Cheers, pal. Reminds me of the cadavers we worked with at the Kelvin Institute. Well, those were a lot tidier, but you still develop a strong stomach for this sort of thing. OMG, is that an authentic bratwurst stand? Come on, let's get hot dogs.'

'Nah, you're alright, pal,' I say, still a bit queasy.

'Jomo, hot dogs?' she shouts above the noise.

He turns back, all ashen, and heaves like he's going to puke again, but manages to keep it together. Just.

'It's me and River then,' Priya says.

We take a spot at the counter where a Kraut-passing Fifer about my age takes her order, complete with a faux German accent for effect. Hard to believe all these people can be so cheery when not five minutes away there's a dead guy glued to a ceiling.

I scan the crowd. Have this weird feeling that someone's watching. More Spidey sense than anything tangible. Sure, this is Edinburgh, and no doubt there's a couple of thieves about looking for easy marks, but it feels viscerally like surveillance. But I don't see anyone I can pin it on. Maybe I'm just being paranoid.

'This is an orgasm wrapped in a bun,' Priya says, ripping into her hot dog. 'What say you, River?'

River replies by wolfing down her sausage.

'Come on, let's get out of here,' I say. I'd feel more comfy out of the crowds. Too many faces here.

'That heat coming off Bumblebeam reminds me of Max Wu,' Priya says.

'Then they had the same condition?'

'Different prognosis, though.'

I get that. Max hasn't ended up with a Shaka the Zulu execution.

We're up on Calton Hill, which is dead this time of the night, and I'm relieved there ain't no soul living or dead on our six. Bit of a mission hoisting River onto the pillars of the unfinished replica of the Parthenon. She backs into me as Priya and Jomo disappear through the portal.

'Come on, girl, it's just a doorway. You're telling me you were cool as a cucumber with the dead guy at the Advocates Library, but not this?'

I pick up River, loving the feel of her soft fur against my body, and then in we go. Poor lassie's in a bit of a state when we make it through the other end. Squirming about and nipping the air. I wisely put her down, lest she decides I'm the enemy and bites my nose off.

'What do we have here?' say the watchman in the bellhop outfit, noticing River. 'Such a beauty. Don't be afraid, little one, it's always unsettling the first time, but you get used to it.' He turns to me. 'Look after this one well and she'll take care of you; some beasts have been gifted with will, same as us, and she's one of them.'

'Erm, thanks.'

I don't remember him going gaga the first time I came through. But whatever he's saying works on River, because she calms, even allowing him to stroke her.

Jomo and Priya are already waiting by the archway leading to the steps that descend into the Library. I still have to give the watchman my ear to punch in before I go through. Doesn't matter how many times I've come through this way, he always asks to see the damned thing. Then again, folks who work for the Library are anal about things.

'You'll be due a new one soon,' he says, handing it back.

River's already bounding along ahead of us, gaining confidence, as we make our way down the gigantic stairs. Jomo's got his arm around my shoulder, putting serious weight on me, and Priya's chair clunks and clutters as we head down, past the walls with Ethiopian iconography. We reach reception, and, lo, Callander is already there.

'What took you so long?' he asks.

'We stopped for some hot dogs,' Priya replies.

But that only took a minute or two, so there's no way he could have arrived before us. We took the most direct route. I'll wager he has a secret twin and they're messing with us . . . Nah.

'Mr Evelyn, is Pythagoras about tonight?' Callander asks the librarian behind the desk. This one is a pudgy fella well into his fifties who wears purple robes.

'I believe the *head librarian* is proofing in his private carrel,' Mr Evelyn replies coolly. Then he turns to Jomo. 'He is always hard at work in the service of the Elgin, unlike his son, who I fear lacks the same level of diligence.'

'I was just on my break,' Jomo replies, cringing.

He scampers ahead to get away from Mr Evelyn's criticism. We weave our way through the labyrinthian corridors outwith the main hall of the Library. This section gives me the sense of being down a disused mineshaft, albeit one held up by rows of bookshelves instead of normal timbers. Even on a warm summer's night it is cool down here. Blessed relief.

We wind up in front of a carved circular door. Its grooves and lines resemble a numberless clock face.

Sir Callander knocks.

'Enter.'

We follow into the massivest, swankiest carrel I've ever seen. The room is a perfect cube carved out of the same rock that makes the hill. Its dimensions and symmetry are so perfect that were it not for gravity you couldn't tell up from down, left from right. Dr Maige is bowed behind a massive stone desk, all elegant straight lines and right angles. Not a sound penetrates from the outside. There's nothing on the walls to distract the occupant either.

Dr Maige is reading a small notebook, occasionally scribbling something down. I can't make heads or tales of what he is drafting because it's dense with mathematical notation I've never encountered before.

'Dr Maige, I—' Callander starts, but the head librarian holds out his hand and continues with his work.

There's always some kind of power play going on between the head librarian and the secretary, and the annoyance registers on my mentor's face. Maybe it's because the Library and the Society are independent but interdependent, as Eilidh Logan suggested. That's bound to generate friction from time to time. Dr Maige keeps us waiting a good while. His scarlet robes, bright against the black stonework, exude his power and authority in this place. It's his Library.

'It's not his fault,' Jomo whispers to me. 'Proofing is hard work.'

'What?'

'That's what he is doing. It's one of the most important things the Library does for Scottish magic,' Jomo answers with pride.

'I still don't get it, man.'

'Surely by now you've encountered the term proven or unproven spells?' Priya chimes in.

I nod, because I've seen such in my reading, but not thought all that much about it. Easy for this lot, who get to learn magic full time. I'm trying to do it on top of a million things I'm meant to be doing, and there's only so many hours in the day.

'It appears your dominie is allowing gaps in your knowledge, Miss Moyo, so I hope you will permit me to remedy that,' Dr Maige says, placing his pen down. He adjusts the sleeves of his robe. 'Librarians are natural philosophers in the mould of Maxwell, and one of our key functions is to wed magic to mathematics. In fact, the very best of us spend very little time on the upkeep of the Library and most of it proofing. Magic is not created but discovered, young lady . . .'

'There really is an urgent matter we must discuss, Pythagoras. Perhaps you could deliver this lecture another time?' Sir Callander says, exasperated.

'You recall our conversation on my dissertation when you were new here, Miss Moyo?' Dr Maige says, blanking my gaffer. I cringe, caught up between these two. 'When I came to Scotland from Tanzania, it was to do a doctorate on the number symbolism of the Pythagorean Brotherhood in the ancient world. They believed that numbers were imbued with magic. So we know even in antiquity, different cultures noted how the spells you weave with words are merely a linguistic expression of universal mathematical law. In the beginning was the number, not the word.'

It makes sense to me since the fire spell, which is the first thing everyone learns, is underpinned by the Somerville equation, which describes the words of the spell in mathematical notation. I've seen mentioned in some texts that something called 'decoherence' is the process by which mathematics passes into magic. I don't fully understand it, though, to be honest. Not yet, anyways. Proper geek stuff. I would love to lounge here and blether on about it all if my mentor wasn't so pissed. Not that that's stopping the good doctor.

'Every spell must be mathematically proven for us to comprehend the fullest Platonic truth underlying it. When a magician discovers a new spell, they send it to us for proofing, because only when its underlying mathematical structure is known can we truly differentiate it from other spells. It is not uncommon to find that what is thought of as a new spell is in reality merely a new linguistic expression of an already known phenomenon. The vast majority of common spells have already been proven. A few, such as Rachman's esoterica, which I'm sure you'll come to learn of in time, continue to elude us. Which brings me to my role. Without proofing, magic descends back into the dark ages of mysticism and superstition. But now I find myself interrupted from this critical work. So, Sir Callander, how may a servant of this august institution be of service to you tonight?'

Ouch.

That's basically an F.U. gift-wrapped in Valentine's Day paper. But everything Dr Maige said leads me to another theory of magic that riffs off the Mathematical Universe Hypothesis, which, to me, is sort of like the Simulated Reality one, only in that one the world we live in isn't a computer simulation but rather the result of mathematics, which is hardcore, 'cause it's like saying the universe isn't described by mathematics, it actually *is* mathematics. Gets me wondering, though, like if librarians can show magic as mathematics, then surely the converse is true? Rather than waiting for magicians to create spells, they could work the reverse and use mathematics to suggest new ones, right? Not that I'm going to ask this question in the middle of a pissing contest.

'I regret the intrusion,' Sir Callander replies, tone all wooden-like. 'But I would not come to you unless it was a matter of grave import.'

Dr Maige interlocks his fingers and reclines.

'Dad, there's—' Jomo starts.

'It's *Dr Maige* to you, Mr Maige,' his father says, cutting him off. 'Your position is with the Library, not the Society. You'd do well to remember that, young man.'

Jomo looks down, crestfallen, and I'm thinking his father doesn't need to do him like that. Can't be easy for him. This sort of bull kills the spirit, and Gran says there's nothing worse in this world than a soulless being. I want to say something, but that ain't what we're here for the now. And I don't see how it would make things any better.

'I need you to make a book,' Sir Callander says.

'Of whom?' Dr Maige snaps to attention.

'Bo Bumblebeam, a recently deceased unlicensed practitioner.'

'Out of the question.'

I'm confused. They want to make a book out of a person? This doesn't make any sense, so I keep alert for clues.

'It's a matter of extreme importance. Bumblebeam is tied up to a nefarious scheme and lives are at stake. This is a question of mutual aid between the Library and our Society,' Callander presses.

'There are strict criteria for what books are published by this institution, and I don't need to explain to *you* that those rules exist for a reason. Mutual aid does not override these considerations, and you know this very well,' Dr Maige replies forcefully. 'Now, if there isn't anything else, I must return to my work.'

Sir Callander exhales loudly through his nostrils, before abruptly leaving. There's nothing else for the rest of us to do but follow with our tails between our legs.

XXX

Callander's scowl hasn't lessened much by the time we reach the central balcony in the main section of the Library. I imagine he is a man used to getting his way, but then I still ain't at all sure what this talk of making books and all that is really about. Our shadows sway in the flickering candlelight, and the air is thick with the scent of wax. Out here you are swallowed in the staggering vastness of the Library, and the readers in the lower sections appear small as dolls.

The subterranean structure of the Library makes it feel like many different things at once. A mine, sculpture, temple – hell, sometimes I feel like I've won the golden ticket and am inside an Easter egg. I rest against a pillar, cold rock rough against my skin.

'There isn't much else we can achieve here tonight,' Callander says at last. 'Miss Moyo, you will continue with your enquiries and report any progress to me. And, in light of these events, I strongly suggest you urgently acquaint yourself with the practicalities of Clifford's *Self-Defence*. Call upon me should you need aid.'

With that, he strides away briskly, leaving us to it. He is right, I must be more careful from here on if I don't want to find myself at a sticky end. We all have to. So many pieces in the air at the mo. I'm gonna have to do some serious thinking, so we can be done with it. Then I can catch my golden egg and make a nice omelette. To think I nearly lost my nerve and gave it up.

I'm afeard to the max right now. If it were anyone but Bumblebeam, I'd venture into the everyThere to find him and strike a bargain with his soul. But I saw what he did the last time I was out in the astral plane. Venturing in there would be some kamikaze shit. Even Brother Musashi in *The Book of Five Rings* counsels caution against folks like that . . . but what's the alternative?

'I'm sorry about everything, guys,' Jomo says.

'It's not your fault your dad's a bit of a knob,' Priya replies.

'What's this book Callander wanted anyways?' I ask.

'I have an idea,' Jomo whispers excitedly. 'How about *I* make the book? I've seen it done a couple of times, and I'm sure I can do it now.'

'Are you out of your goddamn mind?' Priya says.

'I can do it.'

'Hold on,' I say. 'How is publishing some book going to help? Plus, we have to save Max now, not in a year's time.'

'This is the stupidest thing I've ever heard in my life,' Priya snaps back at Jomo. But she throws me a crumb too. 'The highest-ranking, most skilled librarians can channel the memories of a dead subject into what they call a book, because those memories can then be "read". If we had a book of Bo Bumblebeam, it might give us clues that could help save Max. But Jomo's dad said no, and Jomo—' she stops to glare at him

'—has *never done it before*. It's been a rough night, and Sir
Callander's right. Let's leave this silly talk behind, get some
kip and work something else out in the morning.'

Jomo shrinks, head down like a beaten dog.

He only wanted to help, but the way Priya speaks don't
leave no room for further discussion.

Jomo's proper low from being knocked back, so I punch
him playfully in the shoulder to snap him out of it. But Priya's
right all the same. We need a half-time break, and somebody
better bring out the oranges.

'Right, I'm heading home. We'll catch up tomorrow, hey?'
Priya says, taking off the brakes on her chair. 'Jomo, we good?'

'Yeah,' he says.

She leaves us, headed for reception, and I figure there's
not much reason to linger here anymore.

'Come on, Jomo, chum me down to the underHume. I
need some practice.' I also need to message Gran to let her
know I'm staying in town tonight. No point in heading out
and then making the trek back in tomorrow morning. Great
thing about the Library is you've got loads of nooks and
crannies to crash where nobody can disturb you. Some
evenings I even hear snoring coming from dark corners, so
I'm not the only one who does this.

Me and Jomo head all the way down to the bottom floor of
the Library, then further down into the basement – if an
underground location can be said to have a basement. The
practice room is a bare cave made of rough-hewn walls that
exude an ultra-primeval air. Nothing like the swank of Dr

Maige's carrel down here. It's the only place they'll allow you to practise magic within the Library, and I get why now. It's to protect the books and other users from mistakes.

I take out my copy of Clifford and toss my bag to one side. Jomo leans against the wall, still looking annoyed with everything. But hey, it's been a long night, and maybe River can cheer him up, 'cause I don't see no way the now.

'Okay, old man. Let's see what you've got,' I say, taking my scarf, Cruickshank, out of my pocket and holding it in one hand so it dangles.

The way I see it, I've got my katty for range, my dagger for close-quarter action, and Cruickshank's somewhere in between. If I can train it to punch and grapple or even distract my opponents, that should give me an advantage when I'm in action.

'Wake up, Cruickshank,' I say, and immediately the lower end rises up. 'Now punch.'

Cruickshank rolls into a ball and sucker-punches me in the gut, making me topple over.

My poor tummy.

Jomo slow-claps my humiliation as I slowly get up.

'What the actual fuck, Cruickshank? We're supposed to be shadow-boxing, but if you're gonna be a dick about it then it's the sin bin for you,' I say, tossing the scarf on the floor. I swear the cheeky git curls into something resembling a smile. But I refuse to be baited. Instead, I open up Clifford's *Self-Defence*, flicking through the pages to find the spell for concussive blasts.

Priya used it at the Edinburgh School, and I figure it'd be a great way to knock out opponents.

253

'Fancy a cuppa?' Jomo says with a yawn.

'Sure thing,' I reply instantly, before seeing his angle. 'Hang on, are you trying to get out before I cast this spell?'

'Maybe try it a couple of times before doing it with me in the room. No offence, Ropa, but I've heard your fire spell's a bit, shall we say, scattershot.'

'Whatever, man, just make sure you've got lots of sugar in my tea.'

Good thing he's out 'cause I can now fully concentrate. Magicking requires laser-like focus. Your mind has to be centred on the spell, the underlying science, the intended effect, et cetera.

Okay, so concussive blast is essentially a powerful soliton that you generate to take out an opponent. I'm looking to create a calibrated long-wavelength atmospheric soliton, sort of like what happens when there's an explosion and the air blast knocks things out around it. The funny thing is that this type of wave, the soliton, was discovered by John Scott Russell in the canal near where I live. The soliton is stable over long distances at a constant velocity, whereas ordinary waves are prone to flattening and interference.

Clifford writes that you can aid the spell by using an open palm gesture and thrusting forward to direct the air current.

Okay, here goes.

I go into a stance, feet shoulder width apart and left leg slightly behind my right to absorb the recoil generated in my own musculature. The more powerful the blast, the more intense your recoil, which limits how hard you can let this thing fly.

Breathe. Find your nexus point.

'Hunched against the elements, show your strength, Boreas, and take this man's coat off.'

I thrust my hand forward and it jacks backwards immediately. A pneumatic *pfft* sets off a foggy indentation of my hand veering to the left. It smashes into the wall with a thunderclap, pretty close to where Jomo'd been standing.

Oops.

Not exactly where I was aiming, but at least I sort of got it to work.

I focus and try the spell again, with the same result. Hmm. Why is it veering left like that? I'm bending over to pick up Clifford's book when someone speaks behind me.

'Unless you have a compass with you, I would hesitate to invoke the Boreas variant. He is, after all, the god of the north wind, and so will only work towards that cardinal point, just as Zephyrus goes west and Notus south. If you invoke a more general anemoi spell, though, it would be slightly less powerful, no doubt, but much more wieldy.' It's a jarring, reedy voice I'm not acquainted with.

Standing in the doorway is a lad in a blazer, shirt and dress pants like a geriatric. I home in on his mop-style haircut.

'Also, your hand coordination is all wrong,' he continues. 'It comes after the spell, when you really ought to be moving in rhythm with your incantation so you reach full extension with the final word. Otherwise, you're out of sync, which overall results in a more limited entropic shift.'

Rory MacCulloch. I've spent ages trying to get hold of him – his phone number, his school, his friends. And now he's just strolled in here, easy as. Last time I heard of his movements, he was with Bo . . . and look what happened.

Got a real bad feeling about this. I snatch up my scarf, just in case he tries anything.

'Rory MacCulloch, you owe me some answers. And they better be bloody good, 'cause I—'

I stop suddenly, sensing something's off. There's a glint in his eye that ain't human. And from past experience, I think I know what it is.

'I am addressing the entity within this boy. Who am I talking to?' I say with Authority.

'I was invited here, Ropa Moyo. That won't work on me.' His voice is grating, and a twisted smile appears on his face.

The face morphs, and something like a second pair of eyes flickers on his cheeks. One moment his mouth appears to smile; the next it looks as though it's screaming, like some great battle's raging within. He steps inside the room with a strange walk, knees bending too much, his ankles twisted. He should be rolling in agony, never mind walking. The motion of his arms seems random and his head flops around on his neck. It's like watching a string puppet move.

'Who are you, and what have you done with Rory MacCulloch?'

He laughs like nails scratching chalkboard, jaws hanging down like they are dislocated. This must be who I sensed skulking about on the High Street earlier.

'Little witch, you, who are in league with the One Above All, dare to question my presence, even as you lay down the red carpet for him in blood and pain and suffering? Such hypocrisy.'

'Don't know what you're on, pal, but I ain't in league with anyone.'

'Is that what you believe?'

'Why are you here?' I try to reassert my Authority by asking the question.

'The Monks of the Misty Order danced on my grave, disturbed my remains and kicked my skull around like a football after they performed dark magic they understand nothing of. They are bound to me now, and I will use them as my vessels to save Scotland from a peril you are all too blind to see. Then, maybe, I too will be allowed to move on at last.'

'Yeah, right. You're just a friendly ghost out here to play hero. Your so-called "vessels" are facing death because of whatever it is you're doing to them.'

'Don't you know everything has a price?'

I very nearly answer when I recall Gran's advice on dealing with wayward spirits, the ones that resist Authority. The more questions you answer, the more Authority you cede, and if you allow the conversation to go on long enough, eventually you will be powerless over them. And that is especially dangerous here. Most spectres are invisible, save to folks like me; then you have those that can manifest. Or poltergeists, the bams that'll do dodgy shit like banging doors and toppling furniture. Touching the material world is the next level up according to Gran.

But whatever is inside of Rory is, like, the worst ever. It's ancient, angry and malevolent, so I have to be careful. It thinks whatever it's doing will redeem it from something, allowing it to move on. But taking possession of people's bodies is a big no-no in my books. I don't even need my mbira to hear him since he's speaking through the mouth of his human vessel. With them lot there's no negotiation, no redemption. You cast them out to the Other Place. One-way ticket to the land of gnashing teeth, wailing and all that other biblical bollocks.

It's much harder to cast them out without a name. I never even saw Gran do it, but I have to try all the same.

River stays low, quietly circling to get behind him.

'I will cast you out tonight, pal,' I say.

Now, Brother Musashi said a great many things, and none of them involves telling your adversary your intentions, especially when you need your mbira to do the work and said instrument is in your bag next to said adversary. So I'm kicking myself when this spirit incants a spell, blazing up the mother of all thermospheres in his left hand. The fire illuminates the room, sparkling fierce orange like sunset. Screw this. I'm reaching for my katty when Jomo bursts into the room holding two cups of tea.

'Stop, both of you, right now,' Jomo shouts.

Rory cocks his head and turns, which gives me enough time to load and aim. I whisper a Promethean fire spell, infusing it in the rock so it'll explode into shrapnel mid-flight. He's not getting away from me.

'That means you too, Miss Moyo,' Jomo says, startling me with his formality. 'This Library is a sacred space where all practitioners may enter without prejudice, and no violence is permitted within its walls. Is this clear?'

'Jo— I mean, Mr Maige, this isn't Rory, it's a spirit that's taken over his body. I have to cast it out.' The rock is burning my fingers.

'Doesn't matter. The Library allowed Mr MacCulloch in as a member since he is a student of the Edinburgh School. As such he is protected by its rules . . . as are you.'

Rory, or whoever the hell is controlling his body, extinguishes that almighty thermosphere. I'm tempted to take my shot now, but the look on Jomo's face stops me.

'Sensible girl. I am not here to fight with you. But if you continue to interfere with my work, there will be consequences.'

'Like what you did to Bo Bumblebeam, hey?' I say.

'How dare you accuse me of that!' it shouts in anger. 'Bumblebeam was an excellent vessel. I shall avenge his death.'

I ain't buying what he's peddling. Spirits like this lie all the time.

'Tell me your name,' I command.

It snarls and leaps back.

'That's enough, Miss Moyo,' Jomo says firmly. Almost sounds like his old man. 'Mr MacCulloch, this practice room is occupied, but you are free to use any of our other facilities unmolested.'

Jomo moves out of the doorway and allows the body of Rory and its driver to walk out with that awkward puppet gait. Once it exits, I throw my ammo in the corner of the room. There's a pop as it explodes.

I have to flex my reddened fingers 'cause the stone was hot. Quickly, I grab my gear, backpack, Cruickshank too, and I call River. I make to follow, but Jomo prevents me, offering a cup of tea.

'He's getting away,' I say.

'I wouldn't do anything just now, Ropa. There is another way,' he says.

XXXI

My nerves are shot. It's been mad today, but there's nothing a nice cuppa can't fix. Me and Jomo are sat on the hard floor of the practice room, while River's still alert, eyes fixed on the door. My mind's in overdrive though. That orange flame made by puppet Rory doesn't exactly correspond to the flames Detective Balfour clocked at the Advocates Library. But it's got to be him, and anyway, surely it's easy to mix up orange and yellow. I don't believe anything puppet Rory said. He did it alright.

We were wrong about what these boys were doing in the astral plane. It wasn't an object they brought here but a soul. Hence the interest in King James's *Daemonologie* and that forbidden magic angle.

But it's still just a ghost at the end of the day, and that's my speciality.

I'm going to have to speak with Callander about the Society's blind spot when it comes to this side of things. Kinda like how doctors in the day refused to treat feet and teeth because they felt it beneath them. The Society values manipulatory magic above all else, that is, the ability to effect thermodynamic changes in this world. And I was told that as a ghostalker I was no different to a telephone line. Hardly magic at all by their standards. No wonder Bumblebeam, with his interest in the astral realm, found himself an impoverished practitioner working on the fringes.

Now, Priya stated Bumblebeam's body was radiating heat, which sounds to me like the same thing going on with Max Wu and Doug Duffie. They may have all been possessed by the same spirit then.

'What are you thinking?' Jomo asks.

'You know why it's cold whenever there's a ghost nearby?'

'Nope.'

'See, in order to manifest from the everyThere, they have to fix in their harmonic resonances with our dimension. But 'cause of the laws of thermodynamics which apply in our world, this takes energy. So they normally draw from the local environment, lowering the temperature in their surroundings.'

'What's that got to do with all this?'

'I reckon if a ghost were to manifest within your body, it would have to go into overdrive to provide the energy for such a high-level symbiosis. Then what happens when it bails on you? You're left in this state of fever due to an imbalance in the entanglement field of your soul and body. You've been jacked out of alignment.'

'Sounds alright, but there's a massive hole in your hypothesis. If that was the case, there'd be no spirit mediums and the like, innit? They'd get sick after one possession.'

'Not necessarily,' I reply. 'Mediums are trained individuals, skilled practitioners, as it were. Also, mediums are only possessed for, like, a couple of minutes before the spirit leaves. Not days and days.'

'I think you're onto something there. If you're right, the spirit is possessing the Monks of the Misty Order one by one, burning them out in turn. We should tell Priya. It might help with Max's treatment.'

'You do that, Jomo, and let me know what she says.' At least that will get the two of them loved up again, after that tiff over the book. He's up in an instant, but I recall something. 'You said there was another way to find out what was going on?'

'Let me call Priya first, then I'll fill you in. We can meet tonight – I'll text you a time,' he says, rushing out.

So much to do. But if I'm right, at least I've solved the thing that started this whole mess in the first place. Naturally, Callander will have to be told. Allah, I wish I was getting paid for this gig. That'd be me cashing out now, but bloody Cockburn shafted me good and proper.

You know what? Screw Rory MacCulloch. Him and his pals invited this thing in, so let them deal with it. I don't like loose ends, but I've done my bit. I've fulfilled my commission; mission creep ain't an option. Let the possession bollocks be someone else's problem. It's clear to me now that the Paterson fortune's the only way I get out of this rodent race, and that's what I should pivot to, period. Sir Callander's done right by me, but I can't pay the bills or keep Izwi at home with goodwill.

Get it done right and I'll be laughing all the way out of the bank.

XXXII

I've had a nice shower 'cause Jomo snuck me into the staff quarters, so I'm feeling fresh in yesterday's gear. Seems like the librarians are cool with indoor plumbing since it's been there since Roman times, but they draw the line at electricity. A bit of kip's done me good, and I'm recharged and back on the grind, taking River down the sneaky steps leading to Holyrood. I have to stick to the right side of the path 'cause the vegetation sticking out of the stone wall's getting out of hand.

Today's a scorcher, and I keep a bottle of water with me. Heat rises off the tar, making Edinburgh feel like an oven. When it gets really bad folks faint on the pavements, especially the elderly. I'd love to stay in the shade, but I have work to do. Gotta pick up Tom and be the tour guide once again. I also have to find out where the bloody hell Ship Close was and see if it holds any clues about the Paterson fortune. The road itself no longer exists, but there'll be something there, I'm certain. Reckon I'll do that when I get into the bank later this morning to debrief Callander.

My phone rings and I fish it out. Priya.

'Top o' the mornin' to ya,' she says with a poorly done Irish accent. 'I spoke with Jomo last night, and I can't tell you how happy we are with your investigation. Kicking myself 'cause our initial diagnosis was so far off. The human body is the most resistant thing there is to magic. That's because it's a vessel of will, like I told you, but these boys have somehow managed to bypass it. Max Wu and Doug Duffie have a rare case of Schöner's animaluxation. Even Lethington says he hasn't seen it in clinical practice.'

'Now you know the cause, are Max and Doug going to be okay?' I ask.

'That's why I'm calling. I've been up all night at the clinic consulting old texts, since it's hardly ever mentioned in modern literature.'

'But there is a cure, right?'

'It's complicated. We need to realign Max's soul to his body because that's all been thrown out of whack. But to do that, we have to know who occupied the body in the first place. Without that, we can't quantify the levels of disharmony. We need a name, Ropa.'

Fuck's sake, this shit never ends.

'Hello, you still there?'

'Yeah, I'm here.'

'You heard what I said about the name of the spirit, right?'

'I'll have it for you soon,' I reply.

'Brill, time is of the essence.'

There goes my exit strategy. Lame to even think I was anywhere close to being done with this hustle. It's all tied together, and I gotta unravel the whole thing else nothing works, like when Izwi messes with Gran's wool and I have to spend hours untangling it. I'll get that spook's name one way or the other.

Jomo's plan for tonight better work.

'When's V-Day, lads? Are you winning?' I ask Rooster Rob's sentries. They're manning the barricade near the Meadow-bank side.

'We're mopping up already, Ropa Moyo,' one of them replies triumphantly. 'Were it not for this heat we'd be done already. Maybe you could lend us that fox of yours to hunt down the last few. That'll help us finish this thing off for sure.' He winks at us.

'Sorry, but she's already got a job.'

Summer mornings like this, Camelot's a riot of colour, from the bright yellow gorse to the vivid green, red and blue polyester tents dotted about. There's clothes hanging out to dry, stretched out on bushes, and skinny-dippers bathing in the Dunsapie Loch. They've got sheep and a couple of goats grazing here too, some porkers in a pen. I need to get myself invited to a barbecue here sometime. That's just my tummy talking.

A steady stream of men carrying wares descend the hill to sell in the city. They move slowly and deliberately under the unrelenting heat. It'll be a mix of pilfered and legit goods, I reckon. That's just how things work up atop the hill.

I get to the double-decker bus.

'Tom, you good to go?' I call.

I knock on the folding doors, making a racket, but don't get no response. Then I peer through the windows, trying to see if there's anyone on the lower deck. Knapf. It's empty. No choice but to enter. I call out as I ascend to the top deck.

He's not here.

Still early. He could be somewhere around the hill, taking a dump or doing whatever. I'll wait a couple of minutes. I lounge on the front bench and check out folks going about their business. A bearded tinker's busy shoeing his mule. Boys flying home-made kites high up in the air like they don't have a care in the world. Good for them. I seldom have time to fanny about or do anything fun.

Come on, Tom, let's get going already.

I give it half an hour and mess about on my phone before deciding to look for him. Can't be far. He's not supposed to leave the hill without me or a member of the Clan looking after him.

'Out we go before the ticket inspector catches us, girl,' I say to River.

There's a big old circus tent nearby, the grandest on the hill, and that's Rob's hame. I roll back the tarpaulin and go in, through a narrow aisle with terrace seats on either side. Smells like a tavern in here. There's stacks of television boxes and others advertising gaming consoles. Stolen, obvs. The boxes of mobile phones catch my attention too.

'Hail to thee, thane of Camelot,' I say. 'This war must be wearying business.'

'Heavy is the heid that dons the croune, for it be made o' razor an' thorn,' he replies.

Rooster Rob's sat in an old-fashioned metal bathtub at the far end of the tent. It's not connected to any plumbing or anything like that. He picks up a small pail filled with ice and uses it to top up his bath. A couple of goons are hanging out in the tent, already in various states of intoxication.

'A man cannae get nae peace with yous aboot, Ropa Moyo,' the Rooster complains.

'There'll be plenty of that when they plant us.'

'Odds are it'll be yous first, at the rate you're going.'

Here we go again.

'Where's Tom?' I ask, changing the subject.

'Do I look like a nanny?'

'Christ, Rob, cut me some slack. Your money's coming, and last I checked, Tom was paying you quite a bit for this glamping experience.'

'You two,' Rob orders his goons, 'go find Tom so I can get some peace. Nae one comes up or down this hill without me knowing of it.'

He sinks into the tub, submerging himself fully. The stress of the war must be getting to him 'cause he's a bit more meh than usual. In a tent like this you can almost imagine an army camped out, adjuncts coming and going with orders and battle plans. Surviving in Edinburgh's a forever war, that's for sure.

I wait on the terraces, and after a good while, the goons come back with word they can't find Tom.

'He isnae anywhere on the hill, Rob,' one of them says.

The Rooster sighs long and loud.

'You lot only had one job,' I say, pinching the bridge of my nose.

'Spread word for the lads tae find his arse in one piece an' haul it back here,' Rob says to the goons. Then to me, 'I'll give yous a bell when I get word.'

Great, now these guys have lost the golden bloody goose. Of course the war's disrupted them, but that's no excuse for any of this. Nothing for it, I have to keep moving, but not before I swipe one of the mobile phones from the pile of pilfered wares. That's payback for the retainer the Rooster took off me.

XXXIII

I'm proper raging by the evening 'cause the Clan still ain't found Tom. They have eyes and ears throughout the city, but they've only got so much bandwidth, given that they're in the final stages of a war. I've been all over the city myself trying to locate him, and have duffle bags filled with thin air for my efforts. Even went down to the archives and was told he hadn't been. That's a whole day down the drain, and now me and Jomo have to be making moves while I've got all that swirling in my mind, like.

So we're on a tricycle Jomo procured, parked up at the arse end of the Cowgate before it turns into Holyrood Road. At least it's still the city centre, 'cause I've been tramping about so much I couldn't be arsed going any further than this.

Poor Jomo's shaking like a leaf despite the heat. I can tell he's all nervous, and I wish it hadn't come to this, but I'm not seeing too many other options at the mo.

'Pull it together, you've got this,' I say.

'Maybe Priya was right. I've never even cheated in an exam, and now I'm playing Burke and Hare with you. I'm practically a grave robber,' he moans.

Jomo explained the plan to me earlier, on the phone. I can't say I love it, but we're all outta options. Basically, the book Sir Callander was after is the 'essence' of Bo Bumblebeam. A book of all his memories, thoughts and what have you. That way, we can find out who possessed him and the others – and who's in Rory's body now. Find the name, cast out the ghost, cure the teens and Bob's yer uncle. Problem solved.

But to create the book, we need Bo's body. Bit gross, but I don't see how else we're going to save those teens.

'Hey, this bodysnatching was *your* plan. It's for the cause, and your paperwork seems legit, right?'

'I stole it from my dad's office. He's gonna kill me if he finds out.'

'It'll be fine, trust me.'

He swallows hard, and I finally come out of the trike's cab. The body of the cab's signed 'West Port Sundries & Deliveries'. We chain the thing down, because, you know, Edinburgh. And then we head for the grey brick office. It's only two storeys high, a little removed from the street, with a car park in front of it; bland post-war shit that makes no effort to blend in with the traditional architecture of the Old Town. There's a massive shuttered bay door, but the entrance is glass.

A small weather-beaten plaque on the wall says 'City Mortuary, 297 Cowgate'. Jomo buzzes, and when he announces he's from the Library, the door unlocks.

The godawful smell of putrefaction mixed in with bleach hits me soon as the door swings open. Makes me want to puke, but I scrunch up my face, cover my nose with the sleeve of my jacket and soldier on. Rats scurry out into hidden nooks along skirting boards. The fluorescent lights flicker and I catch shadows, a handful of lingering souls milling about the place. Deados are attracted to places linked with death because it's somewhat easier for them to tether to this world. But they can't travel far in the summer, when the everyThere's pull is strongest.

'The power was off during the heatwave this afternoon, and, for that matter, most other days too,' a slurring voice says from somewhere within. 'Half my fridges are broken, and the council don't want to know, then you've got all them bodies they keep bringing here. Cut-throats in the fleshmarket dump them right outside in the car park some weekends. No room left at the inn even if baby Jesus, Mary and Joseph were to come round here looking for a place to stay. I've got bodies lining up the corridors. You're the young librarian. I remember you from last time.'

'It's nice to see you too, Mansoor,' Jomo says.

'Who's she? Where's Sneddon? What're you playing at?' Mansoor emerges from within, pale, bald, looking like a corpse himself. 'Thirty years I've done this job, and I ain't never seen no female librarian before.'

'Congratulations, you've seen the yeti,' I reply.

Mansoor retrieves a rollie from behind his ear and lights up, regardless of the dated 'No Smoking' signs on the walls.

He regards us suspiciously with bloodshot eyes, then says, 'Paperwork.'

Jomo hands over a sheaf of papers all filled in, along with some crisp banknotes, which Mansoor pockets immediately. The old man grunts and nods.

'You tell them it takes some doing to replace a corpse as

271

distinctive as the one you're after. Them peanuts don't cut it no more, not if I have to be stuck out here all night mutilating someone's da so I have something for the pathologist in the morning. On top of that, you lot don't pay me enough for all them ears I keep sending you. What do you use them for anyway? You know what, don't bother answering that. I don't want to know. Our arrangement's got to be changed. It's only fair. Now go outside. I'll open up the loading bay for you.'

Turns out, as Jomo reveals while waiting for Mansoor, the librarians are part-time 'resurrection men' and they've been at it for centuries. Back in the nineteenth century, industrious types used to steal dead bodies from Edinburgh's graveyards, selling them on to the medical school for dissection. Grim trade, but as long as it was done quietly, the law turned a blind eye. You can still see the results in Edinburgh's old graveyards, where some of the graves have iron bars round them to deter the resurrection men. Burke and Hare took the grift too far, as everyone knows. Them two were like, why wait for people to drop dead when you can knock 'em off yourself, guaranteeing a fresh supply of corpses . . . I wonder what the Library's stance on that is nowadays.

'Come on, you two, I've not got all night,' Mansoor says, rollie dangling off his lips. He has a trolley with a body bag on it. 'This the right one?'

He unzips it, and sure enough, Bumblebeam's there bearing the stigmata. Jomo's method better work, 'cause I ain't chancing trying to find the dead guy's soul in the every-There. That and the fact that there's another ghost mixed up in all this means if I went through, I wouldn't know what sort of reception I might receive. Normally ghosts just shuffle aimlessly. But I'm not about to jump in and find myself sandwiched between two hostiles on their own turf.

Jomo frowns and nods, pushing the cycle into the bay.

'Quickly now, I don't want any more flies getting in here,' Mansoor says.

'Have you sorted the body for us already?' Jomo asks.

'I've been doing this from since before you were born. Innards out, save for the heart and the brain, same as always.'

'Thank you,' Jomo replies.

'Thank yourself and get on with it now. My friends are inside waiting for me. It's poker night.' As far as moody morticians go, Mansoor's in a league of his own. I just hope he ain't playing poker with the dead, that's all.

I grab the legs while Jomo holds the upper half, and we lift on three. Doing my back in with this. Bumblebeam still weighs a bit regardless of his missing insides. Give me ghosts any day. I don't think anything in life quite prepares you for the experience of trying to load a stiff onto a tricycle hearse on a hot summer's night in Edinburgh, that's for sure. Of course, rigor mortis has set in. Mansoor watches us with some amusement as we stumble about trying to get Bumblebeam in the cab at the back of the tricycle.

'You know, you two could have just slid it straight on from my trolley,' Mansoor says, lowering his trolley to wind us up.

'Thanks a lot,' I reply.

He laughs heartily, before falling into a coughing fit. I swear, working amongst the dead like this is bound to make you lose your marbles. Soon as his lungs are clear, he takes another drag from his fag and waves us off. The shutters to his loading bay make quite the racket on their way down.

There's no more room left for me on the trike, and I'm cool to walk alongside while Jomo pedals. I've done enough cycling today, and my knees don't wanna do it no more. Still, as I'm walking, I keep an eye out for Tom, just in case.

XXXIV

The librarians' entrance – not the Society one on Calton Hill – lies in David Hume's mausoleum in the Old Calton Burial Ground. Back in the eighteenth century, a Jewish dentist by the name of Herman Lyon was looking around for subterranean real estate for him and his wife, since they weren't allowed to be buried in the Christian cemeteries, and the city hooked them up with this spot. It became the go-to joint for non-believers too. It's a dope location with stunning views over North Bridge across the New Loch, right through to Edinburgh Castle.

Couple of ghouls are milling around, watching, as they do. One thing the dead have on their hands is time, lots of it, and I envy them for that. Jomo unlocks the mausoleum, the gate's hinges squeaking as it opens. He kneels and presses on a secret rock that opens the underground entrance.

'Back in a sec, I need to get the ramp for the trike,' he says, descending into the darkness.

I hang back, waiting under the quarter moon hanging in the sky. Doesn't take long, though, before he returns, and I guide the trike down the ramp into the long, sloping corridor with ancient symbols marking the walls. Torches light our way as we descend, until we find an annex where we leave the bike and carry the corpse ourselves.

This late at night, every sound we make echoes, and my heart's thumping like a bongo drum.

'I'll go first,' I whisper as we reach the stairway that ascends into the Library proper. Figure whoever's bottom will bear the brunt of the weight.

'Yeah, only if you know the directions,' Jomo replies.

Fair point.

And so I end up bottom, with Bumblebeam's legs over my right shoulder. I have to lean in and give it everything I got. Both arms in it and my back's killing me, but we make progress, trying our best to be quiet. Easier said than done on hard stone floors.

'Stop,' says Jomo when we near the top.

The sound of footsteps on the landing is just as unbearable as this weight I'm carrying. Once they pass, Jomo gives the all-clear and we emerge onto the middle tier of the Library. There's a reader leaning on the balcony of the lower tier, absorbed in her work. Luckily, she doesn't look up, else we'd be busted. We keep to the shadows as best we can, but it's damned hard to be inconspicuous lugging a corpse between us.

Jomo scurries into a corridor and we hide behind one of the bookshelves carved out from the rock of the hill itself. I lean the body against a shelf to relieve some of the weight as a set of footsteps goes by.

Then we're off again, struggling along until we get to an archway with Arabic-looking script and a large double door dotted with brass studs. Jomo pushes it open, and we walk into a massive, brightly lit room, candelabras dangling on sparkling golden chains from the ceiling.

I shut the door behind us, using my foot.

The room is long and rectangular like the nave of a Gothic cathedral twice as large as St Giles'. But it doesn't give you the silent chills of a church, nor the dignified quiet of the Library. I sense rumbling vibrations. Not sound or anything like that, but something akin to waves crashing into one another, a churning ocean. This room makes you feel submerged deep down, as though when you leave you're sure to come out with a severe case of the bends.

'Move, man,' Jomo says, 'cause I'm lingering. 'It's okay, there's no one in here. You have to book a slot to be admitted into this reference section, and I checked the list earlier.'

'You nearly took me in here the first time you brought me to the Library, but your father stopped us, remember?'

'Ropa, you've not seen half the Library. You wouldn't be allowed in anyways. You're just an associate member, not a full member.'

'Cheap shot.'

'No hard feelings – all students are associate members of the Library. Only registered practitioners get full membership. This is the actual Library of the Dead.'

'—?'

'I know, I know, everyone calls this whole place the Library of the Dead. But in reality, you have two libraries in here. Out there, that's Calton Hill Library, where we keep the texts. This place here is the actual Library of the Dead, where we keep our books. You may borrow texts, as you do, but you can't ever borrow our books. Doesn't matter who you are. You read them here and here alone.'

This place, man.

The floor is worked into intricate geometric designs sprawling out in a seamless style like Moroccan tiles, only the polished patterns are cut into the rock itself. And in the pattern's grooves is the most incredible flow of metallic filler which keeps the floor even. It's like that kintsugi thing they do to fix pottery with precious metal in Japan, only here it goes right along the floor, the silver a sharp contrast to the black rock of the hill. It shines in the candlelight, giving the illusion of flowing rivers of mercury. The channels are like veins and arteries, capillaries branching off. Takes my breath away.

There are no windows, naturally, but where the main Library section makes do with chisel-marked stone walls, here artists have worked in classical reliefs polished to perfection. I'm having a hard time keeping this body aloft and checking this place out at the same time.

'Pretty cool, hey?' Jomo says.

'It's alright,' I reply.

The figures on the wall are so lifelike their robes appear to be fluttering in the wind. Maybe a trick of light, but goddamn. Running beside us are channels of water. The surface of the liquid ripples in waves agitated by the vibrations in the air. Maybe this is what it is like to be sat inside a human heart, because this room feels alive.

Jomo leads us through a tunnel with smooth walls that descends until we find ourselves in another small room that resembles a morgue. But I feel an intense longing, as though something's tugging me into the large room again.

I want to feel those vibrations.

To feel life.

We place Bumblebeam's body onto a stainless-steel mortuary dressing table.

'I need to go back upstairs to check that Library out, Jomo.'

'You're feeling the pull, aren't you? There's a reason you book a session – because sometimes a librarian has to kick you out for your own good. They say in the past, some magicians starved to death reading, unable to tear their eyes off the books. Librarians are trained to resist, so be careful, Ropa. Anyways, I need your help right here.'

Jomo unzips the body bag all the way down. The smell is indescribable. He heaves and runs to the bin to puke his guts out, saying, 'Sorry, sorry, excuse me,' between bouts. I pat his back until he's done. Then he straightens up, eyes glazed like a zombie's, and grabs a bottle of water. He swigs and spits into a barrel at the back of the room.

'My dad . . . Dr Maige thinks I'm not cut out for this,' he says.

'Doesn't matter what he thinks.'

'But, hey, if I can't qualify as a librarian, he says the Library will always need cleaners. I guess that's something.'

'Screw him, man. You know yourself better than anyone, and that's all that matters.' I poke him in the chest and hold my finger there. 'Under the sword lifted high, there is hell making you tremble. But go ahead, and you have the land of bliss.'

'What does that even mean?'

'Just something some old Japanese geezer told me.'

'Whatever. I'm going to make this book.'

We kit up in aprons, gloves and goggles available in the

room. Makes us look like pros. Jomo asks me to help him turn Bumblebeam's body onto its left side. Then he goes round to the back and rolls the body bag under it. After that, we heave it to the right and I take the body bag away. There's holes in the back of Bo's body, exit wounds from the attack.

'You've heard of Sculptor's Cave, right?' Jomo asks.

I shake my head, clueless.

'Hundreds of years ago they used to sacrifice people in caves here in Scotland. Powerful ritual stuff. They even sacrificed kids, and they'd let them desiccate where animals couldn't get to them. I know you talk to ghosts and everything, but after they cross over, it's a mission to locate them. That's why you need the body, because it contains knowledge that simply rots away unless something is done to preserve it. Spirits can mislead you, but the body never lies. It's the source of ultimate truth. What we do in the Library of the Dead is turn body language into books.'

The chat seems to distract Jomo from the gruesome nature of the work as he launches into talk about anthropomancy and slinneanachd, the ancient practices from which the Library of the Dead derives its craft. There's a vigour and an enthusiasm about him too, something between an artist and a mad scientist. He has an array of instruments on a tray that don't look wholesome. Like, old surgical stuff, bone saws and scalpels.

'You good?' I say when he wipes his brow with his sleeve.

'I've seen Dr Maige do this a couple of times and I remember every step of the process. I'll show him.'

Jomo starts cutting into the skull, and now I feel like I'm the one who's gonna void my tea.

XXXV

Shattered don't even begin to describe it when I emerge from the Library at dawn with River. I've left Jomo hard at it 'cause the process of 'making a book' is no mean feat. Kinda seems like he wants to outdo his dad more than anything else, and I can't blame him for it. It's a toxic fuel to burn, but it's got him motivated and we need to get this job done anyhow. By the time this is over, I'm splitting what I receive from the fortune three ways, and maybe that'll buy Jomo freedom too. Just gotta find Tom first.

Another braw day and all. Reckon I need to touch base with my peeps, maybe catch some zzz before I head back into town. Jomo says the book will be ready tonight.

'Spare some change, please?' a beggar asks me at the foot of the hill.

I stop, fish through my backpack and give him two plums and a crab apple. That's all I've got.

'Bless you,' he says as I ride away.

Maybe that's what I'll do with some of my dosh, give it to folks without a plastic bag to their name. Me, Gran and Izwi don't need much. Just something to get us set up. A house with running water, meds for Gran, school for Izwi, steaks for River and maybe a new pair of boots for me.

A car toots behind me as I'm cycling down Princes Street with River trotting along. I'm already on the verges, so I keep on going. It toots again. I'm about to give it the finger when I turn back and spot Callander in his Bentley. I swear this city's too small.

'We really should stop meeting like this,' I say.

'Put your bicycle in the boot. There's been an incident at the archives,' he says.

'I don't think your boot's big enough.'

'Haven't I already taught you something about splicing space, Miss Moyo?'

Duh – magic.

He pulls the Bentley up beside me and I dismount. The electrics behind honk furiously because he's straddling lanes and they can't get past, but he doesn't seem rushed.

Once I'm done loading the bike, I jump into the leather seat beside him and have River sit on my lap. We leave slowly, the engine rumbling like a beast. Once I have cash, I'm definitely getting myself a licence . . . when I turn sixteen. I'll be able to buy an electric car with all that money. Only important people like Sir Callander are allowed fuel for their cars. Everyone else has to make do with horses, bikes or trotters.

'A magician attacked the archives, and as you can imagine, the bank is demanding answers from the Society.'

'Rory MacCulloch?'

'Relations with the RBS are strained enough as it is without some rogue practitioner burning down one of their facilities. As you can understand, this also places us at odds with the

282

OUR LADY OF MYSTERIOUS AILMENTS

Library. Such a situation should never have been allowed to occur.'

There's a great deal of irritation in Callander's voice, fury in his eyes, as he takes us down the West Approach. The top's down and the wind blows against my face. Blue skies horizon to horizon, sunshine, and in this warmth I worry the ice I'm skating on's getting thinner by the moment. The whole thing's falling apart. Eilidh is gonna spill the beans and I'm busted. I've told Callander about everything except Tom. What if he's missing 'cause Rory got to him up on Camelot? I have to consider that possibility. So puppet Rory snatched him, extracted information about the fortune, and now he's hunting for proof from the archives. That's got to be it, surely?

But what would this ghost be wanting with all that cash anyway? Unless . . .

Fuck me.

Priya said she needed the name of the ghost to heal the Edinburgh School boys. I fish my phone out of my pocket and text her: 'Try William Paterson!'

It all makes sense now. The Monks of the Misty Order, Bo, Max Wu – all of it. Bunch of schoolkids messing about with shit they don't understand, and now Paterson's using them to reclaim his fortune. How could I not have seen this before? I've been dealing with ghosts since I was a little girl, and one thing I know is that the number-one reason they linger in the everyThere, refusing to move on, is because of unfinished business, usually involving a grave injustice. Figures. At long last, Paterson wants his money back.

'Is there something you want to tell me?' Callander asks.

'Oh no, I'm good,' I say.

Now you've gone and made a mess of it like a right muppet, Ropa.

Of course, the man calling himself Thomas Mounsey probably isn't even a descendant of Paterson. He's an imposter. The Paterson family got fobbed off a long time ago and haven't come for this money since then 'cause they couldn't prove nothing. I just heard a foreign accent and bought it hook, line and sinker like a mug. I was too busy chasing bucks like my middle name's Diana. This is not good. I can hear the ice cracking under my feet.

I'm such an eejit.

I have to fix this.

Okay, so this Thomas Mounsey guy's trying to run the scam of the century and he manages to piss off the ghost of William Paterson, who comes back with great vengeance and furious anger. So now we've got Bo Bumblebeam dead, an attack on the archive, Max Wu and Doug Duffie hanging by a thread. I'm gonna catch the blowback when this almighty clusterfuck comes tumbling down.

'Roger that,' Priya texts back.

I just need to calm down and think, find some way of sorting this without compromising myself in the process . . . In for a shilling, in for a ducat.

The electric gates are already open when we swing into the archives. There's some mean private-security types in Kevlar holding automatic weapons. They wear black fatigues with no identifying insignia as to who they work for. A fire truck. No police cars though. Looks like the bank's keeping this in-house. Makes sense. If it's a cash robbery, they'll have the law seek it out, but they don't want anyone snooping around in their holy of holies in ways they can't control. If the police make this a crime scene, they'll have access to everything. They are the state, and the state is the monarchy.

This city, man – it stinks.

The look on Eilidh Logan's face when she sees me makes me want to turn tail, but ain't nothing else for it now. She's standing in the car park with some executives in sharp business suits. They're three middle-aged men with the sort of corporate similarity that makes them look like they were manufactured in the same factory. A firewoman in fatigues is explaining something to them.

It's there again, that chemical scent, kinda like burnt plastic, harsh at the back of your throat.

'Please excuse us,' Eilidh says to the firefighter when we arrive.

'Was anyone injured? What was taken, and how bad is the damage?' Sir Callander gets straight into it.

'This was done by one of your people,' the tallest of the corporate geezers says.

'An attack on the bank by a magician leaves a very sour taste in everyone's mouth,' says the one to his left. 'The Society is supposed to *protect* our assets.'

'The security of this facility was never entrusted to us,' Callander says. 'You have lessened your reliance on us, and the bank pushes us further to the fringes with each passing year.'

'That was the king's decision, and you know exactly why. Your position was untenable.'

'He froze our stake. But there's nothing in the edict that directed you to remove our seat on the board and withdraw cooperation in other areas.'

'So you admit then that you planned this attack to get back in,' the man on the left says. 'Two guards, badly injured. Men with families, all so you could try to overturn—'

'I'd be very careful before I started making such accusations,' Callander says, lowering his voice to a growl.

There's quiet, and I notice no small amount of discomfort on the face of the banker who challenged him. Sir Callander can be intimidating like that. He's not your sweet grandpa; he's the sort you know can deck you if you push him.

'The Society also keeps important records here,' Eilidh points out.

'That may be true, but our CEO demands answers,' the tallest banker replies, retreating from his allegations.

Just then, a small two-door electric vehicle drives through the gates at speed and parks beside Callander's Bentley. Out springs Dr Maige, moving faster than I've ever seen him. The archivists are part of the Library, after all. It makes sense he would be concerned about their welfare.

'The collection,' he says . . . Or maybe not. It's the documents he is more concerned about.

'Most of them are safe, but we've lost a stack of correspondence dating back to the Equivalent Company, which received the charter to create the Royal Bank of Scotland. We don't know which letters specifically, just now, but the whole team is looking into it,' says Eilidh. 'A fire was set in the front office, but there's nothing there we can't replace.'

'Were the documents digitized?' Dr Maige asks.

'Requests for funding to do that have been made over the years, but none has been forthcoming.'

'We have to find out who did this and retrieve our lost property. The bank will authorize whatever monies are required,' the tallest banker says.

From what 'Tom' told me, the Equivalent Company holds a special place in the bank's history. The theft of these documents must be an attack on its very soul.

'The culprits will be found and dealt with accordingly,' Callander says severely.

That earns me a look from Eilidh, for bringing Tom into their midst, but she doesn't rat me out. Thank the Buddha for that.

'Excuse me, but who on earth is this little girl and why is she dressed in a lab coat?' the second man asks, noticing me.

'She is an employee in our General Discoveries Directorate,' Callander replies.

'I've seen it all now,' the man says.

'Perhaps we should concentrate on facilitating the retrieval of any and all lost documents,' Dr Maige says firmly. It's clear what his sole focus is.

'And then maybe we can get round to ensuring this does not happen again,' Eilidh adds.

While the office was destroyed, we still have CCTV footage, and we huddle around a small LCD screen as one of the security men presses play. It starts with a figure approaching on the desolate South Gyle Crescent. I recognize the puppet-on-a-string gait instantly. Ominous and yet strangely purposeful.

Rory MacCulloch inspects the gate for a moment. The image isn't really sharp and he's obscured by the metal bars on the gate, but you can clearly see him hold out his hand, and then the gate blows inwards. The first guard rushes to meet Rory in the car park. He moves swiftly, crouching, firearm pointed. There's no audio, but I get the sense he is shouting something, orders, a warning maybe.

But he hesitates. Makes sense, 'cause what he sees in front of him is a teenager, a schoolkid. Then Rory waves his arm and something throws the guard high up in the air, out of camera shot.

Inside the facility, the footage is a much better resolution. The second guard manages to radio for help before he too is dispatched. Rory MacCulloch looks up at the camera, at us, and gives us his twisted smile.

XXXVI

When stuff comes rushing at you there's a temptation to jump in and go, like a dog chasing cars. You speed up when you really ought to slow shit down, step back and take a look at the picture from a different angle. After I leave the archives, I head home. It's just a stone's throw away, and I'm well frazzled. So much pressure. I have a headache, and nothing's going my way.

Need to recharge, restrategize and regain the initiative.

'Good to be home, hey, girl,' I say to River as she saunters into the comfort of her own burrow beneath our caravan.

I open the door of the cara and toss my bag on the counter.

'Ropa!' Izwi shouts, pouncing on me.

'Hey, sis,' I say, lifting her up.

Brahma, Vishnu and Shiva, she's a skinny little thing just like me, but she still weighs a ton. Must be 'cause I'm knackered like this. I carry Izwi across the cara and sit us down next to Gran, who is busy doing some crocheting. Thing about my sister is, when she blows her gasket, hot lava fizzes out, and that shit scalds like nothing else. But when that lava cools, our island grows a little larger and we find we have new fertile soil in which to grow our relationship.

'You've been gone for ages. Are you angry with me?' Izwi says.

'No, never. I love you too much for that, sis. I was working, that's all.'

'Talking to ghosts?'

'Sort of. I'm trying to find some missing items for some very important people.'

'Gran says when you lose something, you should always look in the last place you left it. Isn't that right, Gran?'

Gran chuckles and says, 'It works for me.'

'You know what, I might just try that. Thanks, sis.'

'Izwi, warm up some oats for your sister. She sounds exhausted.'

I yawn. More than you know.

But this is me, this is my life. Everything I do, I do for them two, and I wouldn't change that for anything in the whole wide world. Mornings like this in the eye of the storm, I just wanna freeze time. Here, now, this moment. Me, Gran and Izwi. That's my real fortune, and I wouldn't place it in any bank in the world, 'cause I keep it right here in a vault in my heart.

'Have you considered Gary O'Donohue's invitation yet?' I need to take my mind off work.

'Don't rush me,' says Gran. 'Is he paying you, is that what it is?'

I laugh. 'I'm busted, Gran. You know I'm a sucker for fresh tubers and bulbs. He's really nice.'

'I've already been married twice, Ropa. The first time was long before you were born, so don't you go about teaching me to suck eggs.'

'I'm never getting married,' Izwi says, rejoining us and handing me a bowl of oats. 'Boys are disgusting.'

'What about your boyfriend, Eddie?' I taunt her.

'Eww,' she says, and we laugh. Gran louder than us two, filled with mirth, so much that the caravan rocks back and forth.

These guys are so worth it. I have my oats, delicious 'cause Izwi added a teaspoon of home-made bramble jam, just the way I like it. We shoot the breeze, listening to dope beats off the Shanbehzadeh Ensemble Gran's been playing. They play bagpipes, but not the Scottish sort; theirs are even more whiny. Makes me think of geese for some reason. Gran ululates with the musicians in the song, and it rings out loud. She says that's a thing they used to do at celebrations when she was a little girl growing up in rural Zimbabwe. I've tried it too, but it kinda sounds weird coming out of my lips. Izwi's much better than I am at it, and once her and Gran get into it over the percussion, we've got a party going on. When I've had my fill, I fish out my mbira and start jamming along with the Bandari bangers coming out of our speakers.

After a while, the party starts to fade and I shuffle across to my berth. It don't take long before I'm knocking out them zeds.

I listened to a podcast a while back where this guy said he'd discovered the real reason behind everything that was wrong with the world. It wasn't our fault or nothing, that was just how it was. He had what he called the theory of the eternal spin. Like, the earth is spinning on its axis at unfathomable speeds, so we live our lives like children spinning around until they get dizzy. To top that off, we're on this merry-go-round situation circling the sun. Once every year we go yay, and then we're back at it again. All this spinning, these cycles – that's what drives everyone nuts, or so he thought. It's some sort of horrific amusement ride. The guy saying all this, Bill Hicks, was a comedian, and I don't know if he was serious or not, but I'm certain he was on to something when I wake up.

Izwi's not here, probably gone off to Eddie's to play. Gran's taking a nap. Sleeps upright with the crotchet still in her hands. I take the fleece that I was using and put it on her. Then I check my phone and see a message from Priya asking me to call her.

I don't wanna disturb Gran, so I step outside to make the call.

'Please tell me some good news,' I say, soon as Priya picks up.

'Using William Paterson's name didn't help the boys. He's not our ghost, sorry.'

What? That don't make sense. What other ghost would be interested in the Paterson fortune?

'Are you sure?' I ask.

'As sunshine. Sorry, but he's a dud.'

Knapf.

'I need more time to work another angle,' I reply.

'Max's organs are failing, Ropa. I don't think we can keep him like this much longer.' Priya's sombre, and that's not a good thing.

'I'm on it,' I say, hanging up.

Then I message Jomo to tell him I'm on my way.

I feel an overwhelming sense of sorrow checking out of the caravan again. Can't even say goodbye to Gran and Izwi properly. There's something Brother Musashi says about not letting yourself be saddened by a separation, but I can't seem to do it. He was all about not forming attachments and not stressing about material things, which is proper hardcore.

Most of what he says is true, but I just can't get myself to buy into this other stuff. The dude was a proper samurai, wandering about feudal Japan kicking ass, and I admire him for it. For walking the walk. Not too many folks can say they've done that. And there's a lot of what he says that I get with, but not that. I'm attached to my family, and I guess that makes me a different kind of warrior.

What Brother Musashi saw as a weakness is actually my strength, my reason for being here.

XXXVII

Head back up to Calton Hill Library with River and meet Jomo. So many people about the now. Magicians on their books looking posh and mysterious. This makes a change, 'cause there's days I come in and see no one else save for the librarians. Jomo takes me into the Gothic cathedral that is the Library of the Dead, and those seductive vibrations hit me again.

In the morgue, what I see laid upon the stainless-steel table makes my jaw drop to the floor.

'There's your book, Ropa,' he says, beaming with pride.

There's a certain look in his eyes. It's almost beatific, the sort a marathon runner has after the race is over and they know they've crossed the finish line.

I walk up to the table, not quite believing what I'm seeing.

There is a book . . . of sorts. Nothing like anything I've ever seen before. It's the size of them super-large church tomes, two and a half feet in length, another foot and a half in width. Nearly a foot thick. There's a dark beauty to it. Repulsive, yet enchanting, this strange artefact of bone and flesh gently pulses upon the steel table.

It's alive.

The spine is made from Bumblebeam's vertebrae, and the bones outside the book spread around it, a kind of exoskeleton. Running from this spine, right up onto the cover, are rib bones broken and reset. And that cover – made of flesh that looks so alive with moles, freckles, stubble, scar tissue, veins. It's all held together with hair woven into thread.

'Jomo, what have you done?'

The cover is Bo Bumblebeam's face. The book pulses softly, and I reach out to touch it.

'No, not yet,' Jomo says, grabbing my hand.

He digs in the pockets of his white robes, pulls out a pair of silken gloves and puts them on.

'Books are read in the Library, not down here.'

'I can't take my eyes off it,' I say.

'I already warned you, man. Tell yourself to resist the lure. Be ever mindful of it. The older books are even more alluring. That's why this section is reference only. No one's allowed to take these books out, like, ever.'

'I now know what it is to gaze upon the One Ring,' I say, shaking my head and pulling myself together. It takes everything I've got, every ounce of will, to turn away from the book.

Jomo takes the book carefully in his gloved hands and we ascend through the smooth corridor. He's struggling 'cause the book is weighty, but soon we find ourselves back in the splendour of the Library of the Dead proper.

The shelves rise as high as the ceilings and are made of dark, polished hardwood, carved in intricate designs. Pillars at their fringes make them resemble narrow four-poster beds.

But they have lace curtains in front of them so you can't see the books properly.

Probably for the best. In here the tug is strong, almost as though the books are calling to you, begging to be read. That's what it feels like deep in my core. I shake my head. *Get it together, Ropa.* It's the bloody lure . . . That's what they are: sirens. These vibrations are their music, and if each book is singing with its own pulse, then inside the Library you have the harmonies of a celestial choir calling underneath the burning lights of the candelabras.

I turn around, do a full three-sixty and keep following Jomo, but all I really want is to pull those lace curtains back and take one. No, I want to read them all, even if it takes me the rest of my life. I would stay here surrounded by this . . . Nah, that's crazy talk. I know Jomo's warned me, but the lure tugs at some place beyond reason.

'I get the sense sometimes that the books are watching,' says Jomo. 'Sneddon says when you read one it reads you right back.'

'Have you ever read one?'

'Nah, librarians aren't allowed to read the books, not even my father. Our role is that of custodians. We just keep them here for the readers. Don't get me wrong, I've been tempted. They say it's like being in someone else's mind. Can you imagine what it must feel like to be authentically inside of the head of a genius, to feel their thoughts formed like sparks setting off an inferno? They say it stretches the dimensions of your own mind, changes you forever. You have no idea how much I've wanted to try, but I'm becoming a librarian and I've learnt not to come in here unless I really need to. It's easier when you're with someone else. Sneddon says we librarians are bibliothetic priests and the price for admission into this clergy is our celibacy from the books . . . not that I've ever, you know . . . with a girl . . .' he says, face reddening, 'but I guess he knows what he's talking about.'

'He's a good egg, Sneddon.'

Jomo turns left into a gap between the shelves and steps over the small channel of water that runs alongside the main aisle. In front of us is a large white marble table, distinct against the dark rock behind it, almost like an altar.

My knees go weak.

I can hardly feel the ground beneath my feet, and I sway from side to side in a drunken shuffle. Being sandwiched between two aisles with shelves of books calling out is the equivalent of being the rope in a game of tug of war.

Have to remind myself of the mission.

I need to extract a name from the remains of Bumblebeam so Max Wu and Doug Duffie can be cured. Then get more details about the Monks, where Rory MacCulloch might be hiding out and what he's up to. Where they went, what they did, anything at all that I can use. That's the mission, and I repeat it like a mantra. The lure can't get me that easy. I've been hanging out with the dead for a while.

'Since the very beginning, the Library of the Dead has sought to harvest and preserve in perpetuity the cream of Scotland. Not just their work, their writings or biographies, but the very essence of their being,' says Jomo, very obviously echoing what someone else must have told him. 'We have them right here: academicians, doctors, scientists, inventors, mathematicians, leaders of all stripes from kings and politicians to military men and trade unionists; we have artists and composers, sportsmen too; magicians, naturally; every trade, every occupation, original thinkers of every stripe. The Library takes precedence over the remains of Scotland's dead, and these are the books in which the true history of Scotland was played out and its future penned and prophesied.'

These books are living things, life born out of death. Jomo gently places Bo's book on a velvet-lined missal stand upon the great marble table. Behind it, dropping all the way from the ceiling, is an incredible tapestry embroidered with scenes from key moments in Scottish history. The last third of it is bare, as if waiting to be updated.

I stand before it all in awe. And I see just how small I am. A mere stitch, barely visible to the naked eye.

'You ready to read, man?' Jomo asks.

'Sure thing, let's do this.'

For all the book's awesomeness, the fleshy cover wraps right round, even the middle bits where the pages are supposed to be, so you can't quite pull it open.

'Hold your palms out straight and slot them right there in the middle where there's no stitching.'

'Kinda like reading braille, right? Okay, here goes,' I say.

I plug myself into the book. The soft flesh warps and stretches, allowing my hands to go clean through.

It's like my body's been reversed and I'm floating through space. Only it's warm and I can taste nature all over myself, as though my tongue were my skin and I'd licked a meadow bursting out in the glory of spring. It feels wonderful, until I fade away, like a sentence chewed by a backspace key. My thoughts and being falling off me, away from me, out of me . . .

And then it hits me.

Loud, anguished screams. Rage and horror beyond language. A jolt, like touching a live high-voltage wire.

I'm immersed in the bodyscape of anguish. Drowning in fire. Looming over me, watching and inflicting, is the shadow of a spectre in a dishevelled horsehair wig. Pain like I've never experienced before explodes through my skull. It hurts. The spectre laughs and I smell death and decay. I need to let go. But my arms aren't my own. I'm frozen in a wave of agony. I want it to stop. Jomo's shouting but I can't make out the words. Everything's jumbled up. Oh no.

Make it stop.

Pure torture.

Pain shreds through every nerve, until any other feelings and thoughts are cancelled and submerged into the electric current ripping me apart . . .

XXXVIII

I scream, trying to pull my hands out, fighting with everything I've got. Forget the pain, this is about survival. I'm battling with pure instinct. My catapult? Dagger? My nails. I'll use anything at all. That scent of smoke, I think I'm burning. Bloody hell.

I open my eyes to a bright white light that sears my retinas.

'It's okay, Ropa, stop.'

'Am I dead?' I ask.

'No, you muppet, but you bloody well came close. Now stop thrashing about. You nearly knocked my gnashers out.'

I put a hand up over my eyes to block the light out. My hand. I got it back, in one piece too. And the rest of me, nose, face, ears, two legs; I think it's all there. Phew. As far as bad trips go, this takes the biscuit. Squint my eyes and peek out, colours dancing and swirling in my vision. I can't quite make anything out. Just shapes and shadows. Priya's sat next to me.

'Where am I?'

'Our Lady of Mysterious Ailments, and you don't want to know the bill you've racked up already. Lucky for you, it's all being charged to the Society as an accident at work situation. How are you feeling?'

'Like I've had my skin put back on inside out.'

'Bloody well should after the stunt you and Jomo pulled.'

When the swirling colours in my vision stop, I finally make out Priya sitting forward in her chair. She holds my hand and gently squeezes.

'Your bedside manner is crap,' I say.

'I'm a healer, not a doctor. I shoot straight from the hip. What were you thinking?'

'Things went tits up.'

'Royally. I'm really trying not to say I told you so . . . but I told you so, you silly sausage.'

'Don't, I know it now.'

Priya holds my other hand in hers. A thin film of water in her eyes. I try to smile, but my lips are so dry, I can barely pull the corners up. I'm in a luxurious room, on a single bed with plumped-up pillows. White sheet over my body. That smoke I smelt is some harsh incense in a bowl on my bedside table. Priya lets go of my hand and touches my forehead.

'I'm thirsty,' I say.

She pours me a glass of water from a carafe on my bedside table while I sit up. My hands are trembling, and I struggle to get it to my lips. Priya helps me steady it so I can drink. I swear that first gulp is the sweetest, most satisfying thing I've ever tasted in my life. Pure nectar. River pops up from somewhere under the bed and leaps onto me. Never been happier to see her in my life.

'Hey, girl, you good?' I say as she settles in my lap. Greyfriars Bobby ain't got nothing on River's loyalty, that's for sure . . . hmm . . .

301

I check out the robe they've put me in. One of them hospital ones. Damn, I think I'm in diapers too. Yeah, definitely. And I'm in such a state, I don't even have the decency to be embarrassed by it. We chill for a couple of minutes, but I can tell something's weighing on Priya's mind. It's written all over her face.

'Is Jomo okay?' I ask.

'Sorta, but you know what his dad's like.'

'How bad is it?'

Priya gives me the lowdown straight, without any condiments. Turns out the Bo Bumblebeam book Jomo (and me, I guess) cooked up was defective. It takes years of training before they'll let a librarian make one, and even then it will be under the supervision of their superior. Priya also says that reading the books takes great skill and only the best of magicians have mastery of that ability. The rest keep well away from the Library of the Dead – there's more than enough learning to fill several lifetimes in the Calton Hill Library, so why risk it? Having felt the incredible pull of the books, I see now this can only be right. But what's that they say about hindsight again?

Apparently, I had a wicked seizure after I tried to read the book. Was thrashing about on the floor with the damned thing attached to me, screaming like a banshee. River was having a good go at the book amidst it all, and that was enough to convince Jomo we'd screwed up badly enough to get help. The master of the books is Dr Maige, so I can only imagine how that went down. Anyways, the good doctor managed to salvage me in one piece, and they rushed me down to Our Lady for treatment.

What a ride.

'They want to see you, Ropa. I have to tell them you are conscious now. You feel up to it?'

No, I really don't, but I nod anyways. I can do this now or have it hanging over my head. Best to get it over and done with. Priya leaves the room, shutting the door behind her, and I look past the incense smoke, through the window to the garden outside. Brother Musashi says, 'Truth is not what you want it to be; it is what it is. And you must bend to its power or live a lie.' Time to face the music.

Sir Callander walks through the door. His face is unreadable. Dr Maige trails in close behind with Lethington in tow.

'How are you feeling, Miss Moyo?' Callander says, taking a spot at the foot of my bed. With the librarian to my left and the healer to my right, I'm surrounded.

'I've had better days,' I reply.

'You have the best care in all of Scotland,' says Lethington. 'No lasting harm has been done. Consider yourself lucky, young lady.'

'Miss Moyo, the Library is very disappointed by your actions,' Dr Maige says.

'Surely this can wait. The girl has been through enough as it is,' Sir Callander says.

'No, it cannot. Such breaches of trust are intolerable and go against everything my institution stands for. Ropa Moyo, I have come to the understanding that your association with my son is detrimental to his development. I must ask henceforth you cease any further association with him.

Furthermore, your membership of the Library has been suspended until we can ascertain you are able to comply with the rules.'

'This is ridiculous.'

'Sir Callander, when this young lady joined the Library, it was on the condition you would monitor and control her behaviour. It shall be made clear in my incident report that you have failed to fulfil that obligation. We have every reason to expect better of our patrons. That is all I have to say on this matter. Gentlemen, Miss Moyo, I bid you good day.'

Callander lets out an exhausted sigh as Dr Maige leaves the room. I get it. He's stood up for me as my mentor, but my actions impugn his credibility and standing. This whole thing's an almighty clusterfuck.

'Right, I shall leave you two to it then,' Lethington says. 'There's a call bell on the bedside table if you need anything.'

He leaves me alone with Sir Callander and my shame. Heaps of it. And the shame's a hell of a lot harder to bear compared to the razor strokes slicing into my nerves. Callander closes the door and sits on the chair beside my bed, so we're side by side. He crosses his legs and locks his fingers into a church steeple, resting the tip on his lips. He studies the painting of the Forth on the opposite wall, with the Bass Rock jutting out of the churning sea.

'I'm sorry,' I say.

'Hmm.'

There's nothing else for it. This is my mess and I have to own it. Here goes. I tell him everything, absolutely all of it: Thomas Mounsey, the Paterson fortune, along with the stuff he already knows about Rory MacCulloch and the Monks. The deal I struck with Tom and how I was seeking to profit from this whole situation. I leave nothing out, and when I'm done, I feel naked. Exposed.

Fuck my life.

Callander remains contemplating the picture, until I can't take it anymore. Must be what it's like standing in front of a firing squad. Only I've already taken several shots. Now I'm just tired.

'I already knew,' he says at last. 'I was waiting for you to tell me yourself. Eilidh Logan is my goddaughter. She came to me immediately with the information because she was worried about your safety. After your visit, she did some investigating, and I'm sorry to tell you, but Tom Mounsey isn't who he says he is. Paterson has no living relatives by that name, and we found no records of him at all.'

My stomach sinks. After all that, turns out the golden goose lays crappy pyrite eggs. Should've known better. Should've asked more questions.

'You've got yourself entangled in matters of which you know very little. Naturally, I was disappointed that you tried to deceive me, even though you know very well that I am ultimately responsible for your welfare in all matters pertaining to scientific magic.'

Earth swallow me whole; there's a strange sensation in the pit of my stomach. I can't bear the humiliation. It's over for me. I know I'm getting the sack. Guess that'll be for the best then, 'cause I've made a hash of things.

I look down at my legs and hope this meeting's over soon.

My mobile rings from the bedside unit, but I can't answer it right now.

Callander waits until my phone stops ringing.

'You are highly intelligent and resourceful, Ropa, but you would do well to remember that while you may use deception in the course of your industry, the relationship you and I share must be built on the bedrock of trust and integrity. Otherwise, we are only wasting each other's time. Recall next time that my name and my position are the cloak you wear upon your shoulders.'

Callander gets up. Wait a minute, is that it?

'I'm not fired?'

'That would be the easiest solution, wouldn't it? But I've lived a while, Miss Moyo. You are young, and your errors of judgement, while disappointing, are not unexpected in someone still learning. What is important now is for you to recuperate with haste and set about rectifying these costly missteps.'

I could almost cry. And when Sir Callander leaves, I do.

XXXIX

I've made a proper arse of myself, and I don't even receive the mercy of a dishonourable discharge. I could mope and staple donkey ears to my head, but I can't sit here feeling sorry for myself. Miyamoto Musashi says, 'Do not regret what you have done.' I think he doesn't mean for you to brush it off, but that you learn, grow and move on.

I have to fix this.

The question is, how?

I call Gran to let her know I'm good and out working. She'll be worrying otherwise, and I don't need that extra serving of humble pie for my dessert. I replay all the events over the last several days. In the midst of my pain and discomfort, I still have to work this thing out. The facts are all there, so it must be I've missed something crucial. If I was Sherlock Holmes I'd withdraw inside my mind palace, sorting shit out.

An orderly brings me food, but I don't want it.

What did I miss?

The image I saw reading the book of Bo Bumblebeam Jomo made. A spectre wearing a dishevelled horsehair wig. Who was it? That could be any nobleman from the seventeenth or eighteenth century. I need more than that.

When I first spoke with Lewis, he said Max had a theory that the Monks of the Misty Order don't tap you up. You have to find them. There's a clue I missed in there somewhere. They are secret, but they'd have to be discoverable for the Edinburgh boys to join.

I'm not looking for anything elaborate. Heard on a podcast about something called Occam's razor. You don't shave with it or anything like that. William of Ockham was some English Franciscan friar from back in the olden days. He came up with the idea that when you have a problem and you're setting up various explanations for what went down, the solution with the smallest number of assumptions is usually the correct one. They use that shit everywhere, in science, philosophy, medicine, whatever. Simplify. Don't overcook things. I like that, because it clears out all the noise, and there's been quite a racket kicking off the last couple of days.

William of Ockham . . .

Why am I so bothered by him?

Nope, I shouldn't allow myself to get distracted. My brain can be all scatty sometimes, but now's not the right time. Maybe I won't have my meal, but that jelly and custard sure looks nice. Need glucose for the noggin 'cause I'm thinking, innit?

Delish.

I give River the plate with the rest of my meal, and she gets stuck in before I even set the plate on the floor.

'Make sure you eat all your veg.'

Come on, focus. Follow the money.

This whole thing's about the wonga, and both Rory and Tom are treasure-hunting after the same loot with no maps.

To get to it, they have to prove its existence first, find the paper trail that leads all the way back to the Darien Scheme, the Equivalent Company and the bank. Now I know Rory's stolen stuff from the archives. I imagine this contains things Eilidh Logan didn't hand over when we went there, which means he has a certain edge.

When me and Tom went out there, he mostly went through ledgers and financial documents. We didn't find the smoking gun, so to speak.

What does this mean then?

Fuck's sake. My phone rings, breaking up my chain of thought. I fish it out of my bedside table.

'Well, hello there,' I say when I pick up the video call.

'Ropamatron!'

'Erm, aren't you banned from talking to me forever?'

'I was going out of my mind. My dad won't let me leave the Library, so I've literally been wandering about the place trying to find some cranny with a signal. And I found it right at the top, near the entrance. Are you okay, man?'

'Super-duper, never been better. Not every day a book tries to devour you.'

'I am so, so sorry.'

'It's not your fault, man. Schooled me, so next time some kid tells me to stick my finger in a power socket I really ought to give it some thought.' He sniggers, trying not to make noise. I can just about make out his face projected against a dark background. 'How's things with your dad?'

'Fam, he was livid. I got read the Riot Act. Can't blame him too much, though, 'cause you were looking like a goner proper. I shouldn't have made that cursed book. I swear, never again.'

'No use flagellating yourself, man. It's done.'

'I'm so happy to see your face.'

'Don't cheese out on me now, Jomo, we've got work to do. The only way I get back in is if I fix this mess.'

'Just say the word.'

'Keep checking your phone. I'll holler when I've got something for you.'

I'm about to hang up when Jomo says, 'Hey, Ropa . . . you look like the Bone Collector in that outfit.'

'He was the baddie in the film. I think you mean Lincoln.' I end the call.

I text Priya to come through when she's got a minute. Must be doing her rounds with other patients. She pings back her shift's through in an hour and she'll come round then.

Where was I?

Think.

Build up my Sherlockian mind palace once more and put everything in its rightful chamber. Now I'm outside that shit, looking down with a God's-eye view. No good wallowing in the mix like I was earlier. That's the kind of thing that got me in this five-star hotel inhaling weird incense.

It's all about the money.

Stands to reason both Tom and Rory, whoever the hell they really are, each hold pieces of the jigsaw. If Rory hadn't hit the archives then Tom would have found a way. He's got research that his father supposedly did, but it's not enough. This whole thing kicks off when he comes into town looking for this cheddar. Whatever he holds must be such an essential piece of the puzzle that Rory was willing to go after him.

Still something's missing. I can feel it throbbing harder than the pain coursing through my shot nerves.

Then there's Wilson and all this talk about someone else who's in on this racket . . . Rory ain't working for himself. It's clear he's serving some spirit. But if Tom's not really a Paterson heir, then who's he working for? Who stands to gain the most from this heist?

An invisible hand. Someone who can't act openly, of course.

Something that's been guiding our collective greed.

My leg's jiggling in the bed 'cause I'm revving up. What am I not seeing here? It feels so close, at the tips of my fingers. Tom's got the hypothesis about the existence of this cash, which sets this whole shitstorm off.

Still, that's not enough to facilitate restitution.

Because?

This is the world of finance, and it's the numbers that matter at the end of the day. They do all the talking. You have to have the accounts *proving* where the money went. But Tom said the family was shown this over a hundred years ago, so that's a dead end . . . unless . . . Oh my God, I'm an eejit.

'Ele-freaking-mentary, my dear River.'

This was right there in front of us when we went to the archives, and I totally missed it. We need to go back to the very beginning, right where this whole thing started. Tom even mentioned it, but I was so focused on the wonga in front of me, I couldn't see the invisible money behind it.

Because if you are running grift, cooking the books, you still need to keep oversight of where everything is. You keep one set of accounts for the taxman and another for yourself. That's how it's always been done.

The simplest thing is to find them ledgers with the original figures. Voila, there's all the proof you need in order to file a petition for restitution with the king. But these accounts could be anywhere.

Like in their original, booby-trapped safes.

Ship Close. And I'm sure I know that name.

Send Jomo a text, like, be my Alfred from the Batcave and get me the info I need. Then I throw my covers off and swing my legs over the side of the bed. Steady, I feel woozy. Hold on to the bedside unit for balance, rock back and forth a few times, gaining enough momentum to stand up.

'Hey, hey, where do you think you're going, Lady Lazarus?' Priya says at the door.

'It's party time. Put on your dancing shoes. We're going for a night out on the Old Town.'

XL

Feeling like a baby gazelle just birthed onto the savannah 'cause my legs are wobbly as spaghetti. Got my gear with me, backpack, katty, scarf. River's checking me out, like handle your drink better, and Priya's saying something about leaving against medical advice. But when a girl's gotta go, she gotta go.

I take a peek into Max Wu's room through the glass plate on the door, thinking, *Hang in there, wee man.*

I hold onto the walls as we make our way out 'cause I ain't steady yet. But I'm getting there. River stays close to me. Figure there'll be plenty of time to veg when they plant me, but I ain't doing that anytime soon. And soon enough we find ourselves out of the clinic in the warm summer air infused with scents coming off the herb garden.

Grab my bike and off we go.

Surprised by how out of breath I'm feeling as we come onto Bruntsfield Place. I'm having a hard time keeping up with Priya, sweating like an oinker too. My T-shirt's drenched. But at least we've got a nice downhill stretch towards Lothian Road.

It don't take too long before we're in the Old Town proper, heading up the High Street, where I dismount 'cause of the crowds. Loads of bunting flying mini Union Jacks in the air. Banners declare:

ONE NATION, ONE PEOPLE, **ONE KING**,
ONE FLAG, ONE DESTINY

Unity . . . right. I'm just here because of one schoolboy, one ghost and one wanker who called himself Tom. Sod the rest of it.

'Where to now?' Priya asks.

I check my phone and read the coordinates Jomo sent me. Legend – he'd have had to go up and down those awful stairs in the Library to get back to a place with reception again. That's what besties are for.

'There, the whisky shop across from St Giles' Cathedral.'

'Why aren't the shutters down? Shouldn't it be locked up for the night?'

'Let's hurry.'

Priya gives me cover while I retrieve my bag of tricks to work the lock, but the door's already unlocked. This closed sign upfront ain't gonna keep the horde from the liquor for long. They just ain't noticed it's open yet. We go in, trying to be as unobtrusive as we can. Past the counter. Bottles of single malt and hundreds of other alcoholic beverages on display. I'm tempted to grab a couple to sell – old habits – but that's not why I'm here.

A pair of dusty footprints on the linoleum floor.

Leading to . . .

The far corner, the door to the basement. Edinburgh's a

liar. She presents a prim front as though she's been forever frozen in time, but the reality is there've been many changes over hundreds of years. She's like Theseus's vessel, slowly morphing. And one of her old haunts was Ship Close, which is still here, but it vanished off the map long ago. If it weren't for Jomo's access to old city plans in the Library, it'd have been hard to find, but here we are on the site of what used to be the very first branch of the Royal Bank of Scotland. But what if, among these vaults of low ceilings and stone, the secret ledgers are here, hidden away for posterity? Those ledgers are the final piece of the puzzle as to what happened to the Paterson fortune.

I smell something harsh and acidic.

So much dust in the air, making it hard to see as we descend into the basement. It's already coating the bottles. I have to squint because it's irritating my eyes.

'Careful,' Priya whispers.

We wander past the stocks of merchandise, boxes and crates, until we find, right at the back, a massive hole blown through a false wall. Bingo, bitch.

Dark inside; it's impossible to see.

I turn on the torch on my phone and shine it through the hole.

Someone coughs from within. I duck to the side just in case and take cover by the wall. Priya disappears behind a shelf.

'Help me,' a weak voice calls from within. Sounds like a Londoner. What the hell is one of them doing here?

'Who's there?' I ask.

'Ropa? Is that you? Please help me.'

How do they know my name?

I've never heard that voice in my life. And yet something about it nags at me. I shine my torch once more through the swirling dust and debris within. I look at Priya, and she shakes her head. Too dangerous. River goes in without hesitation.

'Please,' they say.

I step in, navigating past the rubble, to find deep inside the cavity behind the false wall a large open vault. The door is thick, and rust has been eating away at it for centuries. The laboured breathing grows more intense as I enter the vault with Priya. The smell of burning flesh hits me.

'The Monks got me,' the man says. 'That kid with the weird haircut does spellcraft like a demon, mate.'

And now I know who it is. Tom Mounsey: swindler, conman and liar, but definitely no Paterson heir. Can't believe I let myself buy his schtick. Wasted so much of my time on this guy.

'You ain't no pal of mine.'

'So you figured it out. You're real smart, you know that? I'd have recruited you to the spooks after all this was over. They told me you were the weak link, which is why I worked you, but they were wrong.' He tries to laugh but winces in pain. 'Nothing personal. I did what I had to do for king and country.'

Spooks? King and country? A spy.

'I knew something was off with your accent, but I thought, what do I know about Canadians?' I say. 'You didn't intend to honour our arrangement. As soon as you discovered Ship Close, you bailed on me and the Clan. Then you came here

316

and spent time disarming the booby traps protecting the safe. But you didn't know Rory would find you.'

Looks like Tom got the short end of the stick.

He's scorched all over, and it's grotesque to see. My own skin burns at the sight of him like this, clothes seared into his flesh. Small tufts of hair remain. It's horrific, this, and I kinda liked him too.

But nothing about our partnership, our heist, was ever really true. I was just a mark to him. Those eyes. His real accent. An Englishman in Edinburgh.

Priya stares at him for a sec before her medical training kicks in. She reaches under her seat of her chair and retrieves her medical pack.

'It's too late for that. Water, please,' Tom moans.

I grab a bottle from my backpack, unscrew the cap and put it to his lips. He winces as I pour, trying to avoid his scalded lips.

What a mess.

'Here, give him this. It'll ease the pain,' Priya says, handing me a small dried sprig of some flower I don't know. I offer it to Tom, and he chews it with some difficulty, then immediately gives a sigh of blessed relief.

'There's a pack of fags in my right pocket,' he says.

The pocket's fried, along with the rest of his clothes, but I spot the singed packet next to him. Must have fallen out. I open it and find a cigarette that's been burned in sections but looks salvageable.

Place it in Tom's lips.

Can't find the lighter though.

Tom whispers something and a bright yellow flame appears in the air. I'm an absolute tool. Flashback to the first time I met him, I sensed something but didn't make out he was a practitioner. Of course he is. This is why Callander asked Balfour about the colour of the flames at the Advocates Library. I'd bet the entire fortune that Tom was responsible for Bumblebeam's death.

I was too busy chasing money to think too hard about who he was. It blinded me to the fact he knew my name when we first met. But now I get the distinct impression of a chameleon that's been changing colours all along, making me see what I wanted instead of the truth in front of my eyes.

'I'm guessing you weren't after the Paterson fortune as the long-lost heir,' I say. 'But what do "king and country" have to do with it?' I frown. 'What's the king got to do with anything?'

He laughs, but it turns into a cough. 'See, I knew you were smart. The kid with the stupid Beatles haircut has everything now. The little bastard got me.' He tries to smile and his lower lip splits. 'I didn't mean to lie to you, partner, but my superiors expect results, and sometimes, well, you get collateral damage.'

Hmm. Does this mean the king is the One Above All? Wilson did say I was working for him. By this he meant working with Tom, surely? Lines up with them 'taking care' of things at the Advocates Library.

'Priya,' I say.

She shakes her head. There's nothing she can do. We got here too late.

'Who's the One Above All?' I ask. 'Where did Rory MacCulloch go? Were you working with a man called Wilson?'

'Whoever holds the purse strings of magic holds Scotland itself. And—' Tom looks at me, those bright eyes dimming. He exhales for a long time, a steady stream of smoke, then air. Then nothing. Doesn't take another breath. The cigarette remains glued upon his scalded lips.

He's gone.

'Can you talk to his ghost?' Priya asks.

'It's too soon. The newly dead are without form, confused as newborns. It will be a few hours before we can get anything from him.'

'We don't have a few hours! Max won't be long after Tom if we don't hurry.'

'Is there anything here we can use?' I say, looking around the empty vault.

Nothing but dust, rubble and the lifeless body of the spook who called himself Thomas Mounsey. We were too late. Those footprints I saw upstairs. They must have been heading out of the store, because the dust came from down here. But they'd disappear in the crowds on the Royal Mile . . .

Would Rory go back to the Edinburgh School? Nah, he can't be that stupid. If only we'd been a few minutes earlier. All this happened 'cause I couldn't cycle fast enough. I put my hands on my head.

'Hate to be the devil's advocate, but it looks like we got outplayed,' says Priya.

'What did you just say?'

'We were outplayed.'

'No, before that.'

'I hate to be the devil's advocate?'

319

What was Bo Bumblebeam doing in the Advocates Library? It's just around the corner. Searching for something or seeking refuge in a familiar place? He wouldn't have been Bumblebeam then, I remind myself. He would've been possessed too. And the Monks of the Misty Order. So bloody obvious. I am a total dunderheid.

'We need to go now,' I say.

The vultures are already inside the shop, grabbing free bottles, by the time we emerge upstairs. The shop's heaving, and everyone's so busy looting, hardly anyone notices us as we slip out.

XLI

Me and Priya bomb through the crowds on the Royal Mile, and then down onto George IV Bridge with River bounding along behind us. Screw the pain, I'm busting a gut, high on adrenaline. It was right in front of me the whole time, but I missed it. Kicking myself 'cause of that spanker, hindsight. *Monks of the Misty Order.* An odd name for a bunch of school-boys to come up with, yet there I was thinking it was some random toff bollocks. How would an Edinburgh student find the fraternity in the absence of any other information by which one can join?

Grey is the colour of mist – there's your 'Misty'.

The answer was sparked by my elementary-my-dear-Watson gene when I was thinking about William of Ockham, earlier.

Where do you find monks in Edinburgh?

They're extinct, all except for the so-called Monks of the Misty Order.

But they were there, once upon a time, before the Reformation, back when Scotland was still Catholic. William of Ockham was a friar, and they are similar to monks. The only difference is that they serve in the community while monks choose seclusion. It's not Ockham who was bothering me; it's this religious dimension. He's the key that unlocked the puzzle for me. We veer right into a narrow access lane between an old pub and a bookie's, through the black wrought-iron gates into Greyfriars Kirk. I dump my bike on the ground and retrieve my mbira from my bag. There used to be a Franciscan monastery here, before it became the kirk.

Monks of the Misty Order – grey friars.

These grounds are freezing cold despite the warmth of the evening. A sure sign of spectral intrusions.

Whoever's been possessing the schoolboys must be buried here, and I damn well know who they are now.

The great building of the kirk looms ahead of us in the dimming summer's light. Its face is dominated by the five windows inscribed within an arc, like a handprint of glass. Less serene, the kirkyard is eerie, filled with graves and tombstones, memorials taking up every inch of available space. Some of the graves are covered with iron rails, mort safes to deter grave robbers and wanton librarians.

I hate coming here more than any other graveyard in the city 'cause the deados are proper mental, like. There's a dark energy here. They refuse to wax and wane with the seasons, drifting in torment and confusion.

Everyone in Edinburgh knows its bloody history. Minority Presbyterians resisted the changes to the doctrine imposed by Charles I. Four hundred of them were brought here to be tortured, starved and broken back into the king's peace or face banishment. Many died or were executed for treason.

You can sense the anguish and despair that leached into the very substance of this place, creating a thick blanket of dread. The suffering and horrors those men endured has scarred this place for all eternity.

I turn to the right, and in the distance, amidst the graves, is a figure with his back to us, standing in front of a small fire. He is near a grand mausoleum capped with a classical dome. Its decorations are far more elaborate than David Hume's mausoleum at the Old Calton Burial Ground. I know who's buried there.

'Stay behind me,' Priya says as we approach.

Rory MacCulloch keeps very still, watching the flames, smoke rising up into the night air. His hands are clasped behind his back in the stance of a gentleman at leisure. Within him I see the wigged halo of the spectre I saw in Bumblebeam's book. The flames burn atop Tom Mounsey's open briefcase, and a large pile of documents has been stacked to fuel the bonfire. We have to be quick or we'll lose it all.

'Sir George MacKenzie of Rosehaugh,' I say. 'Lord Advocate, founder of the Advocates Library.'

'You have my name at last, little necromancer,' he replies. 'I admire your persistence, but it won't help you, I'm afraid.'

He turns round to face us, one leg forward, the other still stuck the wrong way round. The way he moves like a puppet on strings is disconcerting and repulsive. MacKenzie looks from me to Priya. He inhales deeply, taking in the smoke from the burning papers.

'It's time for you to leave this realm, never to return,' I say.

'I served my king and country better than most, for which they named me Bluidy MacKenzie. Now I do it all over again only to be insulted by a little girl still wet on the nose with her mother's milk?'

'You will leave Rory MacCulloch's body, or I will send you to the Other Place by my Authority. And, trust me, no one comes back from that realm.'

He begins to laugh, loud and long, shattering the quiet. His eyes move out of sync as though each of its own accord. Within his being I glimpse the shadow enveloping Rory's aura. It's gonna be a mission expelling MacKenzie without hurting the body. I had hoped that maybe with a name it would be possible to scare this spectre off.

I prefer bargaining to battling.

'You pathetic fools still don't understand!' he shouts, face so contorted it ceases to resemble anything human. 'Everything I have done, I have done for this nation. Yet you who are in league with the One Above All continue to impugn my good name and cast Scotland into shadow. For years I've watched while time after time your people tried to crush our glorious nation by any means necessary. Your children played *football* with my skull. Now I return to protect us once more – and I will not be thwarted by a little girl.'

Boohoo, ghosts and their bloody grievances. Bollocks to that.

MacKenzie holds up his right hand and a thermosphere bursts alight. It shoots towards us, leaving a tail of bright sparks in its wake. Priya whispers something quickly, and the fireball crashes into a transparent greenish screen in front of us, the heat dissipating in a wave of bright orange sparks. It's a heat shield, a countermeasure spell I'm yet to master. But even with it we still feel the flames.

'Ropa, you need to get this ghoul out of here,' Priya says. 'You saw what happened to the other guy in the whisky shop.'

'I'm on it.'

I twang a note on my mbira, trying to disrupt MacKenzie's harmonics, the invisible tether that ties him to this world. He howls in pain and leaps back, scrambling onto all fours. Nailed him but not square enough. I hit a few more notes, driving him back. The mbira is an instrument that's been used for centuries to deal with spirits, but I feel his resistance hard against its musical notes. The metal keys are rigid underneath my fingers.

MacKenzie launches a concussive blast at us, churning the atmosphere. It comes at us as a whooshing shield of grey, and Priya casts herself forward to absorb it. Her wheelchair rolls back, riding the impact of the blast. She spins three-sixty and mutters an anemoic incantation, launching it back at MacKenzie with twice the fury.

His eyes widen as the blast catches him in the chest, throwing him back several feet. The air about him takes on a green aura.

'Keep him busy while I save the documents,' I shout.

'On it,' Priya replies.

She's already whispering incantations, creating an almighty entropic shift. Damn, girl.

I run behind her amidst the tombstones, towards the bonfire rising high into the sky. The chemical smell is so intense, I choke and cough. Now if only I could remember that Poseidon spell.

Stuff that. I kick the heap with my trusty boots, knocking

it over. Beyond me, strobes of green and orange backlight the kirk as Priya duels the spectre. I stomp on the books and papers burning beneath me like I'm at a ceilidh, but the magical fire seems impossible to stop.

'Heads,' Priya shouts, and I instinctively duck.

Searing heat as Halley's Comet flies over me, and I'm singed by the sparks shedding off its tail. The thermosphere hits MacKenzie's mausoleum and explodes, leaving burn marks on the walls. Bloody hell, I could have been barbecued. MacKenzie dashes back and forth, trading spells and counters with Priya at a furious pace I could never hope to match. The air around them has turned foggy with an industrial smog that grows thicker the longer they duel.

Oh shit, the documents.

I throw down my backpack and quickly take off my lab coat to smother the burning papers.

Something flashes in the corner of my eye. Before I can sort myself out, I'm hit by an incredible blast square in the chest. It lifts me clean off my feet. As I hit the ground flat on my back, I'm thinking I've taken punches before but never anything like this.

Flames spinning all around me.

My head's foggy.

The sweet temptation to close my eyes and lie here for a little while. No. I'm not going to pass out. Force myself to get up onto my feet. The ground's unsteady. Now I know what a boxer who's taken one to the back of the head feels like. I look up just in time to see Priya driven back by a ferocious blast. She's knocked clean from her chair.

'I've always stood on the side of justice,' shouts MacKenzie. 'This is all for Scotland.'

He throws a thermosphere, but Priya quickly rolls left, away from her wheelchair, and takes cover behind a gravestone. He walks towards her, prepping the next attack. Without her chair, she can't get away.

I run towards them and, without thinking, throw my mbira as hard as I can. It hits MacKenzie, and he turns to me with bared teeth, all fury and rage. The veins on his face are incredible to behold. His eyes have turned red with blood. Rory's body resembles the monster within.

River emerges from the darkness and bites into MacKenzie's calf, just as he's about to launch another spell. He cries out in pain and kicks her, throwing her off.

It gives me just enough time to close the gap. I leap, throwing everything I have behind my fist, and catch him on the jaw. There's a satisfying crunch as he reels back. My hand stings from the impact. He staggers a few feet and smiles, spitting a couple of molars onto the ground in front of me. That should have knocked a bull out, but not this prick. I reach for my dagger, then remember that I'm fighting MacKenzie but the body in front of me belongs to someone else. So I go back in with my fists, quickly, before he can incant.

He ducks and catches me in the ribs.

Ouch. I thought this guy was supposed to be a lawyer.

Before he nails me again, I kick him in the shin with my steel toecaps. As he staggers back, he sends a concussive blast my way. I hold out my hands, like I saw Priya do earlier, and try to ride it backwards. But instead of absorbing it, I slam into a massive tombstone. Hurts like hell.

'Prometheus,' I shout, setting off a firework display of piercing white sparks.

MacKenzie shields his eyes against the glare. The air is so thick with noxious smog it's getting harder to breathe. I roll and duck before he recovers, fishing in my pockets for my katty.

When I come back out, katty loaded, MacKenzie has vanished.

River trots up to my side.

Priya joins us, back in her chair, ready to rumble.

'Where is he?' she asks.

'No idea. Keep your eyes and ears peeled.'

She grins. 'I love this shit.'

'Psycho.'

She picks up my mbira and stuffs it in the gap on the side of her seat.

I'm shitting myself as it is. This is his turf. He's rested here for centuries, and probably spent a fair chunk of that time wandering these grounds, so he knows them intimately. Nothing but unease knotted in my stomach, nerves on edge, and I ache every-which-where. My eyes smart from the brightness of the Promethean fireworks. The smog makes it even harder to see as I scan the kirkyard, finding nothing but gravestones, trees and desolation.

Footsteps behind us. I turn suddenly and fire my katty, loading a Promethean spell. The stone explodes mid-flight, spraying grapeshot.

Nothing there.

Quick reload.

A shadow fleeting in the corner of my eye . . . nothing but an old ghoul risen from beyond to watch the show, dead-eyed as a cow in a meadow. A few others are slowly rising in the graveyard. Makes it harder for me to focus. MacKenzie could be lying in wait behind any of the hundreds of tombstones planted in the ground. And he knows we can hurt him, which makes me super anxious and him more dangerous. I'd rather the enemy I can see any day.

We walk down the sloping graveyard, keeping near the boundary wall. He's got to be here somewhere. I can sense him watching, waiting to make his move.

River goes up ahead of us, sniffing the air.

That's my girl. Find the wanker.

God, I hate old graveyards.

A tree rustles beside me. I look up to see a dark figure leap from the foliage and we tumble atop a grave. Thank Yahweh for the soft grass, but not the hands around my throat. Can't breathe.

Priya yells a spell, but when River leaps onto MacKenzie, she can't let fly. My girl does enough to distract the ghoul and he leaps off me, running towards the old church. I give chase as he scales the walls, ascending unnaturally, until Priya nails him with a concussive blast. He responds with a hail of thermospheres, forcing me to take cover.

'I've had quite enough of being disrespected by you, little girl,' MacKenzie shouts. 'Time to finish this.'

His barrage forces Priya back, threatening to break the heat shield she's conjured. Flashes of raging orange fire eat away at her fragile green barrier.

I leap out from behind my cover and run at MacKenzie, whipping out Cruickshank as I go. MacKenzie's rage is aimed at Priya, but when he sees me waving the scarf like a lasso over my head, he raises his hands to take aim.

'Cruickshank, bind him,' I command, letting fly.

The scarf strikes MacKenzie in the face, rapidly wrapping itself around his head then pinning his arms to his sides. MacKenzie writhes about furiously, but Cruickshank has him tight as a python on its tea. For good measure, I knock him to the ground with a kick in the chest.

'Here,' says Priya, tossing my mbira at me.

I catch it and thumb furious notes, pinning the possessed boy to the ground and cutting off MacKenzie's tether to the everyThere. He howls in pain from behind the scarf as I play 'Muzambiringa Munenyemba' just like Gran taught me. My thumbs work fiercely, channelling those ancient harmonies that connect the living and the dead, which are the hallmark of Shona magic. Subjugating MacKenzie to my Authority. He falls into a fit, jerking around like a rag doll, but I've got him now. The keys of the mbira soften underneath my calloused fingers as my own power grows stronger. Each note is a link in a chain clicking into place.

'De, de, zengene uyo ndiani, Rory MacCulloch sengerudze peya tsve . . .'

'Please, no more,' MacKenzie cries out. 'Let me return in peace to the everyThere. I shall trouble you no more, little witch.'

'We're beyond that now, Sir George MacKenzie,' I reply.

'Have mercy, I beg you. Everything I've done in my life

and beyond, I've done for the good of my people. For the glory of Scotland.'

'You're not the first person to make such a claim, Lord Advocate. But because of you, men are dead, with another boy going that way. And it won't happen on my watch, you hear me? Not while I remain a ghostalker. You have overstayed your welcome.' I place my right hand on his forehead. It burns, but I grit my teeth and hold firm. 'Sir George MacKenzie of Rosehaugh, I bind you by my Authority and hereby break the bond of obligation upon Rory MacCulloch, Max Wu, Doug Duffie and anyone else in the Monks of the Misty Order.' I have to include any others, just in case, because I can't be sure how many students are in the fraternity.

A harsh wind rises with fury, kicking up dirt and debris, violently shaking the trees.

'I expel you from the earth and I cut you off from the every-There, for you have broken natural law. And by my Authority, I cast you out to the Other Place, the realm from which there is no return.'

There's a loud crack like thunder, and in the sky a dark portal opens just beyond the treeline. It's a formless void of darkness so complete it's unbearable to look at. And it exerts a terrible gravitational pull, ripping MacKenzie's soul with such violence that Rory MacCulloch rises two feet into the air. MacKenzie fights with all his might to hold on to his host. His grotesque spirit transforms into an old man with a powdered wig as he battles against the irresistible pull of the Other Place. But there's nothing he can do now.

T. L. HUCHU

Once his soul fully leaves Rory's body, the boy falls limp to the ground.

MacKenzie is lifted up into the air.

Desperately, he searches for anchoring, but I return to playing my mbira, ensuring his harmonics cannot find the everyThere. There's only one place for him now. A nonplace.

Up he goes, into that monstrous void. Feet first, then the rest. Yet still he fights to hold on, hands gripping the event horizon. Only his head and shoulders remain, distended and disfigured by the overwhelming pull of the Other Place.

'You don't understand what you are doing, necromancer. The One Above All will get you. You've doomed this city, doomed Scotland and this entire realm.'

I stop playing and flip him the V as he's finally swallowed by the hungry Other Place.

The wind settles down.

A weight lifts from this kirkyard.

The portal closes, shrinking to a full stop, then nothing. No one comes back from there. Ever.

'Wow, that was mad,' Priya says, grinning. 'You know, you kick arse for a rookie.'

'And you've got fancy moves . . . for a healer.'

'Look at us, sucking each other's dicks in a graveyard of all places. How cool is that?'

I think Priya enjoys this stuff a little too much. I'm just happy to have made it in one piece. Not a big fan of this crazy shit, but a girl's gotta do her job. There's got to be easier ways to earn a living. I get a lot of satisfaction from finding out who was behind all this, but I won't lie if I say I'd prefer cool cash. Satisfaction don't buy you no bread and milk from the corner shop.

I take Cruickshank off Rory's face and throw the scarf round my shoulders. Then I step back to let Priya examine the kid. His body's blazing so hot it could fry an egg. But there's a peaceful expression on his face, and none of that darkness remains in his aura. It's the serenity of a fighter who's been knocked out cold.

Priya reaches for her medical bag under her chair, takes out a crystal and places it on Rory's chest.

'Is he going to be okay?' I ask.

'Yeah, I'll call the clinic to send someone over.'

The air is filled with ash falling to the ground, scraps of paper, burnt pages.

Oh no.

I rush over to the remnants of MacKenzie's deranged bonfire. But it's a smouldering heap of ash, blackened pages and some covers. I manage to save a few books, and there are some singed documents that might be salvageable, but most of it is beyond that. There goes the paper trail.

Nothing else for it now. I take out the napkin with Tom's signed contract and whisper a Promethean fire spell. A flame crawls up the length of the napkin until it threatens to burn my fingers. Only then do I let go and watch the ashes tumble away in the wind.

You win some . . . you lose some.

I message Jomo to send his father or the archivists to Greyfriars Kirk. Dr Maige ain't going to be pleased about his precious documents, that's for sure.

I pick up my singed lab coat and put it back on, then kneel down to check on River. The air's filled with smoke and ash, but maybe somewhere above us the stars are still burning.

When I get up, the graveyard is packed with forlorn ghosts from a different era. All around me, the grey shadows of men in shackles wearing hideous dress. These are the Covenanters, men who were persecuted for their faith. I realize they've carried the sort of pain that won't allow them to move on.

I recall the words my grandmother once used and tell them, 'Go now, my friends. You have no business in this realm anymore. I set you free from your pain and just rage. I bestow on you warmth and love to take to the halls of your ancestors. When you reach their vast lands, where the grass is tall and the cattle are fat, where the sun rises twice a day, once from the east and once from the west, they will weigh your hearts against a feather and find them lighter. Be on your way now. All is well.'

XLII

I pass out in the staffroom at Our Lady's clinic on a couple of chairs while Priya administers her healing. The scent of coffee wakes me, and I'm blinded by the brilliant morning sunlight streaming through the wide windows. Someone's thrown one of them thin hospital blankets over me.

'You snore like a tractor,' Lethington says, stirring his coffee. 'How do you take yours?'

'Milky with lots of sugar.'

'You know, it has been fascinating reviving treatments that haven't been seen on this island in a hundred years. Realignment of subluxed souls, and three in one evening! I intend to publish a piece about it in the *Monthly Sceptic*. If ever you should develop an interest in healing and herbology, I would be more than happy to take you under my wing.'

Still in a bit of a daze, wiping off the gunk in the corners of my eyes. I can smell the smoke from the bonfire snagged in my clothes. But I feel great. Much lighter, in fact, as I receive my mug from Lethington. He peers over his round spectacles and hands me a packet of Jammie Dodgers.

'You're welcome to share my stash anytime, sticky fingers,' he says.

'Cheers.'

'When you're done, come to MacCulloch's room. Your mentor is asking after you.'

I raid the fridge and toss River some cheese before inhaling my biscuits and coffee. Then I fold up the blanket and put the chairs back in their places. Don't ever expect no one else to clean up after you, that's what Gran told me, and I don't ever behave no different regardless of where I'm at.

'Come on, girl. The sun don't stop for kings even.'

Figure the job's done, so I take off my lab coat and return it to the hook on the wall, next to the others. Massive burn on the back, along with smaller black spots where the embers caught. It's probably more of a net now than a coat. I grab my backpack and gear before venturing into the corridors towards Rory's room.

Spring in my step as I wander past the soothing artworks on the wall.

Fragrant scents of herbs and aromatics fill the air.

I get to Rory's room and wait in the doorway. Callander's stood at the foot of Rory's bed, next to Cockburn and a man who must be Rory's da. He calls me in, then places a hand upon my shoulder.

'Lord MacCulloch, allow me to introduce you to Ropa Moyo from the General Discoveries Directorate. She was instrumental in finding your son's cure.'

'I have nothing but the utmost gratitude,' the lord says in a voice so posh it's practically folding its own napkin. He takes my hand and shakes it vigorously. The Piaget on his wrist is tempting. 'You are a credit to your institution, young lady. I was away in Europe on His Majesty's service when this dreadful mess occurred.'

He is a short, round man, dressed in a double-breasted suit, tailored, of course, with a ruddy face and a button nose fit for a pug. Rory is sat up in bed on plumped-up pillows, eyes closed and looking all beatific.

Cockburn says, 'There are disciplinary considerations. Unsanctioned consorting with extranatural characters is a serious matter for the Society.'

She's not my favourite person in the world, but after everything that's happened, this wee bastard deserves his comeuppance.

'The boy is a student of the Edinburgh School. As such, responsibility for his discipline falls to us,' Wedderburn says quietly. He stands near the window. But I recall earlier how he said the school wasn't responsible for the kids during the holidays.

'This matter is far too serious and must be handled by the disciplinary committee within the Society,' Cockburn presses.

'The rector is right. Unless the Edinburgh School wishes to pass the buck to us, it falls within their jurisdiction,' Sir Callander says.

Cockburn shoots him an aggrieved glare. 'Then what does the school intend to do?'

'No lasting harm was done, I'm sure. This loyal servant of the king should be very grateful if you would look at certain mitigating circumstances that factored in my son's uncharacteristic behaviour,' Lord MacCulloch says. 'The boy lost his dear mother recently and has been suffering greatly. Surely we can all agree mental health problems are a grave issue affecting the youth today, and layered atop grief, one must be moved towards feelings of sympathy and understanding.'

'He was consorting with vengeful entities,' says Cockburn.

'Then you agree that these actions were not entirely his own. He was acting under the influence of something ancient and malignant.'

'That's not what I meant.'

'It's implied in your choice of words, unless you wish to withdraw them. Of course, I am the boy's father and take some responsibility for not having monitored him properly. But you must understand that the strain involved in undertaking the king's work in Europe means my attention was diverted in this instance.'

Lord MacCulloch keeps mentioning the king, reminding everyone here of his standing with the monarch. Punish my son and answer to a higher power, is what he's really saying. It's not subtle at all. But we have rules, right? There's no way this whole thing goes without punishment. I suspect at the very least Rory MacCulloch will be excluded from school. Back when I was in formal education, I saw kids go down for a lot less, so I wait for Wedderburn's reply.

'Having considered all the information before us, I believe that our actions must always be proportionate and in the best interests of our pupils and the community we serve. And so I agree with Lord MacCulloch that mental health is a very serious issue. Rory is a grieving young boy led astray by his cunning peer Max Wu, whom we will expel from the school. However, Rory's return to the school is conditional upon his good behaviour, and he is to attend regular sessions with our school counsellor. I believe that is a fair, firm and satisfactory resolution. As for Doug Duffie and the rest of the so-called Monks of the Misty Order, if there are any, we will find out who they are, abolish their clandestine fraternity and seek to rehabilitate them on a case-by-case basis.'

'Boys will be boys. But rest assured, I will be severe with Rory once he's on the mend and comes home,' says the lord in a satisfied manner. He turns to Rory. 'No more video games, internet, rap music, and certainly no pudding for the rest of this summer, young man.'

Wow. This shite's pure sham, like. Max Wu gets expelled even though he wasn't the one who went about town barbecuing folks, I get suspended from the Library, and all Rory gets is the threat of missing his pudding. What a fix.

Callander is blank and Cockburn is seething, but Wedderburn is pretty relaxed, like a member of the old boys' club.

'Well, I'm glad this matter has been resolved to everyone's satisfaction. Alas, there is no rest on His Majesty's service, so I will take my leave. Rector Wedderburn, please see me out. I read in your last newsletter that the school was soliciting donations to renovate the rugby pavilion? Let me see if I can help with that,' Lord MacCulloch says, turning towards the door.

I'm stunned and pissed off as anything. Yet we have to pretend like it's all gravy when this thing's ranker than the New Loch.

'Sir Callander, I must—' Cockburn begins.

'As far as the Society is concerned, the Edinburgh School

has resolved the matter accordingly,' he replies, following Wedderburn and MacCulloch out of the room.

Cockburn is seething, but composes herself, readying to leave. I decide to take a chance with her, seeing as I've done some heroic shit and am due one.

'Any chance I'll be taking my test again soon?' I ask.

'Never, if I have anything to do with it,' she replies before sweeping out of the room.

Bollocks. It was pointless to even try with her. I'll sort it out with Callander anyways. When I reach the door, I turn back and see Rory open his eyes. The minger smirks and gives me the finger.

Sometimes you gotta remind yourself to stay in your lane, else you gonna be fretting and stressing about stuff that ain't got nothing to do with you. Reckon it was Reinhold Niebuhr who said something about that. Still holds true. I've done my bit and the rest is up to them. Not much else I can do about this fudge, 'cause I'm just an unpaid intern at the end of the day.

I find Sir Callander waiting for me in the corridor. His expression is neutral, and I know it won't do no good talking about any of this with him. From the first time I entered the Library and then joined the Society, I learnt this whole magicking bollocks runs on its own logic that seems to defy common sense. They'll tell you black is white and white is black. That's just how they roll.

It's exhausting.

'You have done very well, Miss Moyo,' Callander says.

Doesn't feel like it, though. Rory gets off free, and any

chance of me getting a nibble of the fortune went up in ashes.

'I'm not sure we've seen the end of this. This thing about the One Above All keeps bugging me,' I reply.

'Lower your tone.' He looks around. The corridor is empty, though.

'I can only think of one person who fits the description.'

'And who would that be?'

'The king,' I whisper.

Callander gives me a long hard look, and I give it right back. But who else sits above us all to a man? Who else has the power to use spies to do his bidding? This is cloak-and-dagger stuff. Reminds me of what I read about the Soviet Union and the Americans during the Cold War. Tripping each other up in the shadows.

This whole business was a battle to control the Society of Sceptical Enquirers by grabbing their assets. I know the Society can't transfer their share of assets in the bank elsewhere. But the king still can't take that share outright. Not legally, anyways.

Proof of the Paterson fortune was key, though. It would have been all the excuse he needed to seize it. English monarchs are really not averse to that sort of thing . . . just ask the Catholics. But if the king did this without just cause, he would only succeed in alienating all of Scottish magic. And that's how shit kicks off. No, this was the cleaner way of doing it. It didn't matter that the spy who called himself Mounsey wasn't a true descendant of Paterson. All that was needed was evidence of the Society's misdeeds for a 'confiscation' of the Society's assets at the bank. But there's more . . . Post-catastrophe, the Royal

Bank of Scotland is a shadow of its former gigantic self. So I figure it wouldn't have had the funds to cough up that debt owed to Paterson anyway. We're talking missed dividends and interest over three hundred plus years. So if the king pressed for restitution of the fortune to Mounsey, aka the crown in disguise, the crown's holdings afterwards would be enough to take over the whole bank. The debt would also totally bankrupt the Society, as I can't imagine it would have had enough assets tucked away elsewhere to cover it. True, Callander is prickly when it comes to the Society's independence. But whoever holds the purse strings calls the bagpiper's tune. And so Scottish magic would be in the king's pocket for ever after, and Scotland even more securely under his thumb.

There'd be no getting out of that hole, and I came so close to facilitating it. I get cold at the thought.

However, the king's actions were so egregious they touched the spirit world. So the avowed monarchist Sir George MacKenzie rose from his grave to try to redeem himself – to save Scotland, in a sense. MacKenzie then killed the spy who called himself Thomas Mounsey. And in the process, he destroyed the evidence required to further diminish Scottish magic . . . I guess in some perverse way we *were* on the same side. This despite the fact that I was actively working with the other side. But he was killing the kids to achieve his goals. I had no choice but to cast him out.

'You will tell no one of your suspicions, not even your friends, you hear me?' Callander looks grim and disturbed. 'My predecessor in the Society struck out against our current monarch, just as he came into his power during the second

Restoration. It was a disastrous mistake and cost us dearly. It seems the king has not forgotten when Scottish magic stood against him. I have spent my entire tenure as secretary of the Society ameliorating the effects of this misstep, assiduously avoiding further confrontation with London. We must be very, very careful. Do you understand what is at stake here, Miss Moyo? The independence of the Society and the future of Scottish magic itself.'

I nod.

'Good. Now, if you will excuse me, I have a lot on my plate. I'm sure you can imagine. Please ready your family; I shall pay you all a visit tomorrow.'

'One more thing,' I reply. It's insane, but the institution I work for is built on stolen money. I at least have to salvage something out of all this. 'When do I get to take the test again so I can become a proper apprentice?'

'There'll be plenty of time for that later. Right now we are to deal with more weighty concerns.'

My mentor leaves with a troubled expression on his face. That's all above my pay grade, though. Still, I'm left hanging. Not really sure what my place in the Society is. I can't go on being an unpaid intern forever. I need to earn real cheddar, else I have to go back to being a fucking ghostalker. Again. Nah, that's a step backwards, and I've learnt too much to go back. Maybe I still have to pay my dues, but one way or the other, I'm gonna make it in this bitch. Screw it – I remember I have one last thing to do before I leave this clinic.

◎　◎　◎

It's warmer, like normal room temperature, when I enter Max Wu's room – just as I finish sending Lewis a 'Mission Accomplished' text. The crystals have been removed. He's up, looking a bit worse for wear, but I've seen crazier sights on the fleshmarket on a Friday night. His mother, Connie, is sat on the bed next to him, with Bing taking the armchair nearby.

'Hero of the hour,' says Priya as I walk in. How she looks and sounds so fresh having pulled an all-nighter is beyond me.

'Are you planning on messing with ghosts again anytime soon?' I ask Max.

He shakes his head, embarrassed.

Anyone with a sense of shame's not beyond redemption, as far as I'm concerned.

'Once I figured that the name of the Monks points to Greyfriars cemetery, all I had to do was visit the place. Then I found the headstone with our school's beithir on it for the next clue. It felt like a bit of a game. A dork like me doesn't get invited to parties, let alone secret fraternities, so I though it was great when I got in. We were doing cool arcane magic, the sort of mysticism forbidden at the school. It was brilliant, visiting graveyards, hopping across planes, expanding our consciousness. We were just messing around. Then . . . then came Sir George MacKenzie. We knew we'd let someone very bad in and were scared. I would see the ghost in the mirror and stuff, haunting me, following me everywhere.'

'You won't need to worry about that anymore,' I say.

'He's been expelled,' Bing says bitterly. 'Thank God. And thanks to you, Ropa.'

'I think I'll try my hand at something safe instead, like

investment banking,' Max says soberly. 'No more magic for me, thank you very much. I can't believe I was so stupid.'

I can't help but notice how easy the leap from magic to high finance seems for a former student of the Edinburgh School.

'Kids join gangs all the time. You just happened to be in a posh one, that's all.'

'At least they weren't the sort to go about trashing restaurants,' says Priya with a laugh.

Connie looks at me with tears in her eyes. A mother's relief. That makes this worth much more than anything else in the world. I ain't got a mum or dad for that, but what I'm seeing in front of me is the real, unconditional deal. Bittersweet shit, makes me sad and happy at the same time.

'We know we're not allowed to pay you, but I checked with Mrs Cockburn and she did say a small token of our appreciation would be permissible under the rules. Please could you accept this,' Bing says, going into a wee bag beside him. 'It's a nice poster you can put up in your room.'

He hands me a postal tube.

'Cheers,' I say, sticking the poster in my bag. 'Max, you need to holler at your pal Lewis. He misses you.'

'Did he really say that?' he asks.

'Didn't need to,' I reply. 'But I know it.'

I'd rather have dough any day, and I ain't got no room of my own for a poster, but as they say, it's the thought that counts. At the end of the day, I can hold my head up and say I did right by the Wus. A job well done's got to be reward enough by itself, I guess. Doug Duffie wasn't no client of mine, so I'll let someone else worry about him. Sign my time sheet, I'm done.

XLIII

'Come on, Gran, you're doing my head in. We're going to be late,' I say, banging on the bathroom door. 'Izwi, are you done packing your suitcase yet?'

'Stop hustling me. You're razzing everyone this morning,' Izwi fires back.

'I'm with the kid on this one. Chill, Ropa,' Jomo says.

'Shut up and make those sandwiches, man. It's not like I've asked you to do a five-course dinner.'

'What am I supposed to be doing?' Priya asks.

'I already told you, the basket.'

Christ almighty, it's like herding cats, and I'm not talking about the musical. Everyone wants to do their own thing. *Mother of God, Gran, you're killing me here.* It's a madhouse, but I still can't believe at eleven in the morning on a Thursday folks want to be dragging their feet.

'You're putting cranberry sauce in with the egg mayo? Who does that?'

'I'm not even supposed to be here,' Jomo protests.

His dad's banned him from hanging with me, but Jomo was, like, screw that. Not to his dad's face or anything that bold; he just got sneaky. We're day ones. Anyway, what's the worst that could happen? They already got him cleaning the Library. Same shit as cleaning out King Augeas's stables as far as I'm concerned.

'On top of that, my book was expunged,' he says bitterly.

'Duh, what did you expect?' Priya replies.

'It's going in the incinerator. That was my first . . . never mind.'

'Gran!'

A sharp click of the lock. The bathroom door opens, and Gran emerges wearing a short-sleeved floral dress. Jomo wolf-whistles. She looks stunning, dressed up like she's the Horae of summer herself. I stand back and check her out. The moles and freckles on her skin look like seeds scattered from the bountiful meadow depicted in her outfit.

'I'm feeling that number,' Priya says, taking a pic on her phone.

'You look amazing,' I exclaim.

'I'd look nineteen if only you'd given me a couple more minutes.'

'Priya, help Gran put on her sandals.'

'I thought I was doing the picnic basket.'

'I'll do it myself,' I say, shoving Jomo from the counter so I can pack the grub.

'Ropa's so bossy,' says Izwi, and they burst out laughing. Not me though. I've got stuff to do, like always.

Takes a few more minutes of cajoling and corralling before I finally get them all organized, and then we're out of the caravan into the glorious day. I make sure Gran's got her straw hat on in case the sun gets too bad. Then I lock up the cara and warn Jomo to be careful with the picnic basket. Izwi's riding along with Priya in her wheelchair. And River joins our crew, dashing ahead to explore the thickets and bracken. We walk slowly 'cause Gran's hips ain't in good nick and she leans on me for support. Her eyes ain't much good either.

I've let my locks down and am in shorts, flip-flops and a Shatter the Shibboleth T-shirt Jomo brought along so we could be twinnies. In return I gave him the poster Bing Wu gifted me 'cause there ain't no space for that on my caravan's walls. It's a fair trade.

All around us, Hermiston Slum's going about its business. Children playing in the dusty alleyways. Already a few green-fingered fiends are working their allotments, and folks wave or say good morning as our wee party goes by.

We go over the old stone bridge to get to the footpath on the other side of the canal.

'Well look at yous,' Gary O'Donohue says, waiting on the verge for us.

He doffs his panama hat, looking like the man about town in a navy-blue suit and winkle-pickers. Man's even worn a tie for the occasion, bright yellow like the corn marigolds lining the path.

'Morning, Gary,' I say.

'May I?' He offers his arm like them Casanovas in the black-and-white movies, and I place Gran's hand on it.

'Giving away the bride,' Priya says.

'Shut it.'

Undeniable though, Gran and Gary look super cute

together. Their backs are bent, their clothes a size or two too big, but they take that footpath like it was a catwalk and I snap a pic of them from behind. Don't need to be told to give the two of them space while we cruise along at a snail's pace. Nosey me wants to listen in to their convo every time I hear Gran cracking up so loud birds take flight.

'Never thought I'd be chaperoning your nan on a date,' Priya says.

'We've got to. You can never be too careful with these old people. Look at his hand, what's he up to?' Jomo says.

'You lot are disgusting,' I say.

'Repugnant.'

'Vile, even.'

Priya grins. 'We'll wear that as a badge of honour.'

We make way for a cyclist heading into town and press on, past the farmhouse on one side and the newest bit of the slum on the field adjacent to the M8. Nothing's nicer than hanging out with your pals like this. All the pressure just peels off you.

'You see these hawthorn berries that grow in abundance along the canal?' Priya says.

'Yeah.'

'Make jam with them. It'll be good for your nan's heart.'

'Will do, though low-sugar jam goes off fast and wouldn't see us through the winter. I'll figure out an alternative way to store them.'

'I'll get you capsules instead, and I've got some fennel tea too, which'll be good for her waterworks. I'll see what else I can rustle up from the panaceary.'

'You're a diamond, Priya. I really mean it,' I say.

'I'm a sapphire,' Izwi says.

'I guess that makes me a ruby,' Jomo adds.

Not exactly the point I was trying to make, but this gang's full of it. Reckon the exercise is great for Gran too, getting her out of the cara and away from all that crocheting. Slow and steady, we get to the field by the wee burn passing under the canal. Cows are grazing in it; you can smell them, and they watch as we set up our picnic blanket.

All sorts of insects buzzing in the air.

I'm hoping the midges are gonna be kind today.

'Oh, my poor knees,' says Gran as Gary and me help her onto the blanket.

Then we're all settled, ready for Jomo's famous picnic fare. Munching grub and hearing Gary and Gran reminiscing about the old days before the catastrophe's like listening to an audiobook. They drag time to a halt by tethering to the past.

Not that Izwi cares; she's grabbed a couple of sarnies and nipped down to the burn, chasing butterflies and frolicking with River.

We're an hour in, enjoying our picnic, when Gran tells me to call Izwi over.

'It's time,' she says softly.

I look up and see two figures watching us from the footpath. There's a sinking feeling in the pit of my stomach. Take out my phone and photograph Izwi bounding through the field, coming back to us.

'Come here, my sweet, sweet child,' Gran says. 'Give me a hug.'

I'm doing everything to hold it together when Izwi throws her arms round Gran's neck and buries her face in her shoulder. 'Be good, and may the blessings of your ancestors forever flow in your veins,' says Gran.

Didn't think it would be this difficult. If only I knew a spell, one so strong it could hold a moment in place. But in this world, time's a river carrying us aloft, and its current's just too strong to swim against.

XLIV

Sir Callander's waiting on the footpath with a woman. She's attired in a fitted red dress with a wool cape which runs to her chest. She has red hair and wears red lipstick, and I sense something thoroughly modern about her, an economy about her movement, crisp lines, a definite intelligence. The woman smiles warmly when she sees my sister.

'Izwi Moyo, I'd like you to meet your new head teacher, Mrs Featherstone from the Aberdeen School of Magic and Esoterica.'

'Such a pleasure to meet you, Izwi. I've heard so many wonderful things. Our school is delighted to have you,' Mrs Featherstone says, bending down to the same height as Izwi and offering her hand.

Little sis doesn't reply, but she doesn't front either as she shakes hands. Gran had a word with her and convinced her this was a great opportunity. She wouldn't have listened to me otherwise. Now I ain't so sure, to be honest. I mean, I know why we have to do this, but it still sucks arse. If only I'd gotten my hands on the fortune . . . but what's the use?

'We are grateful for the scholarship,' I say when it becomes clear Izwi isn't interested in speaking. The kid's stubborner than a mule. I flash an awkward smile.

'Don't worry, she will be well looked after. There are plenty of little girls her age at our school, and she'll make friends in no time.'

'Her belongings?' Callander asks.

'They are in the caravan. It's locked; I'll come with you to get them.'

'That will not be necessary,' he replies. 'You have done well. Izwi, hold my hand and take Mrs Featherstone's as well. There's a good girl.'

Callander stares wistfully down the valley, watching Gran and Gary chatting away on the picnic blanket a distance away. There's a melancholic air about him. It's almost as though there's a chasm he cannot cross. Usually, his face appears hard and set, but the softness of it now moves me.

'Would you like to talk to my gran before you go?' I ask.

He hesitates.

'No, Miss Moyo. There's nothing more I can say today that I haven't said before,' he replies. A door shuts, and his voice hardens to its normal tone: 'Mrs Featherstone, we will take our leave.'

'Wait,' I say.

I take out a phone. It's the one I pinched from Rooster Rob's tent, and I've got a SIM card for it too, so it works now. I show it to Izwi and then put it in her pocket.

'That's for you, sis. You can call or text me anytime.'

'Outside of lessons,' Mrs Featherstone says.

I kneel and give my little sister a great big hug.

Hard to let go, but I do.

'I love you, sis,' I say.

353

Izwi answers with a silent kiss before she takes the grown-ups' hands.

'Bye, River,' she says softly, before glaring at me with a frown. The kid blames me, and she's right. If I'd worked harder, been smarter, made more money, sis could have stayed.

Before I can say goodbye, there's a blur like someone waving their hand very fast. A rush of air blasts my face. When it clears, Izwi, Callander and Mrs Featherstone have disappeared into thin air. And I am left staring at the empty space where my little sister was.

'The Hermes's walk. That's some next-level sorcery,' says Priya. 'I wouldn't even try it.'

I don't care. All I know is I'll miss Izwi an awful lot, and I know Gran will too, loads more than me because the two of them were always together when I was away. Proper companions. But sis is off to a good school, one that can give her better opportunities than I ever could. And that's all that matters.

'You okay, man?' Jomo says.

I nod quietly. He has a couple of whiskers on his chin. Fancy, I'd not noticed them before.

'Come on, let's get back to the picnic. See what the lovebirds are up to,' Priya says with good cheer. Jomo puts his arm round my shoulder and leads me back to the field.

I'm spaced out, chilling with these folks, thinking about Izwi. Gran and Gary have some good craic going on, but I'm just not in the mood now. I need to think about the next hustle to keep my nose above water 'cause this interning bull won't pay my bills. Not sure what to do just yet, but I'll make a plan. I have to.

'Fam,' says Jomo, checking out the poster I gave him. 'This is vintage. I can't accept this for a two-shilling T-shirt.'

'What do you mean?' I ask.

'Look it up, Priya,' he says.

She searches for it on her phone. 'Whose signature is that?'

'Some guy called Alex,' Jomo replies.

'An original *A Clockwork Orange* poster signed by Malcolm McDowell, who starred in it, goes for a fair mint, you know.' Priya shows Jomo her phone.

'Wahey,' Jomo says, giving me back the poster. 'Looks like Bing's sorted you on the sly, man. Come on, I know a place on West Nicolson Street that trades in this kind of thing.' He jumps up, ready to move. 'Sorry, Gran, but we've got to go. Gary, be a gent or you'll answer to me.'

Priya shrugs and Gran bursts out laughing, the sound of it ringing through the trees and valley, running with the burn.

'These young people,' she says.

Soon it's me on my bike, Priya in her wheelchair, Jomo on his skateboard and River on her trotters, making a mad dash into town to sell the poster. It's a bloody braw day, and there's kids dancing in the spray of a burst water main. Maybe this summer's gone the way it's supposed to. I'll leave all my troubles for autumn to sort out.

Acknowledgements

Jamie Cowen, superstar agent, your belief in my writing and ideas, your support – and the work you do in the shadows – made this series happen. You're a legend, and I cannot thank you enough.

Bella Pagan, editor extraordinaire, working with you is like being put through a top-spec industrial washing machine cycle. I feel dizzy after your edits, but the novel comes out clean, mean and lean. Thanks to you and team Tor, on both sides of the Atlantic, for your belief in Ropa and her story.

Jamie-Lee Nardone, awesome publicist – you've kept me busy and the book busier still.

I am really grateful to Sally Cholewa, and the RBS Archives, for your immense help with banking history and your knowledge of the Darien Project. Your archive is a much more welcoming place than the version depicted in this novel.

My writer/reader buddies Jeanne-Marie Jackson, Mohammed Naseehu Ali, Summaya Lee, Chikodili Emelumadu and Michelle D'costa. Your support and keen eyes have sharpened my quill over the last few years.

Jane Morris and Brian Jones of amaBooks, for your immense support of my work over the years. Your anthology *Moving On* published my story, 'The Library of the Dead', which I cannibalized for this series.

Maximilian Musavaya, Hildegard Musavaya, Rugare Murwira, Patrick Musavaya, Pascal Musavaya, Paul Musavaya, Shingi

Mugadza, Jane Mugadza, Ropa Mugadza, Kuda Kuwanda, Upenyu Kuwanda – ndimi vanhu vacho!

Jasper, Dylan and Mandy at Waterstones Princes Street. I am grateful for the chai lattes and the enthusiasm you have for *The Library of the Dead*. And all the booksellers, librarians, reviewers and bloggers who've been shouting about the Edinburgh Nights series, you really warm an author's heart. Thank you.

Shout-out to the e-zine *Electric Spec* where I published my story 'Ghostalker', which contained the proto-Ropa.

Edinburgh, the city that keeps me dreaming – I'm glad to call you home.

AN INTERVIEW
WITH T. L. HUCHU

Meet the author and find out more about the Edinburgh Nights series and its inspirations. We hope you enjoy these insights into Ropa and her world.

How long was the series developing in your mind before you wrote the first book, *The Library of the Dead*?

Circa 2015 I published a short story titled 'Ghostalker' in the e-zine *Electric Spec*. It was about an unnamed girl going around my hometown of Bindura delivering messages for the dead. She was the proto-Ropa. There was something in her zingy voice that stayed with me. I felt she had legs, but didn't quite know if I could manage the marathon of writing a novel, let alone a whole series. Two years later, I published another story called 'The Library of the Dead' in the anthology *Moving On: and Other Zimbabwean Stories* published by amaBooks in Bulawayo. This contained a version of what would become 'the Library' and an acolyte who would be Jomo Maige. But that story was set in Harare.

I immediately knew the two stories were set in the same universe and any attempt to write a novel would involve combining them in some way. The final piece of the jigsaw came to me in early 2018, when I realized that moving these pieces to Edinburgh would give me the perfect canvas. And by mining Scottish history, I'd have enough material for a series. And it had to be a series, because the ideas contained within couldn't be sufficiently expressed in a single instalment.

If you could sit down for a chat with any of your characters, who would it be and why?
Melsie Mhondoro, Ropa's grandmother, has secrets – and getting them out of her is a pain. Who is she really? I think Ropa takes her for granted because she's her grandmother and so she misses key details. How come at the start of *The Library of the Dead* Gran was knitting a cardigan that happened to be the right size and fit for Ollie, the missing kid? Gran is always knitting and Ropa just happens to get a magical scarf from Callander, too? Maybe it's just a coincidence, I don't know . . . When I was a teenager, I took my one living grandparent for granted. What could possibly be interesting about old people? At that age you're pretty much the centre of the universe, and it's hard to make that leap to see the elderly have the same rich experience of life that you do, even for a smart kid like Ropa.

It doesn't help the situation much that Ropa isn't always honest with her grandmother. I suspect this might be because her grandmother isn't always honest with her either. She had to have picked up that trait from someone. And so, I'd love to sit down with Gran over a nice cup of tea and have her tell me her life story.

359

T. L. HUCHU

What were your biggest influences for the series?
I read voraciously, so with a lifetime of that behind me, my influences have started to blur somewhat. The most obvious one though is Ben Aaronovitch's *Rivers of London*, which is a very playful police procedural, infused with magic. Once you strip it down to the nuts and bolts, you have an exquisite schema that you can retro-engineer to suit your aesthetic preferences. The old cliché – 'talent borrows, genius steals' – is pretty apt and many authors have taken this to heart. I had the stories, I had the characters, I had Edinburgh, but the engine that drives this narrative is perhaps adapted from Aaronovitch. He's not the only person I've 'stolen' from, I'm afraid to admit.

I regret dissing Dan Brown when I was younger, brash and a bit of a prick. I regurgitated the stuff I read in the broadsheets about how he was a dreadful writer, etc. No one writes rollicking tales bringing a historical quest into a contemporary setting better than he does. This is a crucial element to what I'm doing here. And for pesky ghosts – see M. Night Shyamalan. For language – Anthony Burgess's *A Clockwork Orange* is a novel I love, and so I riffed off his inventive take on 'youth-speak'. I won't even go into the various historians whose work I'm pilfering as I bring this thing together! The process is very much like being a nightclub DJ. You're mixing up various beats as you go. And if you do it well, then at the end of the night, your set is a work of art in its own right.

Ropa has such a brilliant voice – witty, dead-pan and full of energy. How did you go about crafting her character?
Her voice is so much fun to work with! It's one of the things

I love about writing this series. I trade in contradiction, messiness and inconsistency because the world we live in has no neat edges. Ropa is potty-mouthed and uses slang drawn from Edinburgh, London and some Americanisms. She'll throw around a bit of the Scots, which is all around her, and Shona words picked up from her gran. She's also an autodidact and will discourse happily on science and history. Most creative writing advice tells you to avoid clichés, but Ropa revels in colloquialisms and will never try to create a 'fresh metaphor' when there's a ready-made phrase to pick off the shelf.

I wanted to create something sonically interesting, tugging in different directions simultaneously. Kids – hell, even adults – do this sort of code-switching all the time. The language you used in the playground with your friends is different to the language used at school or work. Notice how Ropa swears an awful lot, but never does so in front of her grandmother or Callander. But the language also serves to tie this book to the place it's set. Everyone in Scotland understands what's meant by a 'dreich' day. Language represents a way of seeing the world and is specific to a culture or people. In Ropa's case, hopefully the reader can also experience some of the frantic energy only possessed by the young.

Ropa inhabits a dystopian, somewhat futuristic Edinburgh that's seen better days. What made you choose this setting?
I wanted to find a new way of playing with time in this novel. Most works I've encountered fracture the idea of linear time by playing games with chronology, messing around with the timeline as they go. I have an interest in psychogeography

anyway – the effect of a geographical location on the emotions and behaviour of individuals. But I thought – what if altering the landscape and culture also allows me to play with time? There is a reason *The Library of the Dead* starts with the house where the historian Thomas Carlyle spent his honeymoon. It was an overt signal to the reader that I am telling a history set in the future. People also say 'God save the king' in Ropa's world, so we know this is set after Elizabeth II's reign. Then again, the reader knows plenty of kings reigned before her, and this setting seems authoritarian, so they might wonder if this is history repeating itself at first. But either way, the reader knows we are not in our 'now'.

We see that Princes Street Gardens, in the centre of Edinburgh, has reverted to the Nor Loch that used to be there prior to the nineteenth century. Edinburgh today is a quaint, rich, touristy city, but prior to the Union of 1707 it was a dirty, smelly, crime-ridden cesspit in the poorest nation in Western Europe. Its old name, Auld Reekie, is back with a bang and my version of Edinburgh closely resembles that of the eighteenth century. Would we have called Edinburgh dystopian back then? This is a city in which some things function and others don't. It's only dystopian in the same sense Delhi or Hanoi or Lagos or São Paulo can be said to be dystopian. At least, that's my thinking. If you go to the third world, you see these things more clearly. I can leave Harare, a modern city with skyscrapers, and twenty minutes later I am driving past areas where people live in traditional mud huts. Some readers may find it jarring if you put electric vehicles next to horse-drawn carts in this version of Edinburgh.

But isn't it equally strange that theatre, radio, television and the internet all sit next to one other in our world? If you walk around with your eyes open, the past and the present are already intermingled in surprising and delightful ways.

Did you discover any interesting facts about Edinburgh while writing the Edinburgh Nights series?

I've lived in Edinburgh for over fifteen years now and I feel like I'm barely scratching the surface. That feeling intensifies when I write about the city. It's not the largest city in the world. But what it lacks spatially, it more than makes up for temporally in the depth of history contained on every street. See, I'm not just interested in the Old Town and New Town, which is what most people think makes up Edinburgh. That's what they put on postcards for tourists to send back home. They'd never put Granton, Niddrie, Restalrig or Wester Hailes on there. And it's for that reason that I'm interested in these spaces. This is a multifaceted city, a divided city in many ways – socially, culturally, economically. This is why I needed a character at the periphery to help in its exploration.

A lot of the stuff I learnt hasn't made it into the Edinburgh Nights books. But some things did . . . I spent a lot of time fascinated by the history of quarrying in Wester Hailes. This was a massive pit, where they extracted much of the sandstone that built the New Town. Later it became a landfill site, then it was covered up and repurposed into the sprawling housing estate that's there now. When compared to the posh city centre it was exploited to build, Wester Hailes is radically different, so the contradiction is glaring. In these sorts of spaces, you find communities with their own stories and voices. Some of those voices I borrowed to help create Ropa's. Writing this series means I'm becoming more deliberate in my research and explorations of the city. I try not to miss anything. However, one lifetime could never be enough to learn everything there is to know about this wonderful city.

Do you recognize yourself particularly in any of your characters and, if so, was this deliberate?

They say all fiction is autobiographical and all autobiography is fiction, don't they? Also, 'write what you know'. A work of literature is an expression of self, no matter how far you want to distance yourself from it. But the self is a multifaceted thing and our consciousness can't perceive it all. So it's not as if there's a 'me' character in there. Yet there are portions of the text where I recognize something true from within myself.

If you could use any magic from your series in everyday life, what would you choose?

Callander hints tantalizingly at the prospect of reversing entropy – or going back in time. But I'm not quite sure he can really pull it off. It all depends on your interpretation of the 'Maxwell's Demon' thought experiment that he describes in the text. But I think if you could reverse it, then there'd be no limit to your powers!

What advice would you give to aspiring authors?

It's really hard to condense years of practice into anything pithy. The great thing about the age we live in is that information is freely available via the incredible invention we call the web. But reading is very important for anyone who intends to be a writer. That's your foundation . . . engaging with as much literature and non-fiction as you can, across different genres. Nothing is ever wasted. I didn't know my love for popular science would one day come in handy when creating this magic system. Likewise, I've used history and pop-philosophy in my books. Hoover up as much as you can. Once you've done that, you can start on your writing. A cursory search on Google will reveal plenty of information on how to be a writer, as well as industry stuff about approaching publishers and so forth. Likewise, YouTube has a wealth of material too – videos, courses, author talks, interviews, etc. You can pretty much get your MFA by consuming this content. But, ultimately, there's no substitute for doing the work. There are people out there who enjoy talking about writing, but don't do the actual work. They might grow bitter as time goes on because they want to be a writer without developing their work and engaging in the labour that it actually involves. Don't be that person!

Do you plan your work or make it up as you go along – or in other words, are you a plotter or a 'pantser'?
I make lots of notes before any actual writing begins. Random ideas come to me and I record them. And I spend quite a bit of time thinking about a project before I dive in. For *The Library of the Dead*, I had over 10,000 words of notes jotted down. But once the writing starts, a lot of that stuff goes out the window. That's because, with each keystroke, the story develops in ways that can be quite surprising. For example,

my notes had focused on the fact that the Library would be
under Calton Hill. So, I researched this location and considered how the Library would be constructed. When I set out
to find a suitable entrance for it, I wandered through the
nearby cemeteries and picked a big round mausoleum I liked
the look of. But guess what? That was David Hume's mausoleum, so everything had to change! I knew about his ideas
on scepticism and empiricism. So, suddenly, the magical
society I'd planned as one thing became the Society of Sceptical
Enquirers. The magic system then had to be built around
this. Who was Hume's BFF? Adam Smith, of course. So now
Scottish magic was wedded firmly to commerce, and out of
that emerged the plot of *Our Lady of Mysterious Ailments*. I
have ideas but constantly have to make course corrections in
reaction to the unexpected stuff that comes in. You can do
all the plotting in the world, but as the contours of the world
you're building start taking shape, you better be ready to
pantser your wee heart out.

**An author has as long as it takes to write their first book, but
readers want the next book in a series more quickly! Did this
pressure change your writing methodology?**
This is a good problem to have. It means you're not writing
into the void any more, and must be grateful to those readers
for taking such an interest. I consider this a privilege, since
no one forced me to be a writer. I like working within a
structure, so I'm on that grind five/six days a week. I'm doing
the best work I can, same as I would be if I were employed
as a checkout operator or a cleaner.

Do you like to listen to music while you work?

Nope. I prefer silence and solitude when I write. This helps get me into that zone where I can hear myself think and my characters' voices clearly. There's this beautiful moment when you're *on* and the ideas are flowing and the writing is going well. You're in this pocket where you can get to your desk day after day to create. It's pure bliss; there's nothing else quite like it.

Did writing this series feel different to writing your earlier books – and, if so, why is that? Or maybe you discovered quirks that will always be part of your writing process?

The younger me revelled in self-flagellation and playing the tortured artist. It is fashionable, isn't it, to say woe is me; how hard is this writing life? But it's creating art and working with words – that's a beautiful thing. It's a privilege to be able to do it. It's play. I'm having a blast writing this series and I hope that enjoyment filters across to the reader. I've combined my writing with running, a newly discovered passion of mine. The two are similar in many ways. You can't be a tortured runner; people would think it ridiculous. To be a runner or a writer involves turning up and doing the work, day after day. Then the results will come. I find that if I look after my body, my mind's sharper; the younger me preferred mind-altering substances and a couch-potato lifestyle. Looking after my body and mental health is now tied in to doing my work. The process is becoming more holistic. I won't claim I've achieved the perfect balance but I'm striving, and as a result I'm enjoying what I do.

367

For you, what is the most challenging part of writing a book?
I find the challenges are always external to the work itself.
As I've said, writing is the same as running; the two are
indifferent to externalities, in my mind. With running it's all
about putting one foot in front of the other, until you do your
twenty-six miles and finish the marathon. With writing, you
lay one sentence after the other until you have a manuscript
at the end of it. It really is that easy. But on certain days, as
a runner, the wind blows against you, on other days it's too
hot or too cold, or the route is too steep, or you ache and
your muscles hurt. The list of excuses you can conjure is
endless, but the work remains the same.

Likewise, with writing, you get challenges too – not enough
time, self-doubt, neurosis about publication, the laptop breaks
down, procrastination, friends come calling uninvited, eating
up your time. Here too the list is endless, but the work remains
the same. It's indifferent to all that. So, to restate, the most
challenging things are external to the process itself. The 'challenges' we acknowledge as a writer's lot would be laughable
if we transposed them onto the work of bus drivers, plumbers,
accountants, nurses or any other 'key worker'. At least that's
what I think. What helps me grind through is taking owner-
ship of the work I do. I chose to be a writer; this isn't
something that was imposed upon me. And so, I do whatever
it takes to get the job done.

**When you published the first book in your Edinburgh Nights
series, was there anything about the publishing process that
surprised you?**

Maybe I should try to speak holistically about my experience, but to be specific – I was really surprised by how positive everyone is and by the energy they put into the work they do. The human element is key to everything. I can't speak to everyone's experience of publishing, but this has been true for me . . . Engaging with really hard-working, passionate people who want your book to succeed far exceeded my expectations of how all this would go. There's the editor who brings so much to the experience, sees things you wouldn't see and works with you to refine the manuscript. First structurally, then line by line.

Then you have the copy-editors, who I believe are locked up, ball and chain, in the basement. They comb through stuff forensically, leaving you doubting whether you are proficient in the English language at all. And the proofreader finds yet more stuff, right at the end, leaving you shook! Then you have the cover designer who comes up with a kick-ass work of art that visually expresses your novel and stands out on a crowded bookshelf. There are also the guys in marketing, sales and publicity doing the very necessary work of getting word of the book out there. I'm sure I've forgotten others involved in the process, so please forgive me, but the amount of labour that goes into getting one book out there is incredible. How that entire symphony plays in harmony is still a wee bit of a mystery to me. My name alone appears on the cover and I'm happy to play up the idea of the 'lone genius'. But the truth is that it's such a collaborative process – and without all these people's input, you, dear reader, wouldn't be reading my thoughts on this.

What have you learnt about the editorial process while writing Ropa's story?

The editorial process is very intimate and collaborative, so I did a lot of work with Bella Pagan and her team. I've learnt that you have to go into it with an open mind. It's not supposed to be adversarial. If the editor didn't like your stuff, they wouldn't have bought it. At this stage, the question isn't whether it's good or not, it is can we make this thing great with the reader in mind? So I've learnt to apply the principle of charity during my engagement with the process. This doesn't mean that I go with all the editorial suggestions. Indeed, there are areas where I see things differently. But, broadly, you have synergy there. Once you put ego aside, the editorial process is a lot of fun. I enjoy finding creative solutions to the issues the editor highlights along the way.

Do you have a favourite fact about Edinburgh?

Edinburgh is a literary city. Back in the day, there were luminaries such as Walter Scott, Robert Louis Stevenson and Arthur Conan Doyle to name but a few. Today, we also celebrate contemporary writers such as Jackie Kay, Irvine Welsh, J. K. Rowling, Ian Rankin, and so on. Edinburgh takes writing and writers very seriously. I remember myself as a twenty-three-year-old wannabe writer, stepping out of Waverley station for the first time and seeing the Scott Monument. This was many years ago and I felt something I'd never felt before, something no other place has made me feel since.

Ropa loves listening to podcasts on history, among other subjects. Is there a period in history you find particularly interesting?
The Scottish Enlightenment was this remarkable period in the eighteenth to nineteenth century. Here, this impoverished, backwater state underwent a radical transformation and had an outsized impact on the world. Scotland is tiny – today the population hovers just over five million – but its contributions to the world we live in are immense. Think about Scotland's impact back then on universal education, jurisprudence, banking, health care, philosophy and literature. And that's before we even think about science, technology and the many Scottish inventions. This, of course, is tied up with Empire, colonialism, slavery and that dark history. But you can't get away from the fact that this small country undeniably affected global history.

In fact, I believe it is crucial to study the Enlightenment – and the Scottish Enlightenment – in order to have any meaningful engagement with the age we live in. I also see many parallels between Scotland then and Zimbabwe now. If the 'shithole country' (as it was called) I live in could do all that, and propel itself into the future, there's no reason Zimbabwe or any other small country couldn't do the same. Arthur Herman argues that the very notion of 'human history' is a Scottish invention. And fundamental to that idea is the concept of progress. Many of the debates and disputes that are key to the Scottish Enlightenment are still relevant today. So understanding this period, and how our world was shaped then, is crucial if we are to transform society into something better.

If you could invite one person, living or dead, to a dinner party, who would it be?
Though my Russian is woefully inadequate, it would be Dostoevsky. He'd be the ideal guest, because everyone knows the famous dinner parties in his novels get a bit wild! This is the writer who really ignited my passion for literature in my early twenties. At that point, I was living in a tiny bedsit in Reading, Berkshire, with no idea where my life was going. Reading . . . the town that got me into this had a pretty apt name, don't you think?

I've said before that I think Dostoevsky is the great Zimbabwean writer. His work speaks so viscerally to the contemporary Zimbabwean experience that my first ever attempt at writing a novel was a plagiarism of his *Demons*. It was written in that very same bedsit, circa 2003/4. Maybe some of his doom and gloom rubbed off in parts of the Edinburgh Nights series. There's certainly a great deal of poverty, crime and desperation there. Hell, even tuberculosis . . . so it's a cityscape he'd recognize. Then, after dinner, old Fyodor and I might hit the casino – and suddenly I feel another story coming on. For a writer, there are always more tales to tell!